SWIMM
THE R

JASON GARNER

hyaline

First published in 2004 by Hyaline Ltd,
3 Lower Thurlow Road,
Torquay TQ1 3EL

www.hyaline.co.uk

ISBN 0-9547326-0-X

Scripture quotations are from The Holy Bible,
English Standard Version, published by
HarperCollins*Publishers* © 2001 by Crossway
Bibles, a division of Good News Publishers.
Used by permission. All rights reserved.

Set in Bembo by
Samantha Barden
sambarden@ntlworld.com

Printed by Cox and Wyman Ltd,
Reading, Berkshire

For Sue

Author's note

The characters, churches, schools, organizations and establishments in this book are all fictional. The districts within Dakar are invented. Gorée Island and the Lac Rose are, however, real places, as are the Magic Roundabout in Swindon and the locations and landmarks in North Wales. The story of Gelert is said to have been fabricated as a means to draw tourists to the village of Beddgelert.

Part I

Chapter 1

Paul Trent had a problem. He was afraid of letting other people down. More specifically, he was afraid of the rejection that might come from people whom he perceived could have felt let down by him. He was largely unaware of the problem in his conscious mind, but deep in his subconscious his soul independently took daily decisions on his behalf in order to stave off any possible future rejection from other people. In a nutshell, much of his life was governed by something of which he was only very vaguely aware.

At university, he had a chat with his personal tutor during his final year. The tutor was not in the habit of giving out careers advice, but in Paul's case he decided to make an exception. 'I think you'd make an excellent secondary school teacher,' he said. Paul agreed wholeheartedly – never even having considered it until that moment.

Later, during the practical stage of his teacher training, he was hit by the harsh reality of a future filled with undisciplined, cruel teenagers and classrooms stinking of antiseptic cleaning fluid. But he could not pull out. His agreement with the tutor's suggestion in the final-year conversation had sealed his fate and cemented the course that his life would take; the mere possibility of being thought of badly by the tutor for giving up the course made him feel sick to the core of his being. His soul did not reason that the tutor might not care about a former student deciding to reject his advice, or indeed might not even remember Paul at all. It was an inexplicable disorder – all the more so because it did not apply to members of his immediate family or to his wife, Rowena, in particular.

Here is a typical situation: Paul is getting out of bed to leave the Trent family house at seven-thirty on a Saturday morning to assist another physics teacher with shifting some lab material at school. 'Paul,' Rowena slurs from underneath the duvet, 'you said yourself that Stephen was only *thinking* about moving the stuff today.'

Paul is struggling to pull on a shoe without undoing the lace. 'I promised to help him. A promise is a promise.' Actually he has not made any promise to help, but he remembers the Friday afternoon conversation with his colleague as tantamount to a promise, or at the very least a tacit understanding that he will be there to lend a hand. 'And what if he's down there now, waiting for me? What'll he think?'

'But what about our lie in?' Rowena protests in half-formed syllables, unaware that her husband has already left the room. 'You promised *me* we could have a lie in.'

He shuts the front door noiselessly so as not to wake the twins and drives to the school. It is locked and silent. The colleague does not arrive. Paul waits, hands on the cold steering wheel, outside the back entrance to the physics lab. Half an hour later he puts the car into reverse and heads home in turmoil. I need another hour in bed, he thinks, slamming the front door closed, unconcerned now about waking the children.

Paul and Rowena had met at the Christian Union of their teacher training college. Rowena had a degree in history and was taking advantage of generous government cash incentives that were being thrown at graduates interested in teaching. She had always liked the word "vocation" and she said it to herself sometimes in imagined conversations with friends.

Teaching? It's always been my vocation. As long as I can remember.

The couple were married shortly after qualifying. They moved to Swindon and both found work. Rowena was pregnant ten weeks after the honeymoon and when the twins, Jonah and Eritrea, were born she left work to become a full-time housewife and mother.

So it was that Paul, who had never actually wanted to teach, found himself inextricably tangled up in a teaching career, having to earn to cover mortgage repayments while Rowena, who had dreamed for many years of being a modern-day Anne of Green Gables, was at home with babies that took turns to wake her up through the night.

By the time the children were old enough to go to school themselves, Rowena mustered what vestiges of self-confidence remained within her and mentioned to Paul that she was considering applying for a teaching job. But he would not hear of it. 'It's just not feasible,' he said. 'What happens if we're both working late and the children have to walk back to an empty house?'

'It wouldn't have to be like that.'

'Not at the beginning, perhaps. But that's how it'd be eventually. There needs to be someone at home when they come back from school. It gives them a feeling of security.'

When the twins were nine years old, the Trents were compelled to move. The two-up, two-down terraced house in Swindon was too small for the family; the twins needed their own separate bedrooms and, besides, Paul no longer considered the area of Swindon they lived in to be "safe" for the children. Through Rowena's badgering, Paul applied for a job in Marlborough, at the grammar school. Having had her teaching dream thwarted, Rowena had thrown herself into interior decoration but had exhausted the possibilities in their tiny house. As the juggernauts thundered past a few short metres outside her front door, she dreamt of a house with mock Tudor panelling and a garden filled with phlox. Kitted out in yellow rubber gloves and with a bucket of tepid water by her side, she scrubbed at the insides of the downstairs window frames to remove the noxious soot that always seemed to coat them. What kind of air are we breathing in here? she thought. But as her thoughts developed from worries to fantasies, she closed her eyes and touched cool flagstones by an Aga, smelled the wetness of a freshly mown lawn, heard the muffled swish of wooden curtain rings against wooden rail as flowing white muslin curtains were drawn open, to reveal the view of a walled herb garden from the upstairs master bedroom…

The family moved into their Marlborough home in the spring of the twins' ninth year. Paul and Rowena started looking for a church immediately. The elders at their Swindon charismatic church had prayed for them and "sent them out" to serve whatever new church might be in need of their gifts. It was with this in mind that Paul avoided Marlborough's largest congregation, Glenfield Free Church, which was known to be a thriving community of committed Christians.

'But why can't we just *visit* and see what it's like?' Rowena queried as they were driving back from a Baptist church that was too far away from their house to be worth considering. 'I can't see what's wrong with that.'

'We've talked about this time and again. Don't you think there might be another place that needs us more?' Paul was frustrated that she might not be in full agreement.

'Even big, successful churches need people sometimes,' Rowena said meekly.

Paul gave a 'humph' that contained the smallest note of unwilling acquiescence.

6

The following week he took them to St Peter's Parish Church, a stone's throw away from the house. It was a well-presented gothic church that might have appeared in the corner of a postcard depicting Marlborough's traditional sights. The congregation, too, seemed to sense that it was their duty to fit the romantic ideal of the kind of folk who would frequent such a building. The middle-aged women, dressed in smart tasteful jackets, gathered their grey hair up into elaborate buns, sprayed themselves with rich, stale perfume and snapped closed golden purse clasps as they prepared for Sunday Morning Prayer. The husbands donned musty suits and strode stiffly in through the nave door, with great aplomb.

The services were strictly a question of rote. After the second hymn and the sending-out of whatever children might be present to Sunday school, Reverend Abel Thacker walked into the pulpit and delivered his sermon with measured solemnity and composure, as if being filmed. On the Trents' first Sunday, the twins had been too shy to go out to Sunday school with the other two boys and, in their boredom, had soon started to provoke each other. Rowena had spent most of the service trying to keep them from fighting in the pew, but had not been too distracted to realize that this was the last church on earth she wanted to settle in. She said so to Paul when they were walking home.

Even so, they were back there the following week. This time the children consented to go to Sunday school, thereby doubling its numbers and giving Rowena ample opportunity to size up the congregation, many of whom had left too swiftly for her even to see them the previous week. Very few were as young as her and Paul, though most were better dressed.

In his sermon, Abel Thacker reminisced at length about the "good old days" – days when milkmen served gold top and people could leave their doors unlocked without fear of being robbed. Days when atomic bombs were being dropped and dictators were trying to take over the world, Rowena thought with irritation, shifting in her seat to keep her backside from going numb. The audience sat rapt and attentive, heads cocked in apparent absorption with the exhortation. Their eyes stared at Thacker – through him, perhaps. It was like a scene from *Invasion of the Body Snatchers*.

Afterwards the family walked home together. The children had run on ahead, despite Paul's attempts to call them back with warnings of tramps and drunks. 'The vicar didn't mention Jesus a single time,' Rowena said. 'Didn't you notice? He was on the verge of saying it once, but then bit it back and said, "The Lord", or something.'

'Which is precisely why this church needs us,' Paul answered.

'I don't think he's even a Christian,' Rowena continued.

'All the more reason to pray for him then.'

Rowena wanted to grab him by the arm and say, look, just because the elders laid hands on us before we left it doesn't mean we have to go and join the deadest church in the district to try to start a revival. Why make it into a personal crusade? We've had no guidance that we should be there.

Instead, she said aloud, 'We really should pray about it.'

'Of course we should.'

On the Trents' third Sunday, Abel Thacker invited the family to lunch. His wife served a pot-roast with cauliflower that had been boiled until it was pink, and sprouts that disintegrated into a mush that tasted of nothing but water. She was a small woman in her late sixties who said very little at the dinner table, as though having been reminded over many years that women should keep their mouths shut as a sign of respect for their wiser partners. Behind this starched respect her eyes contained the faintest shadow of a look of surprise or wistfulness, as though she had realized shortly after getting

8

married exactly what it was she had let herself in for and then reacted in a moment's outburst of forbidden emotion. The hint of surprise that remained was like the tic left over after a stroke. It said a lot to Rowena.

Reverend Thacker himself sat like a patriarch at the head of the table. His whitish hair was divided by a razor-sharp side parting that he might have had all his life. The hair around the parting had begun to thin, revealing a scalp the colour of cooked lobster. He spoke to Paul and Rowena about dates: the time he and his wife had left their previous parish in Kent to take on the job at St Peter's, the time the church roof had needed repairing after the worst winter gales on record. As he spoke on, Rowena looked at the wife and thought, poor woman.

With lunch out of the way, the four adults withdrew to the lounge. The children went to play on the vicarage lawn. Thacker threw a concerned look after them, as though fearing that they might tear up the turf or uproot the cherry trees.

Over coffee, Paul was already responding eagerly to his probing enquiries about possibly being a part of the church, joining the electoral role, perhaps even the Parochial Church Council. Rowena was irritated to distraction as she watched him make what she knew, for him, represented unbreakable pact after unbreakable pact. It was like watching a man standing up to his neck in a deep hole in the sand, digging as fast as he could while the tide came in around him.

The previous week, they had indeed prayed about St Peter's – and Rowena had had the sense of absolute conviction that it was not their battle; that they should move on, even to consider Glenfield Free Church. She had a massive sense of foreboding about St Peter's, which was only heightened when she grasped the significance of the look in the eyes of Thacker's wife. She could see from the vicar's body language and the way he stirred his coffee that uppermost in his mind was the outward

9

appearance of the church: how it looked to the rest of the local community, and how the presence of a young couple with degrees and teaching qualifications might alter the carefully sculpted order and image of the place.

Although she was not entirely wrong in her assumptions, Thacker had other motivation, too, for encouraging them to commit: for a while now he had been worried that one of the only other members in their early thirties, Nigel Stephens, might lose heart and leave if other like-minded people did not join soon. Abel did not like Nigel much, considering him to be one of a new breed of people who took the Bible altogether too seriously. But Nigel was the Sunday school teacher, and the only person who could conceivably be responsible for any children that came to St Peter's – and if there was one thing that Abel Thacker disliked more than people who believed the Bible, it was children.

During the meal, the sight of Jonah and Eritrea fidgeting with boredom had almost been enough for him to discourage the Trents from joining. But, he thought prudently, if they stay the children will obviously go out to Sunday school, and the friendship between Nigel and the couple will keep Nigel from leaving. And even if he does leave, perhaps by then the wife will be settled enough to consider taking over the running of the Sunday school.

At the time, the Sunday school only had one other member who could truly be considered a regular. But in Thacker's mind there had to be someone, some contingency plan, to keep the children of any visiting couples out of the service proper. If not Nigel, then Rowena. Thacker tried to weigh the negative aspect of the twins' presence against the potential assets that Paul and Rowena could be by joining the church. It was a fine line all right. If only they didn't have any children.

Paul's thoughts were developing along other avenues: Rowena is right, he thought, this man has never had a conversion experience. He does not know what it means to be born again.

He saw in his mind a picture of himself and Rowena walking up and down the church aisles, praying for revival before the service started. He saw Abel Thacker and other members of the congregation kneeling in repentance and having their eyes opened spiritually to the state of the church. Outwardly, he nodded and agreed with the vicar's words that flowed over his head, as the vision developed into a picture of the heavy nave doors open and swarms of people rushing in to worship. And he was there in the pulpit preaching to them, guiding them. It made his heart beat fast with anticipation. For a moment, he even forgot the deep misgivings that Rowena had shared with him during their prayer time.

As the Trents left, Paul and Abel shook hands in a decisive kind of way.

Later, when Paul and Rowena were sitting in their own living room, Rowena said testily, 'So I take it we're staying?'

'I didn't say that,' Paul replied.

No, but it's what you implied, she thought. She considered giving vent to her feelings about his methods of committing himself to people, and her dislike of Abel and the church in general. 'You know full well,' she said aloud, 'that if he knew our intention in joining the church was to change it he'd never have invited you to be on the Parochial Council. It's false pretences, that's what it is.'

They exchanged a few more comments before Paul started on a long spiel about being equal to the challenge and the calling given them when they had left their Swindon church. He used words like "divine appointment" and "spiritual breakthrough". Rowena looked at the plastic curtain rail. It would have to go. Perhaps Marlborough had a shop that sold rails made of polished pine. Paul continued his monologue. Rowena nodded and emitted monotone 'mm-hmms' in the right places, her mind on curtain rings. She eventually agreed that St Peter's was where they should be, hoping that it would shut him up. Anything for a quiet life, she thought, visualizing double-glazed uPVC windows with leaded trimming. But, she wondered, what kind of a deal would we get if we had them fitted throughout the house at the same time?

Chapter 2

Abel Thacker was not essentially a bad person: like most disagreeable characters, he was merely a victim of circumstance. He had grown up in a family environment where structure and moral discipline were considered the be-all and end-all of human existence. His father had been the kind of man who would not tolerate disobedience in any shape or form. When Abel, as a two-year-old child, began to develop conscious understanding of the world beyond himself and to test his limits, his father saw it as the beginnings of planned insubordination and made it his duty to nip it in the bud. When the boy was moved from a cot to a bed he sometimes climbed out, as toddlers do, and wandered to the door in the hope of hearing his parents moving around downstairs. But whenever his father discovered him loitering out of bed, he gathered him up violently and pushed him back, forcefully and with harsh warnings, face down on to the mattress. There were also beatings for stepping out of line.

With time, Abel learned, subconsciously, that limits were something to be cherished, and everything else to be feared. As a boy he attended Canterbury Cathedral with his parents. As a teenager he developed a love not for adventure or self-expression, but for the order and routine of the traditional service liturgy in the *Book of Common Prayer*. He found solace in the architecture of the Cathedral, in the planning of the church calendar and the formality of the congregation. His father saw these things as proof of a successful upbringing, and was satisfied – never once considering the tragic reality that his child-rearing strategy had, in fact, killed his son's spirit.

Abel became a confirmed traditionalist and trained as a vicar. He filed away his sermons for future reference. He loved the sound of words like "Maundy Thursday" and "Second Sunday before Lent".

So, when he discovered that Paul was a Bible-believing Christian of the very worst kind – much worse than Nigel – he was angry. He was angry with himself for having made such an error of judgement in welcoming the Trents into his safe haven of order. He was angry with Paul for having duped him. Really, he was afraid.

When Paul first joined the Parochial Church Council he sat quietly and minded his own business, while the other members banged their fists on the table, coughed until their rheumy eyes filled with tears and argued bitterly about leaky cisterns in the church hall or moulded plastic chairs. However, after a few weeks Paul began to make comments and suggestions – but always implicitly and innocuously, from the flank. At first, these suggestions – mostly about prayer meetings or get-togethers with other local churches – were a cause of some surprise to Thacker. Then, as they became more obvious, the vicar realized that the Trents had pulled the wool over his eyes regarding their motivation for being in his church. He was not pleased. One Sunday, he saw Paul's hands raised slightly in worship during *Crown Him with Many Crowns* and was so agitated that he had to fight to keep from telling the organist to stop playing.

Rowena, though not on the Church Council, signed up on the flower rota. The two other women responsible for the flowers were not too much older than herself; one of them was the mother of Tom, the other regular boy in the Sunday school. But it quickly became clear to Rowena that any ideas she might have had about friendship between herself and the two women were wishful thinking: they treated the flower-arranging meetings as a front for horrific gossip sessions about other churchgoers, and they were loathe to allow an outsider into their world of intrigue and malice. When Rowena joined them for the first time she was puzzled by their distant superiority. She almost asked them why it was that they were so unwelcoming, since they took it in turns on alternate Sundays to interrupt the notices with sarcastic comments about how – despite having asked on numerous occasions – they still had no assistance with the flowers. It was completely incongruous.

Rowena bore it for a time, sometimes even daring to make tiny hints about Christian matters, in the form of comments about her favourite hymns or the church fixtures. These comments were greeted with arched eyebrows, or looks of appalled pity. When she told Paul how they were he was tempted to sympathize, but he knew that if he openly criticized the church or its members in any way it would give Rowena the impetus she needed to bring up the subject of leaving altogether.

She was perfectly aware of this, of course, but had by now resigned herself to a long stint at St Peter's. And Paul, in recognition of her resignation, had given her free rein over the decoration of the house and more money than he would normally have considered prudent, to spend on fittings. There was a tacit agreement between the two: Rowena would permit Paul to continue his crusade if he, in turn, let her have dominion over the house. This made the prayer times they had together about the spiritual state of St Peter's highly contrived and stilted.

The flower arrangers were a fair representation of the general female population of the congregation. It became clear to Rowena that the women were only interested in church activity as a means of bettering their social standing. In her mind, Rowena often pictured them as a mass of bodies clambering over each other in a desperate attempt to reach the top of the pile, scratching and spitting hateful abuse at each other. In practice, the abuse came in the form of barbed comments made by immaculately dressed ladies over a cup of tea after the service. But it was the same to Rowena. Bored to distraction by being unable to establish a single meaningful friendship, and disinclined to get involved in the church fêtes, treasure hunts and various other activities – all of which were merely smokescreens to provide the women with opportunities to bolster their social status – she turned her attention to the men of the church, and, more specifically, to Nigel, the Sunday school teacher.

She knew from having overheard snatches of whispered conversation at church that Nigel, like the Trents, was pitied and considered an oddity for taking his religion too seriously. Nigel was a young man, a year or so younger than Paul. He was a typical single Christian who burned the candle at both ends, doing charity work at the local hospital in addition to having a full-time job. But, as he was dedicated to the Sunday school and fairly open about his faith, Rowena approached him as an ally in the war against deceitfulness in the church. He agreed that, yes, gossip was rife and that something would definitely have to be done about the lack of Christian charity in operation. 'Paul and I pray about the church anyway,' Rowena said. 'You could join us if you wanted.'

So, for a while, her waning spiritual stamina had been fanned into flame by meetings that took place once a fortnight at the Trents' house.

But as the private prayer times between Rowena and Paul were strained, what hope could there be of prayer succeeding with a third party? Nigel's interest, too, inevitably began to fade and the meetings became more irregular before dying a death.

With time, even Rowena began to consider Nigel somewhat of an anomaly. She wondered how he could sit back and observe the spiritual sickness that epitomized the church without taking a stand or simply leaving. He's just worn out, she told herself, what with all his other commitments. In truth, she did not want to think about it too much, because thinking about his situation brought her too close to considering her own: her unspoken arrangement with Paul and how it had placed her in a position of compromise. By now, the home, with its parquet floors and kitchen spotlights, was too precious to her. In the recesses of her heart, beyond her conscious mind, she feared that having it out with Paul would signal the end of his willingness to provide generous home improvement subsidies. She might lose control over the house…

A few months after Paul joined the Church Council Nigel left it. 'I just can't cope with any more of those meetings,' he confessed to Paul, as the two walked out of the church car park late one Thursday. 'I think I've spent about three years trying to persuade Abel to reform things.' He paused. 'But it feels like a hundred.'

Paul said, 'Early on, what kind of things did you suggest?'

'Getting a youth music group together, more upbeat meetings. You know, turning the clock forward to the twentieth century. But he wouldn't ever have it. None of them would. They never will.'

'You can't leave.' Paul was unable to keep the note of shock from his voice.

'Look, it's just the PCC,' Nigel said. 'We should see it for what it is. It's not the spiritual pulse of the church.' He rubbed his forehead above his eyebrow with two fingers. 'Anyway I'm tired of finishing these evenings with a headache and acid indigestion.'

To Paul, Nigel looked like the kind of person who was always fundamentally tired – just holding up, as it were, but valiantly seeking to draw attention away from this fatigue by endeavouring to give the impression of having a limitless store of energy at the ready to commit to some worthwhile cause. His demeanour and body language were always accommodating, in line with this endeavour: he desired to show that he could give one hundred and fifty percent of himself, if need be.

Really, Paul knew that this apparent dynamism was a sham. Even so, seeing Nigel like this, with his guard so obviously down, he couldn't keep the disappointment from registering visibly on his face.

'I'm sorry,' Nigel said. 'I know it's not what you wanted to hear. I'll pray for you. I really will, but for the time being I just have to be away from it. Otherwise I'll really start hating Abel and that won't be any good for anything or anyone.' He had reached his car and unlocked the door. He seemed to be anxious to make a move. 'You could consider it as you taking the relay for a while,' he ventured.

Paul opened his hands in the gesture of a shrug. He said carefully, 'I suppose you need the break. You always do too much. I've never known how you juggle work, hospital, church, the prayer meetings. But it'll be hard without you.'

'I'm not leaving for good. I needed to know there was someone else here who could make a stand for the right things while I'm out of it. It makes me feel better about doing this.'

'I understand,' Paul said. 'And for goodness' sake, don't lose any sleep over it.'

So, two years have passed and the Trents are still at St Peter's. They sit in a pew on the left-hand side of the church. Rowena has experienced every describable negative feeling – and some indescribable ones, too – regarding the church. Every week, there are two hymns followed by the notices before the children leave for Sunday school. Then Abel Thacker strides into the pulpit and dispenses his sermon with all the enthusiasm of a caretaker emptying a bag of rubbish into a bin.

Without any Christian friends, Rowena has long since withdrawn into herself. She and Paul do not pray together any more. In fact, Rowena does not pray alone either. She watches Paul sitting, head strained forward and slightly on one side, with a ridiculously counterfeit expression of fascination, mixed with hopeful encouragement, on his face. He looks like a teacher in a Year-Seven French oral exam. Perhaps he is trying to communicate to Rowena his conviction that one day Thacker will speak some words of truth. But nothing that has left the vicar's mouth has ever given them the slightest shred of hope and they both know it. Rowena knows, too, that Paul's unwillingness to recognize St Peter's as a lost cause is as much due to his fear of reneging on the commitment he made to Abel Thacker two years previously in the porch of the vicarage, as it is to his pride. He's probably scared of letting Nigel down too, she thinks. How can a wife possibly fight against such a combination of fear of man *and* hidebound spiritual pride? He'll never let us leave. The sense of failure and guilt would be too much for him.

Sometimes, when sitting in church, Rowena is so disgusted with him that she feels nauseous. After the final hymn she goes to the back of the nave and drinks a cup of tea, eats a biscuit. She psyches herself up to starting a conversation with one of the socialites. She views this as a challenge and an act of self-sacrifice – as does the socialite with whom she speaks. The conversation, which is limited to only the most banal and trivial of subjects, jolts along awkwardly as both parties wonder how they can bring the dialogue to a swift end without it looking as though the encounter has been a challenge for either of them. Then a voice inside Rowena says, how dare you?

It says, for two years your husband has been struggling to bring about change in this church. He's prayed and fasted and dedicated time and energy so that my will be done at St Peter's. What have you done? Have you been a good supportive wife? No you haven't. You've been boiling over with anger towards him. You've opposed everything that he's tried to do. You could have helped him, but you've made his task impossible. The reason there has been no change here is because you've been nothing but a millstone around his neck.

Rowena is racked with guilt: she has lost the ability to discern whose voice this is. She alters the tone of her voice, takes more of an interest, tries to think how she could win over this socialite for God. Afterwards she smiles kindly to Abel's wife, standing alone by the baptismal font, and makes a ghastly attempt to be cheerful when the wife – another pariah in the church – comes over to speak to her.

When the children and the husband have been rounded up, the family leave and walk down the road back to their house. As soon as she steps in through the front door, Rowena smells the rosemary on the roasting lamb and forgets about her inner conflict. Later, she pours the meat juices into a saucepan, crumbles in a stock cube and thinks, now where did I put that whisk? As she is adding the greenish water from the courgettes she watches, through the window, the children scramble up into the close-knit branches of the maple tree at the bottom of the garden.

Later still, when the four are finally sitting at the table, Rowena spoons a generous helping of mint sauce on to her plate. She has forgotten that St Peter's even exists.

One Saturday night in July of the Trents' second year at the church, Rowena had a dream. The evening was uncommonly hot and sticky. All the windows in the upstairs of the house were open but there was not a breath of wind. Rowena had thrown off her side of the duvet and lay flat on her back with her hands folded over her chest, like the stone statue of a saint on a tomb. She listened to the sound of an irate dog barking a few houses down and then looked over at the red LED of the bedside clock. Three o'clock on a Sunday morning, she thought as she drifted into oblivion.

Then she was back in the Trents' pew at St Peter's. Abel Thacker was walking towards the pulpit in his exaggerated formal gait. He started preaching. 'I am tired of people who claim that the church of God is the people. The church of God is this architectural masterpiece, built by craftsmen who have dedicated years of their life to making it beautiful. It is the cornerstone of the parish and a place of refuge and comfort to those seeking inspiration.' The customary feelings of weary frustration began to boil up within her. She turned to her husband, who was sitting bolt upright, his eyes void of expression. Then, inappropriately, the two flower arrangers were standing beneath the pulpit snipping carnation stems and gossiping over the vicar's voice. 'And that Rachel must have been sleeping with so-and-so from the choir for at least seven months.'

'Oh I *know*!' the other answered joyfully, like a flame licking over a dry piece of paper. 'When I called her the other day it was only eight in the morning and *he* answered the phone.'

Other people, too, were now gathered around in twos and threes under the pulpit with coffee in hand, whispering, leaning towards each other like conspirators, looking over their shoulders distrustfully at the others. It seemed as though the service was over, but Abel continued to speak on, unaware.

The sound of tittle-tattle and scandal swelled to a crescendo the way the sound of voices does following the final hymn and blessing. It filled the chancel. It rose into the roof. Rowena wanted to poke her husband and say, don't they realize the service hasn't finished yet? But then she saw a man standing alone over by the lectern in the south transept and her voice died in her throat.

He was standing still, watching Rowena intently and seemed, perhaps, to have been waiting for her to look in his direction. But as she focused on him she realized with a profound shock that he had tears in his eyes.

Rowena had only ever seen a man cry once – her father had wept twenty years ago, after being made redundant. But those tears had been tears of self-pity and fear. This man was crying completely unselfconsciously, not for himself, but for her and out of sorrow. The sight of him unpretentiously weeping was overpowering and terrifying. She couldn't recall anyone ever having expressed that intensity of emotion over her. The sound of the gossiping and the sermon faded into the background, becoming like fragmented excerpts of radio news drifting from an empty, far-off room. The man stepped towards her and she panicked and stood up. 'Don't cry about me,' she called out, desperately. 'I'm not worth it.' In turmoil, she stumbled past her oblivious husband and ran towards the man. She was already crying herself as he caught her in his arms and held her. A dam deep within her burst and she sobbed uncontrollably, pathetically on his shoulder. For a time the pressure, long withheld, seeped out of her in tears of bitterness and regret.

After a while the pressure began to ease. Rowena's sobbing died down. She held tightly to the man and, as awareness slowly returned, she sensed within herself the tiniest hint of calm and resolve, a feeling she had not had for some years.

Though she wanted to look up, she kept her face buried in his shoulder. He held her for a long time.

She sensed that he was going to speak. She wanted to hear his voice, but she was afraid, too. He seemed to know this, but eventually he said, 'Child, are you willing to help him now?'

Rowena glanced over to where her husband was sitting in the pew and was touched once again by the old feelings of annoyance. Paul, so stubborn and pig-headed, bribing me into joining his crusade.

'But you went along with it,' the man said.

'And he always makes himself feel indebted to people.'

'You could have faced him with it.'

'Oh, but I couldn't. He makes it impossible for me to say anything. He does, you know, he makes it impossible for me to raise the issue. You see –'

'I only want you to be *ready* to speak to him.'

And she knew it. The self-justification died on her lips and she understood that she had never even let herself entertain the possibility of receiving the right frame of mind. Instead of making peace with Paul, she had held on tightly to her resentment and kept it as something that she could lord over him, to make him pay for being proud and a slave to other people's expectations, without ever taking her feelings into consideration. Oh yes, and, above all, for depriving her of a career. Paul was aware of what he'd done. Why else would he have given her extra money for the house? Ah, but she took it, and not only that, she also reserved the right to punish him later for his weakness...

Rowena cried again, so hard that her chest ached. She cried until she knew that, by her compliance, she was responsible for what had happened. She could not accuse Paul.

The man took her shoulders in his hands. He said, 'Are you ready to help him now?' Rowena was mortally afraid to look into his face. She nodded and glanced up at him, and was surprised to see that his eyes were filled not with severity but with love, and with something more than that – acceptance. He led her to where Paul was sitting. Paul saw neither of them, but continued to gaze at Abel Thacker with dead eyes. Rowena and the man watched him for a while. Then the man said, 'You will help him, but first you must take your children and leave this church, and you must do it right now. Can you do that?'

Rowena looked at him. 'I don't know. I… I think so.'

'You will have to be strong for him, too. Because he can't be strong for himself.'

Rowena nodded.

When she woke in the morning, her pillow was cool with the wetness of the tears, but she had forgotten the dream.

'We mustn't forget to ask Nigel to walk the kids home after the service next week,' Paul said, as he and Rowena settled into their pew.

'I'm sure they can walk home on their own. They *are* going to secondary school in a few months' time –' the organ began to play the introit and Rowena lowered her voice to an insistent whisper – 'and anyway they'll be furious. They won't have it.'

'Well that's just tough, I'm afraid. I'd rather have them angry with us than murdered by some drug addict in the park.'

'Don't say that. Don't be ridiculous. You always exaggerate.'

'And what about that girl in Bath? Stabbed twelve times outside her local newsagent. Nobody thinks anything like that could happen until it does.'

'You're obsessed. You can't go through life trying to –' but Paul cut her off with a dig in the leg, motioning with his head to the familiar figure of Thacker exiting the vestry.

Rowena seethed her way through the first hymn, the notices, the reading. There was another hymn and the children rose to go out to Sunday school. As the congregation was standing up to sing, Rowena turned to her husband to deliver a cutting remark about him being morbid, but, from the corner of her eye, she noticed the lectern. She opened her mouth to speak and then shut it again. Something about the lectern made her intensely uneasy. She stared at it, feeling her pulse speeding up and adrenalin building in her body. The man! Her throat constricted and her eyes welled up.

'Paul, we have to leave. We have to leave *now*,' she hissed.

He shot back a venomous look. 'There's no need to be childish and make a show in front of everyone just because you don't agree with me.'

'It's got nothing to do with *that*. We have to go.'

'We're not going anywhere.'

'Paul, we must go. Jesus told me that we had to.' The words sounded hugely melodramatic when she spoke them out loud.

The third and final verse of the hymn began. He leaned towards her and whispered, slowly and deliberately, 'You are not going anywhere and I am not going anywhere. After the service, when we get home, we're going to have a talk.'

The congregation sat down and Rowena fought back tears. Every muscle in her body was poised to enable her to spring up out of the pew. The vicar's dreary voice set in. Silent words rang in her ears: You must take your children and leave this church, and you must do it right now.

When the final blessing was over, Rowena stood up slowly and started to walk out. Paul plucked at her arm to try to stop her, but she shook him off. 'You still want to make a show of this?' he said, but she walked away, even as he was speaking. She walked straight out of the doors, turned left and doubled back around the building. She reached the place where the nave wall joined the transept before falling on her knees and weeping.

Eventually, she came back to herself. She began to feel the heat rising from the moist grass. A bee landed on a daisy in front of her hand and the whole flower dipped with its weight. In the distance, the steady, lulling hum of a lawn mower could be heard. The sound of it rose and fell on the warm summer breeze. She drew a ragged breath and reached for the handrail of the stairwell leading to the outside door of the vestry.

After the service, Nigel walked across the yard from the hall to the church building. Instead of entering through the front porch door, he checked himself and went around the side of the church, between the oak and the south side of the nave. He walked to the south transept, head down, intending to go in through the vestry door, but then almost stumbled into Rowena. Her eyes were puffy and bloodshot. He stopped dead in his tracks.

'Nigel,' she said, exhaling. She was not expecting to see him.

'Rowena? You're crying.'

She struggled to her feet and opened her mouth to speak but – not for the first time that morning – the words stuck in her throat. She stared at him idiotically, with mouth open, for a moment. Had he been looking for her?

'I… It's partly my hay fever. I can't do anything about it.'

'You're sure?' He didn't believe it for a second.

'Yes.'

'Well, if I can help in any way…' his voice trailed off.

They stood awkwardly for a moment. Rowena fought the bubble of sadness and conviction back down. Get a hold of yourself, she told herself. Aloud, she said, 'There's something I meant to ask you. Next Sunday morning, Paul and I have to meet his sister in Swindon. I don't think the children really want to go, so if we drop them off here on the way, could you walk them back home after church?'

Nigel hesitated. 'You only live across the road.'

'I know,' she replied acerbically. 'It's just my husband being idiotic. If it's any trouble it doesn't matter, we'll ask someone else.'

'No, no. Not at all. How long will you be?'

'Oh, you don't have to stay with them, or anything. Paul's not that paranoid.' She spat out the words. 'All you have to do is make sure they get home safely.'

He touched her shoulder. 'If there is something the matter, you must tell me. You will, won't you?'

She nodded. She couldn't understand her emotions. Why couldn't she speak to Nigel?

They faced each other for a moment longer. 'Well,' he said and patted her on the shoulder, clumsily. He looked as though he was going to say something else, but then thought better of it and slipped past her, down the mossy stairwell and through the vestry door.

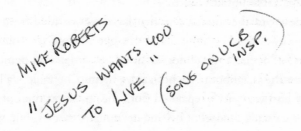

Chapter 3

Jonah and Eritrea spent much of that summer playing in the garden. The six weeks between the end of primary school and the beginning of secondary school were timeless days of lazy heat and dandelion milk, drowsy wood pigeons and cuckoo spit.

The garden of the Trent family house was an exciting place: the French windows at the back end of the dining room looked over three levels of lawn, layered like shallow steps down a hill sloping gently towards a muddy stream that all but dried up in the August heat. A narrow, shady passage surfaced with greenish concrete ran down the left side of the house, providing access to the kitchen door. Beyond the door it met a crazy paving path that lay in the shadow of the hedge on the left side of the garden. The path ran parallel with the lawns and was interrupted only by steps between the levels, all the way down to the stream. The first lawn was divided from the second by a large hydrangea and the second from the third by clumps of catnip and tall dog daisies. The garden was hemmed in from the neighbours on both sides by impenetrable walls of privet, and was partly separated from the stream at the bottom by a sprawling hedge of an indeterminate species, but with such thick, sinewy branches that Paul could never be bothered to cut it back.

The top lawn belonged to Paul and Rowena. On sunny afternoons Paul sometimes sat and marked books there, and the pages of the shabby orange exercise books lying on the brittle plastic picnic table flipped over in the breeze, as though the wind were looking impatiently for a particular word or picture.

The second layer of lawn was no-man's land: too shady for Rowena and Paul and not private enough for the children. The grass was not kept short and grew in unkempt tufts here and there. Rowena was not overly concerned about its appearance; the hydrangea mostly hid it from view.

The lowest level was the twins' territory. Here the weeds grew unchecked. There was a balsam with its miniature spiked pods that exploded when touched, showering seeds far and wide and leaving traces of the plant's sickly odour on fingers. There were swathes of goose grass, groundsel and tottergrass. Down in the cooler, shadier area where the garden met the brook there was an abundance of red campion with its rose-pink flowers and fuzzy stalks. The twins loved it down there. It was a kingdom of overpowering aromas and it was theirs and theirs alone.

Rising from the mess of hedge was the trunk of a stunted maple of some kind with branches stretching over the tiny brook. It was a sorry sort of tree that seemed to be there almost against its will, bent over with the effort of fighting the onslaught of nature. Growing near the base of the tree was a mass of summer jasmine that had, perhaps, been carefully nurtured by previous owners, but which now burgeoned wild and abandoned. The hedge and the jasmine had grown up around the trunk of the maple and, over the years, almost completely submerged the tree. Now, all that could be seen was a bushy beard: a tree encased in something like a vast shaggy rubber-band ball.

During the Trents' first summer, Jonah had climbed up, fought his way into the branches and hollowed out a nest. It had grown in shape and become the children's favourite haunt. The maple branches spread like open hands and the flattened hedge and jasmine formed a dense cradle between the wooden fingers. The twins could lie back, surrounded and hidden by the lattice of green vines on all sides, but with the blue sky above and the sun on their hair, or they could lean forward over the brook, feel the thrill as the weaker branches gave under their weight and smell the faint odour of wet, dark leaves down below through the heady fragrance of jasmine flowers.

They called the den "the secret place" and the brook "the dark lands". In the August before starting secondary school they seemed to spend almost every waking moment down there. Rowena had to shout herself hoarse from the kitchen window before they finally trudged up the path to eat their tea. As they sat sun-dazed, eyes unaccustomed to the dark interior of the dining room, eating their food in drowsy silence, she thought, they can anticipate the autumn term. They don't want to grow up.

The Trent family's exodus from St Peter's to Glenfield Free Church coincided with the start of the twins' first term at secondary school. Jonah, who was naturally better at remembering it was broth, as opposed to soup, that too many cooks spoiled, scraped a place at Marlborough Grammar School, although he wished he hadn't. He dreaded the idea of having his father for maths or physics and he refused point blank to take a lift into school with him. Instead, it was Rowena who dropped him off on the first rainy Monday: a pale boy looking like a shorn sheep with his close-cropped curly brown hair, and with worry shining in his eyes. He looked vulnerable as he walked from the car to the main gates of the school, his blazer so long that it hung over the knuckles of his hands, but his old primary school trousers so short that there was a good inch of sock visible between the hem and the new black shoes that pinched his ankles.

He had inherited his father's sense of indebtedness to others, so when he found himself sitting next to a boy from his new church in more than one lesson, he felt that the coincidence constituted some kind of irrevocable bond between them and that they must be friends. The boy, James Dow, was an endless talker whose eyes were never fixed on the person he was addressing but roved here and there, always looking for trouble. He was quickly branded a moron by the popular clique in the class but his friendship with Jonah was, by then, too much of an established fact for Jonah to be able to consider doing anything to end it. Besides, he provided Jonah the opportunity to exist unnoticed; if James talked, Jonah could be silent. And James liked to speak for other people.

Marlborough Grammar was modelled on what the head-master imagined great English schools – not the comprehensive school he had attended – to have been like in the 1950s. He was a shameless autocrat who lived in an absurd fantasy world that revolved around house crests, Latin maxims about excelling beyond the humanly possible, and stern discipline. The school groaned under the weight of rules: there was a one-way system that had to be adhered to and anyone caught eating so much as a crisp indoors would receive a detention. The system was enforced by an army of seventeen-year-old Oxbridge hopefuls who flaunted their prefect badges as though they were Olympic medals.

All but hidden from other people's view by James's tireless attention-seeking, Jonah melted into the system, wearing his apprehensive look as he changed for gym or stood in the dinner queue waiting his turn for a portion of processed mashed potato that looked and tasted like concentrated wallpaper paste, complete with pockets of dust.

Considering that it was possible to be in breach of school rules merely by turning around and walking the wrong the way down a corridor, his class 7R were soon labelled as "difficult" by the staff. Once, in morning assembly, the school sang *All Things Bright and Beautiful.* Where the words went: *The purple-headed mountain, The river running by*, Jonah's class laughed so loud that the pianist lost his concentration and ground to a halt. This earned them a group detention, which Jonah resented deeply as he was the only one who hadn't even sniggered.

Perhaps it was because 7R had Mr Trent for maths that Jonah made it his business to be totally invisible. He became the kind of unobtrusive boy that the teachers could never remember as having existed, a straight B–grade student who filled out the numbers in the school photo: people's eyes always passed over him looking for someone else.

Jonah was meticulous in his approach to Christianity. There was a strange similarity between his evening prayers and the concise, clinical entries in his homework diary: *Read Wilfred Owen poem and write own small poem about trench life, finish results and conclusion for experiment on copper sulphate crystal, simultaneous equations exercise 9.* After cleaning his teeth he went into his bedroom, shut the door and looked over the back garden before drawing the curtains. Sometimes he opened the window and strained to hear the rustling sound of the brook. Then he climbed into bed, plumped up the pillow behind him, linked his hands around his knees and prayed. He had a list of requests engraved on his mind: Dear God, please let my uncle and aunt become Christians, let things go all right at school, look after my family and friends.

Sometimes he came to in a daze, as if sucked back through a long tunnel, and realized that he had been sitting for minutes at a time with his mind blank, the dull overhead bulb casting a gloomy orange light over the bedroom. Rowena had stopped coming in to help the twins say their prayers when they were ten and Jonah was beginning to flag, but he stuck to the task tenaciously. He could not comprehend God. Sometimes, to keep his mind from wandering, he tried to visualize something to pray to. He pictured the sallow facial contours of the carved marble crucified Jesus that had been behind the communion rail at St Peter's, but even that did not keep him from sometimes losing track and slipping into a void of empty thoughts, an underground cellar labyrinth of vacant white rooms, each one the same as the others.

He walked home with James, of course. It would have become a daily tradition, even if Paul had not forbidden him from walking home alone in his first year.

Almost every day, the two friends sat in the bedroom and Jonah listened half-heartedly while James's thoughtless thoughts poured from his mouth in an unchecked flood of verbal diarrhoea, covering every subject from the desperate, unconvincing fantasies about what he had done with a nameless girl he'd apparently met on a family holiday, to the blood-fests of the videos he kept in his bedroom. He talked frenetically, with obsessive zeal.

'Anyway, this guy's waiting above the hatch in the elevator shaft with the Uzi. He waits 'till the other guy's come in through the door and is standing right underneath. Then he opens fire, point-blank range, on the guy's head, through the hatch –' James sells the image point by point like a door-to-door salesman – 'blood explodes all over the walls of the lift, but really thick and crimson, like it's got pulped-up brain in it –'

'Cup of tea?'

'Then he jumps down through the hatch, other guy's lying on the floor, no head and… Yeah, all right.'

The two trudge downstairs and find Paul sitting at the dining room table, a pile of books at his elbow. They give off the trademark school smell of stale disinfectant and make James think of the machine with the revolving pad that is used to clean the black lines of shoe rubber from the linoleum in the corridor outside the canteen. He says, 'Hello Mr Trent,' with sycophantic reverence, hands behind his back.

Jonah flicks on the kettle switch and watches the steam rise, imagining the consistency of dark blood running down elevator walls. He opens the biscuit tin and takes out four digestives, the edges of which have inexplicably eroded. He thinks, is there some kind of tiny parasite I don't know about that eats away at them?

Eritrea's blurry, distorted form is seen through the opaque square of glass in the kitchen door, framed against the background of privet. The spring in the handle whines as she tries it. It is locked, so she bangs impatiently on the glass. James leaps forward and turns the key and Eritrea steps over the threshold, pointedly ignoring him and giving her brother a look charged with thunder. 'You could've opened it.'

'I'm trying to make tea for our guest,' he replies acidly. 'Or perhaps you'd prefer me to be rude to visitors?' The question is left hanging and James looks mortified.

Eritrea runs a hand through her dark curls and takes her bag from her shoulder. Her white school collar peeps over the blue jumper. Underneath the zigzag creases of wool are the enticing curves of young girl budding into young woman. Green eyes look impassively through thick lashes at the visitor. Nose slightly turned up, a light covering of freckles on her cheeks. 'Can I come past, please?' A totally neutral voice, now: she is twelve going on sixteen.

James steps backwards and Paul marks away, oblivious.

Jonah slops tea on the stairs on his way back up. In the safe confines of the bedroom, James holds forth about pre-pubescent encounters with girls, a distant look in his eyes. 'On the last day when we were kissing in the caravan she took her top off so I could feel her up.' He talks on, going into more lurid details. Jonah wonders how he can blatantly speak such rubbish, riddled with inconsistencies, without feeling deeply embarrassed.

'You really fancy her, don't you?'

James knows from the disgusted tone that the reference is not to the fabricated female. 'What, Eri? No way. She's not my type. Anyway, she's your sister. It'd be gross.'

Jonah is not convinced. He wants to say, you're such a liar, you know. Don't think I can't see through you. He shakes his head in disgust and blows through his mouth, an imagined retort bringing the involuntary reaction. He is sitting on the window sill and looking over the garden: three squares of lawn. He has never shown James the den in the maple tree.

Paul and Rowena entered the doors of Glenfield Free Church like prisoners freed from a two-year stint in a windowless jail. Spiritually, they blinked and groped their way forward, unused to the light that suddenly surrounded them.

The pastor stood on a carpeted stage and preached with microphone in hand. There was no pulpit.

'Sometimes,' he said on the Trents' first Sunday, 'we carry all kinds of baggage around with us and we naturally think that it's a part of our character.' He had a habit of roving from one end of the stage to the other as he talked, addressing people personally, it seemed. 'Galatians is a great book,' he continued. 'A life-changing book. Not the kind of book you can read and then put down and forget about. It forces you to take decisions. One of its main messages to us is that our slavery is *over*. But we don't seem to understand what this really means.' He paused for a drink of water. 'Someone – a Christian – came up to me recently and manifested a completely unprovoked temper tantrum. I couldn't believe it. I said, "That's unreasonable and I won't stand for it," but this guy responded, "That's just my character. If you don't like it you're hampering my personal growth and not letting me be who I am." '

He shook his head. 'Hampering my personal growth. Those are the very words he used. If people have had an uncontrollable temper for years it doesn't mean to say that it's *just* a part of their *character*! Jesus has given us freedom from the slavery of those things, but we just don't seem to realize it. We say, "Oh well, that's just my character," but it *isn't*. In Galatians, Paul says, "Stand firm therefore, and do not submit again to a yoke of slavery." The slavery ended as soon as we gave ourselves to Jesus.'

Paul and Rowena were sitting together. The corporate feeling of conviction that touched them both through the pastor's words made them want to keep from looking at each other out of embarrassment. Something like the beginnings of an apology began to form in the back of Paul's mind, but it was still difficult for him to think clearly. Had he acted out of line towards his wife? He remembered shouting at Rowena about something a while ago, but his thoughts were somewhat indistinct and evaded him: he was still not used to hearing anything that sounded like truth.

After the calamitous service at St Peter's on the Sunday morning following the dream, Rowena had gone home, sat in the bedroom and cried. The children, sensing that something very bad had happened between their parents, had been deadly silent – almost fearful – on the way home, and had gone straight out into the garden. Paul had stood in the living room, uncertain as to what to do while the chicken cooked dry in the oven. He felt foolish and angry and sorry and confused. There was something frightening about the way that the conventional pattern of the day had been torn asunder by the outburst at the church; it was as though he were standing looking at the broken pieces of a precious vase he had smashed quite unnecessarily.

Eventually, he walked purposefully up the stairs and opened the bedroom door. Rowena was sitting on the bed, facing the window. He could tell from the way she leant on her arm that she was all cried out. He knew how her face would look. 'I know I sometimes overreact about the twins' safety,' he began uneasily, in his best conciliatory voice.

Rowena shook her head. 'You really are a child sometimes. What I had to say had nothing whatsoever to do with the children walking home alone.' This comment was addressed to the window. Then she turned around. 'You sent Nigel to come looking for me after the service, didn't you?'

'No, of course not. I didn't know where you were. I had no idea…'

For a while the two remained motionless, Rowena sitting looking out of the window and Paul standing behind her, every muscle in his body tensed. After an eternity, Rowena said, distractedly, 'They're playing in the tree. You can see the branches moving from here.'

Paul stepped up to the bed and touched her shoulder. 'So why did you say we had to leave in the middle of the service?'

Rowena turned and looked at him with a straight-faced expression that asked, are you really going to listen to me? I doubt it.

'Please,' he said.

37

They stood, mute, for a time. Then she told him about the dream.

Afterwards, he said simply, 'Okay, so we'll leave.' He was silent for a moment, before opening his mouth to speak again, but his words were drowned out by the smoke alarm.

A month passed while Paul fought a bitter battle with the guilt and fear. It rose up within him, a dark, intent force, strangling him during lunch break in the staff room, the way the jasmine strangled the maple tree in the garden. It waited for him in the car when the final afternoon bell rang. It greeted him in the morning when he stood, stupid with fatigue, under the shower.

The imagined scenario of the unavoidable conversation with Reverend Thacker stalked him. It grew and changed, depending on how he was feeling. Sometimes it became so convoluted that Nigel found his way into the images, standing behind the vicar and saying, 'If you go it'll all be finished. There'll be nobody left to pray for the church. You'll have let the side down.'

Then there was Rowena sitting on the bed, shoulders slumped in defeat. 'It wasn't an option,' she had told him. 'He said we had to go.' The feelings swirled around and got jumbled up in a bewildering maelstrom. He clenched his eyes shut during morning assembly, wishing he could be free of it.

By the first Sunday in September he had decided to speak to Abel, if not from conviction then from the utter frustration born of being plagued by incessant guilt. His hands were trembling when he approached Thacker, who was standing by the porch after the morning Communion, holding a cup of watery church coffee. Paul said, 'Could we have a word?'

They went to the lady chapel and Paul sat down, palms sweating. 'Rowena and I have been *thinking* recently –' he laid the emphasis on the word: he had meant to say, "praying" but knew the vicar might think he was being patronized spiritually – 'and we really feel that it's time for us... to move on.' Blood thumped in his ears.

The corners of Abel's mouth were creased down. He looked at the cluster of bubbles in the centre of his cup and sighed softly: it was a sigh of relief, but Paul interpreted it as one of disappointment.

'I know we said originally that we'd be committed to St Peter's for a lot longer, but Rowena, ah, I mean *we* think it would be best to... to...' the sentence ground to a halt.

Thacker tried to think of a suitably judicious response, but his mind was taken up with one thought: this interfering family is finally going to leave. He said, 'Well, this comes as a somewhat of a surprise, I must say.' He cleared his throat the way Paul's university tutor used to and looked up with a raised eyebrow. 'The way we do things here never has suited you, really.' It was not a question.

'No, no. It's not that. It's just...' Paul fell silent again, unable to find a single thing to say to support the lie.

There was a moment of silence. It dawned on Thacker: that's the last of the two troublemakers off the Church Council. But Paul was leaning forward, looking intense and worried. He needed a formal acquittal.

The vicar sipped his coffee. Perhaps he could say something about how their departure might affect the church in a negative way? The only thing that came to mind was that it might signal the end of the Sunday school, Jonah and Eritrea being the only two regulars. And if the Sunday school ended, then perhaps Nigel would leave, too. And if Nigel left there would be no facility for children, so that visiting families with children would never stay. It was a satisfying train of thought. He sniffed deeply and said to Paul, 'I think if you've thought the matter over carefully then you must move on.' He coughed and gave Paul a solemn look, trying to find some spiritual-sounding words that would round off the meeting nicely, but nothing came to mind.

'Personally, I don't necessarily think you should go. Not just now. Why be so final about it? I mean, for one thing, the kids are settled.'

'Yes, that's true.'

'Things *have* been slow, but there's so much to do here.' Nigel had paused. 'It's not because the prayer meetings fell through, is it?'

'No. Anyway, that was ages ago.' Rowena wanted to tell him about the dream, but it seemed oddly inappropriate. 'We're just acting on what we feel God wants us to do. I'm convinced he wants us to be somewhere else. I can't really put it any clearer than that.'

'You were crying a few weeks ago. Outside. Did that have something to do with all this?' There was apprehension in his voice.

'It... Yes. Sort of. I didn't mean not to tell you. I was only crying then, I suppose, because I somehow felt we'd been wasting our time here.' She did not want to bring her argument with Paul into the conversation, but she realized that by not doing so Nigel might easily misconstrue what she had said as being in some way negative about him, so she sought to mitigate the comment. She touched his arm. 'I know that sounds terrible, doesn't it? I didn't mean that *you* might have been wasting your time here, too. I just mean that we have to go. But I'm quite... concerned for you. Honestly. How are you going to manage?'

'I'll soldier on.' He shrugged. 'But of course you must go if God's told you clearly that that's what you should do.'

At Glenfield, it was difficult for Paul to come
his feelings. In August he had still considered
warrior, the last bastion of the true Christiar
church. Now he felt rather like a precocious c
admired his achievements alone and then sees w
doing.

There was no longer any immediate need to assume an
attitude of grave spiritual attentiveness during the service, nor
to intercede silently for a spiritual breakthrough during the
sermon. He was slightly depressed. On the outside he thought
it was because he felt redundant; just another bum on a seat in
a big church. The real reason was that inside, his soul pined for
the feeling of self-importance that had rooted itself in his
heart the moment he had seen the vision of Reverend Thacker
on his knees at the rectory two years earlier.

There was a peaceful, unaffected spirit at Glenfield that
made him feel inexplicably self-conscious and shy. Having
been away from other Spirit-filled Christians, yet having,
at the same time, considered himself at the pinnacle of his
personal Christian development, he now found himself feeling
embarrassed and even afraid when there were times of open
prayer or song. The Holy Spirit told him that the discomfort
he felt was actually something to be welcomed and accepted,
but His voice was still very quiet, and Paul was not yet able
to tell the difference between the Spirit's whisper and the
impatient, insistent call of his soul to do and say other
apparently spiritual things. Early on in the autumn, his soul
had led him to share – or rather boast – about how his time at
St Peter's had put him more in tune with spiritual warfare. But
as the scales gradually began to fall away from his eyes, the Holy
Spirit suggested to him that if he really *had* been discerning
or wise about such things he would never have talked about
them so openly anyway. He realized that perhaps the Glenfield

..e was trying to impress over post-service coffee were d aware of this already. So he shut up.

Paul was still a long way from realising that his attitude towards Abel Thacker, and especially his inability to broach the subject of leaving, had been symptomatic of his fear of being rejected – not only by the vicar, but by Nigel, too. Instead, he convinced himself that he had been wisely biding his time to act on Rowena's ultimatum. He was unable to see that the commitments he had originally made to the vicar had put him in a kind of bondage, so he chose to believe that he had been incredibly sensitive and patient towards Thacker for the last two years. Sometimes, he tried to pick his way through the intricate strands of incentive and motivation in his mind. It was not easy. The one thing that sometimes made him stop and think was the fact that, after all the time spent worrying about ending two years of commitment, the break itself had been like the snapping of a dry twig: an inconsequential anticlimax, over in a second. But he was unwilling to entertain the thought that God might not have wanted them to be at the church in the first place.

The fact that it had taken Paul a whole month to summon up the nerve to free the family from St Peter's, even when it was manifestly obvious that they were not really wanted there anyway, was something that Rowena was angry about for a long time. More infuriating still was that he had insisted *she* tell Nigel they were leaving. 'It doesn't make any difference who tells him,' she had said. 'If we make a decision as a couple then I can speak for you and you can speak for me.'

'If it doesn't make any difference, then you can tell him.'

'Why do you care so much about what he thinks of us? It's not like he's taken any initiative to get anything done in the church recently.'

Paul had greeted this comment with silence.

So Rowena had talked to Nigel, but only on the express condition that Paul go to Abel and tell him personally that they were leaving, rather than write a letter, as he had originally suggested.

When she arrived at Glenfield and saw how good it was, her first reaction was one of bitterness towards Paul. The unabashed sincerity of the services and the warmth of the fellowship only underlined the meaninglessness and futility of St Peter's. Gradually, however, the warmth began to penetrate her heart. After the Galatians sermon, she sat at home and read the whole letter. The passage about finishing in the flesh what had been started in the Spirit touched her and made her think about the time at the teacher training college when she and Paul had sat up together and prayed, not out of duty but out of joy and longing. It reminded her of a Paul that she had not known for some years, and she felt slightly less bitter towards him.

The following Sunday she fought and fought with herself, but was unable to keep from shedding a few tears during the worship. Judith Morewell, the youth group leader, noticed and approached her after the service. 'Come and have lunch with us,' she said.

Chapter 4

From the moment Eritrea stepped through the classroom door on her first day at secondary school she was worshipped. She seemed to be enveloped in an aura of exhilarating promise that reached out and touched the other two-dimensional people around her, animating them with light and colour whenever she turned her attention to them. And they longed for her to do so, because Eritrea did not speak to people so much as confide in them; giving them, if only for a moment, the feeling that they were fundamentally significant when she addressed a few words to them in her soft, perfect voice.

People leaned towards her as flowers bend towards a nourishing source of sunlight. The boys in her class grew up, became accountants, married and had children, but still sometimes lay awake in the small, cold hours of a shadowy Monday, filled with regret that they had not captured her.

But Eritrea could not be captured. All the males in her class had, lodged in their mind, minute sensory snapshots of the elemental Eritrea: her fine long-fingered hands holding a pen, the motion of a curl falling irresistibly over her face as she leant over a book, the alluring, fleeting perfume of her cold cheek in a queue in the corridor on a winter morning. They nurtured these tiny memories, but they could not possess the whole Eritrea. And they knew it. What was in her was genuine and compelling – so much so that her peers adopted an almost reverential attitude towards her – but it was also tantalizingly intangible. The quality defied description. It simply was.

She was not subject to the politics and pecking orders that bound the rank and file of her class – she sometimes spoke to the lowliest and most despised pariahs. Any other girls in the class who crossed the lines of popularity by talking to such outcasts would only have been providing the physical evidence that they had fallen from popularity and were desperately seeking to secure some kind of recognition from anyone who would give it, to protect themselves from further rejection. But when Eritrea sat next to an outcast it was an act of charity and an assertion that her status could not be affected by anything she did. The other girls looked on, confused and somewhat afraid that someone could consciously violate the immutable laws that bound the classroom together.

The fortunate two she selected as her confidants were Paula Heathfield and Nicola Lee, two of the other most popular girls in the form. Together Eritrea, Paula and Nicola formed a female triumvirate that ruled the class, providing the boys with a target audience for their ever more desperate offerings of juvenile bravado and bullying.

At weekends Eritrea preferred to spend time over at the girls' places, although her parents' house was larger. Saturday evenings were spent in a bedroom dissecting the attributes of screen actors and making endless comparisons with the various males, school and otherwise, that they knew.

'He's so *slimy*. I don't know how she lets him just run his hands all over her body,' Paula shivers with a grimace. 'I wouldn't let him put his tongue in my mouth for a million years.'

'Paula, you're talking about Brad Pitt not *Rowan Atkinson*,' Nicola replies, in a voice charged with the kind of patronizing sarcasm that only an attractive pre-pubescent girl can pull off with style. All three girls are staring at the silent grey frenzy of dancing specks on Nicola's TV screen after a film. 'Anyway.

You're jealous. You know Eri could have Brad Pitt if she wanted him. Couldn't you?' She is lying face down on her bed, chin in her hands, bare feet in the air. She leans forward on her elbows and blows on Eritrea's head. 'Couldn't you?'

'Yes, that's right. He wants a twelve-year-old from Marlborough. Actually he called this evening and I had to put him off. Silly of me, because I wind up watching one of his films anyway.' Eritrea is slumped in a bean bag, propped up against the bed. She sits forward and tries to form the polystyrene contents of the cushion into a more comfortable shape. 'Shit!' She has knocked the dregs of her juice on the carpet.

'Don't worry about it.'

'Well, Eri can have him for all I care.'

'But I don't want him. This is a stupid conversation.' She has wiped up the juice with a handkerchief and is rinsing it under the tap in the bedroom washbasin.

'Anyway, I'd rather kiss Neil Baker than Brad Pitt,' Paula continues slyly, inviting comment, as she shoves the next video into the machine with a clatter.

'Oh, why don't you tell us something we *don't* know,' says Nicola. She and Eritrea laugh.

Contrary to his assertions, Jonah's friend James was hopelessly and inextricably in love with Eritrea. The adrenalin rush he experienced when she entered a room was akin to physical pain. When he was away from her, he suffered the conventional dull ache that most desperate suitors feel when they know that they are chasing a dream that will never become reality.

Mentally, he tried to clothe his desire in romantic respectability, thinking that if Eritrea could read his mind she would see that the decency of his intentions was comparable in nature to her own purity in spirit, and then acquiesce.

Really, however, his intentions were far less innocent than even he could admit to. He wanted to kiss her, to touch her, even during church. He could not sleep sometimes.

One afternoon he arrived at the Trent house alone. Rowena had come to the door in an apron. 'You could wait for him in the living room or upstairs if you want. He should be back in a few minutes.'

James wandered into the living room, examined the carriage clock on the mantelpiece, picked up a magazine from the coffee table and flicked through it. Snatches of conversation drifted from the kitchen over a running tap and the scrape of a potato peeler. 'I can't believe it's entirely wasted time.'

'No – you mustn't think like that. There'll come a time when you'll look back and see that there was a reason for it. I remember when Phillip lost his job. He didn't know what to do. He was *destroyed*. A year later, though, he was thanking God for it.'

'You say that. I'm sure he didn't say, "Thank God I lost the job." '

'Not *like that*. But later he admitted that it wasn't what he'd really wanted originally. He even recognized that he'd got so caught up in it and proud about it that he couldn't let go of it himself any more. He needed God to take it away.'

'Yes, well, it's taken Paul over a year to admit he's more concerned about what people think than what God wants. But he'd *never* say that he was too proud to let go of St Peter's.'

'Give it time. With Phillip, I think that if we hadn't prayed and given that job over to the Lord before he started, He'd never have taken it away. He'd have just let it wear him into the ground.'

Water was poured down a plughole. 'But when *we* prayed about St Peter's –'

47

James felt uncomfortable. Usually he was a shameless eavesdropper, but a private conversation between his youth group leader and the mother of his best friend was simply too close to home. It made him feel profoundly uneasy. He stepped lightly through the living room door and up the stairs.

His intention was to turn into Jonah's room, but then he felt a sharp tick of electricity in his chest on noticing Eritrea's bedroom door ajar. He paused for a moment, hand on the banister, battling with base instincts. Then he took a deep breath and tiptoed across the landing to her room.

An enthralling, almost imperceptible fragrance blended with the air as he pushed the door open. He saw the shaft of afternoon light reflected on the parquet slats, a plump white cushion in the corner by the window, a paperback thrown open, spine up, like a miniature paper tent. He held his breath and stepped in. Gradually the divine surroundings soaked in. A print of Monet's bridge by the dresser, pine chair with *her* jeans slumped inert over the arm, hurriedly made bed with the bottom corner of the duvet touching the polished wooden floor like a lover's gentle finger tenderly brushing its partner's shoulder. James might have sat down on the bed, but he did not want to defile it. Slowly he let out his breath, relaxed his shoulders and tasted again that wonderfully feminine scent. Then, behind the sink he noticed a round wicker basket – the type that might have housed a cobra had it been standing in an Indian street. His heart pounded and a black veil of desire swathed his common sense, then took control. He crossed the floor, opened the lid and lifted out a diminutive white bra. He held it to his cheeks, closed his eyes, pressed it into his face, smelt the stimulating, epicurean smell of perfume interwoven with skin.

'You can keep it if you want.'

He spun around.

'You know, as a memento or whatever.'

Eritrea was standing casually in the doorway with a hand on the frame, watching, a look of mild curiosity in her eyes.

James died a thousand deaths. He opened the basket and laid the article back on top of the other clothes gently and regretfully. He closed the lid and walked back to the door, ears flaming. Eritrea moved to one side to let him pass. For one unbearable second they were both standing side on, in the doorway. Then the door was shut behind him with an innocuous click.

Two people were untouched by Eritrea's charms. The first was Judith, the twins' new Sunday school teacher, and the other was Lucy Rayner, also from the youth group and in Eritrea's class at school.

In the case of Judith, the feeling was mutual. Eritrea could not, for the life of her, understand what it was that inspired the feeling of defensive animosity that rose within her when she was around Judith. She hated to think that someone might take a dislike to her without just cause, a feeling that was compounded by a formless intuitive fear that crept around the edges of her mind when she so much as thought of her.

The friendship that her mother had with Judith made Eritrea's life somewhat complicated. Eritrea was loathe to put her feelings into words – she could not describe them anyway – so they remained on a purely motivational level. Judith was polite to Eritrea, but made no attempt to smooth over the jarring collision of their personalities with a kind word or smile when the two occupied the same space in a room. Nobody else seemed to notice this clash. It was never mentioned, even in passing, and became the closest thing to paranoia that Eritrea had ever felt.

Lucy was another baffling case. At first, Eritrea was convinced that her inability to approach Lucy and have a
conversation with her was because of Lucy's proximity to
the Judith situation. But there was no logic in that, because it
wasn't as though Lucy was particularly close to Judith anyway
– she simply attended the church youth group. Stranger still
was the fact that Lucy was in Eritrea's form group and the two
lived very close to one another. Like Eritrea, Lucy was a
Christian, but was considered a "square" by the rest of the
class. This was a relatively mild verdict, considering the kind
of damning judgement that twelve-year-old schoolgirls are
usually capable of passing on someone for being in any way
different from the crowd, but Eritrea felt guilty for not trying
to protect Lucy from some of the more malicious comments
and slander that sometimes came her way. And for every
week of term that passed without Eritrea making overtures of
friendship there was less possibility of the two talking to each
other at church. The situation just developed, bizarrely and
unaccountably.

'I can't understand why you don't give her a chance. Jonah
walks home with James,' Rowena ventured once, the way
mothers do.

'Yeah, and don't I know it. He spends half his life here,'
Eritrea retorted. And most of that time is spent with his face
in my linen basket, she thought.

Not surprisingly, Eritrea found it difficult to go to youth
group. She felt offended and indignant around Judith, ashamed
around Lucy and disgusted around James. At first she stayed in
the services, much to her parents' consternation. Then, one
Saturday, she stayed the night at Nicola's house and had a valid
excuse not to go to church the following morning.

She walked home from school with Nicola and Paula,
until their paths diverged. Often, Lucy could be seen on the

opposite side of the road, bobbed blonde hair, stooping walk, bag slung over her shoulder, eyes straight ahead. The eyes might have been saying, I won't tell anyone that you go to church if you don't. Eritrea did not know what kind of sign was intended by this pointed, deliberate disregard. Perhaps Lucy meant nothing; perhaps she was simply self-conscious.

In keeping with the school convention of singling out and condemning anything out of the highly pretentious norm, Paula and Nicola poured scorn on Lucy.

'She looks like an alien.'

'Clomping around in those utterly ridiculous shoes that went out with, like, the stone age.'

'But she has to wear them. It's part of her religion, like, I don't know, penance or something.'

The two girls tittered. Lucy loped on, ten metres or so ahead, on the other side of the road. 'Oh *Gawd*, thank you for – inyourgreatmercy – permitting me this *honour* of suffering for thy great sake. Amen.' Nicola mimicked an absurd upper-class accent – nothing like Lucy's real voice – rubbed her chest and panted as though in ecstasy. Eritrea walked on in silence as the two fell about laughing.

Now here was the strange thing: both Nicola and Paula actually knew that Eritrea went to church too, but they were careful to give the subject a wide berth. If Eritrea happened to mention that she was going to be involved in some kind of Christian event, they adopted a considerate, even respectful, tone when referring to it. It was ludicrously hypocritical.

When Paula and Nicola went their separate ways, Eritrea was left to walk the rest of the distance alone. By that time she was usually a hundred metres or so behind Lucy because the girls dawdled. Lucy then turned off to the left and went up the hill to her house, sometimes glancing back momentarily at Eritrea, despite herself. Eritrea walked down her road, through the garden gate, and down the passage between the wall and the hedge. Outside the kitchen door she sometimes wondered why she and Lucy were not the best friends that, in another life, they might have been.

Chapter 5

It was December the nineteenth of Jonah's second year at secondary school. Soaking sleet fell from a lead-grey sky as he stood in line with the other rowdy members of 8R outside the main school building, waiting to be given the order to walk to the bus that would take them to the Marlborough Grammar School carol service. There was pushing and shoving and a general air of festivity. The Christmas holidays were only one-and-a-half hours away.

Only one-and-a-half hours.

When Jonah had heard in a morning assembly a month previously that the church normally used by Marlborough Grammar was unavailable, his mind had quickly led him through the other possibilities and straight to the unthinkable. He had tried to shut it out, imagining that the longer he entertained the thought, the more likely it would be for the school authorities to decide on St Peter's Parish Church.

But they did anyway. It was the only other local church grand enough to befit the head's expectations of what the school, with its reputation, merited.

Like his father, Jonah was subject to feelings of guilt over which he had no control. He had overheard some of his parents' arguments before the move from St Peter's and he knew that, at least for a time, his father had considered leaving the church as tantamount to desertion. He had hardly even been surprised when his father had found himself unable to get out of some task related to cleaning the physics lab, that merely happened to coincide with the service.

Jonah's desire to escape the potential embarrassment of being recognized at St Peter's was so great that he considered faking illness and missing school altogether. But he was incapable of lying so openly, so that had been an impossibility. Perhaps he could do something bad enough to earn himself a detention? But the detentions were to be held back at the school *after* the carol service. It was a truly impossible situation, and at one o'clock Jonah found himself being herded on to the bus with the rest of his class.

His legs were already shaking as he entered the nave doors and smelt the smell of faded hassocks and old wood, saw the green canvas and metal of the chairs that had been brought up from the church hall vault. He kept his head down as he stood waiting in the main aisle, while a history teacher and his form tutor tried to find a way around the logistical problem of fitting the four classes of Year Eight into three pews. Once seated, he closed his eyes and drifted out of his physical body as the boys on his left and right pushed, shouted, howled and swore. Hands slapped at his shoulders. 'He's praying. Look he's praying!' More laughter. The rest of the school filed into the church, filling it as it had never been filled in the two hundred years of its existence. The A-level prefects had the honour of sitting at the back, in the proper chairs.

The service started. 8R's state of restless excitement was further kindled by the obligation of silence. James poked his friend. 'Wake up. It's started.'

The first hymn, *Oh Come All Ye Faithful*, provided the opportunity for more horseplay. During the chorus 8R literally screamed out the final *Oh come let us adore Him*, causing one of the Year Seven form tutors to turn and glower at them. He raised a finger. I'm on to you, it said.

There was a Bible reading, then another carol. 8R became more raucous, attracting looks from other members of staff around the church. Abel Thacker himself scuffed across the dais and stepped into the pulpit. 'This is a very special time,' he said, looking over the congregation of children – his worst nightmare. 'A time for celebration. A time for praise.' Then one of the boys next to Jonah was pushed from behind and let out a loud, aggrieved, 'Ow!'

Things happened very quickly, but later, when the episode played itself over and over in Jonah's mind, everything seemed to take place far too slowly – like actions in a silent, recurring nightmare. The teacher who had raised his finger in warning whipped round. Jonah, who had been keeping his eyes on the red floor tiles, chose that particular moment to glance upwards and met the stare of the infuriated teacher who said, in a voice charged with wrath, 'You! Stand up!' Jonah had pointed stupidly to his chest. You don't mean me. Surely not me. Abel Thacker had stopped speaking. The entire school was poised and on the edge of their seats.

'Yes you, arrogant boy. Stand up!'

Jonah sat, frozen. His top and bottom teeth seemed to have melted together. The teacher rose from his pew, strode over and grabbed Jonah's blazer with a pincer-like hand, making the top button of his shirt cut into his neck. He dragged him from the pew and pushed him into the centre of the aisle. 'You will stand here,' he hissed in fury. Then he went back to his pew, sat down and twisted his head and shoulders in a self-justified kind of way, to straighten his jacket.

A drop of sweat formed in the damp area behind Jonah's knee. It felt ice-cold as it slid down his calf. He stood, rooted to the spot, heart pounding as though it would push itself out of his chest, with the eyes of several hundred pupils and tens of teachers fixed on him. The space that he had vacated quickly closed up as the rest of 8R settled themselves more comfortably in the pew. They were absorbed; they were captivated. Their eyes reflected a sudden serious, mature involvement with the sermon. Butter would not melt in their mouths.

The thirty minutes that followed were some of the most agonizing of Jonah's life. Minute, invisible insects seemed to be crawling all over his body, through his hair, in his armpits and over his feet. He struggled to fight down the bitter-tasting bile that tried to force its way into the back of his throat.

For a long time, he stood motionless in the same stooped position he had finished up in after being pushed into the aisle, and he kept his eyes fixed straight ahead on the steps of the dais, a few metres away. Thacker talked on. Another hymn came and the rest of the school rose and stood, in a strange show of solidarity it seemed. They sat down again. Jonah thought, hazily, it looks like I'll get that detention after all. Then he glanced away to his left and met the gaze of Nigel Stephens, his former Sunday school teacher. Nigel had no expression on his face; he was simply watching him. Jonah lowered his head and the insects crawled with intensity, eating into his flesh, irritating the eczema on the backs of his hands.

Then the carol service was over. The pupils were dismissed, one class at a time, from the back of the church. Jonah's class stood up and filed out with the genteel reverence of monks. As he passed his friend, James gave a slight, guilty shrug and whispered, 'I've got to go, I'm being picked up today.'

Et tu, Brute, Jonah thought. Nobody gave him permission to move. Then the Year Sevens ahead of him rose and glanced at him fearfully as they might look at a leper. There were whoops of joy from the back of the nave and the courtyard: a cacophony of excited voices talking over each other, riotous general hilarity.

Finally, the teacher who had grabbed Jonah strutted over to where he was standing. 'I hope this has taught you to show a little respect for the church.' His voice was dangerously low.

In another situation, Jonah might have sought to protest his innocence, but there was no point; the episode seemed to have been predestined. If the mere thought of St Peter's, a month ago, had been enough to bring him back here and cause this incident, arguing or appealing would only lead to something worse.

'Don't just stand there. Don't you have anything to say?'

'I'm… sorry?' Jonah answered slowly, bewitched.

'Go. Go on, get out.'

Jonah walked slowly out of the swinging double doors, mute and detached. He was no longer the object of anyone's attention. Boys had broken into groups and were making their way out through the church gates. Some threw their bags into the air. Others scuffled and fought with each other as they waited for a parent to pick them up in the family Mercedes. Nigel Stephens was nowhere to be seen.

Jonah slipped around the side of the church between the oak and the wall. The sound of holiday merriment faded. He held the rail above the steps leading to the vestry, as his mother had once done, and felt the sleet on his ears and neck. He leaned forward, smelled the cold smell of wet rusted metal, let the metal touch his forehead.

On rising, the wintry wind struck his face. The grass was the same gunmetal grey as the sky. Perhaps nobody has stood on these steps for years, he thought, hands numb from gripping the bar. There was a bizarre kind of calm out here, behind the church. He stood for a time, breathing through clenched teeth, battling with the urge to empty his stomach. Then, when he was sure the coast was clear he straightened up and stumbled back past the oak, through the empty courtyard and out of the gates.

Instead of entering the house, he walked down the side passage, past the kitchen door and towards the back garden.

Tiny bluish spots danced in front of his eyes and he was so light-headed he felt as though his whole body were being lifted from the ground. The grass seemed not to bend under his feet. Stepping on the dark, slippery stones of the crazy paving, he lost his balance slightly and half fell into the hydrangea, a mass of tangled branches, leaves and brown, rotting clumps of flowers.

The stream was swollen and dark with mud. Jonah crouched down beside it, but then, on reflection, sat down fully and relaxed; he felt the excruciating prickle of droplets falling into his hair, the tickle of water running through his scalp, the uncomfortable chill of damp seeping through his trousers, through his pants. He picked a blade of grass. Then he leaned against the stump of the maple trunk and traced the pattern of the exposed rings with the tip. The tree had only been cut down a month or so ago; there were still patches of wet sawdust on the ground, and the inside of the trunk had not yet started to go dark from exposure to the elements.

It was somehow liberating to sit there in the cold and let the sleet and the mud do as they would. Jonah knew that probably nobody had been down to the bottom of the garden since his father had gone there with a chainsaw to put the tree out of its misery during the autumn storms. And Paul had done a thorough job: gone, too, was all of the jasmine and much of the hedge. There was something sad, desolate even, about the open space that was left behind following the desecration of what had once been their private territory. But Jonah knew that nobody else would disturb him here and he gradually felt his stomach muscles start to unclench, despite the cold. The crashing waves of guilt and revulsion from the scene in the church began to dissolve away under the freezing rain. Soon he would stand up, walk back up the garden and through the kitchen door. He would peel off this wet school uniform and cast it aside, as a snake sheds its skin, and stand under the shower. But not just yet. Over the rippling of the stream he heard – very muted on the wind – the strains of *In Dulce Jubilo* from a neighbour's house and he remembered that the Christmas holidays had started. No, he would not get up just yet.

Chapter 6

The muscles of Eritrea's face were tensed in an irrepressible smile. She and Nicola were standing to one side of the lobby of Bebidas club. All around them teenagers, painfully conscious that they were being watched and sized-up by the many other young people, affected airs, shouted or tried to look detached or uninterested. Clusters of boys slouched together and let out loud, mating-call laughs, almost on cue. There were also safe little cliques of girls: chests wrapped in tight cotton and lycra, legs needlessly shaved. They licked experimentally at the edges of lips coated in blood-red wax, touched their hair, recounted realistic-sounding stories of fantasy males, rolled their eyes and threw their hands up in simulated disgust. He was such a drag. Nothing but a thorn in my side. I had to cast him off. A snap of the fingers: like that.

The sound of a pumping drumbeat from the adjacent dance hall permeated everything and smothered the reality of the situation – nervous youngsters packed together like battery hens, desperately hoping for an opportunity. The air was thick with inexperience. Cracks were appearing in the thin veneer of feigned worldly wisdom; looks of been-there-seen-that were already interspersed with unintentional anxious, darting glances at Justin Stewart, the idol of Year Twelve, and the other older, more experienced, boys.

'I told you it'd be easy.'

'You what?' Nicola shouted, fiddling with the corner of her sleeve.

'Getting in, of course. Nothing to it.'

60

'Yeah, well, if Paula doesn't hurry up and get out of the bog somebody'll see us and we'll all get kicked out.'

Eritrea laughed. 'Who by – a teacher?'

'Maybe. Or that cow Alison – she'd be bound to go running to old Harvey on Monday.' She hung her head on one side and said, in a squeaky, high-pitched voice, 'Oh Mr Harvey, I thought you'd like to know three girls from your class were at Bebidas last Friday.'

'Don't be stupid. How can anyone check up on us?'

Paula emerged from the ladies' adjusting her skirt. 'Thanks for waiting.' The anxiety in her voice gave her away.

In an effort to crack down on the escalation of under-age drinking in Marlborough, the boards of governors of several secondary schools had, against their better judgement, decided to organize an alternative to the Dog and Duck for the local contingent of thirsty minors. An agreement had been made with the ailing club Bebidas for a Friday evening disco, open to anyone between the ages of fourteen and seventeen. The manager had been unwilling. 'How do you expect a club to make anything selling lemonade to teenagers? We're not running a bloody charity.' But his own daughter had recently been caught smoking dope outside the art block at school. On its own, that was not enough to persuade him, but the promise of a surprisingly generous council subsidy to make up for lost alcohol profits finally won him over.

'So what they're saying,' remarked Paul Trent, when the Bebidas plan was mentioned at a staff meeting, 'is that council money that should come to us goes to the kids so that they can hit on each other every Friday.' It was intended as a joke, but nobody laughed.

The project had been spearheaded by the headmaster of the comprehensive school that Eritrea attended. He had been dragged into resolving some of the more embarrassing and repetitious cases of teenage drunkenness involving pupils and was keen to avoid any more of his free time being taken up with it. 'But it won't succeed unless they see it as something exclusive,' he warned, while briefing his teachers. 'If just anyone is allowed in it'll lose all credibility, the kids we're trying to keep out of the pubs won't go to it, and it's back to square one, which nobody wants.'

So the Bebidas initiative was implemented, with teachers from the local secondary schools warning students that anyone under fourteen caught trying to get in would be turned away and their parents notified. 'And don't think that you can get away with it,' Eritrea's form tutor said, trying to sound as though he cared. 'We *can* and *will* punish you here in school if we find out you tried to get in.'

'Of course we're going,' Eritrea said to Nicola during break time.

'Oh yeah,' Paula said, 'and get suspended in the process.'

'Come *on* Eri,' Nicola said. You can't be serious. You –'

'Are you a chicken?'

'– heard all that crap about parents and stuff.'

'So, a chicken, then?'

Nicola gave her a look, come on don't pull that one on me.

'The whole thing is stupid. It's a complete contradiction. Think of all the Year Nines who won't be able to go. Like, half the class are allowed in but you can't go because your birthday's in April. Oh yeah, that sounds fair.'

'It might be unfair if we actually *were in* Year Nine,' Paula remarked.

Eritrea thought for a moment. 'This is nothing. It's *less* than nothing. We'll all go and if we get caught you can both say I masterminded it and forced you against your will, or something.'

'As if anyone's going to believe that.'

'God! It's not like we're going to get chucked in prison. I'll say I had a carving knife in my bag and that I'd cut you if you didn't go in with me, okay?'

Eritrea looked over the balcony at the rolling sea of heads flickering in the strobe light. The plummy fragrance of dry ice and unisex eau de toilette failed to mask a less innocent odour of stale cigarettes and old beer. The incongruent pastiche of smells made Eritrea feel heady. She was queen of all she surveyed. Near the DJ she saw Alison from Year Twelve moving and trying, pathetically, to look provocative for her boyfriend Justin, who stood opposite her and stepped to the music, not unlike a penguin. She thought, all right, so he looks okay but if he kisses the way he dances... One of her favourite songs came on and she wandered down the stairs, through the crowd and started to dance, alone. Two songs later she was tapped on the shoulder. Nicola leaned nervously towards her and shouted, 'And where were you?'

'Here. Where d'you think?'

Nicola was still playing with her sleeve. She'll make a hole in it if she carries on, Eritrea thought. 'Why don't you dance? C'mon don't be so frigid.'

Nicola stood for a moment, looking flustered, and then started to move, hesitantly. She looked edgy and deeply ill at ease.

'Where's Paula?' said Eritrea in the brief lull between songs.

'She saw Neil Baker over there.' Nicola waved her hand in an arc that covered half of the club.

'Neil and Paula,' replied Eritrea sarcastically. Nicola smiled. The next song kicked in.

A little while later, Eritrea walked back up the steps to the balcony surrounding the dance floor. Sweaty, and with a heavy pulse ticking in her ears, she scanned the tables and booths. Neil Baker saw her from where he was sitting in a corner with Paula and motioned for her to join them.

She sat down on a low stool opposite them. Neil's arm was strategically draped over the top of the couch above Paula's shoulders, not actually on them. She looked coy, victorious even. Eritrea took a drink of Paula's lemonade. She couldn't be bothered to shout over the din. After a moment, Paula bent forward. 'Stay here and don't let him go anywhere. I'll be back in a minute.' Then the coy look again. She rose, straightened her skirt over her thighs and trotted down the stairs.

Eritrea watched her slip out of the door towards the toilets thinking, she spends half her life in there. Then she felt eyes burning into her neck and swivelled around to meet Neil's gaze. His arm was still on the back of the couch. The two exchanged looks. Eventually he lifted his arm down and sat forward, putting his hands together like a Mafia godfather. He said something that Eritrea couldn't hear.

'You what?'

'Paula said you threatened to stab them with a kitchen knife if they didn't come.'

'That's right. They're such cowards it was the only way to get them here. It's in my bag. Want to see it?'

Neil gave a sardonic "please" kind of look. 'I'll take your word for it. Just as long as you don't use it on me.'

'Unlikely.'

A silence. Then: 'You know I like you Eritrea.'

'No I don't.'

'That's why I came. I just knew you'd be here. I just knew it.'

She raised her eyebrows. 'On your own, right?'

He nodded. 'Yeah, but I met some other guys from class. They're over there.' He signalled with a thumb. 'So I bump into Paula and I know you're here too. This whole thing is a crock of shit −' his tone assumed complicity − 'but I knew you'd come *just* because they said we couldn't. That's what you're like. Anyway, I guessed right.' He leaned further forward and a lock of hair fell over his face. He combed it back with his fingers. Eritrea thought of Paula fumbling to apply mascara in front of a packed mirror and thought, God help me. She reached up and touched his hand and held it for a moment while he looked back in mild shock. Then, impulsively, she drew him towards her and kissed him.

When she broke off he remained hanging in the air, frozen in the same position with a wide-eyed look on his face, like a gasping trout. They watched each other for a moment.

'Why d'you do that?' he said, trying − and failing − to mask bewilderment. In the eerie half-light of the balcony his face suddenly seemed paler, the skin of self-assurance torn away.

Seeing the effect the kiss had had on him made her feel warm to the tips of her toes, but she gave nothing away with her expression. She simply said, 'Don't tell Paula, 'cause if you do, she'll kill me.'

Neil shook his head. He looked afraid. Then Paula was at the top of the stairs.

Later, when the three girls were together on the dance floor, Paula said to Eritrea, 'An hour ago I'm, like, fighting him off but suddenly he *totally* loses interest. I don't know what's up with him.' She sounded hurt and frustrated. 'And then he just goes and disappears.'

Half an hour before the end of the evening, Eritrea made an excuse and went to the bar. The beer pump handles were conspicuously covered. As she was sipping her drink she felt hands touch her hips. 'Eritrea Trent, just run off and break my heart.' She smiled without turning around and looked into the coppery depths of a whisky bottle hanging upside down on the spirits rack opposite her. 'What is it with you?' The voice attempted to salvage some self-assurance but the hands were trembling. It was touching, almost pitifully so.

So she turned, took his hand and led him to a secluded corner. He followed, like a lamb. She sat up on a high stool and he stood before her. Putting his hands back on her hips he leaned towards her and kissed her, fearfully and timidly at first, but then with more fervour. She gripped his torso between her legs.

Once, he broke away and looked up at her with a mixture of eagerness and apprehension, all guile peeled from his face. Then his lips touched hers again. Hands slid up the smooth, velvet skin of her back, over the tiny alluring bump of a mole, until they met cotton. Then, they moved slowly around to her chest. She offered no resistance as he handled her with his uncertain, adolescent hands, slipping the underwired support of her bra up over her breasts and caressing them, feigning practised expertise.

She let him touch her as they kissed for several more minutes. Then, hearing the anthem of the last song, she took his elbows, gently removed his arms and placed them back by his sides, the way a nurse might take a desperate patient's grasping hands and lay them softly on the bed-sheet. Again she said, 'Paula can't know about this.'

'You don't even have to say it,' he replied huskily.

'We'll go downstairs separately. Paula'll be waiting down in the lobby – that's what we arranged. We'll meet up there.'

Paula was already there. 'Where's Nicky?' she asked, agitated. 'First Neil disappears, then you, then Nicola. God, I sound paranoid.'

Eritrea saw Neil trot down the stairs. Something in his step made him look fragile, as though he were about to come undone. He stood like an obedient but guilty dog, equidistant between the two girls.

'Do we wait for Nicky inside or outside? I've been here five minutes already,' Paula said irritably, aware perhaps that something was not quite right.

Neil looked increasingly uncomfortable. 'Well. I think I'm gonna make a move anyway.' He took the cloakroom ticket from his pocket with his vulnerable hands, not sure whether to look at Eritrea or Paula. 'So... You'll be here next week?' The question was addressed to the air between the girls' shoulders.

'Yeah. For sure,' Paula said, too eagerly.

Then, as he started off towards the cloakroom, she reached out an arm and made as if to say something. But he was gone. 'You see what I mean,' she whispered, hurt. Eritrea looked at the garish red diamond pattern on the carpet.

The girls waited a further five minutes and then headed out of the main door. The other teenagers were dispersing, fading into the shadows. A few were making out ostentatiously under street lamps or writhing in doorways. Unsuccessful boys were still shouting and laughing, but it was more forced and urgent now – the evening was over and their efforts to seduce a member of the opposite sex had been fruitless.

Then Paula saw Nicola and rounded on her. 'We were waiting in there for *hours* looking stupid. You *said* you'd meet us in the corner by the bogs. You –' she saw that Nicola's eyes were bloodshot and grief-stricken. 'What is it?'

Nicola clenched and unclenched her teeth to keep back the emotion. 'Let's walk.' She strode ahead, arms folded and hands gripping the backs of her bare upper arms against the cold. 'It was that bitch Alison. I was dancing, but I thought I'd come and find you, Eri. So when I'm trying to get through the crowd I nearly bump into her, and she goes straight out and comes back in with this bouncer. I'm still looking around for you but the bouncer chucks me out. I couldn't even get my coat.' She paused, fighting back tears of resentment. 'It was so humiliating. I had to give them my name and that bitch, that *bitch* Alison is with Justin Stewart and it… and it… And then I'm standing out here like a fool knowing you're waiting for me inside but what can I do? And then… Alison and Justin come out and she gives me this bitchy patronizing look. The *cow*.' She spat out a string of vengeful curses.

'I saw her about an hour ago but I didn't even think…' Eritrea said. She considered. 'But we'll make her pay.'

'Some consolation,' Nicola said. 'I'm freezing. I haven't even got my coat. I've been out here for years.' She hiccupped and tears sprang back into her eyes as the self-pity took control again.

They parted at the end of Eritrea's road. She slipped in through the front door. 'Paula's mum dropped you off okay?' Rowena called from the living room.

'Yep,' Eritrea lied trotting up the stairs. Suddenly the smell of old smoke on her jeans and in her hair seemed overpowering, a dead giveaway. Removing her top, she flicked her bedroom door shut with her foot, balled up her clothes and tossed them into the linen basket. She could hear her mother talking from the living room, as if she thought Eritrea was still in the hall. Wrapping her upper body in a towel, she opened the bedroom door, went to the top of the stairs and hollered, 'What?'

'That personal stereo under your bed. Where did you get it?'

'Mum, I've asked you not to go through my stuff!'

'I didn't go through anything. It was on the floor under the bed when I was vacuuming.'

'It's Paula's. It's on long-term loan.'

68

'Well, you should be more careful with it then. I nearly sucked it up into the vacuum cleaner.'

Eritrea went to the bathroom and shut the door while Rowena continued to talk, unaware that her daughter was no longer listening.

After taking a shower, she lay back on her bed like a new being, skin soft and dry. The memory of the driving beat filtered through her head and merged with the pumping of her heart. She closed her eyes and let herself sink into the duvet while a distant ringing echoed and reverberated in her ears. Through the musical residue she felt once again the rough graze of delicate teenage stubble around soft lips, timid hands on her thighs and chest. Her emotions were intricate layers of satisfaction, compassion, even sympathy, sandwiched between disjointed fragments of song melody. She felt no remorse for what she had done. Mostly she remembered Neil's naïve eyes again and again. Well, Paula did tell me not to let him go anywhere.

As she was drifting off to sleep, she remembered that she had not prayed for a while. Somehow it did not seem appropriate.

*

The following Monday seemed to Eritrea like an absurd, American teenage soap drama. She walked to school under the spring drizzle with Nicola and tried, in vain, to placate her.

'Look, I told you yesterday that nobody'll mention it. Nobody *cares*.'

'It's all very well for you. *You're* not going to get suspended.'

'And neither are you.'

'Yeah well, we'll see, won't we?'

'Nobody called your parents, did they?'

'Not yet.'

'So forget about it.'

Neil was waiting in the classroom with a well-prepared expression of adoring self-sacrifice tinged with wounded pride on his face, ready for Eritrea when she walked in before registration with a paranoid Nicola in tow. Paula was sitting next to Neil, talking loudly about the events of Friday evening in a desperate attempt to establish some point of rapport between them, for the sake of the others around her. He was having none of it.

As Eritrea had predicted, the day passed without a single teacher mentioning Nicola's incident at Bebidas.

'But I'm not going back next week, and that's final,' she said emphatically as the three sat around empty trays in the canteen.

'P-*lease*,' Eritrea retorted contemptuously. 'Paula's coming, aren't you?'

'Of course,' she replied, remembering words from last Friday that had not been intended for her.

'So there you go. And anyway, if you don't come you won't see Ms Alison get her just deserts.'

Nicola looked thoughtful. 'Well... there is that. If you can find a way to get her back, the bitch.'

Eritrea did have a plan, but it involved talking to Neil. She waited until after French, a class that neither Nicola nor Paula took, and then plucked his elbow in the corridor as the pupils were heading for break.

She watched a crisp packet skidding around the silted gutter at the far end of the junior playground. The drizzle hung in the air like Neil's last comment – a sticky haze.

'I know,' she replied. 'But it's just the heat of the moment. Spontaneous. I didn't think it was anything serious.'

Neil's thirteen-year-old vocabulary prevented him from explaining his feelings. He looked away and Eritrea was shocked to see that he was struggling to contain his emotions. She touched his arm. 'I thought... You know... Everyone gets off with each other all the time. I mean, it's the guy who has to go and break it off on Monday when *she* read too much into it.'

'Maybe. But with you, it's not like that.'

'C'mon, don't take it so seriously.'

They stood in stalemate while the crisp packet scraped its way up and down the wall.

'So... No hard feelings?' Eritrea ventured tentatively.

Another wait while Neil looked at his shoes. He felt clumsy in his school uniform. The bell rang.

He thought, how could I be angry with you? The memory of Friday evening, an exquisite dream of tactile exhilaration and stronger – but less tangible – feelings of yearning submission, had branded itself in his memory, burned a fiery trail through his soul and played itself back over and over again throughout the last two days and nights. He looked at her bare knees, damp from the rain, probably cool to the touch, and felt them again around his waist.

'Even if I wanted to, I couldn't have any hard feelings, could I?'

In school, she had never paid the slightest bit of attention to Justin Stewart, but between Tuesday and Friday she made a few signs to him; some subtle, some not so subtle. On Tuesday, she made sure that she was ahead of Nicola and Paula in the centipede of shoving and swearing that constituted the dinner queue, so that she could choose a table suitably near to where he was sitting. She did not advertise her presence, nor did she once turn to look at him, but she noted with satisfaction that he was not keen for his girlfriend Alison to sit with him at lunch: he was the typical egotist, preferring to eat within safe confines, behind several layers of adoring male cronies.

When Alison brought her tray over to his table on Wednesday and broke the testosterone circle, Eritrea pinned her ears back and heard, over the canteen din and the vernacular shriek of one dinner lady to another, the hint of irritation in Justin's voice as he attempted, grudgingly, to reconcile the opposing worlds of male clique and female interest.

'Have you listened to anything I've been saying?' Paula said. She snapped her fingers in front of Eritrea's eyes. 'Wake up, girl.'

'I'm awake.'

On Thursday, Eritrea was presented with an absolute gift that she was shrewd enough not to squander. At ten o'clock, after compulsory maths, she saw Justin alone in the corridor, opening his locker. It was raining hard outside and the sole window at the bend of the corridor, ten metres away, threw a warped white reflection on to the ugly orange flooring. The strip lights were off and the corridor was filled with the dreary, almost phantasmal half-light that seems to exist only in schools.

She thought quickly. Parts of the floor were still wet from being mopped. Such a perfect opportunity as this called for a piece of outstanding improvisation. She started to walk more quickly and then trot, as if in a hurry. As Justin was turning the key in the locker door she put her foot on a patch of damp floor. She had intended to fake a slip, so she was startled – but not at all dissatisfied – when she actually *did* skid. The bag flew out of her hand, spilling its contents far and wide. One green exercise book skittered and slithered its way across five metres of floor, landing close to Justin's feet. It couldn't have been thrown better.

'Shit,' she remarked stoically, almost to herself, bending down to begin picking up her paraphernalia and ignoring the figure opposite her.

'Here,' a voice said. A hand proffered the exercise book. She stood up slowly, dragging the ringlets out of her face and took the book. Justin looked at her for a moment, but all she saw was a dark silhouette framed against the distant window, greasy with rain.

'Thanks,' she said uninterestedly.

He vacillated. 'You okay?'

'Fine, as you can see.'

'That was a pretty big fall. You sure you didn't hurt yourself?' The tone was brusque, affected; attempting to cover any trace of genuine concern.

'No, I'm fine.'

The last of her possessions, a personal stereo, was retrieved and placed back into the bag. She tied the drawstring in a clumsy bow. Justin said, 'What are you listening to?'

'Jimmy Hendrix, if it still works,' Eritrea replied, already disappearing around the bend in the corridor.

So, she is sitting alone at the bar immediately to the left of the doors that lead from the lobby stairs to the club area itself. She is in a potentially vulnerable position: the Friday clubbers entering can see that she is obviously unaccompanied; she makes a point of displaying none of the signs that might indicate she is waiting for the protective cover of a friend to return from the toilets or wherever. Instead, she watches the girl in the striped Bebidas waistcoat wipe the fake tortoiseshell bar surface that is spotted with bubbly pock-mark cigarette burns. She thinks, that girl could clean all night and the bar would still look sticky.

She scans the crowd and is both relieved and piqued to see Neil already holding Paula's hand, a little way off by the square lights of the cigarette machine. There is something resigned in his stance but Paula looks smug and more than a little self-satisfied. Eritrea thinks, well, talk about not wasting any time. But his chagrined appearance pleases her. Part of him – a lot of him, perhaps – is still suffering.

Then Justin enters with Alison and a number of other devotees in tow. He glances at Eritrea, who does not have a drink. She sees him remember: the girl who tripped over in the corridor yesterday and who listens to Hendrix. Then he and his entourage have melted into the crowd. Did Alison see me? she wonders. Yeah, like I really care.

She walks on to the dance floor and loses herself for a while. Then comes the touch on her arm. She turns and sees Justin. 'Not here,' she shouts. 'Let's go to the bar.'

When they are settled at the bar he says, 'So what's your poison?'

'G and T, extra lemon.'

'Okay.' He signals to the bar girl. A gin and tonic for the lady and pint of lager.'

The girl gives him a tired, not-amused, look. She has heard it before.

'All right then. Orangeade for me. Make it two?' He points to Eritrea.

'No,' she says. 'Anything but that.'

'Okay, one orangeade and one cola.'

They sip the cold, artificial liquid. He says, 'How's your knee?' It is the only point of reference he has.

'Nothing broken.'

'I've seen you around this week.'

Less obvious now. She resists the temptation to say, that's because I wanted you to, you idiot. Instead, she smiles. 'Not the most original chat-up line I've ever heard.'

'I guess not.'

'Why d'you come here? You could be *out* out.'

'I got hammered at The Fountain a few weeks ago and told a barman where to go. They kicked me out and I got blacklisted so I'm laying low.'

'Not impressed.' She really is not.

'You're sure of yourself for someone who's not even supposed to be here... are you?'

'No.' She considers bringing Alison into the conversation; making a quip like, are you going to get your girlfriend to have me thrown out too? Instead she says, 'So.'

'So what?' He moves a little nearer.

'So let's hope you're better at kissing than you are at dancing or chatting people up.'

'Oh, and when did you see me dancing?'

'I was watching you from the balcony last week.' Flatter him. All guys love to be flattered.

'Who says I'm going to give you the chance to find out?'

'Who says I'm going to let you?' she answers as he leans closer.

At the end of the evening Paula and Neil waited for Eritrea in the lobby. When she made her entrance with Justin, Paula nearly swallowed her teeth. 'These are my friends,' Eritrea said, easily. 'Paula and Neil. Paula and Neil, this is Justin.'

'We know,' Paula replied. 'But –' she extended a hand – 'nice to be introduced.'

Neil felt as though a large thumb had descended from the sky and squashed him like a tiny insect: an ant or a fruit fly. He faithfully held Paula's hand and squinted at a poster of James Dean on the wall above the ticket booth as his throat constricted. It was a painful moment.

Then Eritrea saw Alison come through the swing doors with some of Justin's toadies. She was teetering on the brink of rage; fully wound up and ready to explode. From her face it was obvious that she had been looking long and in vain for Justin.

She saw him immediately through the crowd and was about to spit fire when she noticed Eritrea's hand in his. Her jawbone tensed as she bit down hard. Justin had not noticed her. Then one of the friends stepped over. 'We wondered where you were. But I see we should have followed the trail of your marauding dick.'

'Glad to hear you enjoyed yourselves, too,' he replied sarcastically, noticing Alison and disregarding her. The jilt was complete.

Two other toadies made their way through the crush. One of them said to Eritrea, 'You be careful with this one –' a tone of assumed intimacy – 'he only thinks of one thing, and it's not chess.'

'More like "chest" actually,' said the other.

The toadies laughed heartily. Justin did not.

Neil, unable to hear this, broke free from Paula and joined the queue for the cloakroom. The stooges gathered around Justin making loud, offensive jokes – but he did not release Eritrea's hand.

Alison had paused on the stairs, waiting for the one little word or sign from him that could be the catalyst for the outpouring of her rage, but it did not come. Perhaps aware that venting her wrath would only bring further shame on herself, she squared her shoulders and strode down the stairs, looking straight ahead. As she passed the group, however, she could not prevent herself from shooting Eritrea a look of pure hatred. Eritrea whispered to her, 'One all.' Then Alison was gone.

Paula opened her mouth, unable to find words. 'Oh Eri,' she breathed in admiration. 'If only Nicky could have been here. How did you do it? I mean… they were an *item*, weren't they?'

Eritrea leaned towards Paula. Purposefully and quietly, she said, 'I'm not coming back with you. If your mum asks where I am, tell her my parents picked me up earlier.'

'What if your mum calls my house?'

'She won't. She's never called when I've stayed over before.'

Paula opened her eyes wide. 'But what about *my* mum? We agreed... We're supposed to be walking back from the cinema together –'

'Okay. I felt ill after the film, I called my mum. She picked us up, dropped you off and took me home.'

'Fine. But what if your mum calls our place? She'll want to speak to you.'

'Lie. Tell her I'm already in bed, or something. Anyway, she'd never call. Not at this time.'

'You said –'

'How hard can it be? If there's any trouble it's my fault, not yours. Okay?'

Neil came back with his and Paula's coats, quite the gentleman. In the queue he had struggled with the desire to express his hurt with another of his well-practised looks – looks he had only had to develop that week – but he was more concerned that his beloved would not be left with a negative impression of him than he was about expressing the extent of his agony. Tight-lipped, he helped Paula into her coat and muttered, 'Come on, I'll walk you out.'

At that comment, the waves of agitation flowing from Paula to Eritrea evaporated. She said, 'Actually, you could walk me home if you want. I only live round the corner. Eri and I were supposed to be going back to my place, but she seems to have other plans now.'

Neil understood the implications. He almost dragged Paula out of Bebidas, to her delight.

Justin was beginning to grow weary of the tirade of sexual innuendo raining down upon him. It went against his nature to show any kind of affection whatsoever to a girl in front of his followers, but some instinct still kept him from releasing Eritrea's hand. The instinct told him, if you let it go she'll disappear and you'll lose her. To the friends he said, 'I'd love to stay and listen to this crap all night, but I'm not going to. Goodbye.' To Eritrea he said, 'I'll give you a lift.'

There was another 'woah' charged with carnal implication from the boys.

'That would be… nice…' Then she remembered something. 'I've just got to pick up a friend's coat first.'

They left the club with the last comment "cradle snatcher" ringing in Justin's ears. 'Bunch of pricks,' he murmured, searching for his car keys.

Eritrea slammed the passenger door shut and settled into the seat.

He was a flurry of activity, unnecessarily shifting the seat, wiping the fog from the windscreen. 'Heating doesn't work, sorry,' he commented, tapping the key on the metal surface of the ignition column, trying to find the keyhole. 'But then, nothing else does either.'

Suddenly, the activity stopped. There were a few seconds of silence: cold, damp and stale car air, the only noises the ticking of the indicator and the sound of the clutch spring relaxing as Justin removed his foot from the pedal. He turned slowly to look at Eritrea, as if he had just been slapped out of the well-formulated driving test routine. The evening light dimly illuminated her face; the droplets of condensation on the window made it seem mottled. She looked ethereal, as though she might vanish.

For a while the indicator ticked in time to the fading stanzas of dance music. Eritrea, half-shrouded in darkness, sat quietly, her green eyes tranquil. Then she said, 'Aren't you going to drive me home?'

'Who are you?' he said, in a remote voice, staring right through her.

She knew he had released his grip on the wheel – his skin made a chafing sound against the plastic.

'Eritrea. Eritrea Trent.'

'You know what I mean. I'm seventeen and…' He stopped himself before finishing. What he wanted to say was, you're just a kid but you could have anyone you wanted. How can that be? The thought drifted silently into the damp air with the cloud of steam that he breathed out.

They watched each other for a moment more. Then he leaned over the handbrake and kissed her. She responded, gently.

'If you wanted to,' he said, 'we could… go back to mine. I mean just for a bit.'

The engine coughed and stalled as they drove in silence to a destination unknown to Eritrea, a characterless house, masked in shadows; through the front door, the smell of someone else's parents and the traces of another family's evening meal that makes outsider visitors feel like intruders; a vacant white downstairs room, the shameful exposed torso of an adolescent with its patterns of developing adult hair; cold fingers on sensitive shoulders; clammy feet; an intimacy too momentous to be squandered in a clumsy moment such as this, but it is too late now.

Afterwards, Eritrea looked at Justin's face lying against the pillow. Like in the car, he seemed to be looking through her. His face was deconstructed; stripped of all bravado, stripped of secrecy. She was sitting up wearing his T-shirt, feeling sore and needing to go to the bathroom. So this is what it's like, she thought. And I need to go to the loo. She slipped her bare legs from under the cover and stepped lightly to the floor. His hand reached up, the hand of the desperate, grasping patient. She took it in her own and then laid it gently back on the sheet.

Chapter 7

Six teenagers sat ensconced in the back of a minibus that snaked its way around the acute hairpin bends of a North Wales road late one afternoon in midsummer. They were drugged by the heat; jeans stuck to sweating crotches, nerves were wearing thin. Every spare crack and crevice of the vehicle had been stuffed with camping equipment and supplies: tent bags were stowed under seats, the wooden poles of faded windbreaks poked the irritated passengers in the face. A forgotten packet of chocolate brownies wedged up in one corner against the back window slowly disintegrated into a sticky sludge in the July heat.

One of the girls – Lucy Rayner – headphone wire wrapped around her neck, sang, *'Well, I'm a lean, mean, love machine, and I've set my sights on you.'*

Judith Morewell, in the passenger seat, crumpled map in hand, threw her a cautionary look in the rear view mirror.

Lucy, with her thick white legs and conservatively bobbed hair, could hardly be described as lean or mean; as for being a love machine, she was sixteen and had never had a boyfriend of any description, much less been kissed. *Sweet sixteen and never been kissed* – sometimes the words appeared in her mind when she was feeling particularly low about herself. More fitting words for her song might have been *dependable, sensitive, romantic,* though, truth be told, she did have her sights set on someone…

Jonah shifted his numb legs. His soaking socks were encased in the sweltering prison of old trainers. A dismembered hand reached through a pile of sleeping bags and tapped him on the shoulder. James's muffled voice drifted through the flysheets and camping stoves. 'So, what d'you reckon you got in maths?'

'You won't leave it alone, will you? I'm *not* going to talk about exams, end of story.'

'How do you spell silk?' the voice continued.

'S-H-U-T-U-P,' Jonah answered.

'What do cows drink?'

'Rain water. Or any old water.'

'Toast, toast, toast, toast, what d'you put in a toaster?' James continued. He was on a roll.

'Bread,' Jonah answered.

'What about this one then —'

'No. Really. Shut up now.'

Lucy unwound her headphones. 'If I push that pole,' she said to Jonah, 'it'll stab him through the eye. D'you want me to do it, Nest?'

Lucy and Jonah maintained the strange, overly sarcastic relationship that characterizes Christian teenage friends of the opposite sex in a church situation; friends who want to make it quite clear to others — and perhaps to themselves as well — that nothing romantic will ever come of their meeting up and socializing on Sunday mornings and Wednesday evenings at youth group. Perhaps because the incredible heat and three hours of close proximity had melted the ice, there was potential for more forthright and honest conversation. So everyone in the minibus had doubled their efforts to be rude and sarcastic to one another, and nobody more so than Jonah and Lucy. If anyone at her school had made the kinds of comments Jonah had made during the journey, Lucy would have been in tears before they had even reached the Welsh border. As it was, with every one of his cruel and disrespectful comments Lucy, deep within herself, had become more and more convinced that he really *did* feel something for her and was doing his best to mask it.

In response, she had started calling him "Nest" on account of his thick curly hair. To Jonah's annoyance, James and the others followed Lucy's example.

James said:

'There was a young fellow called Jonah,
whose hairstyle was a microphone-ah.
He had an audition with the Jackson Five,
but failed and moved to Pamplona.'

There was a stupefied silence after this and, for a while, all that could be heard was the changing pitch of the engine as Phillip shifted up and down the gears to navigate the hilly road. Then Jonah said, 'That is without a shadow of a doubt the worst limerick I have ever heard in my life. It doesn't rhyme, the rhythm's all wrong –'

'The only reason you don't like it,' James interrupted, 'is because it's true.'

'Yes. Of course it's true. Especially the bit about the audition,' Jonah said. 'And the fact that I now live in Spain, apparently.'

'You could shave it off,' Lucy suggested as they were driving towards Snowdonia national park. 'Then you could sell it as a wig to my old primary school teacher Miss Waldon. She got a perm once a month but it never had so much *body*, such *volume* –' her voice switched to an exaggerated TV advert drawl – 'it's that straight–from–the–salon thickness and body that you *know* elderly women around the globe covet.'

'Quite the comedian, aren't we?' Jonah remarked acidly.

Judith's husband Phillip, who was driving the minibus, realized once again that he was going to have to intervene to diffuse the situation. 'Coming up on your left,' he shouted in a

83

tour guide voice, 'is the famous *Ty Myll*, Welsh for "Ugly House".'

'Alternatively, you could sell it to the owner of the Ugly House to use as thatch,' James crowed from the bowels of the minibus.

They camped in a large, unkempt field in Betwys-y-Coed. It was separated from the road leading into the mountains by a low slate wall that offered no protection against the persistent summer breeze. At one end of the field was a barn that had been converted into a primitive toilet block. The field itself was covered with clumps of plantain that lay on the ground like crouching green spiders. As soon as the group had emptied out of the minibus James started picking the long stalks, looping them around themselves and firing the buds at people by pulling the stalks through the loops.

Jonah and James tried unsuccessfully to put up an ancient green canvas tent. 'You'll have to forgive my scepticism, but I'm finding it hard to believe that your granddad slept in this when he climbed Everest,' said Jonah, 'especially considering the lack of groundsheet.'

'Which is why we use this,' replied James in a voice of great patience underscored with a note of don't-push-it, waving a ragged roll of plastic at Jonah.

The tent was the caricature of a cartoon pavilion, a hideously un-ergonomic green limpet with a full ten centimetres of space between the canvas fabric at the bottom and the hard bumpy ground. When they had finally got it up, Jonah lay inside on the plastic sheet and squinted through the crack across the field to where Lucy and her tent companion Joanne were hammering in the guide ropes around a silvery, space-age dome. 'I've always wondered what a Punch and Judy man must feel like. Now I know.'

James let out an irritated, horsey lip noise. 'If you don't like it you can sleep outside.'

'I might as well be sleeping outside, what with this arctic wind getting three-hundred-and-sixty-degree circulation.'

'In the bus you said you were gonna die of heat exposure and dehydration. Now you're gonna get pneumonia. If you actually bothered to help you'd see that the groundsheet's big enough to go up the sides and cover the gaps.'

Jonah scratched thoughtfully at the light covering of eczema on the back of his hand. He said, 'The fresh air of Wales,' pronouncing it "wheels".

An hour later they picked their way over the dry balls of sheep faeces to camp headquarters: Judith and Phillip's ancient blue family tent with a windbreak in front of the transparent plastic door. The other four, including Lucy and Joanne, were already squatting uncomfortably on the floor eating an incompatible blend of meat stew with gravy and baked beans from red camping plates. The tent smelled strongly of crushed grass.

After supper they sat drugged while Judith got out her Bible. Most youth group leaders would have gone for the minimum cringe-factor exhortation in such a situation, but Judith had never been one to pull any spiritual punches. She said, 'Jesus told his disciples, "I am the living bread that came down from heaven. If anyone eats of this bread, he will live for ever. And the bread that I will give for the life of the world is my flesh." '

As the group sat hugging their legs, mouths twisting out of shape with stifled yawns, she talked to them about how precious it was to God for people to make the decision to dedicate their lives to him while they were still young. Phillip would have got his guitar if it hadn't still been on the floor of the minibus, under a large pile of hiking equipment.

Night began to creep over the top of the hills and soak into the valley and the field. Outside the tent, and sheltered by the windbreak, the stove heating milk for cocoa hissed softly. Seven tired bodies dimly registered the concluding words of the talk as weariness began to take control. They shook from fatigue as they stretched, picked the skin off the hot chocolate and sipped the scalding liquid while Phillip gave them a rundown of the activities for the coming week. 'Tomorrow,' he was saying, 'we go to the outdoor centre, pick up our hiking boots and head off for a nice gentle climb to get us started. Nothing too heavy, just something to whet your appetites –'

'And not before ten o'clock at least,' James interrupted.

Phillip, used to James's constant interjections, continued. 'We'll do our first peak on Tuesday and, depending on the weather, Snowdon on Thursday.' This last comment had been intended to draw a response but it was met instead with an exhausted silence.

Jonah cleaned his teeth in the converted stable block fifty or so metres away from the tent. The stable had, apparently, been renovated by the enterprising farmer who let the field, complete with token flock of sheep, to campers in the summer. From the outside the only sign that the building was anything other than a stable was a steel sink that had been screwed on to the exterior wall, cold tap fixed askew above it.

The sinks inside were made of dirty white china. Years of Welsh winter had infused themselves into the walls, and the damp chill of sleety Januarys oozed from the dark stones, making Jonah shiver. A smell of acrid, prehistoric urine emanated from the toilets, with their black beetle-carapace lids and cisterns perched halfway up the wall. The smell lodged in Jonah's throat, making him choke.

He staggered back to the tent, dimly illuminated by the light of one torch. Inside, James — already wrapped in his sleeping bag — said, 'Shut the door, Nest.'

'Give it a break,' Jonah answered. 'Unless you want me to give *you* a break. A broken arm, that is.' He peeled off his muddy trainers and damp socks and felt the thick grass give under the plastic groundsheet as he rested his bare wrinkled feet on it. He pulled the string that was tied through a corner of the groundsheet and rigged through a metal ring in the top of the tent. The plastic moved up over the gaping hole at the tent entrance, shutting out most of the breeze. Then he climbed wearily into the sleeping bag and wrapped it around his face. James had already fallen asleep.

The sun shone with some uncertainty the next day as the Glenfield youth group climbed Little Tryfan, a weathered slab of rock some sixty metres high, perched in the middle of a valley like a wedge of grey cheese. Jonah was about halfway up, roped to a terrified Joanne who clung to the rock five metres below him, wailing theatrically. 'I'm not going to do it. I've already cut my hand. If I fall now I'll bust my neck for sure.'

'Joanne, *stairs* are steeper than this,' Jonah said to the top of her head as she continued the drama.

'Come on,' Phillip called loudly, in the practised cheerful-but-commanding voice of a hiker used to such histrionics. He tweaked the rope. 'If you move to one side Joanne can come past you,' he said to Jonah.

Jonah worked his feet along the crack in the rock. His neck was absolutely killing him. Too late in the early hours of the morning, he had realized that he was lying slap bang on top of a particularly malicious root that dug sharply into his neck. When he had woken and turned his head he had felt a pain like someone inserting a sharp knife into the top of his spine. 'It's just a crick,' James had commented, unsympathetically.

'My head's about to fall off and you say it's just a crick,' Jonah replied.

Now he was standing with both feet side on, wedged in a tiny crack, and with a hysterical Joanne attempting half-heartedly to climb past. He closed his eyes and tried not to move. The slightest tensing of his neck muscles sent agonizing, persistent twinges down his spine.

The pain had hardly diminished by that evening when he and James sat in the relative luxury of Joanne's tent. She, fully recovered from her ordeal on Little Tryfan, cleaned her glasses on her sleeve and started shuffling a pack of worn playing cards. Lucy was resting on an elbow, fully dressed but swathed in a sleeping bag. 'Last night Jo had a fit.'

'Which Jo?' James replied.

'Jo, not *Nest*. Anyway, there's this scratching outside the tent about two in the morning and something's poking at the fly sheet. Jo starts hyperventilating and says, "There's a ghost outside." '

James whistled a poor impression of an owl hooting.

'Are you listening or not? Okay. Well she starts whimpering and crying –'

'I did *not* –'

'– and goes, "Lucy! This thing's tearing up the ground. It'll kill us both! And –' she laughed long and loud – 'I unzip the tent and there's a sheep grazing outside.'

'You liar. I *never* said we were going to get killed.'

'What're we playing?' Jonah asked, as the girls argued.

'I refuse to play rummy,' said Joanne, dealing out the cards.

'Well, don't start dealing until we've decided,' Jonah said.

'We could play bridge,' James suggested.

88

'Oh *yah*, bridge,' snorted Joanne. 'Maybe I could get you a glass of Bord-*oh* while we play.'

'Idiot, it's only like whist.'

They settled on pontoon.

'So about those GCSE results…' James ventured, shifting weight from one elbow to the other.

'You obviously think we came out here because we like sheep defecating outside our tent and cleaning our teeth in a former pig trough,' said Lucy. 'I'm actually trying to *forget* about exams.'

'Seriously though, I reckon I got an "A" in music at least,' Joanne said.

Lucy rolled her eyes heavenward and threw the sleeping bag over her face. 'Call me when this conversation ends,' she huffed through the material.

'I wouldn't get your hopes up,' James commented to Joanne. 'You're gonna fail them all. Especially music.'

'That's so kind of you,' she replied in a syrupy voice. 'Have you got any more encouraging words you'd like to pass on?'

'Enough!' Lucy shouted through the sleeping bag.

Later on she crossed the field to the stable block with Jonah. 'You look like Frankenstein.'

'Frankenstein's monster,' Jonah corrected her. 'Frankenstein was the doctor.'

'You know what I mean.'

'Well, so would you if you had a crick like this.'

'It can't be that bad,' she said.

The following morning, however, she trotted to catch up with him during the hike and asked, 'So how's the neck today?'

The group, led by Phillip, was walking over the windblown heather towards the slope leading to Big Tryfan. Behind them, the previous day's conquest, Little Tryfan, looked remarkably tame in comparison with the mountain ahead of them. The sun hung heavily in the sky, surrounded by a thick summer haze and the calls of the birds were caught up in the criss-crossing zephyrs and blown across the hikers' faces. Joanne straggled at the back and Judith walked with her.

'Not as bad as yesterday,' Jonah answered.

Lucy tried to think of a reply, to keep the conversation going, but couldn't.

They marched on in silence for a while. The track sloped upwards and became difficult, demanding more concentration. Feet turned on loose shingle, hair matted into damp spikes, temples pulsed from exertion.

'It's gross to imagine that last week someone else was wearing these boots,' Lucy commented to Jonah during the lunch stop, hauling her legs on to an egg-shaped limestone rock and revealing bare shins striped with raised red welts from gorse scratches.

'And someone else the week before that and so on all the way back to when they were bought,' Jonah replied, taking a long drink of warm apple juice. He inspected the inside of his bag.

'Great. My sandwiches are squashed and there's chocolate all over everything.'

'Well,' Lucy replied, 'whoever had these boots before me obviously never washed their feet. When I took them off last night they stank like, I don't know, mushroom soup or something.'

'No, you're all right – that's just you,' called James gleefully from a rock above her. 'I was going to say something about the hum in the tent last night, but I thought, nope – it'd be rude. Seeing as you finally admit to your foot problem now, however…' Lucy picked a thistle and threw it at him. It missed and hit Tina, one of the younger girls, on the shoulder.

Lucy watched Jonah trying to wipe the melted chocolate from the inside of his bag. If she had known the word "phlegmatic" she would have used it to describe him. His personality, his demeanour – everything about him reminded her of a lizard standing serene in the sun: lazy, wary eyes, but every muscle poised for action if need be. His sarcasm, too, was dry like a reptile's skin or like sandpaper. When he laughed it sounded like someone striking a match.

But Lucy found the carefully constructed package of deadpan humour and aloofness particularly appealing. Underneath the façade there was clearly something repressed; something in him that desired to be mothered. It was almost completely hidden, but not quite. Sometimes this tenderness or sensitivity was visible in his eyes as a slight look of shock or fear when he was upset or hurt, or had been surprised by something and was momentarily caught off his guard. Like the lizard that has been knocked on its back, he seemed to kick helplessly for a moment before righting himself again. When these sincere expressions of his sometimes pierced the constructed shell of indifference, he seemed entirely vulnerable. And Lucy loved it. His inability to control fully the face that he showed to the outside world – when everything else about his demeanour was so meticulously inhibited – made her want to throw her arms around him and hold him tight. She rubbed at the itchy red lines on her legs and decided to try to nudge the friendship up a level. 'You're nothing like your sister.' She spoke more quietly so that James would not hear.

Jonah gave her a suspicious look: it seemed to require an explanation.

'I only mean that you're so different, being twins and all.'

'Well? Nobody said twins have to be the mirror image of each other.'

Lucy thought of Eritrea. Eritrea who occupied the same prosaic space as other people but who, at the same time, lived on an altogether higher plane. Eritrea who was treated with an almost ludicrous respect that Lucy had never been given. If a boy from her class had ever spoken to her with the same reverence he used when addressing Eritrea, people would have thought he was sick in the head. 'She doesn't even notice it,' she said, half-thinking aloud.

'Notice what?' Jonah replied. The difference? he thought.

Lucy did not answer that, but eventually said, 'What's she doing this week?'

'She's got a pub job, as a kitchen porter if that's what you mean. Usually, though, I never know what she does from one day to the next. When she's home, she's on the phone or up in her room with Nicola and Paula.' A thought occurred to him. 'They must be in the same class as you, right?'

It seemed strange to Lucy that this small fact – that they were in the same class – should be completely unknown to Jonah. Unknown and unimportant to him; so much so that he had only just thought of it. But for her it had been five years of pain and heartache. Five years of unjust discrimination. Five years of battling with feelings of righteous indignation, of fighting back tears in chemistry lessons, of walking home alone. The feelings flowed back into her soul, making her heart pound. They were not feelings that she wanted to be having halfway up a mountain in Snowdonia with the pink heather and the sun, sitting next to the boy she thought she might love.

'Mmm,' she responded perfunctorily. 'Or at least they were.' After all the exam tension and the end-of-term rush, it dawned on her for the first time that she might not see the girls again. 'Even if we wind up doing our A-levels there we probably won't be in the same classes any more.' Hopefully, she thought. 'Is it because of them that she doesn't come to church?'

'What, Nicola and Paula?'

'Yes.'

'I don't think so. They don't *help*, of course. Mum and dad have never liked them. They reckon they're a bad influence on her. They kicked up such a fuss when she started staying over with Paula on Saturday nights.' He paused. 'We've had our fair share of drama about church. But when Eri stopped wanting to come, mum and dad could only force her for so long. I think they realized it was counterproductive.'

'So why did she stop coming?'

Jonah gave her a look. 'You *must* have some idea.'

'No. Honestly.'

'Oh come on. Surely.'

'Stop messing around with me and tell me.' She dug him in the leg.

'Well, he's the main reason,' Jonah signalled towards James with his head.

'What... him?'

'That's right.' He mouthed the word "obsessed", shaking his head and making his neck twinge again.

Lucy was not surprised. 'You never told me. It's nice to hear a bit of gossip,' she admitted with a sly smile.

Jonah liked the smile. So he said, quietly, 'There's really nothing to tell. He just fantasizes about her day and night. Even if she still went to church she'd never have come on something like this because of him.'

'Funny,' Lucy said. 'I never got that impression when she still came.' She was encouraging him to say more.

'He never did anything to her at church. But he used to spend hours over at our place after school hanging around her and stuff. It was pathetic and gross. It's been going on for years. Believe me, it's really not worth talking about. Honestly.'

'I thought she stopped coming because she didn't like me,' Lucy ventured, more boldly. Then she instantly regretted saying it.

Jonah shook his head. 'It doesn't have anything to do with you, but…' He let the thought go.

'But what?'

'Nothing really. I just can't believe I didn't know how near to us you lived until Judith picked you up in the minibus the other day.' The words might have run on: if you and Eritrea were friends I might have known, we might have seen more of each other. They hung in the air, unsaid but implicit.

'Hmm.' The party was beginning to pack their bags to continue the climb. James had already gone on ahead with Phillip. Lucy thought quickly: if James was not around she could, perhaps, walk with Jonah for a while without drawing everyone's attention to the fact that they were together. As they set off, Lucy watched Judith and Joanne haul their rucksacks on to their backs. They would be the last in the group. She stood up. To her satisfaction so did Jonah. The two started walking, keeping themselves at an equal distance between the main group and the two stragglers. By this act he had given her the physical proof that he had feelings for her. It was his miniscule, undemonstrative way of saying, I do care. You read the sarcasm right. She would have taken his hand if she thought she could get away with it. Instead she asked, 'Is there some kind of special bond between the two of you?'

'What, because we're twins?'

'Yeah, if you like.'

He considered for a long time. So long in fact, that Lucy thought he was not going to answer at all.

'You've been watching too many of those documentaries about Siamese twins in Texas,' he said at last.

Lucy laughed. 'Idiot. I hardly ever watch TV.' They walked on, the only sound their effort-laden breathing. 'Well,' Lucy persisted. 'Is there? You still haven't answered the question. As usual.'

'In a way there is... I think. We don't see each other much nowadays. But nevertheless.' Suddenly, uncharacteristically, he turned to her and his eyes were full of unrepressed anxiety. 'She's a good person, you know –'

'I know, stupid. You don't have to tell me that.'

'Don't judge her because of her friends. She's never personally done anything to hurt you, has she?'

'No, not *her*. Of course she hasn't. And I don't.'

Jonah realized he had crossed a line. He shrank away internally. But Lucy saw both the thought and the reaction. Out of respect, she too took her mental distance from him and looked ahead. They had been walking faster without knowing it and had almost caught up with Phillip. She looked back and saw that Joanne and Judith were far behind.

Soon the path petered out, turning into a crack in the rock that the group could only scale in single file. Lucy climbed behind Jonah and stared at the worn soles of his boots. Conversation was out of the question.

Eventually, she clambered up on to a plateau, panting. The others were sitting, fatigued as Phillip told them about the next part of the ascent. 'This is the highest peak next to a main road in the whole of Britain,' he was saying. When Lucy showed her face he asked, 'And the others?'

Lucy needed a moment to get her breath back, but she pointed back to where she had come from. 'Not too far behind. Joanne got stuck again but she's okay now. I could see them from just down there.'

When Joanne and Judith did arrive Phillip gave them ample time to recover. Lucy noticed him give Judith a husband-to-wife look of, you sure you're alright? She nodded back in the affirmative.

The next part of the climb was known as "Bristly Ridge", a spectacularly jagged crest of rocks sticking out like the plates on the back of a stegosaurus. As the group advanced, the increasing cloud cover began to work its influence and chill the sweat from the exertion down in the valley.

Once at the top of the ridge, Jonah and Lucy scrambled together over a sea of rocks, like a graveyard for gravestones, that spread as far as the eye could see into the dense fog of cloud. It was a bizarre, hostile wasteland; not the same world as Betwys-y-Coed. They were too tired to talk. Lucy saw a ring of ancient lichen on one of the rocks. Like the ring of eczema on Jonah's hand, she thought, breathless, as the blood beat in her ears.

At the peak of Tryfan the hikers silently took it in turns to jump from Adam to Eve, two monoliths almost on the edge of the precipice that fell away to the road far below, beyond the rippling folds of stone and valley. Joanne hung back, afraid, until Tina – who was only thirteen – had made the prodigious jump. 'I'm not going to be shown up by a kid,' she muttered as she stood on Adam and tried to summon some strength into her weak legs, her heart in her mouth.

That afternoon rain came to Betwys-y-Coed in a solid curtain that swept down the road as Judith drove back to the campsite. It lasted for two hours, during which James and Jonah discovered that their tent was not waterproof. The rain brought a plague of midges that rose from the wet grass in a thick, hungry cloud and dogged the campers.

'They're mosquitoes, really,' remarked Joanne as James slapped at his neck and complained.

Those of the group who could put up with the bloodsuckers were standing in a circle around James playing French cricket. 'They're in my hair,' he yelled, scratching his scalp and dropping the bat. While he was off his guard, Joanne took the opportunity to throw the tennis ball. It bounced off his shin.

'Out.'

'No way,' he grumbled.

'Tough, you're out.'

The two immediately launched into a full-scale argument. Lucy, who had been trying to avoid looking at Jonah that afternoon in an attempt to honour his desire to maintain some degree of formal distance, took the opportunity created by the diversion to glance in his direction and was overjoyed to see him quickly avert his eyes from her.

At dinner she did not taste the casserole. Nor did she hear the post-meal exhortation. She did not even complain when Judith asked her to help with the washing up.

In the tent that night, James was overcome by a rare fit of open-heartedness. 'Joanne's all right isn't she? I mean, when she's not wearing her glasses.' Jonah, utterly exhausted, had tried unsubtly to shut his tent companion up by responding with a half-asleep 'hmm' to every comment that was made. The rain, which had started falling again, had easily soaked its way through the canvas and dripped on to the boys' sleeping bags.

Jonah felt ill – very ill – but said nothing to his companion. If I can get to sleep, I'll be okay. I'll be okay if I can just get to sleep, the thought ran through his head as the plastic groundsheet slowly sank into the quagmire beneath them. His heart thudded fast, the way it does when the body is gearing up to empty the stomach. The saliva came thick and fast into his mouth. Suddenly he knew it was unavoidable. Jumping up, he pushed the plastic cover from the mouth of the tent and lurched out in bare feet. A few metres from the tent he bent over and was sick.

Straightening up, he felt the cold mud between his toes for the first time. I have a fever, he thought. Standing here in the rain like this is strange. I have done this before. Stooping to enter the tent, he took a drink from a half-empty bottle of mineral water, its label damp and peeling from the rain. He swilled his mouth out and spat.

Inside, James said, 'Good grief, I only said I thought she's all right, but if she makes you puke –'

'It might have occurred to you I was feeling ill anyway,' Jonah said, shivering.

'You want me to wake Phillip? I will if you want.'

'No worries.'

'I will, honestly.'

'Don't worry about it, I'll be fine.'

'You don't sound fine.'

'Look, I'll be fine,' Jonah insisted.

Wednesday was another wet day. Phillip had his contingency plan ready and took them rock climbing to a place called the "Fire Escape" – a deep, gorge-like slit in the hillside, lined with dark rock, wet with rain. Jonah had kept a low profile that morning and had managed to keep down a bowl of cornflakes, but he took one look at the Fire Escape and knew that he could not climb it. He let James go first, followed by Tina's tent companion Anna, and then Lucy. The rain fell persistently while Phillip, standing at the top, called down words of encouragement to the climbers. 'Okay Jo,' he shouted as Lucy unclipped the karabiner on her harness, 'your turn.'

Jonah squinted up through the rain at Phillip. 'I'm a bit too tired,' he said.

'Come on, it's a piece of cake. Judith'll get you clipped up.'

Jonah shook his head and Lucy poked her head over the edge. Her bobbed hair hung over her face as she called to him, 'If I can do it, anyone can.' The words drifted down with the rain to where Jonah stood, looking up, the droplets spattering in his eyes. There was something warm and slightly mischievous in her voice. Feeling it touch him through the rain, Jonah wished for a second that she was down there with him.

Then James tapped Phillip on the shoulder. A few words were exchanged at the top, thrown away into the wind. Jonah saw Phillip shrug his shoulders. 'All right. Tina, you want to have a go?'

The wet weather persisted into the afternoon. Phillip was running out of ideas, but Judith drove the minibus to the village of Beddgelert, to see Gelert's grave.

Now, the rain seemed not to fall from the sky but to seep from the ground and from the walls of the village cottages. As the group argued about whether to go to the grave or the shops first, Lucy let the rain fall on her waterproof and cast an eye over the blurb on a signpost near the stile leading into the field where the grave was located. It read:

Beddgelert may be no more than a handful of cottages against the backdrop of Snowdonia's magnificent mountain scenery, but this tiny village was home to Gelert, perhaps the most faithful canine ever to have lived in Wales. Many years ago, Prince Llewelyn departed on a hunting trip, leaving his infant son in the charge of his devoted dog, Gelert. On returning, the prince was greeted by the sight of Gelert, his muzzle soaked in blood, and the beloved child nowhere in sight. In a fit of rage and desperation Llewelyn attacked the dog, which fell to the ground in a pool of blood. No sooner had he done this than he heard a cry. He ran in the direction of the cry only to find his baby lying safe and sound in his cradle. Next to the cradle, however, was the body of a large wolf that had been slain by the hound Gelert. The prince ran back to where his dog was lying. The dog faithfully licked its master's hand and died. It is here, in this very field, that Llewelyn buried Gelert. And it is here that the dog rests, to this day.

Charming, she thought, and then noticed that the others had already made their way into the field. She hopped over the stile and trotted to catch up with Jonah, who, to her delight, was at the back of the group.

They picked their way through the muddy puddles along the path. Lucy said, 'James told us you were sick last night.'

Jonah nodded. He watched her drag the ropes of wet hair out of her face.

'You're still ill, aren't you?'

'It's nothing. I must have overdone it climbing Tryfan or something.'

But it was not nothing. The invisible teeth of nausea were gnawing at his empty stomach and the pain he had felt from the crick had somehow returned – with a vengeance.

She saw how he crouched feebly into the wind and read between the lines of his indifference. The desire to mother him suddenly overwhelmed her. She touched his arm and he flinched, involuntarily. 'From where I'm standing you look pretty ill.'

'Please,' he responded. But he did not need to explain: Lucy at least knew him well enough to understand that the thought of people making a fuss on his account was anathema to him.

As they stood over Gelert's grave, she wanted to do something to show that she cared. But the desire not to upset him prevailed and she said nothing.

Some of the tourists were videoing the gravestone with pathological determination. Lucy's feelings of worry for Jonah mingled with other thoughts: it's nothing but a stone. Later, they'll watch those videos and wish they'd taken more footage of their families…

They walked back from the grave in silence and looked through the tourist shops: an overabundance of plastic Welsh dolls with black felt dresses glued clumsily to their garish pink torsos, dragon tea towels pinned to doorposts and flapping feebly and damply in the wind, the rust from the tacks running into the cotton, and vast quantities of other useless paraphernalia: wooden spoons, china cups and yellow, weathered postcards depicting Snowdon in winter, Snowdon in summer, Snowdon by night.

'Weather's clearing up,' Phillip remarked, slamming the back door of the minibus shut.

At breakfast the following morning Jonah knew that he was not going to be climbing Snowdon. He tottered towards the Morewells' tent, his neck aching dully. The sun was startlingly bright that morning; the previous days of rain over, the sky was a clear, brilliant blue and the midges died a silent death in their millions. James was behind the windbreak bent over a gas ring, which was covered by a round black griddle. He offered Jonah a piece of raw bread branded charcoal black with the distinctive pattern of the griddle. 'Toast?'

Jonah raised his eyebrows. 'You call that toast?'

James said, 'You were raving like a lunatic last night.'

When Jonah reluctantly told Phillip that he was not up to climbing Snowdon there was the usual fuss about going to the doctor. It made Jonah writhe inwardly to be the centre of attention. 'Please,' he implored. 'It's just a twenty-four hour bug and this stupid crick in my neck. If I still feel bad tomorrow

I'll go then, okay?' Strike a deal, he thought. The idea of disrupting Phillip's well-planned hiking schedule was too much for him to take.

There was more discussion before they eventually acquiesced. 'But I'm staying here at the campsite with you,' Judith said.

An hour later, Jonah was disturbed from a fitful sleep by the noise of the plastic at the entrance of his tent being pulled back. Lucy looked in. 'I'm staying, too,' she said.

'Why are you so stubborn?' she asked. The two were sitting up against the slate wall at the far end of the camp site. The field stretched away ahead of them, the tents dotted here and there like weird hunched creatures. Over by the stable block Judith's form could be seen leaning over the makeshift sink. The intermittent clatter of breakfast plates floated over the grass. Jonah was wrapped in a picnic rug up to his chin.

'She's keeping an eye on us. She thinks we're going to get off with each other,' Lucy said with a smile. It was the most daring thing she had ever said to another person. She couldn't help it; she was overwhelmed by the desire to protect him. His sickness had dissolved the phlegmatic shell and he seemed fragile – as if he could be blown away in the breeze at any moment.

'With me feeling like this?' Jonah replied after a moment. He had been thinking of his empty bedroom in Marlborough, the tiny particles of summer dust suspended in the rays of sunshine that shone in through the window which looked over the back garden. Empty and silent. 'Do you pray much?' he asked.

Lucy was shocked by his directness. 'Yes,' she answered. 'I pray.'

'How much?' he persisted. 'Every day?'

This seemed like a rather incongruous question. Lucy picked at stalks by her feet and tried mentally to quantify. Did the arrow prayers she made when it looked like she would be the last chosen for netball count? What about the prayers she prayed when psyching herself up to enter the classroom on a Monday morning and face the abusive insults that were always waiting for her? Then there were the long silent talks she had walking home from school. Or the times when she sat in her room swathed in the surreal shadows of those dark, mysterious afternoons of spring rain watching the silver birch outside her window. Could she even consider those times prayer? She closed her eyes and felt goose pimples form on the back of her arms, remembering the sound of the rain on the window and the sight of the graceful leaves of the birch dipping under the weight of the raindrops, the slender trunk with its parchment-thin rolls of bark. Those moments were her most intimate moments with Him – the moments when neither she nor He spoke at all really, when she existed in a place of knowing that He had made this tree and let this rain fall. Sometimes, He would tell her, I know what you've been through, Lucy. I'm the only one who does...

'Do you find it difficult sometimes, like you... you don't really know who you're praying to?' Jonah asked.

'No,' she replied distantly, staring across the field and brushing the grass from her hands. Then she turned to him. 'No,' she said with absolute conviction. 'I know who I'm praying to. More often than not its *me* I don't really know.'

Jonah's eyes registered uncertain curiosity, perhaps even a hint of fear. 'What do you mean?' he asked.

She shook her head. 'I couldn't put it into words. Even if I tried, I couldn't.'

'Try.'

She searched his face for any hint of the customary sarcasm, but saw none. 'Okay,' she said carefully. But where to begin? Hesitantly, she told him of the first day of term at the comprehensive and being stung with the sick feeling of righteous injustice when she had first been singled out to be bullied. The feeling had already grown and budded into a flower of loathing and disbelief before she had started praying with any real sense of urgency.

She told him about the ache of eating alone at school, of being ostracized in class, of hoping against hope that she would be praised for something – anything... 'I've been a Christian for years,' she said, 'but I didn't really start praying seriously until things got so bad at school.'

'I never knew,' Jonah said. 'You never said anything at church.'

Lucy gave him a slightly patronizing look of, oh come on. 'Do you really think I would have made a thing about being bullied? How pathetic would that have been?' And especially in front of Eritrea, at the only place I felt accepted in some way, her thoughts ran on. But she did not speak this aloud. Instead, she said in a voice charged with irony, 'What really makes me laugh is the way that people go on about Christians being the weakest people around because they need faith to shield themselves from the realities of life. Do you know what I think? I think God wants us to be weak. I think he's desperate for us all to realise that we're weak and incapable so that we'll turn to Him. Like, people say that Christians are spineless and pathetic when the truth is exactly the opposite, that having to trust yourself completely and totally to God is what actually makes you strong.'

Jonah said nothing.

'It wasn't until I finally gave up the idea that one day people at school might start liking me that I started to get to know God. It's like, He'd always been saying to me, "Why is it so important to you that they like you?" That really hit me.'

'God spoke to you?' Jonah interrupted.

Lucy considered. 'Yes.'

'What, you heard an audible voice?'

'No. Not like that, but I knew He was speaking to me. Don't you know what I mean? Haven't you ever had the same thing?'

He gave a slight shrug and his expression was once again clouded for a moment by the self-protective cover of neutrality.

He really doesn't know, Lucy thought, shocked. 'It's like suddenly knowing something inside so certainly, that it couldn't possibly be you,' she said gently. 'It's like waves of reassurance and this sense of peace. I can't explain it, really.'

The detachment in Jonah's face was replaced by the trademark frown. Lucy wanted to stroke out the lines. 'I've never talked to anyone about it,' she said. 'I don't think it's something you can easily put into words.'

'You know,' he said, in a voice that was not like his own, 'sometimes I feel like when I pray I'm just praying to a wall, a really high wall that stretches on and on. I can't even see the top of it. And the things I say just hit the wall and bounce off or get absorbed into it, or something.'

He scratched at the back of his hand. The damp had affected the eczema, too; under the dry patches of red skin were small crimson pinpricks – fresh, it seemed. 'I know I'm a Christian. I know that Jesus died for me. I know it in my head, but it doesn't do anything for me. It's like, I could even talk to people about God but it's not from my heart – not from in here,' his hand motioned to his chest under the rug.

Lucy looked at the freckles on the pale skin of his face.

'When I was sick two nights ago,' he continued, 'it reminded me of a time when… a time when I was humiliated in front of my whole school.' He paused. 'Years ago I remember hearing my parents arguing about leaving our last church to come to Glenfield and dad said he felt like he was deserting them and stuff… and… I think that's possibly how they – you know, people at our old church – felt too. I felt bad for him, kind of guilty, like, it was as if the spiritual well-being of the church depended on him and mum or something. Anyway, a couple of years later our school had our carol service there – at our old church – and this kid behind me shouted and I was made to stand out in front of everyone else and our old vicar saw me. It was terrible… So humiliating.'

Lucy put her hand on the rug over his knee.

'Anyway, the point is, sometimes I feel God's like that teacher who made me stand in the aisle. Who had me out in front of other people. Isn't that stupid?'

'No, it's not stupid.' She thought for a moment. 'But it's not true. That's not what He's like.'

They sat in silence, the wind blowing Lucy's hair into her eyes. Across the field Judith sat in a metal-framed garden chair, a paperback in her hand.

'Eritrea's a good person,' Jonah said.

'You don't have to tell me. You know that.'

'I do have to. She'd be so upset if she knew how hard school had been for you.'

'Listen. One of the reasons I haven't talked about it is because I haven't wanted anyone – least of all you – to think that I blame anyone for the way things turned out.' She stopped. 'This is embarrassing for me,' she said shortly.

'I'm sorry.'

'Don't be. I'm not. Eritrea is popular and I'm not. But that doesn't mean that she's to blame or anything.'

'In some ways it's hard for her, too. She's stuck with those awful friends. And I've seen the effect they've had on her over the years.'

This comment seemed strange to Lucy, but she said, 'Look, I hate the idea of people thinking I'm a charity case just as much as you hate people making a fuss over you.'

'I wasn't saying that. I –'

'It doesn't matter. And that's the point. Ultimately, it really doesn't matter. I can look back and not mind about anything that happened, because if things had never been hard I'd never have chosen to get close to God.'

'Do you ever think you and her might have been friends?'

Lucy shrugged with her lips. 'I used to wonder how things might have been different if we were. But it doesn't do any good thinking like that. Anyway, we're too different from each other. I just couldn't pretend to be anything other than what I am. I'd be an embarrassment to her other friends.' And not just that, she thought. She tried to imagine a scenario of her and Eritrea together: in Marlborough centre gossiping over a pizza or at the pub with one of Eritrea's older male friends in tow. The idea seemed laughable. 'It could never have worked,' she said. 'For a start, I don't have an older experienced boyfriend.'

'I could be your boyfriend.'

Lucy laughed caustically. 'Yeah, right.' She glanced at him, but there was still no hint of the sarcasm.

'I'm cold,' he said suddenly.

Lucy felt helpless. 'Why don't you let someone take you to the doctor?'

'No.'

'Jo, please,' she said, surprised to hear herself use his name.

'Tomorrow,' he said, after a struggle. 'If I don't feel better.'

Later in the afternoon, when he lay in the tent in a daze, feeling the cloying humidity envelop him, he heard the sound of the others playing French cricket again, the thump of the tennis ball, the indignant calls and resentful responses. Laughter. These sounds came to him, disjointed and broken, through the noise of the loose tent flap buffeted by the breeze. When Lucy came in to ask him if he wanted dinner, she sensed she should stay with him for a minute. He looked so weak that she was afraid. She took his hand. 'Judith says you're going to the doctor tomorrow and that's final. Actually, she says we should go tonight, now that the minibus is back.'

'No. not tonight. Tomorrow morning. It's just 'flu.'

She stayed until Joanne's voice called everyone for dinner.

That night Jonah was both awake and asleep. The tent wall next to him shifted and grew until it became like the wall to which he used to pray. It rose vertically around him, growing to dizzying, insurmountable heights. He reached out his hand to touch it, but it was somehow beyond his reach. Then, with the pattern of the fever, it shifted in form, wavering and crumpling into the shape of the Fire Escape, a sheer rock face riddled with cracks. Water seeped into the fissures, ran down the stone and dripped from ledge to ledge, before landing on the floor of the gorge. He looked up and saw, many metres above him, the shape of Lucy's head with her bobbed hair obscuring her face. 'It's easy,' she said. 'If I can do it, anyone can.' He tried to call out to her, but no sound came from his mouth. As he looked up, the rain fell thick and heavy on his face and into his eyes. He wiped them with his hand and it came away covered in blood. For a moment, he stared, transfixed at the crimson on his hand. I can't do it Lucy, he wanted to say. The rocks are bleeding. It's too slippery. But the rain fell with greater persistency, blood-red and warm. It stung his eyes, blinding him, so he had to close them. He opened his mouth to call again to her, but it filled with the inevitable metallic taste, choking him. He could feel the blood around his ankles filling the valley, making pools that joined to other pools, eating up the dry spaces and forming streams that flowed thick and dark like the brook at the bottom of the garden, after the autumn rains. He felt it rising to his knees and heard the sound of its chaotic rushing, like the sea. Then the rhythm became steadier and began to match the persistent thumping of his own heart. The blood rose to shoulder level and he felt his feet being lifted from the floor of the gorge. As he was being turned around in the inexorable current, he suddenly knew what was happening to him and he began to cry, silently. Lord, don't let me go like this, he begged in his mind. Please don't let me go like this. He felt his own tears on his cheeks for a moment before the river of blood closed over his face. Then he was sinking down slowly until his shoulders touched the floor of the valley, the only sound now the distant thud of his own pulse. I'm so lonely, he sobbed. The pain of crying burned his chest. Then he felt an arm under his head lift him gently up. He reached out frantically and touched a shoulder. Another arm reached under the hollow behind his knees and lifted his body from the ground. Jonah clung to the shoulders. I'm so lonely. He let himself be picked up and held, limp as a rag doll. I'm so lonely. Then came the answer; compassionate and reassuring: I know. Of all the people in the world, I'm the only one who really knows. Jonah buried his head in the shoulder. But you don't have to be lonely any more. You're with me now.

He was dragged from those arms by a shaking that threw layer upon layer of pain through his body, especially his spine. His eyes seemed not to be a part of him any more but he willed them back into existence and forced the heavy, numb lids as far open as his strength permitted. James stood over him stricken, a look of terror in his tear-stained eyes. 'Wake up Jo, wake up,' he was whimpering. Jonah glanced down at his hands and saw that they were still stained and blotched with the blood from the valley; the index finger of his right hand was crimson, as though dipped.

James half fell out of the tent, crying and shouting. Lucy heard him and was up like a shot. In her pyjamas, she whipped open the zip of the tent and rushed across the dewy grass to the green marquee. Then, a moment later, she was back in her own tent rooting through her things, emptying her bag on to the groundsheet. 'Oh please God, oh please sweet Jesus,' she whispered, her hands trembling uncontrollably. Joanne woke up. 'What's happening?' she croaked in a distant voice, heavy with sleep.

'A glass. A glass,' Lucy wept. 'I need a glass. Or something made of glass.' Joanne passed her spectacles over, perplexed and befuddled.

Lucy ran back to Jonah's tent, tripping on the guy rope of her own, falling, and breaking the glasses. She scrabbled in the grass and found a lens. She grabbed it and ran into the boys' tent. The tears flowed freely and blurred her vision as she pressed the glass against a red stain on Jonah's arm. But it did not fade.

Eritrea had been unstacking dishes at the pub where she worked when the phone in the corridor began to ring. The dishwasher had been left on automatic wash the night before and a glass had been smashed inside the rotating drum, the centrifugal force spraying the shards around it and into the corners of the machine. After lifting out the drum, she gingerly reached into the corners and began to pick out the bits of glass one by one and drop them into the bin. Then one embedded itself cruelly and deeply into the flesh of her index finger and she swore. The phone stopped ringing as she nursed the injured finger with a tissue to stem the blood. Hurried steps could be heard, heeled shoe against floor tile, and then, 'A call for you.'

Eritrea stepped through the corridor and took the receiver.

She listened for a minute and felt the edges of flesh on her forefinger moving against each other as the blood flowed freely through the paper tissue, down her hand. She shook her head in answer to the silent voice on the phone. 'Dead?'

Then the receiver fell from her hand. It hit the floor and broke, sending a shard of plastic skidding across the tiles. Shards of plastic, shards of glass, she thought while a vindictive, singsong voice from somewhere within mocked her: Suicide, suicide, suicide, it jeered.

Part II

Chapter 8

Two of the unlikeliest figures imaginable walked down a dusty street in the remote district of Rufine, east of the Senegalese capital Dakar, on a sunny January afternoon. One, a tallish youth with unmistakeably Nordic features and a mop of blonde hair, still too short to fit properly into a pony tail, seemed to be remonstrating with his companion, a shorter, fattish teddy bear of a man with a dark complexion and a heavy five o'clock shadow. The balding, sunburned head of the shorter man was covered with droplets of sweat but his expression was completely masked by impenetrable black Ray-Bans.

On the other side of the street, three local teenagers sat against a wall taking in the sun, their feet extending over the kerb and resting in the sandy gutter. They followed the strangers with languid eyes, laced with the slightest hint of curiosity.

The two aliens walked to the end of the street, which opened out on to a derelict field, empty except for the odd gnarled baobab tree and the jagged brown carcasses of corroded gasoline cans. Here, the Europeans seemed not quite to know what to do. They did not appear to be sure of where they were going, but neither did they seem completely lost. They paused at the edge of the field. The blonde-haired one looked with grim pencil-lipped dejection at the petrol cans before plucking his fellow by the sleeve and pulling him into a parallel side street. Without a word, the two started walking back in the direction they had just come, but there was something extremely self-conscious in their gait. They walked jerkily as if in a hurry, but trying desperately to give the impression that they were not.

When they reached the other end of the street they paused again, this time outside a small kiosk of corrugated metal. It had been painted a garish yellow and had the word *Choco* daubed over the rusting lintel. Inside, a small Wolof boy sat hunched on a stool, his chin in his folded arms, which were resting on the token counter. At his elbow lay a greyish baguette next to an unappetizing-looking plastic bucket of chocolate spread. In the afternoon sun the contents had dissolved into a gooey black liquid that currently served as a watering hole for tens of ravenous flies.

'Take off your sunglasses,' the Scandinavian insisted in Canadian French.

His companion shook his head, in the negative.

Håkan tried a different approach. 'How can you talk to people if they can't see your eyes? Please take them off.'

'No,' came the reply.

'Marcello, please. For me.'

'The sunglasses stay,' replied Marcello definitively.

They stood for a while at an impasse. Håkan's stomach churned with terrible apprehension and his temples pulsed. He thought, what am I doing here? What would I be doing on a Tuesday afternoon like this if I were back in Stockholm?

Marcello doubled back down the main street, walking with purposeless purpose and with Håkan trotting at his heels. When he reached the spot where the three teenagers were lounging he stopped. Their expressions of vague curiosity broadened into open surprise as he squared his shoulders like a gunfighter and headed towards them.

Standing over them, and with Håkan waiting anxiously to one side, he began to speak. 'Behold, O beloved brethren,' he declared loudly in French. 'We are here on a mission from the Lord and Saviour Jesus Christ to rescue lost souls trapped in the bondage of sin and death.'

Håkan felt his heart drop out of his chest. He wanted to poke Marcello in his fleshy side, slap him on the head, shout, what are you doing, you clown? But the shocking unexpectedness of Marcello's introduction had completely thrown him off his guard. He opened his mouth slightly and glanced askance at the boys, expecting them to stand up and punch Marcello in the gut. To his surprise they sat and squinted up at him impassively. If anything, their demeanour said nothing more than, could you move slightly to the left? You're in our sun.

'After having given His life as a sacrifice for us on the cross,' continued Marcello unperturbed, in his curious Swiss French, 'He ascended into heaven, where He sits on the right hand side of God and intercedes for the saints. One day He shall return to judge both the quick and the dead.'

Following this baffling monologue there was a pregnant silence. Håkan wondered if it might be possible to slip away unnoticed.

'But we are Muslims,' said one of the youths with a finality intended to bring the encounter to a swift end.

This was Marcello's invitation. He squatted down in the sand, next to the speaker. 'But the Lord Jesus Christ is the Son of God. He is the way, the truth and the life. Only through Him can we be cleansed from our sins and have eternal life.'

'Allah has no son,' grunted the second youth eventually, somewhat reluctant to be forced into the conversation.

'Ah, but Allah is not God,' Marcello said, wagging a finger at the two youths like a lecturer at a theological seminary.

By this time, Håkan had been overcome by a stupefied sense of calm. He stood next to Marcello wondering vaguely how his partner could put his foot in it any further.

The comment had the desired effect. The two who had spoken raised their voices in incredulity. '*Mais non, mais non, qu'est-ce que tu racontes?*' they retorted with smiles of amazement on their faces. Marcello began speaking over them, but with quiet resolution this time. Håkan had a picture of his partner digging at a fat hornets' nest with a stick. He sat down next to the third African, who was slightly away from the altercation and had not yet opened his mouth.

'*Nanga def?*' *How are you*, Håkan said, trying out his faltering Wolof.

'*Mangi fi rek,*' came the reply. The boy was half-chewing, half-cleaning his teeth using the yellowed, split fibres of a root of some kind.

'*Nanga tuddu?*' Håkan asked.

'*Mangi tudd Mohammed,*' the boy replied, neutrally. Marcello's sing-song voice ran along in the background, punctuated by derisive rebuttals from his audience.

'My Wolof isn't so good,' Håkan said in French to Mohammed. 'I haven't been here long. Can we speak in French?'

Mohammed gave the semblance of a shrug. '*Bon,*' he said.

Håkan struggled to muster a shred of composure. Doing his best to ignore the argument going on next to him, he said, 'We're from PCOM – Practical Christian Overseas Mission – an organization that does missionary work around the world, and we're working with a local church here in Rufine.' He pointed back up the street, beyond the kiosk. 'It's over there,' he said. '7b Rue de la Cité.'

Mohammed looked at Håkan as if to say, so?

'I was wondering if you'd be interested in coming along to a Bible study or a church service there. Just to see what it's like.'

'You are Jehovah's Witnesses,' Mohammed said.

'No,' Håkan replied, horrified. 'We're just Christians.'

Mohammed nodded. 'Yes,' he said. 'There were some Jehovah's Witnesses just like you here a few months ago. But they went away again.'

'We're not Jehovah's Witnesses,' insisted Håkan. The situation seemed to be slipping away from him. He decided to change tack. 'What do you do?' he asked. 'Do you study?'

'No,' Mohammed answered.

'Do you work here?'

'No.'

Håkan opened his mouth and shut it again. The only question left in his head was, nice weather, isn't it?

'You have a strange accent,' said Mohammed unexpectedly. 'Even stranger than your friend.'

'I used to live in Canada. My mother's French Canadian.'

'But you live here now.'

'Sorry?'

'Over there,' Mohammed said, dipping his head. 'At Rue de la Cité.'

'No… We don't live there.'

'But you're staying there?'

'No. We're staying in Croix Blanche about twenty minutes' drive from here, but we're going to be coming here to work with the pastor of the church at Rue de la Cité.'

'So,' Mohammed answered. 'You don't live there and you're not even staying there, but you want us to go there for a study.'

Håkan's soul drooped. 'That's right,' he admitted. Then Marcello was tapping him on the shoulder.

'We have to *rendez-vous*,' he said.

'Already?' Håkan stood up. 'Can we talk again tomorrow?' he asked Mohammed. The boy shook his head slowly; Håkan didn't know whether this meant "no", "I don't know" or was simply an expression of bemused speechlessness.

An hour later, Håkan was sitting in the back of the battered blue Toyota camper van that had been used to ferry Marcello, himself and six other missionaries to Rufine. The vehicle lurched its way forward, the perished springs wheezing their complaints against the bumpy road. Håkan looked out of the window at the palms and the battle-scarred local buses groaning under the weight of passengers hanging from the windows and squatting on the roof. Marcello was sitting at the opposite window still wearing his sunglasses. During the feedback session in the back yard of the Rue de la Cité church, their driver and leader, Didier, had asked if the first day had gone well. There had been vaguely positive noises from the rest of the group.

'How about you and Håkan?' Didier had asked.

'An absolute success,' Marcello had answered.

Now, sitting in the van, Håkan was tempted to lean over, open the window and throw the Ray-Bans out.

He was a painfully introspective person, always examining his own motivation and never quite living up to his own high expectations. Apart from being a very harsh judge of his own character, Håkan often suffered under the weight of self-imposed guilt for a long time after having done something he considered serious, but that others would probably consider inconsequential. Sometimes, years later, he would remember an episode where he had done or said something bad and would squirm with embarrassment. Once, when he was twelve, he had called a younger boy fat at school and made the boy cry. Now, periodically, the memory of that and other similar incidents leapt into his mind and made him cringe. The thought that some kind of malicious force might be deliberately exploiting his weakness to make him suffer had never occurred to him, because he had not yet reached the point of spiritual maturity where he might understand that there was something altogether unnatural about the frequency and speed with which such memories flooded his mind. Instead, he allowed himself regularly to be crippled with humiliation, accepting it as some kind of penance that he obviously still needed to pay.

He tried to convince himself that he had low self-esteem and adopted a suitably respectful, even reverent, attitude towards other Christians, who read his deference as a sign that he needed guidance. Håkan therefore found himself the target of all kinds of exhortation and more than a few conflicting words of advice from fellow Christians, some of whom were less mature in the faith than him. It was one such word of advice that had led him to apply to do a School of Evangelism with Practical Christian Overseas Mission, though this had mercifully been from one of the wiser influences in his life.

Håkan took the words of guidance and leading on board with good grace. On the surface, he thought, these people are further on with God than me. They know better. Deep down, however, in places that were beyond the reach of his own ruthless self-appraisal, he stood back and admired his own nobly submissive attitude. Not only did he feel proud of himself, but usually considered himself better than the very people who gave him the advice.

So it was that he had left Stockholm the previous autumn to spend November and December in Lyon, with a team of nineteen other School of Evangelism students, learning about the nature of God and the religions of West Africa. He made endless notes during the teaching on developing the heart of a missionary. He was told that it would be an affront to the locals if he wore shorts, carried his Bible in his left hand or put it on the floor. He was warned against developing exclusive relationships with the opposite sex, for these would undermine the morale of the team, and when he was prayed for by the leaders he felt the touch of God on his heart. In tête-à-têtes, he admitted openly to his leaders and the other PCOM students that he knew he still had a lot to learn. He genuinely meant what he said, but in reality, he had no idea just how much.

Before returning to Sweden for Christmas, he was injected full of a cocktail of anti-hepatitis drugs that was almost as lethal as the disease they were trying to ward off and that made his arm ache for two days. When he arrived home in Stockholm, his parents – both committed Christians – found him much changed: quieter, more prayerful and earnest, and just a shade supercilious, perhaps. He did not expect them, or the rest of his family, to understand the relevance of the many hours he had spent in Lyon interceding for the nations. He sometimes left the living room, offended by the Christmas films, and withdrew to his room to pray about the seven weeks he would spend evangelizing in Senegal on the practical part of the school.

Two days after New Year, his parents dropped him off at Västerås airport, somewhat perplexed. As he waved goodbye, his mother tried to dispel the thought, if he's almost insufferable now, how will he be when we next see him?

Just as the sun was dipping below the horizon, the Toyota pulled into a cul-de-sac in Croix Blanche and spluttered to a stop outside a large whitewashed villa, situated within a small compound. The flat roof of the house was walled in with crenellations that extended a little over a metre above the level of the roof. The property as a whole was reminiscent of a crude fort that a child might make out of an empty shoebox.

Håkan stepped out of the van, through the gate and in through the front door. The members of the other two teams working different parts of the city already seemed to have been back for some time; Rufine was the only one of the districts they were working that was not within walking distance of Croix Blanche. As his eyes adjusted to the relative darkness of the large downstairs room, Håkan saw Lauren sitting at the table chatting to Brigitte, one of the French members of the group. Lauren broke off her conversation and said, in English, 'Well?'

'I'll tell you later,' he said. 'I've just got to chill out for a bit.'

'Don't be long,' she answered. 'Brigitte and I got dinner ready half an hour ago. We were only waiting for you guys to get back.'

'Great,' he replied, already out of the main room and heading up the tiled stairs to the bedroom, with only one thought in his mind: falling on the bed and grabbing five minutes shuteye.

Arran, his roommate, was already there sitting barefoot on his sponge mattress, guitar in hand.

'Hope you don't mind me having a go,' he said, laying it back on the bed at his feet. He leant over and dragged the open case towards him, to put back the guitar. The case scratched the sand on the tiled floor in a way that set Håkan's teeth on edge.

'Whenever you want. I told you.' Håkan pulled off his shoes and tried to throw them through the half-open French window that led to the balcony. One shoe landed sole up with a clunk on the balcony outside; the other hit the window, making it quake, and fell back inside.

'So, first day over,' Arran said, as Håkan fell on his own bed. 'How did it go?'

'Don't ask,' Håkan breathed, closing his eyes.

'I just did.'

'How was yours?'

123

'Uh. I asked you first.'

Håkan put his hands behind his head. 'Disaster,' he said. 'Total disaster.'

'Right.'

'It wasn't good. Marcello really is mad. Mad, mad, mad.'

'Two cans short of a six-pack,' Arran said. 'But that's something we know already.'

'Don't we just. We talked to some guys and he gunned them down with his special culture-friendly theology, i.e. *not* Paul addresses the Greeks. Offended them in just about every way possible. We were lucky to escape with our lives.'

'It can't have been that bad. It's just one afternoon.'

'It *was* that bad. He was like... like Charles Wesley on speed. He did everything they told us not to do in Lyon.' Håkan gave his roommate a brief synopsis of the afternoon's conversation. 'He didn't take his foot out of his mouth for long enough to say anything that could've built a bridge. Nothing.'

'Penniless Christians Offend Muslims,' Arran laughed.

'Paranoid Cretins Overrun Mali,' Håkan snorted. 'So how was Tufala?'

'I was with Brigitte,' Arran said. 'She's more tactful than Marcello.'

'And?'

'And nothing. We knocked on a few doors. Talked to a blind piano teacher for a bit, but she had a lesson so we couldn't stay. I let Brigitte do the talking mostly.'

'You want to swap and work with Marcello?'

'Let me consider.' He considered. 'No.'

'It wouldn't be so bad if he didn't insist on wearing those sunglasses.'

Arran said, 'Huh. He was probably just as terrified as the rest of us.'

'You know, I actually hadn't thought of that.'

'Well, you should've.' Then he said, 'You know they're going to enforce that curfew they talked about the other day?'

'I don't remember them saying there'd be a curfew.'

'You'd better believe it. We're not allowed out of the compound after eight o'clock.'

'Oh come on, we're adults.'

'Apparently not.'

Something in the tone made Håkan open his eyes and look over. 'It's a big thing for you.'

'Damn right it is. It's pathetic. How are we supposed to meet people if we're not even allowed out?'

To Håkan, Arran seemed the antithesis of what a Californian should be. He was terribly opinionated about certain things and once he had the bit between his teeth, could almost never be persuaded to let it go. Yes, he was laid back too, in a nonchalant way – almost pathologically so sometimes – but it was a tactic, of sorts. When he had stubbornly refused to back down over something, he cocooned himself in an impenetrable blanket of nonchalance which could not be pierced, even when he was subject to the full force of someone's frustrated will. Not being a strong enough person to run truly with his convictions, Håkan saw this trait in Arran as a strength, and was a little in awe of him for it. He rubbed his eyes and groaned. 'We should go and get something to eat.'

They walked downstairs to find the meal all but over. Lauren gave Håkan a look. I did tell you, it said.

This is how Håkan's daily routine at the Croix Blanche house begins: at seven o'clock comes the nasal ululating of the Muslim morning call to prayer, a phantom voice without a body, floating over the rooftops of the city. This sound merely grazes the outer skin of his sleeping consciousness, sometimes intertwining bizarrely with his dreams of silent snowfall and the bone-dry static electricity of Nordic winter.

Half an hour later, the gate of the villa compound squeaks with the Pavlovian promise of warm bread, brought by Patrique from the Croix Blanche bakery. This sound wakes Håkan properly. He lies completely still for a few minutes, drinking in the reality of the situation: he is in Africa.

Then, as he is putting on his clothes, he shakes his roommate, as requested, but to no avail. Arran, inextricably wound up in his sleeping bag, is always late down. Sometimes he misses breakfast altogether.

The PCOMers converge in the main downstairs room, sandy-eyed and with tongues of nighties hanging out from hurriedly pulled-on jogging bottoms.

After collecting a plastic mug and filling it with a concoction that tastes of water marinated in bread crusts but that purports to be coffee, Håkan sits down with the others, cuts himself half a baguette and coats it with margarine and jam, or chocolate spread. The baguettes are still warm from the bakery but have to be eaten quickly, because if left uncovered for as little as ten minutes they turn into bread-shaped loofahs that no amount of chewing can break down. The margarine is a bright and horrifically unnatural yellow and tastes of wax. As for the spreads, there is a black, oversweet and sticky jam of mysterious origin and buckets of the same chocolate spread that is sold at the kiosk near Rue de la Cité. When Håkan spreads the margarine on his bread he thinks of vast cauldrons bubbling full of the stuff; cauldrons housed in factories like the ones he passes on the way to Rufine, that pump out clouds of toxic black smoke.

Lauren said once, about the margarine, 'The body can't break down the hydrogenated vegetable fat. It's too complicated for the digestive system to cope with.'

'It coats the roof of my mouth,' said Natalie, another American member of the group.

'A failed attempt at alchemy,' Arran commented when he first saw it.

'But they might've got gold if they hadn't added so much hand cream,' Lauren said, and everyone who understood English laughed.

The English speakers are noisier when they joke together. Sometimes the French members of the group ask, 'What was that? What were you saying?'

After breakfast, Håkan trails back up the stone stairs with a cup of filtered tap water for cleaning his teeth and for keeping down the yellow fever tablets; unfiltered, the tap water is slightly brown and some of those who have drunk it straight from the tap have had a stomach bug.

He enters the bedroom, usually to find Arran sitting up in bed, bleary and indistinct, looking not dissimilar to illustrations of Piltdown Man. Håkan takes his tablets with a swig of the water, places the cup on the floor, picks up his Bible and heads out of the sliding French window on to the balcony, which looks over the strip of paved front garden and the front wall of the villa compound. He walks to the end of the balcony and opens another door, this time leading to another tiled balcony, that is also the roof of the garage. The balcony is walled in to shoulder height on three sides, with the fourth wall being that of the house proper. Private though the balcony is, anyone standing on the eastern side of the flat roof of the house can, if they lean far enough over the wall, spy on whoever may be down there.

Håkan shuts the door behind him and begins his hour of prayer and devotion. He paces around the roof in a figure-of-eight while he prays. Sometimes he leans on the wall and looks over the confused mass of roofs and crooked television aerials that spreads out before him to the east of the city. At other times, he sits on the step with his back against the door to the balcony, watching the vast disk of sun emerge ponderously over the messy urban sprawl. It warms his face and hands, spilling light into the shadowy alleyways and the gaps between the roofs, as liquid metal is poured into a mould.

He prays for his family and for his friends, especially those in his church youth group back in Stockholm. He prays for the success of the PCOM team: that God will lead them to the right people, that he and Marcello will be a blessing to the locals in Rufine, that he will overcome his fear of street evangelism. He prays for his own personal issues, for the way he knows he draws attention to himself. Sometimes he is racked with guilt from memories of recent scenes involving his own tactlessness, especially those at the Croix Blanche villa. More than anything, he wants to be rid of the things that impede him in his walk with God. As for the vain pride buried deep within him, if he knew more about it he would try to rid himself of that, too. But the Holy Spirit has not yet uncovered that particular stone in him. And the Spirit is biding His time, waiting for Håkan to see the reality of it, in its ugliness. The Spirit knows all about times, events and collision courses and is a patient guide; He will not permit Håkan to understand it until the right time, so that Håkan will not try to deal with it in his own strength and fail.

Håkan has a ring-bound book which serves as a diary. It is in here that he writes of the secret battles with his motivation, of answered prayers and of the fears that sometimes plague him. But he writes all this in Swedish, to ensure that anybody stumbling across the book will be none the wiser about who he really is.

After prayer comes worship in the large downstairs room, which is also known as *la salle de louange, the worship room.* Although Håkan sometimes plays the guitar, worship is usually led exclusively by Fleur, one of the four leaders. She is a portly, peremptory woman with short French-style hair and a laugh like rapid machine-gun fire.

The group sing for about half an hour before splitting into their respective outreach teams for strategy meetings. Håkan heads back up the stairs again, but this time with the other people in his team, to the largest upstairs room that sleeps all eleven of the female students of the school. It is here, under Didier's guidance, that he prays down spiritual strongholds in Rufine, shares daily developments, helps plan the practicalities of a prayer march through the area and discusses how best to go about inviting people to a church service.

The sun begins slowly to bake the dusty, tarred roof of the villa and the trees outside the window are filled with the persistent, cacophonous chatter of a hundred unfamiliar birds. As Håkan and the Rufine team stumble over their basic greetings in Wolof, the smell of cooking *thiebou dien*, or some other local dish, snakes its way up the stairs, permeating the fibres of clothes with its odour: Didier has hired a maid called Fatou who walks five kilometres across the city in flip-flops to cook for them.

On the first day, the reek of fish hit Håkan like a slap in the face and he thought someone had been sick in the kitchen. Then, when he sneaked a peek through the kitchen door at the stew that Fatou was cooking, he recoiled in horror, thinking of the delicate, clinical sides of pink salmon he would get at home. But when he finally plucked up the courage to take a forkful at lunchtime, he was surprised to discover that he quite liked it.

Fatou divides her stew into four large white enamelled bowls, each partly filled with a bed of rice or couscous. With some help from the group she carries the bowls into the backyard of the villa and places each one on its own small collapsible table. Five or six eaters sit around a bowl on chairs borrowed from the worship room. When the call for lunch has been issued, the men lounge around the back door, reticent about going and finding a place at one of the makeshift tables. This looks like a show of courtesy, but they are all waiting for the others to make the first move, thinking, Didier has the appetite of an ox. If I sit next to him I'll get next to nothing, or, neither of the girls at that table eats anything, so even though Patrique and Marcello are there I'll still get a big portion. But then Marcello's fork does tend to stray into other people's territory...

Of course, Håkan is concerned that he might have a problem with being greedy. He and Arran have discussed it in depth. Arran believes that the best way to eat abstemiously is to chew each mouthful more thoroughly. But when Håkan tries this, he sees other faster and hungrier forks encroaching on his side of the bowl. And the bowls empty rapidly, for Fatou's creations are celebrated events. She is in the kitchen from ten o'clock every morning, leaning over the gas ring and muttering in Wolof, working her magic with *thiof*, crude cuts of lamb, dried *guedge* fish and yams. When there is beef, the French contingent fight over the yellow, jellified marrow in the bones, which they eat with gusto and loud words of praise while Fatou looks on from the doorway smiling shyly, curling her toes and hunching her shoulders in embarrassment.

After lunch come chores. Håkan is charged with the task of sweeping the worship room, which he does with fairly good grace, listening to music on his headphones. Every day, the floor is covered with a layer of Saharan dust that has appeared overnight as if from nowhere. Håkan sweeps methodically, making four carefully rounded pyramids of sand in each of the corners of the room, before finishing off the job with a dustpan and brush. Then he collects the chairs from the back yard and places them back around the two large tables. At least he does not have to clean the lavatories, a job that more often than not entails chasing colossal orange cockroaches around the plugholes.

When he has finished the sweeping, Håkan sneaks upstairs to his bedroom, changes into his swimming costume and then pulls on a pair of tracksuit bottoms and a T-shirt. He changes the music in his stereo, grabs his towel and creeps up the stairs to the roof. The brownish scorched tar burns the soles of his feet, but he picks his way gingerly over to the hottest sun-filled corner and lays down his towel. He does not wriggle out of his T-shirt or jogging bottoms until he is quite sure that he is lying flat enough not to be seen over the wall of the roof by anyone in neighbouring houses: in Senegal it is offensive to show one's bare chest or legs in public. Then he coats himself in sun cream or cocoa butter, presses play, closes his eyes, breathes a deep sigh of contentment and plunges into white-out oblivion.

When the other members of the PCOM team discovered Håkan's secret vice there was talk of prohibiting sunbathing during the daily hour of siesta. It would only take one naked torso — if seen by the wrong Muslim — to destroy the reputation of the group. But Fleur secretly admired Håkan's opportunism. And she lamented the fact that she looked so pale and anaemic...

So it was decided that, if they exercised extreme caution, sunbathers could take advantage of the midday heat on the roof, with the proviso that they must only remove their clothes once lying safely hidden behind the wall.

For a week or so there was rather strained male/female cohabitation on the roof, before Fleur decided that she would

131

like her back to be tanned all over without a line from her bikini, so the boys were relegated to Håkan's balcony, which was engulfed in shadow by two o'clock.

Down on the roof of the garage, with the shadow creeping inevitably over his feet, Arran complained bitterly.

Håkan said, 'It doesn't matter that we only get an hour of sun. It's much dirtier up there anyway.'

After getting his fix of vitamin D, Håkan showers the sweat and sand from his skin, blind as a mole in one of the dark upstairs bathrooms, dresses in his respectable outreach trousers and shirt, and heads down to the Toyota. During the twenty-minute journey to Rufine, he looks out through the chinks in the tattered curtains drawn in the back window against the sun, at the children in shell suits armed with machetes and selling coconuts by the side of the road. The Toyota has been loaned to the group by a former member of PCOM who is now the pastor of the church in the district of Tufala, where outreach teams will take turns to work throughout the stay. The loan is a kind gesture, but the vehicle is old and finds the journey challenging. The road is strewn with lethal potholes and, as Didier swerves to avoid them, Håkan does not know whether the nausea he feels is from the motion sickness or the fear of evangelizing.

When the group arrives at the Rue de la Cité church, which is a spacious hut with wattle walls in the back of a garden compound, they listen to an encouragement from the pastor, Isaac. He is slow-speaking, with the kind of low, musical voice that gives Håkan the same warm sensation that he got from the nurse's fingers when his hair was checked for lice at school.

Then, after a prayer, Håkan and Marcello hit the streets, their hearts in their mouths. Håkan has begun to learn not to let his companion do all the talking. Now he does some speaking of his own, mostly to mitigate some of the more perplexing and unfathomable comments that issue from Marcello's mouth.

For three hours they walk the dusty streets talking to unwitting locals, knocking on doors if nobody is out in the road. Sometimes they stay with one person for a whole afternoon; sometimes nobody will speak to them at all.

At six o'clock the group heads back to Croix Blanche, usually arriving late for the cold evening meal prepared by whichever pair has been chosen to stay behind. There is usually boiled potato and salad, with plenty of brownish filtered water. Sometimes, there is the luxury of glass bottles of cola or a tartrazine-laden orangeade called *Schitrus*, which has been the subject of more than a few jokes among the English speakers.

The reality of the curfew has made the villa feel slightly claustrophobic in the evenings, so after dinner people stretch out into the furthest corners of the compound: Patrique and his roommate Damien go to their bedroom. One stands and counts while the other, with naked, sweating torso, does press-ups with palms flat on the floor, index fingers and thumbs touching and making a diamond shape. Arran sometimes joins them in this act of masochism. 'No pain, no gain,' he says to Håkan, but Håkan does not feel welcome in Patrique and Damien's bedroom. He feels there is a touch of animosity in the way Patrique relates to him. It is not in what Patrique says or does, but in what he does not – the fact that he never does anything to put Håkan at ease. When Håkan goes to Patrique's room, Patrique welcomes him in a guarded sort of way. Neither he nor Damien seems to trust him. Håkan had hoped that this jaundiced-eye attitude might have changed when they left Lyon, but it seems somehow worse here in Senegal, so he does not participate in the evening fitness sessions.

The French-speaking girls are often to be found in the backyard, washing their laundry in the stone sink behind the garage. As they wring out their towels and skirts they splash water on the ground and the wet patches whisper gently as they fade into the warm concrete.

Some pray alone in their own secret places; the covered passage running from the front to the back of the house on the opposite side to the garage belongs to English Richard, who shares a bedroom with Marcello. There is a tacit understanding that those who do not wish to be disturbed will be left alone, so, out of respect for Richard, nobody trespasses there in the evenings. As for Marcello, he sits alone in his room, highlighting Bible passages with various coloured neon marker pens. Every now and then he reaches behind his rucksack, which is propped up next to his inflatable mattress, retrieves a bottle of scotch whisky and takes a swig.

Once, during a time of intercessory prayer in the bedroom, Håkan had stumbled across the bottle. '*Vaurien*,' he had joked – and of course Marcello had wanted to know what this was in English. He had tried out the phrase: 'Scalleewag, *scalleewag*.' Now if he ever goes into his room alone, it is probably for a drop of *scallywag*.

Inevitably, the social factions in the house have split into their own language groups. Håkan plays Dutch whist in the worship room with some of the other English speakers. It is a fast and furious game that makes the uninitiated outsider onlookers feel excluded. The aim of the game is to get rid of a set of cards as quickly as possible. The rules are complex and involve slamming piles of dog-eared cards, making it virtually impossible for anyone else sitting at the table to concentrate on whatever they might be doing; writing letters is out of the question. Håkan plays with silent intensity, frowning with the exertion of concentrating. But he is always beaten by one of the girls. This tends to lead to half-serious comments about cheating, and the clamorous accusations that follow can be heard all over the villa.

The leaders have not been so dogmatic as to insist on a time for bed – after the curfew, it would be a rule too far – but by eleven o'clock the worship room is usually empty except for a lone individual ironing with mute determination at one of the tables. Before Håkan goes to bed, he fills a plastic cup with water from one of the large containers by the door to the back yard. As he cleans his teeth in the boys' upstairs bathroom, the edges of his mind are already blurring with fatigue. Lying on his bed, his brain registers the regular pattern of the light filtering through the chinks in the heavy plastic blind over the French window. Then he is asleep.

Chapter 9

Håkan's team finished their two-week stint of evangelism at Rufine with a showing of the film *Jesus* outside Pastor Isaac's church in the evening of the second Sunday. There was a sandy square outside 7b Rue de la Cité that served as a perfect street auditorium. The pastor set up a collapsible screen and an old projector at six o'clock while Didier and the group, still safe within the confines of the vicarage compound, prayed and practised for the worship that would come before and after the film.

Later, Håkan stood to one side of the screen and watched the crowd sitting in the sand staring at the lined and worn images on the crooked, white canvas. The walls on either side of the street echoed with the popping and crackling from the blemished old soundtrack. The Jesus in the film, with his white skin, long, carefully combed hair and beard and beatific, dazzling smile was every inch the sculpted, manicured western archetype. The dubbed Wolof voice, however, was a high-pitched and nasal bubbling that sounded nothing less than absurd.

A 1970s Simon Peter hauled in the bulging nets and said, '*Ba-ba-ba-baa. Ba-baa!*' in a whistling voice, to which the Jesus squeaked, '*Ba-baa. Ba-ba-ba-baa,*' with a commanding point of the finger. The crowd looked on, mesmerized.

When the picture died and the end of the spinning tape reel slapped rhythmically against the projector, Håkan took his cue from the pastor and struck up the chords of a worship song, while Didier changed the reel. Pastor Isaac snuck around to the PA and picked up a spare microphone, into which he bellowed a deep 'Praise the Lord' at strategic points during the singing.

Natalie, who was standing next to Håkan in a print dress, leaned over, pushed a thumb hard into his side and whispered through her teeth, 'He's rapping.'

After the film, Pastor Isaac took the microphone again and gave a short talk in Wolof. Then, when he invited people to come up for prayer, he signalled for Håkan to begin playing again. About four brave souls came forward. The rest of the crowd looked back and forth from the worship team to the prayer team with rather forced and uncertain grins on their faces. Into the third song, Håkan noticed, with a shock of disbelief, that the person Pastor Isaac was currently praying for was none other than the main youth who had disagreed so vehemently with Marcello on the first day of evangelism. The youth's head was bowed and, over the tinny music, Håkan could hear the pastor's voice speaking gentle words. When the youth looked up, he had a strange look in his eyes: no longer the impassive, disinterested look, but something altogether different – afraid, but as though something had just dawned on him.

Håkan had the memory of this look in his mind as he put his guitar away and helped Didier wrap up the leads for the PA, when the group said their goodbyes to Pastor Isaac and when the Toyota pulled away from outside the church. Natalie was sitting next to him. She adjusted her dress under her sticky legs and said, 'You know, this is the first time we've been out later than eight.'

Mondays were days off anyway, but the Monday following the showing of *Jesus* in Rufine provided the PCOMers with a day's breathing space before the three evangelism teams moved on to their next area of the city. Following a leisurely breakfast, Didier ferried them, in two trips, to St Sébastien beach. He drove the Toyota through the industrial area of Dakar, past the forbidding factories that stank of ammonia and that probably manufactured margarine, and past the desolate shanty towns. Once at their destination, the group peeled themselves out of the van, layer after layer, with those who had been unlucky enough to have had someone on their lap stumbling out on to the sand last of all and stamping to get the blood flowing through their legs again.

St Sébastien was a paying beach in the south of the Cap Verde peninsula and was sparsely populated by the bored, tanned girlfriends of French soldiers, who were most likely sweating their way through military manoeuvres in stuffy barracks somewhere near the coast. The beach was fenced off to prevent beggars and con artists from harassing the tourists, but a number of enterprising Wolofs had nevertheless created a lucrative business on the fringes of the city side of the fence. Anyone visiting the beach had to drive or walk through a complex of buildings before approaching the toll gate, and the walls of these buildings were covered with strange murals depicting fantastic dreamlike landscapes peppered with entranced local wizards, African babies emerging from ostrich eggs and greedy-eyed US presidents, pockets bulging with dollars, standing over the African continent like Machiavellian puppeteers. One had to applaud the artists' opportunism: the immediate reaction from almost every person willing to pay to go and sit on a beach, and thus pass in that direction, was to whip out a camera and snap frantically at the murals. But underneath most of the paintings was a wheedling sentence in French warning that photos could not be taken without express permission of the artist: *No pictures without artist's consent*. Some were less direct: *It's sad to ignore the artist when you appreciate his work*. These cautions were enforced by the artists themselves – or their proxies – who lingered in shadowy doorways to accost the hapless, snap-happy holidaymakers and demand a hundred francs or so, even from those who were only looking. The murals were old and faded and had obviously been painted several years before. Some had been carelessly whitewashed over, possibly as punishment from the building proprietors to the artists for not paying whatever dues might have been agreed. In some cases, the painters had traced over the marks visible under the whitewash to create blurred replicas of the original paintings. These, too, could only be photographed after paying for the privilege.

After taking a furtive snap or two of the unattended walls, Håkan headed down to the beach, laid his towel on the sand next to Natalie's, coated himself with sun lotion and sat down. There was no need to be secretive about bare legs or stomachs here on the beach, and the entire group unfurled under the sun with sighs of self-indulgent bliss.

Håkan tried to strike up a conversation with Natalie.

'Did you notice the pastor praying for that guy in the grey shirt last night?' he asked.

'No.'

'You must've done. They were praying together for ages.'

'Can't say I remember, sorry,' Natalie said from behind her sunglasses.

Håkan considered telling her how confused he felt about the fact that Marcello's bull-in-a-china-shop approach to witnessing could lead to a commitment. But did the guy actually make a commitment?

'I just don't understand how that film could've had any kind of effect on people.'

'Well it obviously did.'

'And you didn't think it was cheesy?'

'I didn't say that.' With her abrupt answers, Natalie was trying to tell Håkan that she wanted not to talk about evangelism, but to relax. He took the hint and lay back.

An hour or so later he woke up from the deepest sleep imaginable. His whole body was coated with a thin layer of sand that clung tenaciously to the sweat and the lotion. He had forgotten to put cream on his lips and they tingled from the burning sun. Slowly, he propped himself up on his elbows, licked his lips and tasted sand. He gingerly removed his sunglasses and squinted as his eyes became accustomed to the brightness. He felt a slight stab of annoyance on noting that most of the towels around him were unoccupied. Automatically, he looked behind him and saw that one particularly large blue towel was conspicuously empty. Then, glancing back, beyond where Damien was lying in a semi-conscious stupor, he noticed that Patrique was not sitting where he had been when the second group had arrived at the beach. He swivelled his head around to check the bar at the other end of the bay. Marcello could be seen, probably taking the opportunity to *scallywag* a cold beer or two. Sitting next to him was Arran, also with a glass of something at his elbow. But there was no Patrique.

Håkan sat up for a while. Should he go and join Marcello at the bar? Perhaps later. He unravelled his headphones and switched on his personal stereo. Closing his eyes and lying back again, he listened to the worship music for a while. As it took a hold he imagined himself in the crowd of people praising along with the band. But then, in his mind, he was the one standing up at the front, leading the people in worship with his guitar. As he played, he saw the PCOM girls standing at the front of the crowd, cheering him on and marvelling at his guitar skills. The fantasy developed for a while, until it dawned on him just what he was thinking. Disgusted, he pressed stop, put the headphones in his bag, stood up and made a beeline for the bar.

This thing that came over him affected everything that he did or said, it seemed. Although he thought that it had only begun during the practical part of the school in Africa, he was mistaken. Sometimes it came in the form of fantasies when he was listening to music, sometimes in the form of attention-seeking comments. Being the way he was, he hated and loathed himself for it. He was repulsed by the thoughts that sometimes ran through his head. He submitted up his guitar playing. He prayed, repented and castigated himself. He even fasted. But the bottom line was that he acted up for the girls. And his behaviour was beyond his own control.

Three months earlier, when he had originally arrived at the PCOM base in Lyon, dehydrated and perspiring from the long train journey from Paris, he had been taken by Didier to his room, where he had dropped his bag on the floor before going for lunch. Then, sitting in the refectory for the first time, he had scanned the faces at the tables. It was such an automatic and habitual impulse in him that he was completely unaware he was doing it. But his eyes settled on a certain person that he watched – or was intensely aware of – from that moment on.

After lunch, the School of Evangelism students had left the refectory and walked up the hill behind the PCOM base. They had begun to converse hesitantly, to find some common ground. When they reached the top of the hill, they sat at a vantage point under the late October sun and looked down over the postage-stamp fields and lines of green vines in the valley below. The person that Håkan had seen in the refectory sat slightly away from the rest of the group, seemingly unconcerned by the fact that other people were making friends and building social bonds. She sat hugging her legs, with her chin resting on her knees and stared mesmerized into the wind. She was so very far away, a person so completely lost in thought, that Håkan held his breath while he watched her. More than anything in the world he wanted to sit next to her, to look into her eyes and have the vital rapport of knowing what consequential things weighed on her mind.

After Christmas, when the PCOM team were waiting at Lyon airport, he knew that she was standing just behind him because he could hear her voice. On the plane she sat far away from him, but if he looked across the aisle he could sometimes see the corner of her hand.

In Africa, he always knew where she was. If, at any point in the day, he lost sight of her, a small part of him began to feel anxious and uneasy and could only relax again when he knew where she was. He thought about her when he took his yellow fever tablets; when the ignition key of the Toyota was turned off and the engine choked into silence after a day's evangelism at Rufine. If he fantasized about being a great worship leader, it was for her. If he drew attention to himself at mealtimes, it was, in some small way, an attempt to establish contact with her. Throughout the two months in Lyon he had never spent any time alone with her and he had only ever spoken to her in the company of other people, but this in no way altered the fact that there was something about her that had his soul prostrate before her. It was the faint smudge of eczema on the skin in the corners of her eyes; it was the cheekbones touched bronze by the Dakar sun; it was the fine white scar that ran along the top of the index finger of her right hand. And it was her name, that beautiful and enigmatic name. Sometimes he spoke it silently to himself when he lay in bed: *Eritrea*.

Chapter 10

A little beyond the outer corner of the cul-de-sac that turned in to the PCOM villa was a wide square of pavement that was, every afternoon from four o'clock onwards, occupied by the *baignet* lady. She was a colossal roll of a woman in a wraparound skirt, with a colourful turban piled up on her head. She and her two helpers – possibly daughters – set up a hibachi grill and a table in the sand and sold their greasy wares to passers-by. One of the helpers, in a green dress, scooped handfuls of lardy dough from a purple washing-up bowl and squeezed balls of it, with a cow-milking action, into the large blackened wok of bubbling fat resting on the grill. The balls bobbed and nodded in the fat until they turned a crispy brown, after which they were fished out, placed into a large bowl and sold to rich Wolof businessmen in white sarongs and flip-flops, who drew up in black battle-scarred BMWs. Lauren and Eritrea often kept secret tryst after the evening meal, creeping out of the gate and down the road to where the *baignet* lady waited with her camping table, a crude bit of cardboard wedged under one leg announcing the prices. The girls became used to timing their trips to coincide with a fresh batch of frying because, as they cooled, the soft golden doughnuts turned into solid golden rocks in the bowl, under the pale evening sun. The other helper scooped ten balls into a paper bag, threw sugar over them from an ancient plastic saltshaker and, holding the bag by the corners, deftly spun it closed.

The *baignet* lady, with a face not dissimilar in appearance to the product she sold, handled the financial side of the business: Eritrea handed her a droopy tobacco-leaf banknote and she placed it into a shabby bum bag, the strap buried deep within the fatty folds of her waist. By the time the girls sat down to eat under Marcello's window spots of oil had begun to appear, dark and shiny, against the brown paper.

'I don't know why I eat this rubbish,' Lauren said, mostly to herself. 'I might as well make quick-dry cement with sugar and pour it down my throat. It has the same effect.'

Eritrea rubbed her hands together to rid them of the sugar granules that clung to them. 'The market has apples,' she ventured. 'But they cost two hundred CFA each.'

'Too much of a luxury.'

'Or you could try drinking water straight from the tap. That would probably relax your stomach.'

Lauren giggled. 'You say the most awful things sometimes.'

'It's true. I should know. I was stupid enough to do it last week.'

'Do you think they'll find out about us and stop us from going out?'

'Can't see why not. It's only around the corner. But it's not like we're hurting anybody.'

'Only our figures,' Lauren said, patting her stomach. 'How often do you get apples?'

'Not often. Like you say, too expensive.'

'But you're lucky to be doing outreach near the market.'

'I suppose. But you don't have to put up with the church at Bougainville.'

Eritrea was working in a fairly wealthy area called Bougainville, under Fleur. Her remit, like that of the other PCOMers, was to invite Muslims to the local church, which was run by Jean Caffal.

But Eritrea was afraid of Jean. On the outside he was an accommodating and smiling man, but try as she might Eritrea could not bring herself to believe a single word he uttered. He had a charming, honeyed voice, but there was something desperately insincere about him. He laughed loudly and too often, and lifted his chin slightly when he leaned towards people, to show that he wanted nothing more than to give them his full attention. But to Eritrea it seemed that his personality was encased in a thick and well-constructed layer of Christianity, like a pancake, and that underneath was a seething cauldron of frustration and anger that bubbled away within him like the *baignet* fat in its battered wok. Sometimes cracks appeared in the armour in the form of irritated telltale comments or glares – mostly directed at his wife. Afterwards, he would turn his attention back to his original audience, a look of timeless gentle benevolence once again seeping from every fibre of his being.

Eritrea could not understand her fear. She simply felt that, very much despite the impression he gave, there was a formless, latent capacity within him for violence.

Though the team had only been working Bougainville for a week and a half, they had already had to endure three marathon church services, each lasting at least two hours. Jean was of the opinion that the church should meet not only on Sunday mornings but on Wednesday afternoons, too. Dutifully, the PCOM team had complied. They crowded into the garage that Jean had converted into a meeting room and sweated their way through the services. Pride of place was given to a cassette player-cum-karaoke machine clogged with sand and mounted on a high table at the front and in the centre, where a pulpit might have been. Next to it was a white board on a tripod. At the beginning of the service was a time of worship. Fleur had been requested not to play the guitar.

Instead, Jean inserted a chewed tape into the cassette deck and switched it on. The music that crackled its way from the speaker, underneath the feedback of Jean's microphone, was the syrupy strains of an American group singing a medley of worship songs in a different space and time. Each song ran into the next with a series of impossible key changes and Jean, who had faithfully transcribed the words from the inlay card, flipped over the pages of the white board while the congregation desperately struggled to keep pace with the ever-mounting tempo and pitch. Jean himself did not sing but grinned, tapped his foot in time with the music and pointed to the relevant verse or chorus with a short bamboo cane; Eritrea imagined he might also use it to beat someone.

After the time of worship came the sermon, an hour of call and response with Jean casting a critical eye in the direction of anyone who did not join in with the 'amens' at the end of his loud assertions. Eritrea's head had usually begun to pound after ten minutes of this. Sometimes, after the sermon there was more painful singing, but Eritrea hardly registered it. The last half an hour of service was a maelstrom of dizzying heat and the sickening smell of sweaty armpits. When she stood outside the door in the shadow of the compound wall she felt as she had done at school after running the cross country; lights danced in front of her eyes and a heavy pulse ticked in her dry mouth.

At the time, she was working with Patrique. The two often talked alone together. In the evening after the second Wednesday afternoon service, they were up on the roof in the corner of the Croix Blanche villa watching the sun set to the west of the city. 'I can't even see what good it is for us all to go to these meetings,' she said in French. 'I mean, if we all go, there's no space for any people that we might bring with us.'

'That's true,' he said.

'And how are we supposed to get more people to go along if we're in a church service instead of out evangelizing? It completely defeats the object of being there at all.'

'Well, we're a guaranteed crowd at the service, if you catch my drift.'

'What? You mean –'

'That maybe he gets off on there being a full contingent at church – you know, boosts his ego – even if none of them needs saving.'

'Ha!' Eritrea laughed. 'That's one way of looking at it.'

'So what do you think we should do?'

'You could mention it to Fleur. Suggest that only half of us go, or something.'

'I could do, but then so could you.'

'I don't think so.' Eritrea did not particularly like Fleur.

'Anyway, we've only got one more service to put up with before we move on. I don't know if it's really worth it now.'

'Sometimes,' Eritrea said, 'it feels like we're missing the point altogether. We're at Bougainville for two-and-a-half weeks and we're spending most of that time cooped up in that garage listening to Jean shouting.' She huffed. 'And, you know, even when we're out evangelizing I feel so useless.'

'Why? Don't say that.'

'You do all the talking. I feel like I'm more of a hindrance than a help.'

During the first week, Patrique had persuaded a local man to let them go to his house and give a Bible study. It was rare for such a thing to happen, so Patrique and Eritrea prepared diligently. When they knocked on the man's door he let them in and led them through to a back room with a corrugated plastic roof. Patrique began to explain the meaning of the cross, with examples from scripture, but the man pointedly ignored him and stared drop-jawed at Eritrea. Patrique had soldiered on for about an hour before running out of steam altogether. 'Come again,' the man said to Eritrea, as the two got up to go. 'Better still, I'll come to visit you. Where do you live?'

This was typical of Eritrea's encounters with the local men in the district. She had grown used to the many hands, both male and female, that reached out to touch her hair and sift through it, as though it were precious silk. More intrusive and difficult to cope with, however, were the ravenous eyes that followed her every step as she walked through the dry afternoon heat of Bougainville. In the evenings after evangelism, she stood under the shower and felt the cool water soak through her scalp, and saw the grey snake of water run down towards the plughole, and thought not of the fingers that had touched her hair, but of the many pairs of hungry eyes that ran up and down her body and of the hands that wanted to touch so much more.

The Bougainville team had been preparing for an open air outreach that was to take place in a park near Jean Caffal's church on the second Friday of their time in the district.

After morning worship, when Håkan's team were sitting up in the girls' bedroom learning Wolof, Patrique and Eritrea practised a PCOM mime called *The Heart* in the back yard, under the supervision of Fleur's roommate Anne. The mime told the story of a man seduced by a woman and tricked into giving her his heart. Once the woman had taken possession of the heart she proceeded to play with it, teasing the man, throwing it up into the air and catching it until it dropped on the floor and broke. Then the man, desolate and sorrowful, turned to God, who gave him a new heart. When the woman came back to tempt him again, he pointed her towards the light and she, too, gave her heart to God.

On the Friday afternoon of the open air, the blue Toyota was commandeered from the Rufine team – who reluctantly resigned themselves to sunbathing that afternoon – and the car battery was used to run the PCOM guitar amplifier. Didier, who would otherwise have been unoccupied, was drafted in to help. He parked the van on the common not far from Jean's church and, with Fleur, hammered four pegs into the dust and tied string around them to create three sides of a square, with the van making the last side. It was within the confines of this makeshift arena that Patrique and Eritrea were to perform.

Crowds of street children watched inquisitively from a safe distance, but as Fleur began to tune up they flocked over and planted themselves obediently on the audience side of the string. Eritrea sat apprehensively in the open side door of the Toyota and watched four boys in the corner of the park stone a squashed rat. They stood in a circle with a chunk of asphalt, each boy taking a turn at dropping the chunk on the rat, before magnanimously passing it on to his neighbour. They wore the looks of rapt concentration that one would expect to see in the eyes of old French men during a *boules* tournament, and were completely oblivious to the activity of the PCOM group on the other side of the common.

When it was time for the open air to begin, Eritrea asked Anne, 'Isn't the pastor going to be here?' as she tied her hair back in preparation for the mime.

'I don't think so.'

'But he only lives around the corner. Surely he'll be speaking, at least?'

'Not as far as I know.'

Fleur led the team in some of the simple French songs, including *The Light, the Light is There*. It went:

The light, the light is there.
The light, the light is there.
If you believe in Jesus the light is there.
If you don't believe in him the light is not there.

Then it was time for the mime. Patrique played the part of the angst-ridden, broken-hearted male with impressive conviction. Eritrea was every inch the wicked seductress, laughing with silent glee as she played with Patrique's heart and looking suitably sheepish when it fell and broke. The street kids, most of whom looked to be under the age of ten, watched with wide, uncomprehending eyes.

When it was over, Fleur and the PCOMers clapped, but the children on the other side of the string were mystified.

There were a few more songs, before the microphone was handed to Didier who, in his nasal Parisian dialect, began witnessing to the now heaving sea of children about how he had come to know the Lord. Shortly afterwards, Eritrea found herself singing again next to Fleur. From the corner of her eye she saw the squashed rat boys still huddled together over their dead catch.

Then the outreach was over and the children were charging over the string boundary and mobbing the performers. Eritrea was pawed and her hair pulled as she distributed John's gospels in Wolof to the tiny, grasping hands whose owners were most likely illiterate. She remembered Didier's words, if you just give out tracts to people they won't value them, they'll just throw them away, but she handed out the booklets on automatic pilot. The group was shrouded in clouds of dust and the Toyota was revving up, adding its own choking fumes to the hazy air. Anne and Fleur were calling over the shouting children and the carbon monoxide, but Eritrea could not hear what they were saying. Then she was squeezing herself into the vehicle; children were trying to climb in and hide themselves under the seats. Others had jumped up on the back bumper and hooked themselves on to the side, clinging on with purpose. The Toyota swerved away, Didier engaged in hand-to-hand combat with the steering wheel, while desiccated faces filled with yellow teeth grinned in through the windows.

The sound of the Muslim call to prayer scared Eritrea. Being a light sleeper, she was instantly woken by it in the mornings. She tried to reason with herself that the call was simply an indication to people that it was time to do something, and that it served much the same purpose as the hand bell that had been rung up and down the corridors of her old school to tell the pupils that it was time for assembly. But however much she tried to rationalize, it still frightened her – more than she cared to admit.

Once awake, she lay silently and watched the other girls. Next to her, on the left, was Natalie on her enormous red and white striped double inflatable mattress that epitomized her personality: obtrusive, loud, inimitable. Then behind her was Lauren on a more sensible-looking Lilo. On her right were Miriam and Céline. They were very close and both looked forward to the summer when they would marry their fiancés, back in France. They often talked together in low voices, like conspirators, about French marriage ceremonies, and their eyes became misty at the prospect of fontanelles and feeding times. It was their defence against the loud, insistent hegemony of the English language. Eritrea hardly knew them.

There were eleven girls together in the long room that, along with a bathroom and a toilet, took up half of the upstairs of the villa. Eritrea sometimes crept into the shower before the morning rush. Generally, though, she preferred to wash the dust and the tactile looks from her skin and hair after outreach. The cool, metallic water was hard, sucking all the moisture from her skin and aggravating her eczema, so she could only take one shower a day.

She was usually one of the first downstairs after Patrique and Didier. She scooped two spoons of porridge oats into a plastic beaker, added a measure of dried milk and filled the beaker from the saucepan of water that Patrique had set to boil on the portable gas ring before going out to get the bread. It was a functional breakfast that she had learned at university: with a couple of stirs it thickened into a glutinous gruel that was infinitely more palatable than the bread.

During her first week at the villa, she had prayed in the shadowy, dank garage under Håkan's balcony. At the far end of the garage was a crude hole-in-the-floor toilet, a watering place for the foul cockroaches that congregated around the rust-stained tiles and twitched their feelers malevolently.

It had been hard for twenty or so people to find a private place for personal devotion. Originally, she and Céline had squabbled wordlessly for possession of the garage, each trying to stake her claim by arriving there first. But the pungent smell that rose from the dark hole of the toilet stuck in Eritrea's throat and, after a few days, she relinquished her claim, moving up on to the roof instead. The other sides had already been taken, but she managed to talk Patrique into giving her his place that looked over the garage roof balcony. 'You can't come here,' he had said. 'It looks east over the city and has great spiritual significance.'

'I know that,' she said. So he gave her the spot, selflessly withdrawing back to the bedroom, where Damien prayed. That had been on the Sunday of their first week in Dakar.

The afternoon of the following Sunday, when the Bougainville team had suffered their last church service under Jean Caffal, Eritrea was told that she could not spend any more time alone with Patrique.

This was how it happened: after lunch that day, Fleur and Anne asked Eritrea to come up to their room. She sat and listened dutifully as Anne explained gently that there was a small issue that needed resolving. Through the wall, Eritrea could hear the muffled sounds of Håkan's guitar; he was practising the songs for the showing of the *Jesus* film that night.

'We don't think it's good for you and Patrique to be spending so much time together,' Anne said.

'What do you mean?' Eritrea asked.

'If *ze uzzeurs* think you have an exclusive friendship with him,' Fleur said, 'it's not good for *ze* morale of *ze* team.' Fleur always insisted on speaking English with Eritrea, even though it would have been far easier for them to conduct their conversations in French. The fact that she chose to speak English now only intensified the irritation Eritrea felt towards her.

Eritrea addressed Anne in French, 'But *you* were the ones who organized for us to be working together in Bougainville in the first place. It's only natural for us to have spent time together.'

Anne looked slightly awkward. 'Yes, you're right of course. But nevertheless, for the good of the whole group, it would be better if you didn't talk alone any more.'

'It doesn't make any sense. You had us doing the mime together.' She took a breath, realizing that she was beginning to sound defensive. 'We spent time together in Lyon and nobody mentioned it back then, so why now?'

'In Lyon,' Anne said, 'we didn't know that you were together so often. And back in France it wasn't the same. Being all together in this one house makes the situation more sensitive. We know that it's not easy for you and we're not saying that you can't *talk* to each other any more. Just try to avoid being alone with him.'

Eritrea was crushed and said nothing.

'It could *coze* a *division* in *ze* team,' Fleur continued. She lacked the ability to express herself sensitively in English, but she liked to practise the words and phrases of Christian jargon that she had picked up in the seminars given by English-speaking visitors during the teaching stage of the school. She talked on, pointing her finger at times. Eritrea felt a lump solidifying in her chest and rising to her throat. It's not fair, she thought. But she resisted the desire to say this out loud.

If Fleur had simply shut up, the matter might have ended there and then, but she was so keen to drive the point home that Eritrea eventually interrupted her and said, 'What about Arran and Brigitte? They spend time alone. And they even pray together.'

'It's not *ze* same *zing*.'

'How come?'

'It just isn't.'

'Why?'

'Because they do not *'ave* feelings for each *uzzeur*.'

Eritrea looked at Anne, slightly open-mouthed, seeking some kind of moral support. 'We don't have *feelings* for each other. We're just friends. Nothing more.'

Fleur made a derisive noise of disagreement and limbered up for another verbal tirade. But Anne touched her on the shoulder. 'Look,' she said calmly to Eritrea. 'This isn't necessarily about what you and Patrique do or don't feel for each other. It's about what it looks like to other people.' She seemed to be choosing her words carefully. 'The fact that you've been together for evangelism has maybe... brought the situation to a head, but that's not your fault. It's ours. And we're sorry for that. The last thing we want to do is to upset you or drive a wedge between the two of you. But you know PCOM policy.'

When the talk was over, Eritrea left the leaders' room numb. That evening she wrote to Lucy Rayner:

I can't believe the way the leaders treat us, as though we were children. I feel so humiliated, especially by Fleur. If you could have heard the things she said about me and Patrique, you'd have laughed out loud. It was as if she thought we were planning to elope before the end of the school. I just keep asking myself why, for goodness' sake, did they have us working together? I'm just grateful they mentioned it today rather than tomorrow. That would have completely ruined my day.

I can see I'm painting a pretty bleak picture of how things are out here and I don't want to do that. The first two weeks have been fascinating. They've been hard, but they've also taught me a lot, I think. Do you remember how we talked about the fact that the supernatural was so much more of a reality in Africa, and that that would probably make the churches feel far more energized spiritually? The funny thing is that the church at Bougainville hasn't been anything like that. Seeing as the pastor organizes two meetings a week, I've had plenty of time to analyse the way I feel and do you know what? Every service has been totally boring. I can't explain it more clearly than that. It doesn't have anything to do with the fact that they don't have the equipment or instruments or any of the stuff we have back in the UK. There's a lot of noise and shouting, but underneath that, nothing. It feels as though the pastor keeps us there for over two hours because he thinks the longer the service lasts the more spiritual it will seem. Patrique reckons that he likes having a captive audience – literally! And that's made me think, especially over this last week, is it really right to subject Muslims to this? I know that Christianity is the truth and I know that the local people here need Jesus more than anything in the world. But what they'll get at the Bougainville church isn't Jesus – it's just legalism of a different kind. I kind of hate myself for writing this, but it really scares me to think that people could be born again, only to go straight into the kind of church that would completely stop them from being able to grow. It would be bad enough for that to happen back home, but think about it: if a person with a Muslim background makes a Christian commitment they're immediately disowned and cut off from their family. And if, instead of being led into the freedom that is theirs in Christ, they get another set of rules what's the good of that? I mean, in the services we get frowned on if we don't verbally respond at the end of every sentence. This morning the pastor went to rebuke someone because he didn't stand up and start praying out loud when he ordered us to… I think you get the picture.

Anyway, I talked about all of this to Patrique – before we got split up – and he reckons that we should have more faith in Jesus' ability to change people inside regardless of what influence their church might have on them. He said that he knew people back home in Quimper who go to the deadest, most legalistic churches imaginable but that they are nevertheless just incredible people whose lives are like a constant witness to the love of Jesus. When Patrique talks to people in the street he's so gentle in the way he approaches them. He's been such an encouragement. He says stuff like, 'Think what would happen if there were just a couple of people in Bougainville who, rather than looking at how tough the services are, just believed that God could work a total change in people independently of what happened on Sundays. And what might happen if those two people got together and prayed for that change to happen…'

But for us, Bougainville is over now. Like I said, tomorrow we've got the day off. In two days' time some of us will be going to Tufala and some of us to Justice IV, which is just across the road. A group is also leaving to go to Dauphin for a couple of weeks. I know that I'm staying here. At least, Fleur and Anne told me that I'd be in Justice IV under Durant. But I've got this sneaking suspicion that Patrique is off to Dauphin. In fact I could stake my life on it, especially seeing as they haven't finalized the teams yet.

I'm writing this to you from the girls' upstairs toilet, outside the bedroom. It's about the only place where I know I won't be disturbed by anyone. I'm trying to think if I've left anything out since I wrote last week. The food is still fantastic – you'd love it. I got over the bug I had last week, but that was just the water. And talking about the water, they made an executive decision not to switch the boiler on, so we can only have tepid showers. I suppose that's not such a big thing, but Natalie (from Florida) says that in really hot weather it's better to have a hot shower because if you're cooler than the air around you, the humidity makes you sweat much more than you would do normally. Having said that, I don't even know if the boiler would work anyway. There's a power cut about once every two days. Sometimes when the light in the worship room goes off we run up on to the roof and watch the city get thrown into darkness...

Chapter 11

Monday was Eritrea's birthday. After breakfast, she sat alone with her back against the wall on her part of the roof while the warm breeze rippled, in fits and starts, over the crenellations. In the opposite far corner of the roof stood Marcello, involved in some complicated and ostentatious prayer ritual, lifting his arms in a gesture of benediction over the south-west side of Croix Blanche. Eritrea watched him for a while, trying to gather her thoughts together and form them into a prayer. She was having trouble reconciling the irritation she felt towards Fleur with the desire to pray; she was still smarting from the injustice and the insensitivity of the previous day. She felt a little self-righteous – almost defiant. But it was hard to hold on to the resentment: the sun was beginning to warm the back of her head, the sky was a brilliant blue. Her birthday had coincided with a day off and Bougainville was now a thing of the past. No more having to share the same room space with Jean Caffal or sit through the services.

For a few minutes she kept repeating the same prayer in her head: Dear Lord, forgive me for being angry with Fleur. The prayer formed and re-formed itself, drifting in and out of her conscious mind, and the wind blew her curly hair around her head. A small bird landed on the very corner of the roof, where the low walls met, and perched expectantly. Then, from the doorway on the roof, emerged the figure of Håkan. He strode over to where Eritrea was sitting and squatted down awkwardly near to her.

'Hold out your hands,' he said. His voice sounded a bit affected, embarrassed. She smiled quizzically and held them both out, palms flat, closing her eyes for good measure. He placed a heavy teabag box into her hands. 'Happy birthday,' he whispered.

She opened her eyes again to see him vanish back down the stairwell.

Well packed inside the box were one bar of chocolate, a roll of camera film, a packet of biscuits, an apple, a toilet roll and a slip of paper that read:

This voucher entitles the bearer to one baignet meal and one bottle of soda in the rustic ambience of a traditional African suburb. Food to be redeemed before February 23rd. This chit cannot be exchanged for cash equivalent.

Eritrea took out the treasures one by one, smelling the chocolate bar and squeezing the trapped air between the wrapper and the bar. She and Lauren had a stash of eight each, one for every week of their stay in Dakar, and one for an emergency, so she knew just how valuable they were. She hadn't thought that other people might have goodies of their own – when she and Lauren consumed their weekly fix it was usually in secret after a *baignet* pig-out and the only thoughts in her head then were guilty ones. As she laid it back in the box she saw Håkan in his bedroom feeling torn and thinking, do I? don't I? Nobody else knows I have this. She appreciated the true sacrifice he had made.

More valuable – and perhaps an even greater sacrifice – was the toilet roll. It was the fat luxurious kind that would usually be advertised with baby geese or lambs, and was nothing like the hard grey rolls that had been sparingly rationed at the beginning of the stay. Standing up, she peered over the wall.

Sure enough, Håkan was back on the garage roof balcony twelve feet below, sitting on the step by the door, with his eyes closed against the rising sun.

Eritrea was in the second group to be taken to the beach. She stood outside the front gate of the compound with Arran, Lauren and some of the French speakers, waiting for Didier to return in the Toyota. In the dip below the pavement curb was a nest of squirming kittens, apparently abandoned.

'It's disgusting,' said Lauren. 'Someone should at least castrate the strays.'

Arran laughed. 'And who's going to do it? You?'

'Don't be ridiculous. All I'm saying is that someone should do something. It's not fair for these poor kittens to die in dust.'

'I never knew cats had such big testicles until I came here,' Arran reflected. 'All the ones back home are spayed.'

Lauren rolled her eyes. 'Feel free to tell us these thoughts of yours whenever they pop into your head, won't you?'

'What? And you're telling me you haven't noticed it?' He turned to Eritrea for support. 'Come on, don't tell me you haven't thought at least once, good grief those cats are well endowed.'

'No, as a matter of fact I haven't. It must be an American thing.'

'A male thing,' Lauren interjected.

'I could try and persuade Didier to let us take them in,' Eritrea said. 'I could say I've always wanted a kitten for my birthday.'

'Six kittens,' Arran said, looking at the nest. 'Tell him you've always wanted six kittens.'

'We don't have to ask him anything,' Lauren said. 'We just move them inside the gate.'

'So you're going to take charge of feeding them, too?'

'I didn't say that. Besides, we don't have any food.'

'You could try giving them some of the doughnuts you two eat so much of.'

'You don't know anything about that,' Eritrea said, sheepishly.

'No, and neither does anyone else in the house.'

'You're a cruel person Arran,' Lauren commented. 'I'm only on a mission of mercy to save these little babies –'

'Babies? I didn't know cats could give birth to babies.'

'– and if I don't move them, they'll get run over by a car. And then you'll feel guilty. Every time you open the gate you'll remember that it was you and your indifference that was responsible for the death of these helpless creatures.'

The argument continued. A group of three itinerant fudge-coloured, horned cows strode casually into the cul-de-sac, like three stately women. They stared around neutrally, the slack skin between their forelegs swaying gently, before bowing their heads and calmly beginning to devour the rubbish that the wind had blown against the griddle fences separating the sandy front gardens from the sandy pavement.

When she arrived at the beach, Eritrea unravelled her large blue towel, laid it on the ground and went straight to the water. It was warm and slightly cloudy, and when she was up to her knees she could no longer see her feet. She waded in up to her neck, holding her hair out of the water. But then she thought, oh well, in for a penny, in for a pound, and ducked under.

After the swim, she lay on her towel and felt the salt prickle as it dried on her skin, under the glaring midday sun. Her ears rushed from the warm brine trapped inside them as the zephyr blew around her. She heard the snatches of contented, purposeless conversation from those around her and the last vestiges of resentment evaporated like the seawater from her skin.

She drifted in and out of sleep for a while, only opening her eyes when she realized that she was no longer in the sun. She sat up and saw a form standing above her so that his shadow fell over, and covered, her body. She shaded her eyes with her hand and looked up as the water trapped in her sinuses began to free itself, tantalizingly. It was Patrique. Had he been standing in her sun in a deliberate attempt to wake her? She gave a cursory glance around. Håkan and Natalie were lying asleep on their towels, as was Damien. None of the leaders was in the vicinity. 'Fancy a walk?' she ventured.

As they watched the seaweed turning over in the shallow breakers at the other end of the beach, near the cliffs, he said, 'Didier told me this morning that I'll be going to Dauphin.'

'Now why does that not surprise me?' Eritrea said acidly.

'Should it?'

'Well, after what happened yesterday...'

'What did happen yesterday?'

Eritrea narrowed her eyes at Patrique, trying to comprehend why he might choose to joke about her embarrassment. Then it dawned on her. 'They told you not to mention it, didn't they?' She shook her head, disgusted. 'Come on, we can at least be honest with each other can't we?'

Patrique stopped in his tracks. 'Eritrea, what *are* you talking about?' he said. His eyes testified to the truth. He really doesn't know, she thought.

'We've been split up. We're not allowed to spend any more time alone together.'

'*Tu blagues.*'

'Why would I make a joke about something like that?' She explained the situation.

'So technically we're disobeying them now by walking along the beach together like this?'

'That's right.'

'And you reckon they put me on the Dauphin team to keep us from having a negative influence on the group?'

Eritrea turned her palms up slightly. 'It certainly looks like it.'

'What's so bad about us spending time together? Everybody else does, especially when they're partnering each other.'

'You try telling them. They think we've got some kind of exclusive relationship going. I told them we're just friends, nothing more.'

Patrique did not respond to this.

'I can't believe that they'd lay down the law like that and then not say anything to you. It doesn't make any sense at all.'

'No.'

'They drag me in there and tell me off like a schoolgirl…' The feelings began to churn in her stomach again. She looked down at the sand. They had been standing still for a moment and she had dug her feet under the dry outer layer of sand and into the cool wet sand beneath. 'I don't want to feel like this. Not on my birthday.'

'Then don't.'

'I can't help it.'

'Look at it this way: I'll be away in Dauphin for the next two weeks with Fleur and Didier. By the time we get back the whole thing will have blown over. And if it hasn't, we've only got a bit over two weeks of the school left. After that we can talk whenever and wherever we want.'

'Yes.'

'We have to toe the line. Think how disappointed you'd be if you looked back and realized you'd let something like their petty insensitivity ruin this for you.'

She looked up at him. 'You're right. What would I do without you?'

'You'll find out tomorrow.'

When they arrived back at where the group was camped out, Eritrea saw Fleur, who had returned from whatever jaunt she had been on. She was sitting on her towel and had clearly been watching them for some time. There was a dangerous coolness in her eyes, as though she were angry about being defied. Well, Eritrea thought, what does she expect if she only tells one of us?

Somehow, it was engineered that Eritrea and Patrique were not in the same minibus home. But perhaps I am just being paranoid, Eritrea thought, as she dusted the sand from her hands and packed the towel into her rucksack.

Håkan sat at the very back of the Toyota and observed Eritrea from the corner of his eye. The two had not spoken since he had given her the present that morning, but she had smiled her thanks to him on the beach, and not even seeing her with Patrique had stopped him from riding high on that brief smile for the rest of the afternoon. His empty stomach had a beer sloshing around in it – courtesy of Marcello – and the alcohol, which had quickly been absorbed into his blood, was fogging his head pleasantly.

As they were driving through the industrial area of the city Arran sat bolt upright in his seat. 'Look,' he said abruptly. On the far side of the road lay the crumpled form of a dead body, clearly the victim of a car accident. The only feature identifying the form as human was an outstretched arm, extended, palm up, from within folds of tattered garment. The hand rested sedately on the burning tarmac, shimmering like liquid through the heat haze. Håkan glimpsed it and it registered like a snapshot in his brain: an arm reaching from a bloodied pile of laundry. The occupants of the Toyota gazed at the broken body and made their hushed remarks, but Håkan glanced over at Eritrea. She had averted her eyes and was focusing her gaze on the inside door handle. The blood seemed to have flowed from her face and the muscles of her jawbone tensed rigid as she clenched her teeth tightly shut. But she did not say anything.

That evening, when the sun was sinking behind Marcello's corner of the roof and the girls' bathroom was empty and permeated with the humid smell of shampooed hair, Eritrea was presented with her birthday cake in the yard outside. The cake was a vast watermelon cut in half and decorated with candles. There was the obligatory rendition of *Joyeux Anniversaire* before everyone devoured the crunchy pink ice and duly spat the pips at each other. Céline's Monday laundry, hanging starchy and rock-solid from a day in the blazing sun, was showered with the sticky pips, despite her protests. Håkan still watched Eritrea, when he thought nobody else might be looking. She was laughing and wiping juice from her forehead, but the mirth in her eyes was a sheen – somewhere underneath was a flicker of apprehension and the memory of a lifeless body; a hand grasping at empty air.

Chapter 12

On Tuesday of the following week, Eritrea stood on the roof with her hands on the low wall, looking down at the four bowls of lunch and the four groups seated around them. As usual, Marcello had finished the food directly in front of him and was beginning to cut away at the cliff face of rice and stew to his left and right. Damien conspicuously scraped his share out of the reach of Marcello's pillaging fork. Anne sat back in her chair, eating nothing.

Eritrea was fasting and praying for a miracle to happen. Since the Dauphin group had left seven days ago, she had spent an almost completely fruitless week evangelizing in Justice IV with Durant, Didier's counterpart. Of all the leaders, Durant was the quietest and least obtrusive, but Eritrea half suspected that she had been put with him so that he could keep an eye on her. The paranoia that she felt about the leaders' decision to take Patrique to Dauphin had been exacerbated by the fact that there was now an uneven number of PCOMers at Croix Blanche to evangelize Tufala and Justice IV; Arran was working alone. More than once during the previous week, she had imagined the last-minute emergency meeting the leaders must have had on the Sunday she was told not to spend time alone with Patrique. 'It's not enough that we separate them,' Fleur would have said. 'Durant, you'll have to partner her for these two weeks to make sure she keeps out of mischief.'

Eritrea came back to herself at that point in her train of thought. 'Oh Lord,' she said silently. 'Why is it so hard for me to concentrate when I'm praying?' She turned away from the wall and paced back across the roof. The base of her neck and the edges of her armpits under her shoulders stung and crept with sunburn from where she had carelessly forgotten to apply sun cream on the beach, the day before. 'Jesus,' she said, into the still air. 'Please make something incredible happen during evangelism. Please do something special.'

Durant was from Alsace. He was a small man with a placid temperament, a soft voice and a well-trimmed beard. He wore a pair of tatty sandals and had the kind of leather-bound Bible that could be zipped closed. It would have been virtually impossible for anyone passing him in the street to mistake him for anything other than what he was: a missionary. At Croix Blanche, he rarely interfered with the daily decisions made by Didier, Fleur and Anne, but Eritrea imagined that, as the most senior of the four leaders, he had ultimate authority. He never took advantage of this authority, but usually aired his wise views as suggestions that might, or might not, be taken on board. He had been a leader for many years and his sandals were coated with dust from the roads of many countries. He never forced his opinions on other people, but when locals gave him the opportunity to speak they listened attentively to what he said, as he instilled an instant sense of calm and well-being in those whom he addressed. Eritrea thought that if anyone made a film about the apostle Paul, Durant would be ideal for the part.

That Tuesday afternoon, they walked the streets of Justice IV. Eritrea had all but forgotten her prayer on the roof, distracted by shooting pains in her stomach from the lack of food and an aggravating headache.

'Shall we try here today?' Durant suggested, signalling down a street. She nodded. To her, all of Justice IV looked the same: rows and rows of one-storey bunkers, joined together in terraces and all made from the same grey concrete. Some had goats tied up outside. They were all identically characterless.

'I don't think we've been down here yet, have we?' Durant remarked.

'I don't know,' Eritrea replied. The two walked for a few metres. Then she stopped. 'Let's try this one,' she said, pointing to a featureless door.

'Why this one, in particular?'

'I don't know… I just… Why not?'

Durant looked further down the street, perhaps assessing the number of houses they might get through if they started here and if everybody was as inhospitable as they had been up until now. 'Okay.'

He knocked loudly and confidently. There was no answer. He knocked again. Still nothing. A chicken clucked in a nearby garden. Standing there, Eritrea began to feel the same sinking feeling she had grown accustomed to in recent days. Durant stood back, seemingly on the verge of suggesting that they move on, but then the door opened.

The man facing them, framed in the doorway, was tall and well-built with wide shoulders and a handsome face. He looked first at Durant, then at Eritrea. 'Come on in, then,' he said unexpectedly, with a bland smile. He waved for them to follow him through a short, pitch-black corridor and into what might have been a living room. 'Please, sit down,' he said, signalling an old-fashioned settee with dark, flat wooden arms. The room smelt strongly of family.

When Durant and Eritrea were settled, he sat down on a plastic chair opposite them and crossed his legs. 'You have something important to tell me,' he said, with an absolutely straight face.

Eritrea thought, he knows we're missionaries and he's about to play some elaborate joke on us. Thank goodness I don't have to do the talking.

Durant said, 'First things first. My name is Durant. I'm from Alsace, France. And this is Eritrea, from England. What's your name?'

'Youssou.'

'Youssou,' Durant said. 'Why do you think we have something important to tell you?'

'Someone told me that you would come and knock on my door.'

Someone, thought Eritrea. Obviously everybody around here has been warned about us.

'Who told you?' Durant continued, unflustered.

'I have a mentor,' the man said. 'He told me that two white people would come and visit me and that I should listen to what they had to tell me because it would change my life.'

'Who is this mentor?'

'A holy and respected Muslim. I'm studying under him to become a religious teacher.'

'Do you know who we are or why we're here?'

The man shook his head.

'And you haven't heard about us from anyone else, except from your mentor?'

'No.'

'We're Christians,' Durant said. He let it hang in the air a while. 'We believe that Jesus Christ, who, as you know, is considered as merely a prophet in the Muslim faith, is in fact the Son of God. God himself in human form.' He spoke quietly and calmly. 'I believe that this mentor of yours was given a revelation by God and that we are here because God wants you to know more about Jesus and what Jesus wants from you.'

'What would Jesus want from me?' the man answered. 'I'm a Muslim. I serve my God and I do all that is required of me by my faith. I am preparing to become a teacher of the faith. So what could Jesus want of me?'

'He wants *you*. Nothing more and nothing less.'

The man looked at them through narrowed eyes. 'I don't think so. It can't be possible.'

'Think about it for a moment. Jesus said, "I know my own and my own know me." He also said, "I have other sheep that are not of this fold. I must bring them also, and they will listen to my voice. So there will be one flock, one shepherd." Your mentor is a Muslim, who probably knows little about Jesus Christ and would certainly not have told you to listen to us if he thought we would draw you away to another faith, that is not the faith you grew up with. But our God is so great and powerful that he has used someone who does not even follow him to speak words of truth into your life. This same God brought us to your door today to fulfil the words that were spoken to you. And he is calling you by name right now.'

The hairs on Eritrea's forearms tingled and her heart beat fast. Silently, she prayed, Lord, is this your answer?

The man sat, dumbfounded for a moment. Eritrea could see in his eyes all the questions piled up in his head, waiting to be spoken from his lips. She had heard them several times over the last few weeks: but Jesus is just one of many prophets, it is impossible for Allah to have a son, the Bible is full of contradictions, the only accurate holy writings are those of the Arabic Koran, in the West the people who claim to be Christians live promiscuous lives, so how can Christianity be right?

'Jesus is calling you by name,' Durant repeated. 'Do you want to hear what he has to say to you?'

The man rubbed his forehead and took a breath. 'All right. I'll hear.'

170

After leaving the house, Durant and Eritrea walked back towards Croix Blanche in silence. Youssou had listened to Durant share his faith for an hour and a half. And, after some persuading, he had even agreed to come and visit the villa the following day. 'But the local genie protector won't let me come,' he had said, apprehensively.

'Don't you worry about that,' Durant had replied. 'Our God is stronger than any genie protector.'

As they were approaching the main road separating the districts, Eritrea said, 'Is he really scared of this genie?'

'Probably a lot more than even he let on.'

'But he's a Muslim, not an animist. He shouldn't even believe in them, should he?'

'The local wizards are Muslims, too, but they're the very people who sell charms to ward off evil spirits.'

'Are they all afraid? Even the wizards, I mean?'

'Of course. The *marabout* wizards exploit people's fear of the local genies by selling them expensive bracelets and talismans, but the ironic thing is, they're probably just as afraid, if not more so.'

'How come?'

'Well, it's quite obvious really. They don't have the Christian's practical understanding of how to deal with Satanic forces. Their knowledge of the way demons work is limited, and they certainly have no authority over them. One of the only things that makes some Africans willing to hear the message of Christ is fear of the devil and of demons. The people here are incredibly superstitious, and the devil takes advantage of it to terrorize them. Ultimately though, God uses even that, because when people are in close contact with – and terrified of – evil spirits, they're much more likely to turn to Jesus once they know that only through him can they have authority over them.'

Eritrea digested this. After a while, she said, 'I prayed on the roof today for a miracle, *tu sais*.'

Durant smiled. 'It's exciting isn't it?'

'It's more than that. It's like a gift.'

'It *is* a gift. To be used like that is something very special.'

'It's happened like that before?'

'Never exactly the same. But similar things.'

'Give me an example.'

Durant touched Eritrea's arm to keep her from stepping out in front of a lorry. 'A few years ago I was with a team of people that went on outreach to Turkey. We were working with the local PCOM base that had set up a medical dispensary in one of the poor districts in Ankara. There was a girl in the team who was like you in some ways Eritrea –' he smiled when he said this – 'but painfully shy.' He paused. 'She was called Sophie. She was so very afraid of street evangelism that we organized for her to be in the waiting room and to look after people who were going in for treatment. One day she felt that God wanted her to pray for an old gypsy who had come in to have her cataracts looked at. She went over and asked in English if she could pray, but of course the old woman didn't understand. So, terrified as she was, she laid her hands on the woman's head and prayed anyway.'

'And the eyes were healed?' Eritrea asked as they turned into the Croix Blanche cul-de-sac.

Durant shook his head. 'No.' He considered and laughed. 'But you would have thought so, wouldn't you? As it happened, she eventually had an operation, which was successful. But I'm losing track of myself. Like I said, Sophie prayed for a bit but felt that God wanted her to pray aloud in tongues – bear in mind that the waiting room was always packed, so it must have been pretty daunting. But she obeyed and, for about five minutes prayed out loud over the woman. Imagine what it must have been like for her. The courage she would have needed to do that. Anyway, when she finished, the old woman was in tears. They had no way of communicating with each other, so Sophie had no idea what the woman was saying through her tears. But –' he broke off and raised his finger at Eritrea – 'when the woman had had her eyes looked at, the doctor, who was a Turk, came out to see Sophie. According to the woman, Sophie's prayer in tongues had been the gospel message in the woman's own language, and the woman's tears were tears of repentance.'

'You mean her – Sophie's – tongue was Turkish?'

'No. And that's the thing. The woman understood Turkish, but she was a gypsy. Sophie had prayed for her in her own dialect, Romany.'

When Youssou came to visit the following day, Håkan was coming to the end of his post-lunch sunbathing session on the balcony. He had pulled a T-shirt over his head, but had no trousers to cover his legs. If I'm quick, he thought, I can nip back through the French window without anyone seeing me. Or I could cover myself up with the towel. He picked it up, shook it and wrapped it around his waist like a sarong. He peeped over the wall to check that no-one was in the immediate vicinity, but there was a man at the end of the cul-de-sac walking purposefully in the direction of the villa. Håkan stooped low for a moment and watched. The man raised his head and looked nervously behind him before stepping out to cross the road.

Then an extraordinary thing happened. Without any warning or sound whatsoever, the man was suddenly thrown backwards into the dust with such force that Håkan heard him exhale as he hit the ground. It was as though a vast, invisible foot had descended from the sky and kicked him full in the chest. He struggled to his feet and tried to advance, but was once again sent sprawling to the ground. Håkan stood, stunned, and watched as the man crawled back to his feet. He stood, dazed, for a moment, steadying himself on a fencepost and taking deep breaths, before trying, once again to cross the road. This time he seemed to be overcome by a fit of dizziness. He faltered, like a man in the dark, and crumpled to his knees, touching his head. At this point, Håkan heard the creak of the gate. Durant and Eritrea went running from the compound and helped him to his feet. As the man lifted his head for a moment, Håkan glimpsed the confusion and the terror in his eyes. Then it was bowed again, as the strength in his legs gave way. Durant and Eritrea draped the man's arms around their shoulders and started to make their way back to the villa. Eritrea looked to be flagging, but then Damien was there to help. Together, they brought him into the compound and through the front door.

Chapter 13

Eritrea was not the only person bothered by Patrique's absence. In addition to sweeping the worship room, Håkan was also allocated the shared task of pumping drinking water for the team while Patrique was away. The laborious job had previously been the responsibility of Damien and Patrique together, but was too much for Damien to cope with on his own, so Durant had asked Håkan to help. Until he had sat outside in the baking afternoon heat toiling away with the pump, Håkan had lived in blissful ignorance of the vast quantities of liquid consumed by the PCOM team. 'And if you think this is bad, imagine what it's like when everyone's here,' Damien grunted, by way of encouragement, during Håkan's second pumping session.

It was a thankless and repetitive task: first, Håkan filled a number of buckets and other receptacles with water and carried them out into the back yard. Then he opened the stirrups of the pump, a contraption like a dynamite detonator with a tap. Inserting the rubber tube that came from the base of the pump into a full bucket of water, he aimed the metal pump tap towards an empty receptacle, put his feet over the foot stirrups to keep the apparatus firmly anchored on the ground, and started to pump. There was no point in trying to pump quickly, because instead of sending a clean jet of water into the receptacle the tap then sprayed the water – like a plant atomizer – indiscriminately wide of the mark. Sometimes Håkan pumped hard anyway, out of sheer frustration, splashing the ground within a radius of anything up to a metre around the bucket with filtered water.

He and Damien investigated the possibility of re-engineering the system by removing the rubber hose from one of the two pumps and placing it over the end of the tap, to avoid wastage. But it was no use: not only were the drawing hoses attached to the two pumps in such a way that they could only be removed by being cut off, but the hoses themselves were clearly too loose to fit over the end of the taps.

'We could cut an inch off the end of the hose and tape it around the tap,' Håkan suggested desperately.

'It'd never work,' Damien had answered. 'And anyway, the tape would get wet and come off.'

'Not if we used masking tape.'

'And where are we going to get that?'

'One of us could go into the centre, or something.'

'During the curfew, when the shops are closed?'

'I don't know. Can you think of a better idea?'

Damien shrugged. 'We can't sabotage the pumps without asking Didier, so, whatever happens, we're going to have to wait until he gets back from Dauphin.'

Håkan gave up and carried on as before. Even when all the drinking water receptacles were filled, the job was not over: the pumps still needed to be opened and the brown silt cleaned with a hard-bristle brush from the porous filtering stone inside.

Apart from his long-running battle with the water pump, Håkan's only other major occupation at the villa during the two weeks of the Dauphin team's absence was honing his guitar skills. As Fleur was away, Håkan was the only person capable of leading worship with an instrument, which he did with judicious self-imposed reservations about becoming proud. So he played standing deferentially behind Anne, who sang and banged a tambourine.

In the evenings, when all the containers were filled with clean water for the following day, he sat in the worship room and practised. In his diary he had drawn a picture of the neck of a guitar with all of the notes written above the frets of each string, and he tried to memorize scales in different keys. With most of the English-speaking contingent – including Natalie and Lauren – away in Dauphin, there were no more games of cards, so by the second week the skin on the tips of the fingers of his left hand had begun to harden up again.

The night before the Dauphin team were due to return he was practising as usual, when Eritrea entered the room. She sat opposite him, rolled down the sleeves of her sweatshirt and folded her arms to listen. She seemed to have just come from having a shower. He played on, more than a little self-consciously. Then she stood up. 'Can we talk?' she asked.

He glanced over at Marcello, the only other occupant of the room, who was absorbed in his Bible underlining.

'Sure.' He laid the guitar back into its case and snapped the catches closed.

'Not here,' she said, and Håkan's heart immediately began to pound. She left the room and went up the stairs, with Håkan following obediently behind. She knocked at his bedroom door as a formality, but there was no answer. 'Is Arran likely to be asleep?'

Håkan shook his head. 'He's probably up on the roof. He usually is about this time.'

Eritrea gave a smile that sent the adrenalin zipping through Håkan's body. She opened the door, walked straight across the room and through the French window. Turning right, she pushed the balcony door open and stepped out on to the garage roof. Håkan sat down beside her on the tiled step, closing the door behind him.

'So this is what it's like out here,' she said.

His brain was filled to the edges with a fluffy haze of nervousness that blanked out any ability to think rationally, let alone formulate an answer. He sat stupid and silent for a while, trying to gain control. 'You've never been out here before?'

'No. But I watch you down here from up on the roof.'

'Really?' He was overcome with gratitude.

'Of course. You walk in a figure-of-eight while you pray every morning. I'm constantly amazed that you don't crash into the wall, seeing as you've got your eyes closed.'

'You watch me?'

'Everybody spies on everybody here, don't they?'

'I suppose so. It's just that when you put it like that, it sounds so premeditated.'

'It's a secret vice that we all share. But you could always say that it's quite justified to watch what other people do, because if you know where they are you can keep out of their way. Give them their space.'

'True enough.'

'But,' she said, 'I *always* know where you are. If I hear the pump squeaking, I know you're in the back yard. If I hear the guitar, then I know you're in the worship room. And if I don't hear either then I know you're up here.'

'I didn't know I was so predictable.'

'I also look at your diary sometimes,' she said, wickedly.

'Is nothing sacred?'

'Only over your shoulder,' she added, by way of justification. 'And, in any case, its just full of "och" and "pa" so I can't understand any of it.'

'*På*, you mean.'

'Alright, *paw*.'

'Spying on people to keep out of their way is one thing. Looking at someone's diary is quite different, surely?' But he was flattered.

'I've seen my name in there sometimes,' Eritrea probed. 'I wonder what you could've been writing about me?'

'That's classified information.' At least for the moment, he thought.

'You should've given me some kind of codename. Some Swedish name that people spying on you over your shoulder won't recognize. Something like Hilda or Brita.'

'Obviously I should've.' He exaggerated the retort. 'Is that what you wanted to talk to me about?'

'No. At least, not directly. We might come back to it, of course, at some point… But I've been wanting to ask you something for a while. You're not annoyed with me about something are you?'

Håkan's head spun with the absurdity of the question. 'Why should I be?'

'You seem a bit distant. We hardly ever speak to each other, and I thought originally that we might've got to know each other a bit better since the others are in Dauphin. But it just hasn't been possible for one reason or another.'

'How could you have done anything to annoy me? I'd tell you if you had. Rest assured.' He was tempted to go on and explain how desperately he had hoped they might speak, and about the last two weeks ticking away without them getting to know each other. But something inside him stopped him.

'There's another thing. I wanted to thank you for the birthday present and get my free *baignet* meal.'

'What, now?'

'Not now. Tomorrow afternoon, say.'

'All right, you're on.'

'I also wanted to get to know you better – as a friend.'

This last comment struck Håkan dumb. When he replied, he said, 'I've wanted to, too, you know. But I didn't feel I could just come up to you and say, "Hi, let's talk" because…'

179

He wanted to say something like, what with you and Patrique being so intimate, and all. But he did not want to bring Patrique into the conversation. He left the thought hanging.

Eritrea correctly interpreted the silence, read the thought in his mind and felt ever so slightly piqued. If he had given her any verbal indication of what he was thinking, she would have asked him, Do you really think that Patrique and I have something exclusive going on? But this would have been overstepping the mark. Instead, she said, 'But *I* did.'

'And I'm pleased you did.' He shifted his right leg, which had gone so dead that it felt like a foreign body. 'I've got terrible pins and needles. Don't you hate it when you get to the stage when you know any movement will be totally unbearable?'

'I know, it's horrible isn't it?' She watched him move his weight cautiously off his leg. 'How are you finding things here?'

'What, things in general, or evangelism?'

'Both. Evangelism.'

'It's okay now I suppose. It was so hard at the beginning, but you get used to it after a while, I reckon.'

'Why so hard?'

'The first afternoon we walked around Rufine I felt so completely out of place. I kept thinking, this time last year I was sitting in a maths class, looking out at the snow and now here I am on the streets of Africa. And then when we finally got to speak to some people Marcello just insulted them. You know how he can be sometimes.'

Eritrea thought about his elaborate prayers and gestures on the roof. 'I sure do.'

'But I think God wanted to use it to teach me something. Not to judge people because they do things differently to me, or something like that, because on the last day at Rufine one of the guys that Marcello offended came to the film and went up for prayer.'

'And became a Christian?'

'I never found out.' Håkan thought about the boy's eyes. 'But I think he did. I'm almost sure he did.' They were silent again for a moment. 'And you didn't find it difficult at the beginning?' he asked.

She shrugged. 'Patrique did all the talking, and he has this way of being able to approach people without scaring them. But I can't say that much happened. Up until we met Youssou this week, nothing seemed to go according to plan, really.'

'But I thought you guys had a really successful time at Bougainville.'

'That depends on who you talk to.' Just saying it made her remember the sound of Fleur's irritating forced laugh filling the converted garage after each and every one of Jean Caffal's humour-free sermon jokes.

'What was so bad about it?'

Eritrea exhaled. 'I got to the point where I thought I'd heard God wrong and that he'd never wanted me here at all. I was so desperate and low about it. That's why I went up on the roof and prayed for a miracle. I really didn't know what else to do. Then, the same afternoon, we go out and meet Youssou. He comes here, he wants to make a commitment.' She paused. 'It's a miracle, plain and simple. Nobody could ever say that it was anything else.'

'You still haven't told me why Bougainville was so bad.'

'I'm coming to that. You see, now I'm beginning to think that perhaps God made sure I was in a situation where I'd start feeling desperate enough about evangelism to pray seriously for a miracle.'

'By making you have a lousy time at Bougainville?'

'No. Well, yes and no. But however tough it was, I still feel that I learned something from it.'

'What made it so tough, if Patrique was so great to work with?'

Eritrea considered. 'The church. There was something about the church that was just impossible.'

'Boring, you mean?'

'That too, but it was more than that. It was as though we were constantly on trial and that we had to perform for the pastor, and that only the people who made the most noise in worship were holy enough. It was so forced, I can't explain it.'

'It wasn't like that in Rufine.'

'It was almost like we were being threatened,' Eritrea continued, a bit distantly. 'Look like you're praising God, or else.' Then she came back to herself. 'I sound awfully judgemental, don't I?'

'No.'

'I've got a friend I write to back home. She says that some churches are legalistic because they're trapped in old routines and that people use the liturgy and service traditions or whatever to keep the Holy Spirit at bay, but she also says there are churches that are just as bad but the opposite, like, charismatic-legalistic. She reckons that those kinds of churches have gone the other way and that people in them are forced to go through the motions of praying in tongues and shouting and prophesying and all that, but that it's just as legalistic, only in the other extreme.'

'For the sake of other people in the congregation?'

'Yeah. She says that most of the charismatic noise is generated to please other people, and that ultimately, it's about being afraid of what other people will think of you if you don't look like you're in seventh heaven during worship.'

'She sounds like a good person.'

'She's my best friend.' Eritrea turned her head away from Håkan for a second, almost as if she didn't want him to see the expression on her face. At that moment, the wind changed direction and carried the faintest scent of her hair towards him. It was breathtaking – the perfect smell of hair that is still just a tiny bit damp from having been washed. He wanted to sit closer to her and hold the curls in his hands and bury his face in them. 'Do you write to her a lot?'

'Once or twice a week. I tell her everything.'

'I've never seen you writing.'

'That's because I'm the only person who's got wise to the fact that everyone spies on everybody else.'

'So, what, you write in bed?'

'Well, I did try that for while. But it's a bit tricky, and then Natalie always complains about the torchlight. I mean, how stupid is that? If she's trying to go to sleep, her eyes are closed, so how is a torch under someone else's sleeping bag going to disturb her?'

'So, not in bed?'

'No. If you must know, I sit in the toilet next to our bedroom. It's the only place I know I won't be disturbed.'

'I don't think I've ever been in there.'

'I should hope not,' Eritrea said. 'Anyway, unlike you I don't have the luxury of being able to write in a language that no-one else understands.'

There didn't seem to be an answer to this. Instead, he said, 'There's a lot that I couldn't tell anyone. Sometimes, I even wonder if it's a good idea to write it down at all.'

'You should do. It's good to get things out of your system, even if nobody else gets to read them.' She gathered the hair that had fallen over the front of her shoulders, twisting it around loosely and putting it behind her head. 'I'm jealous of you, you know. It must be incredible being able to speak three languages fluently.'

The idea that Eritrea, with her emerald eyes and the tiny golden hairs on her tanned arms, could be jealous of anyone seemed absurd. 'They say that if you're bilingual or trilingual you're not actually fluent in any of the languages you speak.'

'Your French sounds perfect to me.'

Håkan huffed. 'When I first went to Canada, my cousins joked about my accent so much that I hardly said anything.'

'You moved from Sweden when you were...?'

'Ten.'

'And you didn't speak any English before that?'

'Not really. Well. Some, perhaps.'

'But didn't you say that you were only in Canada for five years?'

'Something like that.'

'So how can you be so fluent in English when Montreal is French speaking?'

'Well, my parents put me in an English speaking school, for a start. They rotated things: French school in Stockholm, English school in Montreal. In Canada I talked Swedish with dad, French with mum and English at school.'

'How could you cope with that? It sounds impossible.'

'You just adapt when you're young. You don't even think about it. But anyway Montreal isn't just French speaking. It's not like that. Everybody mixes French and English. Even my mother. I heard it all the time, and then when we moved back to Sweden I realized that everyone in Sweden is surrounded by English. Most of the TV shows are from England or the States, and they're subtitled, so even if you don't like speaking it, you still understand everything.'

'If you watch TV.'

'Not even. It's everywhere you go. You just can't escape it.'

'I wish I could speak three languages.'

'Your French is incredible. Much better than Richard's. When I first heard you, I didn't even know you weren't French.' This was a lie, but Håkan wanted so much to mean it, that it did not even register in his mind that he was not telling the truth.

'Even so.'

'I could teach you some Swedish if you want.'

'That would be nice. You know that one of the main reasons I joined PCOM was to use my French.'

'I didn't. I thought you said that you came because of your name, or something?'

'Oh yes, of course there's that, too.'

'I can't really remember.' He remembered perfectly, but just wanted to hear her speak. 'Tell me again.'

'It was just that someone at church gave me a word about remembering my namesake, so I looked into doing something missionary-related in Eritrea. But the situation was so bad at the time and there's no PCOM activity there anyway. So I decided that if I couldn't go there, it would have to be somewhere else in Africa.'

'But French speaking, right?'

'Right.'

'How did you get into French in the first place?'

'You'll laugh if I tell you.'

'I won't.'

'Promise?'

'It can't be such a big deal, can it?'

'No. It really is no big deal at all. It was literally the only thing I was ever any good at, so I thought, what the heck, might as well try and do it at uni, if I get a place.'

'What's so bad about that?'

'Nothing, if you ignore the fact that I'm no good at anything else.'

'I could never believe that.' He looked at her features silhouetted in the semi-darkness and his heart turned over inside him. The desire to hold her close to him was so strong it made his throat constrict. He looked down at her slender hands lying relaxed in her lap. The scar on her index finger shone pale against her tanned skin. More than anything he wanted to run his own finger along it, to feel its raised smoothness. 'How did you get that scar?' he asked. 'I've always wanted to know.'

She turned her hand from side to side, examining it critically from different angles and remembering the barbed shard of glass that had lodged itself deep into the soft tissue of her finger. Just looking at it reminded her of the repulsive painless-but-painful sensation of the exposed edges of flesh moving against each other and the feeling when the splinter was pulled out. In any other circumstances she would have gone to hospital and had it stitched up, but it had been so very inconsequential at the time. Untreated and unstitched, the cut had opened and reopened until she had learnt to write with her thumb and middle finger.

'I'll tell you some other time,' she said.

It was now so dark that he could hardly make out the expression on her face. He looked at the perfect curve of her neck running upwards to her chin, thrown into relief by the whitewashed wall of the villa behind her. Eventually, she said, 'We should start thinking about getting to bed I suppose. What time is it?'

Håkan had to turn his watch to find an angle where the face caught the moonlight. 'Half past eleven. Are you surprised?'

She did not answer, but Håkan could tell that she was smiling.

Chapter 14

The next morning, Håkan woke up and realized that he was no longer looking forward to anything. All of his life, a part of him had craved a certain elusive fulfilment in the deepest recesses of his soul. Ironically, the feeling of fulfilment he so longed for was, in and of itself, a feeling of grasping yearning, but married with an inexpressible sense of elation. The emotion went beyond Håkan's ability to quantify.

He had come close to the desired feeling on occasions, but those fleeting moments had only served to show him that he was not yet there. He had skirted around the feeling, brushed the edges of it. Sometimes, when he listened to particular songs that brought back the warm greens of early summer or the memories of the cool, perfect taste of his first kiss, his finger had been on the pulse of that yearning. This morning, however, as he lay in bed staring at the ceiling, he knew that he would search no longer. How could he describe it? It was as if his soul were resonating in perfect unison with the fabric of reality; as if he were outside of physical time bathing in the knowledge of a great and precious secret that only he knew. It was like a prolongation of the feeling evoked by the cool peppery smell of rain on tarmac after a long dry spell.

His thoughts turned over and examined elements of the physical Eritrea – her knuckles, the way she sometimes pulled her hair to one side of her neck, the perfect, thrilling intensity of her voice – while, deeper down, his soul simmered with an adoration of almost unbearable intensity.

When he went down to breakfast and saw the edge of her knee through the doorway to the worship room, the simmering erupted within him, flipping his stomach like a roller coaster. Sitting behind her at the church service in Justice IV he simply revelled in the knowledge that she was near. At one point, she turned around and gave him a brief, confirming smile, which his soul sucked in hungrily. He sang the hymns loudly and joyfully, bowed his head reverently for the prayers and saw nothing but the outline of her profile.

It was not until after lunch that the elation was tarnished by the first tiny blemish of concern. As the bowls were being taken into the kitchen, he remembered that the Dauphin group would be returning later that afternoon, and that he had only a few semi-private hours with her before the house was once again full. The realization was brief, but it was enough to mar the honeymoon of his fulfilment. The thought of Patrique flashed across his outer consciousness, but he did not associate his concern about the return of the Dauphin group with the deeper feeling of uneasiness that Patrique's presence might undermine his newfound rapport with Eritrea.

Håkan went up to his room to pray but was unable to concentrate, dogged by the thought that if he was not in some neutral place she might not seek him out. He made his way downstairs unobtrusively and sensed that she was in the kitchen. Settling in the worship room, he took up his guitar and played, while the impatience of longing boiled at the edges of his soul.

Eventually, an hour later, she came to him. She was still perspiring from effort. 'Durant made me clean the kitchen walls,' she said. 'He's had me shut up in there like Cinderella.' It was the first spoken contact they had had all day and it was balm to him. 'All that work has made me quite hungry again,' she said tentatively, almost slyly. She left the question unasked, but Håkan was already putting his guitar away. 'Let's go,' he said.

'Do I need my voucher?' she asked as they were leaving through the gate.

'I'll take it on trust this time,' he answered. They crossed the road. 'Let's get something to drink first and then come back for the *baignets*.' They walked a couple of blocks until they found a rusty kiosk with a fridge. 'What would you like?' he asked.

'Fizzy lemon, if he's got any,' Eritrea said.

'Do you have any?' Håkan asked the boy in the kiosk.

The boy shook his head. '*On n'a plus que ça, This is all we have left,*' he said, proffering a bottle of bright orange *Schitrus*.

'Is that okay for you?' Håkan asked.

Eritrea paused. 'I don't mean to be fussy, but I just can't stand orangeade.' She breathed in as if to articulate further explanation, but then said nothing.

Håkan sensed her awkwardness. 'Don't worry,' he said quickly. 'We'll go to another kiosk. There are hundreds of them around here.'

Approaching the cul-de-sac with the food and drink in their arms, Håkan said, 'Did you actually see Youssou get knocked down the other day?'

'Not at first. Durant just happened to notice him from the roof. But you saw everything, didn't you?'

'It was incredible. Like a movie.'

'When Durant told me about the genie protectors, I didn't really believe him,' she admitted. 'Well, that's not it exactly. I just thought it was *unlikely* that there could be demons over particular districts, that could stop people from moving around. Seeing him lying in the road was, like, another confirmation, almost as if God was saying, "*Now* do you believe?" And that was even after the miracle of meeting Youssou in the first place.'

'I'd never seen anything like it before. Not in my whole life,' Håkan said. 'One minute he was walking towards the house and then the next he was literally kicked through the air on to the sand.'

'Durant was talking about Eastern and Western mindsets in the worship room the other day,' Eritrea said. She frowned. 'Were you there? I can't remember.'

'I don't think so.' They were approaching the gate. 'Where can we go to eat these without anyone seeing us?'

'How about here, under the window?' Eritrea suggested.

'Not the most secret of places.'

Eritrea smiled. 'Ha ha. Well at least I haven't been out here since Lauren left.'

'What about Richard's spot?'

'I hadn't thought of that,' Eritrea said. 'We've still got an hour or so before they get back.'

Sitting agonizingly close to her against the cool wall of the passage, Håkan took a drink of his lemonade. The bottle lip was opaque and rough with scratches from repeated recycling. 'You were saying?'

'About the genies?'

He nodded.

'Durant has this theory about the East and the West. He says that in the developed Western world, what with technology and explanations for everything and so on, people live in a permanent state of scepticism and Satan feeds it and uses it to keep them from being able to see the reality of the spiritual realm around them. Even Christians. He says it's like a blanket that covers their minds and that because of that you hardly ever see any miracles. Or at least, not that often. And he reckons that the Western caricature of the devil being red with horns and a tail is something that the devil quite likes, because it keeps people from thinking about what he might really be like and what his strategies are. But he says that in the East it's almost the exact opposite.'

'Meaning?'

'That people aren't sceptical about the devil or spiritual stuff, and they even live in a state of semi-fear of the spiritual realm. And that because no faith except Christianity gives people any real knowledge about the devil, he exploits it and takes advantage of it, just like he does in developed countries, but the other way around. So you see lots of evil spiritual manifestations because the devil knows that, rather than rationally thinking, good grief, what's that?, people are likely to just get more scared, because they feel so helpless against evil spirits and don't know anything about how to have victory over them.'

'Whereas if people saw someone being thrown around the street by an invisible demon in the centre of Stockholm, it would instantly destroy the illusion that there's no spiritual realm.'

'That's it.'

'So in the West it's tactically good for him to lie low and promote scepticism and in the East to make people more and more scared.'

'Exactly. But like Durant says, the devil just exploits the characteristics of the people in any given place. Scepticism in the West is born out of people's pride because they think they've got the world sewn up with technology and every-thing. And fear in the East is due to people's lack of spiritual knowledge. If they knew more about Christianity – even if they disparaged it like people do in the West – it'd probably only take one powerful spiritual manifestation to make them start thinking seriously about Christ.'

'But they do know *something* about Christianity. After all, there are a fair number of Catholics here.'

'Yes, but Durant says that loads of Catholics – not all of them, of course – but a lot of them don't know anything about the authority that they have in Christ. Just like back in the UK there are hundreds of thousands, maybe millions, of nominal Christians who never read the Bible and don't even claim to be born again. What I'm saying is that even a lot of the so-called Christians here are ignorant. So the devil has a field day. If he thinks he can get away with terrorizing someone and make them more scared without them questioning how to be free of the fear, then he will. If he runs the risk of a person turning to Christ for help, he's more likely to lie low.'

'But what about Youssou?'

'That's the exception that proves the point. Think about it: God was already working in him through what the mentor had said. He gave Durant and me the privilege of being the ones actually to bring the gospel to him, but by that time the devil was so desperate not to lose his influence over Youssou that he was ready to resort to absolutely anything, including a noisy and visible thing like what happened on Thursday, and blow his cover.'

'I hadn't thought of it like that,' Håkan said, screwing up his empty doughnut bag.

'And you know, Youssou was terrified of coming here to see us. He said himself that the genie wouldn't let him.'

'The other day you two were saying he wanted to make a commitment. Why hasn't Durant led him in a prayer of repentance or something?'

'He only came on Wednesday and Thursday and Durant reckons it's important for him to know exactly what he's doing before taking that step.'

'Do you do much of the talking?'

'What, when Durant's going over the Bible stuff with him? Sometimes. Durant asks me to share examples of how God's worked in my life and things.' She stood up and wiped the crumbs from her dress. 'What happens if I try to get another meal out of you and claim that the voucher's still valid because I didn't actually give it to you?'

'You might get away with it.'

Håkan was in his room when the Dauphin team returned. He heard the slamming of the Toyota doors and the clash of enthusiastic voices vying with each other for attention about who had had the most successful two weeks of evangelism. Eventually, there was a lull, pierced every now and then by interjections in English and French; Eritrea and Durant were no doubt recounting the events surrounding Youssou.

After half an hour or so, he made his way downstairs and greeted them. In his heart, Håkan did not feel entirely pleased to see them, but he listened to Lauren and Natalie talk eagerly about their experiences. He himself did not have much to say about his own successes. 'Fairly quiet really,' he answered, casting an eye around the room to see where Eritrea might be. When he saw her talking to Patrique, he continued to nod and say 'mm-hmm' to Natalie, but heard no more of what she said.

When he eventually got back to the bedroom, he found Arran sitting on the other bed and a note written on A4 paper lying conspicuously on his own. It said, simply:

Hey Hawk,

We could meet again for a talk tonight, if you want... Say 8 p.m., same place as yesterday?

Love,

Eritrea

When Håkan opened the balcony door leading to the garage roof that evening, he found Eritrea already there, leaning on the wall that looked over the east of Croix Blanche. The day was not yet ready to give in to darkness and the balcony was bathed in a thick, syrupy half-light that framed her form like a portrait.

'Sorry I'm late,' Håkan said. 'I was pumping water.'

'I know,' Eritrea replied, brushing the dust from her elbows where her crossed arms had been resting on the wall. 'I always know where you are, remember?' She sat down on the step under the door and patted the warm tiles as a sign for Håkan to do likewise. He complied.

'I get the feeling the water job's been permanently passed on to me even though Patrique's back,' he said.

'Are you complaining?' She gave him a slight, mocking smile, and looked at him as though over half-moon spectacles.

'No. I guess not. It's just not the most suitable job for me with my hands. Look.' He held them out for her to inspect. The hands were crinkly from the water and the skin on the tips of the fingers was swollen and white and covered with little divots from repeated biting, like the surface of a golf ball. 'When I play the guitar a lot it makes the skin go hard, but when the hard bits get wet I can't keep from biting them and then when I play again it's complete agony.'

'I didn't know you bit you fingers.'

'It's a disgusting habit isn't it? But it's a vicious circle. Once you start biting them you just can't stop. Every time they get wet, the skin comes up white when it's healing and it's too much of a temptation, so you just chew it off again. Then it starts healing up again until the next time you get it wet, and you bite it off again, and so it goes on…'

Eritrea took his right hand gently and looked at his index finger. The touch sent a jolt through him.

'It's an unfortunate pairing of work and hobby,' he said, trying to keep his composure. 'I knew a guitar player who had finger tips that were flat, like spades, and as hard as rock. Mine will never be like that if I keep –'

'You asked me about my scar yesterday.'

'Yes.'

'I want to tell you about it.' She placed his hand gently back on his knee, as though it were made of china.

'You don't have to if you don't want to.'

'I do want to. About six years ago I was working at a pub that had this awful dishwasher. You had to stack the glasses into a drum that spun round when they were being washed. Unless you packed them in really tightly they knocked against each other and one almost always got smashed. Anyway, this one time I was trying to fish the broken bits out of the corners and I felt one go really deep into my finger. It was the most horrible sensation, you know?'

Håkan shuddered. 'Ugh.'

'I'd been washing up by hand just before I started unloading the dishwasher so the skin on my hands was really soft. The other girl who was working there that morning was so squeamish that she didn't have the guts to help me pull it out, so I had to ask the manager.' She broke off and laughed, but it was a cold laugh. 'The end of the shard was barbed. Can you believe that he had to push the barbed end through the skin on the top of my finger and break it off with a pair of pliers before it could be pulled out properly?'

'It sounds excruciating.'

'He made such a mess of it. That's why the scar's so long. It bled and bled,' she continued somewhat distantly. 'Every time I thought it had stopped it opened up again.'

'So why didn't you get it seen to?'

She turned her head slowly and looked at him long. 'I had a twin brother.' The words embedded themselves in the air and stuck there. Eritrea looked out over the roofs with her head slightly on one side, as if considering how to clarify the link. 'He was called Jonah. When I was emptying the dishwasher I got a call that he was dead. The phone was ringing when I actually cut myself. If I'd answered it in the first place I might never have done this.' She traced the line of the scar with the middle finger of her left hand.

'I'm so sorry.'

'Don't be.'

'I had no idea.'

'No. Nobody else here knows about it except the leaders,' she said.

'Not even Patrique?' But he regretted the words as soon as they had left his mouth.

'No, not even him.' She stretched out her legs and rested her head against the worn wood of the door. 'Anyway, that's why I didn't get it stitched up or anything.'

Håkan breathed in. 'What did he die of?' He did not speak with the reverent, respectful tone that Eritrea had grown to hate.

'I didn't know at the time. All I knew was that he was dead.' She lapsed into thought for a while and Håkan sat patiently, waiting. When she spoke again, she said, by way of explanation, 'You see, I dropped the phone and broke it. But I found out later that day that it was meningitis. Type B meningococcal meningitis. He was on a camping holiday and he'd been ill for a couple of days. Then, the morning of the day he died they just found him lying in his sleeping bag with severe septicaemia. He was in a coma by the time he arrived at the hospital. By then it was too late.'

'Why didn't anyone spot it?'

Eritrea looked at her feet. 'The symptoms are just like flu at the beginning, so they had no reason to be concerned And, in any case, the two things that might have alerted people to how serious it was were completely overlooked.'

'What things?'

'When someone has meningitis, one of the first telltale signs is a stiff neck. If you go to the doctor one of the ways they try to find out whether you've got it or not is to get you to move your head and touch your chest with your chin. But Jo had apparently slept on a tree root on the first night and got a crick in his neck, so when he complained about it, nobody thought it was anything bad. How ironic is that?'

'What's the other thing?'

'Septicaemia. It's blood poisoning that first appears under the surface of the skin like little red spots.'

'Why didn't they notice that?'

Eritrea rolled up her sleeve and showed him a patch of red around her elbow. 'Look. We both get eczema. You might even call it a curse. The tent Jo was in wasn't waterproof and it rained during the trip. The damp made his skin condition worse, and when the first red spots appeared, he must've thought it was just his eczema.' She rolled her sleeve back down. 'Freakish, isn't it?'

'But how did he get meningitis in the first place? Isn't it contagious?'

Eritrea looked at the wall opposite and said, laconically, 'Meningococcal meningitis is caused by bacteria that live in the back of the nose and throat. At any given time up to twenty-five percent of the population can carry the bacteria without ever developing bacterial meningitis. But in some cases it goes into the bloodstream and travels to the meninges, which is the lining of the brain. Septicaemia develops when the bacteria that cause meningitis multiply in the blood.'

197

The textbook words tripped off her tongue with practised, mocking ease. 'Nobody even knows why it is that the bacteria so many people carry all the time infect someone from time to time. It's a complete mystery.'

'And this happened what, six years ago?'

'Mmm. And you know, the thing is, he was so stubborn. He never complained about anything. He was the kind of person who'd rather have died than put other people out. He refused to let them take him to the doctor even when he *was* dying.'

'Do you blame him for that?'

'No.' She sighed the word out.

'Why are you telling me this?' Håkan said quietly.

'I want you to know. That's what friends are for, after all, isn't it?'

'I really appreciate it, you know. And I'm so sorry.'

'Like I said, don't be. Everything about it was so unnatural. His death was like a load of horribly implausible factors piled up on top of each other. Statistically speaking, people don't usually even get bacterial meningitis in the summer.'

'I didn't know.'

'Why should you? But then again, why should anybody? Nobody knows anything about these things until they happen. Then you sit down and learn everything, but only when it's too late. The saddest thing about it is that the two of us were hardly talking at the time. I didn't really know him at all. We pretty much avoided each other at home.' She corrected herself: 'I pretty much avoided *him*.'

'I can't imagine what I'd feel like if my brother died.'

Eritrea was silent. The air around them was warm and motionless. In the sky, the stars of the plough burned with fierce intensity.

Eventually, she answered, as if from a dream. 'And even if he did die, you still couldn't. It's like it never happened, or that it was some kind of elaborate joke and one day he'll just come walking back in through the door and I'll have dreamed it all. Jo died when I was sixteen and for the first couple of years that's exactly how I felt. They call that "denial". I hate the way people throw these terms around, especially when they've never gone through anything as painful themselves. And if denial means my heart still doesn't believe he's dead, then I'm still living in it, really. I just don't talk about the feelings any more.' She was silent again. 'I suppose they call that "coping".'

Håkan said, 'I've never suffered anything like that. The only remotely similar thing that's happened to me is when my grandparents died. But that's different.'

'The first time I had any understanding of the fact that Jo was gone was when I got home after my second term at uni. I went up into his old bedroom and it just hit me. I reckon it was because I'd moved out and started something new in my life, and in my mind I thought, he's still here and he's still sixteen. Then I knew that he wasn't. That it couldn't be possible.'

There was a question on the tip of Håkan's tongue. It was: Didn't you go and see his body? He could not ask it.

Eritrea said, 'I always know what you're thinking.'

'You do?'

'Mm-hmm. You're wondering whether or not I saw him after he died and if I did, why I couldn't accept that he was dead.'

'How can you know that?'

'Everybody thinks the same things, asks the same questions, leaves the questions they consider insensitive unasked. You get used to it. It's one of the reasons nobody here knows.'

'I'm sorry.'

'For what? Not asking a question? I don't mind.' She rubbed her cheekbones with the tips of her fingers. 'But just so that you know, I couldn't go through with it.'

'What, seeing him?'

'They told me he looked pretty bad. I didn't want to remember him like that.'

'Were you angry with God?'

'I don't know. At the time I wasn't exactly living what you'd call a Christian life. I didn't even want to think about God. I think I'd blocked him out of my mind altogether 'cause I knew if I let Him in I'd have to do something about the way I lived. As it was I think I, like, held on to Jo's death as an excuse for going on doing what I was doing.'

Håkan did not have to ask what she meant by "what I was doing", but the thought of it wrenched him.

'I suppose I thought, if God ever comes and accuses me about my lifestyle I can point to what happened to Jo and say, "Well, what about this, then?" '

'What brought you back to faith?'

'It happened when I came back from university. The time I went up to his room, you know? I just stood there and was overcome with this feeling of wretchedness. I was there looking at his stuff all tidy on the shelves and thinking, what would he be doing if he was still alive? And then I thought about how I was just completely chucking my own life away, and I felt more miserable than I'd ever done before.

'Ha. It was a bit of a low point for me, that. But God has a way of letting us drink to the bottom of the cup so we can see what's down there. Anyway, it was Easter and Lucy – you know, the friend I told you I write to – came to our house on Easter Sunday with her parents. I think she was surprised to see me, because I used to hate doing anything with my parents, even before Jo died, so I was never at home much during the holidays if I could help it.' Once again she lapsed into thought for a moment. 'She came upstairs and knocked on my door and said something like, "Can I pray with you?" or something. I can't remember what she said, but it was so natural, the way she said it. And, at the time, I really needed a friend – not the kind I had at uni – and I was so desperate by then. She came just at the right time… I think being away from home had something to do with it, too. Kind of like a catalyst. My parents are both Christians so I always felt like their faith was, like, around my neck. They had a lot of rules and I guess I had to go away and find out who I really was before I could be objective about anything.'

'I know just what you mean,' Håkan said. 'I think in some ways it's harder for the children of Christians to come to faith than it is for someone who makes a commitment out of the blue. I mean, at least they can say, "This is the moment when I became a Christian." I used to go up for prayer every time there was an altar call at church.'

Eritrea smiled. 'I can believe that about you.'

'Eventually they had to tell me to stop going forward and just to believe that I was saved. But like you said, it's sometimes so hard to separate what you believe from the framework that your parents create around your life, with all the rules and that.'

'I used to resent them for it,' Eritrea said. 'Especially my dad. He was always fanatical about us being mugged or something. It got so bad that he wouldn't even let us walk to school alone when we were eleven. Can you believe it? There were all these rules about how close to strangers we were allowed to stand, and stuff. It used to drive me mad.'

'Understandably.'

'The ironic thing is that their approach ended up making me want and do exactly the things they were trying to protect me from. It's funny how that happens.'

'Isn't it just.'

'But I don't resent them for it any more. I know they just loved me and wanted the best for me, and I threw it back in their faces. Sometimes, I wonder how heartbroken they must have been during those two years after Jo died. They'd already lost their son and they must have felt like they were losing me as well. What amazes me is that however much pain they were in, they didn't try to draw me back and protect me. Not even dad. I think he knew I was sleeping around.' She stopped. 'Listen, you don't mind me being so forthright do you?'

'Eritrea, I love it when you share with me.' He did not know what else to say.

'It must have been impossible for them. Everything in them must have been screaming to protect me.' She shivered. 'It's getting cold, isn't it?'

'Wait here,' Håkan said, standing up. He opened the door to the front balcony, tiptoed across it and headed back in through the French window. Arran's form was on the bed, swathed in sleep. What time is it? Håkan thought, gathering his own sleeping bag in his arms. Can it really be so late? His body was shaking from fatigue but the insistent longing was calling him back to Eritrea. He slid the door to and headed out.

On the balcony, he sat down next to her and handed her the sleeping bag. She cocooned herself in it and then noticed that he was shaking. 'You're cold too, aren't you?'

'No, I'm fine. Really.' He did not want to say that it was weariness.

'Come here.'

He moved over, as if in a dream, and sat down on the lower step, between her knees. She put the sleeping bag over them both and locked her hands around his chest. For a moment, he kept his back muscles tensed, but eventually, slowly, he leaned back against her chest, feeling the forbidden, alluring softness of her breasts, through her T-shirt, against his neck. For a while, he let the overwhelming feeling soak into his bones and watched the stars in the plough. What he felt most of all was an aching desire to express his longing to her in words. But words were not enough.

For a while, there was no time, just the moment. Eventually, he said, 'You know I'm in love with you, Eritrea.'

'I love you too, Håkan,' she said.

The next day, being Monday, is a free day. The group hire a bus to take them north-east out of Dakar to the Lac Rose, a local tourist attraction reputed to be one of the saltiest bodies of water in the world. At Croix Blanche, the Toyota lies dead outside the villa. It has been slain by its final voyage to Dauphin and back and now rests by the kerb, a huge blue bug slowly baking in the killing sun. Inside, the girls' upstairs room is steeped in a resigned, almost acquiescent, silence and resembles the devastation after an earthquake. The still air is permeated with the memory of ten different feminine deodorants: lily-of-the-valley roll-on, bluebell antiperspirant, Oscar de la Renta. Personal belongings are strewn about the floor in the kind of ultimate chaos that not even the most ostentatious bedroom-scene artist could reproduce. Tortoiseshell hairbrushes filled with fuzzy mats of hair and cosmetic bags lie in a tumultuous sea of clothes. Face creams rub shoulders with Bibles; travel alarm clocks tick away innocuously under duvets or pillows. Next to Eritrea's bed, and half-concealed by her sleeping bag, is a dog-eared card covered with a collage of photos from home. Håkan has already begged her to give him the one of her and Lucy on the steps outside Bath Cathedral – she is thinking about it.

In the girls' bathroom, the mirror is still foggy in the corners and the cold tap is dripping. Across the hallway, beyond Fleur and Anne's room, the first rays of mid-morning sun are beginning to creep through the French window on to Håkan's scrupulously made bed. When he and Arran arrive back later it will feel like the inside of an oven. Håkan's sleeping bag lies neatly on the square of foam that serves as a mattress. Boxer shorts and T-shirt are carefully folded out of view under the pillow. Next to the bed is a rucksack that contains several layers of obsessively ironed clothes, the personal stereo and, of course, the diary. The most recent entry is confusing, for it was written at two in the morning.

Eritrea sits in the bus and feels sweat seeping out of every pore in her body, tickling as it runs down her temples, under her armpits. Next to her, Natalie is talking about the metal bracelet she bought in the market at Dauphin the previous week. 'Look,' she is saying, 'When you get them they're all polished and everything but you only have to wear them for a couple of days before they start corroding on your skin. The guy said it was made of copper but it can't possibly be. And it really stinks, too. Just smell it.' She stretches out a wrist marked black from the metal. 'Didier says we should save our money, get something from a proper jewellers.'

Eritrea's eyes are open and she is staring beyond the arm, beyond the bracelet, beyond the scrub scrolling past the window. She is back in Marlborough, waiting in line at the grammar school to pick up her brother's GCSE results. It would have been easier for Paul to do it. Technically, he should have been there personally to see how his own maths and physics students fared. But he is not yet able to face any of the students, let alone his colleagues – and will only barely be able to do so in September. Eritrea has magnanimously agreed to go in his place, and is clutching a letter of permission in her left hand. If truth be told, her father's carefully chosen words currently sadden her more than the thought of her twin lying dead underground. They are so wretched in their ordinariness. She can see her father sitting, as he sometimes does when deeply concerned, leaning on his elbow and pinching his forehead with his thumb and forefinger, trying to think of how to word the letter of proxy. *To whom it may concern* it reads. *Due to an unexpected family tragedy, Jonah Trent is unable to collect his exam results. As Jonah's father, I hereby give permission to his sister, Eritrea, to pick them up on his behalf.*

'But dad,' she says after reading it. 'I don't need to take this. If the other teachers are there, all I have to do is to explain the situation – if they don't know it already – and they'll understand.'

Paul cannot word an answer, really. His mind is not working in such a way as to be aware of that particular fact. It has taken him an hour to write the note as it is. He shakes his head in confusion and sits back down, defeated, at the dining room table.

Later, standing in the queue and surrounded by braying, cackling sixteen-year-olds, Eritrea feels sick. Some of the boys are already throwing out comments in her direction. One of them makes a filthy proposition to her – on behalf of his friend, of course.

She says, 'Why do you think I'm here, at an all-boys' school, waiting in line like this?'

The boy shrugs, but is pleased to have her attention. 'Picking up results for someone, I suppose.'

'That's right,' she says. 'For my twin brother. He can't be here because he died two weeks ago. So can you back off, please?'

The boy steps away with hands raised, palms forward, as if to prove that he means no harm and the noise around her dies down into the semblance of respectful hush; but only for a moment. Some of the pupils in the queue seem to know something about the incident. The hush gradually develops into a buzz of morbid interest: 'It was that guy who never said anything, you know, thingy, Trent's kid.'

One asks Eritrea, 'Yeah, but what was his first name?'

Another – a comedian – answers on Eritrea's behalf. 'Ruprecht,' he says. 'Ruprecht Trent.' Some of the boys hoot with laughter.

Ahead of her, James Dow looks round in her direction. He has a hunted look in his eyes, which are red and lined. The same thought she had at the funeral flits through her mind: he was there lying next to him when he was dying. She has not spoken to him. She does not intend to do so now. They watch each other for a moment. Then he turns around. It is his turn to get his results.

When Eritrea has Jonah's results paper in her hand she stands to one side and opens it to take a look. After all, she has not received any instructions to the contrary from her parents. She reads down the list of subjects: ten straight Bs.

The Lac Rose glows an impossible vivid pink, tinged with strange blue and purple hues where the sunlight hits it. It cannot be possible, it must be some kind of trick. But there it lies nevertheless, defying nature, in a shallow bowl surrounded by desert flatlands, like a giant puddle of paint water, knocked over by a giant child. The shore where the PCOM team stand is steeped in an intense, dead heat, even worse than the bus. Underfoot are millions and millions of fragments of the shells of tiny sea creatures. They must, one day, have been alive in this place. But that seems even more impossible than the colour of the lake.

Even in this secluded heat trap opportunism reigns: the special mineral-enriched waters of the lake have brought health-mad pilgrims – rich old European men, wiry white hair covering their red sumo chests – who venture into the water hoping for a miracle. Behind them waits a group of locals with buckets of fresh water to wash them down when they come out – but only for a price. It is said that it is extremely dangerous to let salt of that concentration dry on one's skin in such heat.

Eritrea thinks of the salt burning the patches of sunburn under her arms and decides that she will only paddle. Håkan is, of course, watching her from the corner of his eye. He can tell that she does not want to go in the water, but he decides he will venture in all the same. As he steps into the warm brine it prickles his ankles. It is an almost repugnant feeling.

'This is what it's like for sardines in tins,' Arran says, next to him.

They wade out until the water covers their swimming trunks, tickles their bellies, nibbles at their shoulders. Then, as it becomes too deep, Håkan strikes out with a hesitant breaststroke. He tries to keep his hair out of the water but feels droplets sting his cheeks anyway. Carefully he turns in the water to see if Arran is behind him. He lifts his arm to wave. A curious sensation. He tries lifting his other arm simultaneously. He discovers that he can sit out of his depth in the water with both arms raised, and not lose balance or go under. Arran is laughing uncontrollably, floating on his back with his feet and arms well out of the water. At a slight distance Anne calls to Fleur, who is wearing a black one-piece costume. Håkan sees her and thinks, now why should she care about an all-over tan? Who's ever going to see it anyway?

Didier is standing on the shore. Håkan calls out to him, 'Take a photo of us like this with our hands out of the water.'

'I already have,' Didier calls, lifting the camera for Håkan to see. 'I'll put it back in your bag, okay?'

Håkan is about to say, no, take a couple more, but he sees Eritrea trailing her feet in the shallows and the words die on his lips. Something in the way her shoulders are slumped tells him that she is too deep in thought to care about how she carries herself. The idea flashes across his mind: is she regretting what she told me last night? He has already thought it on the bus and experienced all the customary feelings of recrimination, justification. But she chose to tell me. I didn't pressure her. He wants to think things through objectively, but he can't, because a feeling of insatiable exultation overrides everything, resonating in his soul. *She loves me, she loves me, she has turned her eyes to me and chosen me. She loves me.*

Then Fleur calls to Håkan, 'You must leave *ze* water now. *Uzzerwise* it is *dongereuse* on your skin.'

As he wades out, his feet crunching pleasantly on the carpet of crustacean shells, Durant is saying, 'I'm not paying those rip-off merchants a hundred francs for a bucket of water. There's a much better way to get the salt off. Look.' He motions towards a hole filled with greenish water, up at the edge of the beach, near where the scrub begins.

'You must be joking,' Anne says.

'No. It's perfectly clean.' Durant strides over to the hole and plonks himself in. The movement stirs up a cloud of foul black silt from the bottom, which turns the water brown. The other PCOMers laugh loud and crowd around, taking pictures, while Durant sits resignedly in the puddle, his knobbly, whitish knees poking out above the surface of the scum. When he eventually clambers out of the water, Arran waits until the silt sinks back down and then scoops out handfuls to wash the salt from his arms and shoulders. Of course, Håkan has already paid for fresh water.

An hour or so later Eritrea approached Håkan in full view of the rest of the group and said, 'Shall we go for a walk?'

'Why not?' Arran replied. He was lying on his stomach next to Håkan, resting on his elbows and reading a dog-eared book. Håkan threw him an irritated look: can't you see that she just means me? Not anyone else. But Arran glanced back at Håkan with raised eyebrows, feigning ignorance. It was something approaching a dangerous look. He got up, with Håkan, and brushed the shell debris from his legs. Håkan did not want Arran to tag along, but neither did he want to labour the point in front of Eritrea, who made no objection to Arran's insensitivity.

A little way down the shore, Patrique watched the three of them move off towards the scrub and felt something breaking within him. Seeing Håkan at Eritrea's side, he felt as if he were a plate that has been cracked for some time, and that Eritrea was finally and deliberately parting the edges to snap it in two, so that she could justify to herself that it was truly broken and throw it in the bin. Fighting the longing within him, and with a superhuman effort of will, he turned his head away and looked out over the lake. His soul begged and pleaded with him to look back again and to wallow in the self pity and the hurt, if only for a moment. But his spirit said to him, no, don't. Don't do it.

And with that, he entered a new phase in his life. The turning of his head, and its spiritual significance, the relinquishing, was without doubt the single hardest thing he had ever done. But it was the pulling of the tooth – afterwards the pain would diminish, though he did not see it that way at that moment.

Håkan and Eritrea trailed a few metres behind Arran, who was striding through the scrub at a blistering pace. He had taken off his T-shirt and wrapped it around his head like a crude version of a Muslim turban. He looked back impatiently. 'You wanted to go for a walk, didn't you? So come on then.'

209

'I said "walk", not "attempt at the fifteen hundred metre world record",' Eritrea said, perspiring. 'Anyway, you're in someone's field.'

It was true: Arran had already stepped through several layers of droopy seedlings, separated by crude ridges in the sandy soil. Those that had not been trampled were painfully small and looked half-strangled – as though they would shortly die anyway.

'Whoops,' Arran said. He shot an anxious glance in the direction of the scrub, as if expecting an irate farmer to come bursting from a bush. 'Well, it's not as if there was any warning. We'll walk nearer to the shore, that's all.' He hopped between the lines of seedlings and headed towards the lake. The field was now separated from the water by an expanse of dry mud riddled with cracks. As soon as Arran planted a foot on the mud it gave way like an eggshell and he fell, up to his knees, into the black slime underneath. Eritrea and Håkan fell about laughing. 'You and Durant should have your own show, or something,' Eritrea said.

Arran extricated himself from the mire, trampling more crops in the process. 'Laugh all you want. We're walking around the lake and that's that.'

Håkan looked at the shoreline stretching far into the distance until it melted into the shimmering glaze of heat haze. It looked like a film set for the surface of the planet Mars. 'You must be joking. You are joking.' He turned to Eritrea. 'He can't be serious. We've got to be back for the bus in an hour and a half.'

'You,' Arran said, pointing to Håkan, 'are so pathetic.'

'Okay, I'm pathetic, but I'm not walking round the lake.'

'Fine. Try to do people a favour –' he began, and then thought better of it. 'See you later then.' He set off again.

'He's crazy. We'll miss our bus,' Håkan said.

'He will. We won't,' Eritrea smiled.

The two stood there for a moment, soaked in the heat. The only sound to pierce the silence was the whispering hiss of the wavelets against the shore. Håkan wanted to ask her if she regretted sharing with him the previous night, but he knew it would sound stupid. 'I love talking to you,' he said instead.

'Me too.' She turned back in the direction they had come. 'We should make a habit of it.'

They walked back towards the line of scrub. Håkan turned over Eritrea's comment in his mind, trying to decide whether or not it constituted any further profession of love. She carried herself with the same bearing as before; her head was ever so slightly bowed as she picked her way between the lines of saplings to avoid stepping on them. The touch of resignation in her movements added an uncharacteristic hint of frailty to her persona. At that moment he would have done anything for her.

'How do you feel about the others being back?' she enquired.

'What makes you ask?'

'I was just thinking how it changes things in the house. I'd kind of got used to it being so quiet. Hadn't you?'

'I had.' Inside, his soul said to her, you know I wish they hadn't come back. You know I wish Patrique wasn't here. You know that their presence is something that means we can't spend as much time together, so I don't like it.

'Do you think he'll make it around the lake?' Eritrea said, in an uncommonly bright voice, indicating where they had just come from with her head.

'He'll certainly try. He's stubborn enough.'

'I'm working with him this week.'

'Oh. I didn't know that.'

'Goodness knows why they put us together. Durant told me yesterday.'

'What about Youssou?'

'He and Fleur are going to counsel him from now on, apparently.'

'Don't you mind?'

'Well, I spent Friday afternoon at the villa. I don't think there's any point in me being there next week if he comes back every day.'

'But he's, like, "your" convert.'

Eritrea laughed. 'I don't know if I'd put it like that. Anyway, however you look at it, I don't know if I want to spend the last week and a half just sitting indoors.'

It was the first time either of them had mentioned the fact that the time of outreach was drawing to an end.

When they arrived back at the end of the lake where the other PCOMers were camped, Arran was already waiting for them. The mud below his knees had dried in a pale crust on his trousers and his sunburnt torso gleamed with sweat. He looked up from where he was talking to Patrique and Damien about his hike. He had a smug grin on his face and everything about his demeanour said, I told you so.

Eritrea said to Håkan, 'We're never going to hear the end of this, you know.' But what she noticed most of all in that second of eye contact was that Patrique did not look up at them with Arran. The fact registered in her brain, and she was piqued.

Fleur, however, did look at Eritrea. It was not a look that Eritrea liked and, for the briefest of moments, she thought of Judith Morewell.

That week, Håkan was unaware of what was happening to him. The physical Håkan got up in the mornings as usual, ate breakfast, swept the floor of the worship room, prayed with his evangelism group and went around the district of Tufala looking for opportunities to share the gospel. In the evenings the same physical Håkan returned, ate dinner, played cards or joined in whatever the English-speaking contingent were doing, before going to bed. However, the Håkan underneath – the essential one – was in a state of almost perpetual turmoil. The changes that had taken place within him over the course of the school had dissolved whatever restraining elements remained on his heart, leaving him exposed and fully susceptible to the pull of his emotions. Even before he had established a rapport with Eritrea she was already, in a way, the centre of his life. Now that the bond between them had been forged he lived, quite literally, for whatever brief moments of contact he could get with her through the day.

Somehow, the week following the conversations, there seemed to be no opportunity for them to talk alone. Perhaps it was because the house was full again. Perhaps it was because she was deliberately withdrawing from him after having shared too much; he just did not know, and he fretted about it constantly.

What he did know, however, was that he needed her. The slightest look from her was balm on his tormented soul. A smile elevated him, for a moment, into a temporary state of ecstasy. Times away from her were marked by a constant feeling of loss that clawed at him. If she failed to give him the recognition he needed when they were together in company – even in situations where it was completely inappropriate to expect her to – the anxiety within him erupted into feelings of rejection and pure distress. He did not see it in those terms. When he walked through Tufala with Céline in tow, or lay in bed awake, he did not say to himself, this pain I feel, this worry that is eating me up is due to the fact that I have surrendered myself fully to Eritrea. He felt only a blind

213

uncomprehending need for her, the urgency of which blotted out all ability to rationalize.

Eritrea had started working with Arran up at the Quartier Académique, which was a bus ride away from Croix Blanche. Working with Arran was exactly as she had imagined it would be. On the third day, Didier was not able to go with the rest of the group and so entrusted the bus fare money to Arran. When the bus stopped to let the group off, it stalled. Marcello, Lauren, Richard and Brigitte clambered out of the back and Arran and Eritrea went to pay the driver. He took Arran's money, counted it and held out his palm for more.

'What's that supposed to mean?' Arran said, staring at the palm in disbelief.

The driver looked into his side mirror at the other PCOMers waiting on the pavement. 'There were six of you. That's one thousand two hundred CFA.'

'Don't be ridiculous,' Arran retorted. He had one foot in the space where the passenger door would have been – if it hadn't been knocked out or removed – and he was holding on to the window frame. 'It's only a hundred and fifty each. I don't owe you anything. You should be giving me a hundred.'

The driver shifted into first gear as if to drive off.

'Hold on a minute, buster,' Arran said. 'What about my change?'

'I don't owe you anything,' the driver said, self-righteously.

'You were just asking me for more money. Now you're about to drive away. If you were really asking the fair price you'd have tried to force it out of me.'

'I'm in a hurry. I can't keep these people waiting.'

'Hurry?' said Arran disbelievingly. 'I didn't believe there was such a word here. Anyway, I'm not moving until you give me my hundred CFA.'

The driver started the bus, perhaps in an attempt to seem menacing. The engine choked and stalled again. In a fluster, he turned the key and the starter motor grated noisily before coughing into life. 'You rob me of three hundred CFA. I'm going to report you to the police.'

'Arran,' Eritrea said in English, from behind him. 'Is this really worth it?'

He ignored her and addressed the driver again. 'Yesterday it cost a hundred and fifty each. The day before, it cost the same. How about I report *you* to the police for swindling me?'

The driver started to pull away. With his free leg, Arran hopped a couple of steps along the ground to keep himself half in the cockpit. 'Fine,' he said. Glancing around, his eyes settled on a small brass Buddha on the dashboard. He grabbed it. 'We'll do a trade. This must be worth about a hundred.'

'Give it back,' the driver snarled, swiping at Arran with his free hand and making the bus swerve.

'My money,' Arran answered, dropping to the ground and waving the effigy.

Swearing loudly, the driver slammed on the brakes, tore a note from his pocket and flung it at Arran. When he had retrieved it from the sand, Arran tossed the effigy on to the passenger seat.

'What? What?' he said to Eritrea, as they were walking to the university halls.

'You know what.'

'No I don't. Tell me.'

'Like I have to spell it out? What kind of a witness is that?'

'You think I should have given him my watch or something? Jesus never said anything about being taken advantage of.'

'How much is a hundred CFA worth? Next to nothing.'

'It's the principle of the thing.'

215

Later, when they were walking back to Croix Blanche from the bus, she challenged him again. 'So what do you think the Bible means when it says that if someone asks you for your jacket, give him your sandals as well?'

'Jesus never meant we should let ourselves be manipulated. Anyway, it's your shirt, not your sandals.'

'It ruins the point of going out evangelizing if we just argue with the locals,' she persisted.

'I'm not going to agree with you just because you want me to,' he said cheerfully. 'What kind of impression do we leave people with if we go around like a load of gullible idiots, letting them con us whenever they want?'

'I think you have a very interesting way of applying your faith.'

'You can think what you like,' he said. 'There are literally thousands of homeless people and bums where I live in Long Beach. So many, that almost every time you step out of your door you're faced with a situation.'

'So what?'

'So once, for example, this tramp asks me for my jacket so I give it to him in good grace. Then when he's got it and he's looked it over, he goes, "Huh, I threw away one twice as good as this yesterday," so I'm like, "Where did you throw it?" And when he tells me, I say, "Okay, let's go get it, then." So I make him get in the car and we drive to where he says he'd dumped it, and sure enough, there it is lying in a ditch by the sidewalk. And it was better than mine. It was leather.' He let this sink in.

'And?'

'I made him give me back mine, and dropped him off, and told him if he didn't want the leather one he could go without.'

'That wasn't very nice.'

216

'What would you have done? Given him your credit card and the keys to your house and said to him, "I'll be living in a box outside the front door. If you run out of Frosties, come out and let me know and I'll run you down to the shop to get some more"?'

'It's not what you did, it's the attitude.' She knew what she meant to say.

'Being a Christian doesn't ever mean letting yourself get taken for a ride.'

'So what did Jesus mean then?'

'He was talking about people who genuinely wanted help. I'm sure of that. There's a big difference between giving your coat to someone who really needs and wants it and to someone who's just going to throw it away or sell it to get drugs.'

'So you don't ever give beggars money?'

'Eritrea, I don't know what bums are like in England, but if you ever give a tramp money where I come from you can be sure that they'll spend it on booze as soon as you've turned your back.'

'So what do you do, walk on by?'

'No. I ask them if I can get them food or something. I take them to a fast food place. I don't know. I just don't give money. Things aren't as cut and dried as they were when Jesus told the parable. People are more devious now. They've got addictions and options. I don't advocate applying stuff out of context. It's hermeneutics. Exactly what they were teaching us in Lyon, as a matter of fact.'

'I don't know. I think you're harsh and uncaring.'

'You could argue that if I wanted to be really Christian about things I should start up a centre to deal with the root of the problem. Get them off drugs, be a friend to them, help them get deliverance if they need it, lead them to Christ. But then, at the moment, I'm here in Africa, doing what I believe

God has called me to right now. Maybe I'll start a homeless centre in the future, but at the moment, when I'm faced with a situation I do whatever appropriate things I can to help.'

'I just think your attitude is bad.'

'And I think we've wandered off the point. I was only trying to say that there's nothing Biblical about being ripped off.'

Another time, Arran and Eritrea were sitting in the room of a French student. They had been invited back to visit on two consecutive days – perhaps because the student wanted to practise his English – but it gave them the opportunity to share their faith a little. Arran picked up a *djembe* drum that had been lying in the corner and started playing. After a few minutes there was a knock at the door. It was the occupant of the room below, and he looked irritated. 'Tell him to stop banging that drum,' he said to the French student. Arran replied in French, 'Why can't I play?'

'I was asleep.'

'But it's two o'clock.'

'*Mais, en Afrique c'est l'heure de la sieste!*' he replied, incensed.

Arran looked him coolly in the eye. 'In Africa,' he said, 'Every hour is the hour of siesta.'

The student stormed out and the owner of the drum laughed with Arran. Eritrea sat silent and stony faced.

Outside, she said, 'That was well out of order.'

'Don't start on me again.'

'I suppose you call that cultural understanding? The next thing, you'll be going out evangelizing in your swim shorts just because you think it's too hot.'

'He doesn't like me.'

'Don't say that. I'm sure it's not true.'

Håkan and Eritrea were sitting in their place on the balcony. It was Sunday night a week into Eritrea's time at the Quartier Académique and they were talking alone for the first time since the lake trip. He had been waiting there alone, hoping against hope that she would come up and she, seeing Arran talking to Lauren down in the worship room, had seized her opportunity and slipped out.

'He doesn't care much about what people think of him, that's all,' Håkan said, when Eritrea did not answer. 'I'm sure some people would interpret that as him not liking them, but it's not like that. Being blunt with someone and disliking them are two different things.'

Eritrea had meant to say, I'm a bit afraid of him. I feel threatened by him. But she did not understand her own feelings enough to be able to express them like that. 'You could be right,' she said.

'He has a huge amount of integrity.'

'Uh-huh. Pity that integrity doesn't necessarily go hand in hand with sensitivity.'

'At least you know where you are with him.' Håkan said. 'There's not many people you could say that was true of.' This set him thinking. 'I have to ask you something. Please don't take it badly.'

'How can I know that until you ask me?'

'Well… We haven't talked for a while and I was worried – sort of – that you might've regretted telling me about what happened to you, and stuff.'

'I told you because I wanted you to know. I don't regret it.' The insinuation that he might not know where he stood with her concerned her.

'Don't take it the wrong way, honestly. Sometimes I just get paranoid when I don't know if –'

'When you told me you love me,' she cut in, 'what did you mean?'

'What did I mean? I meant that I love you.'

'Yes, but... when people say "I love you" it can mean all kinds of things. It can be quite ambiguous.'

Ambiguous? he thought. What could be ambiguous about "I love you"? Aloud, he said, 'Of the girls I honestly think I have loved, you're only the second one I've ever said it to.'

'The second one?'

'In my life I've loved four, maybe five people. The first girl I loved was called Helena. She was eleven and I was ten. We were at this primary school for French speakers in Stockholm. When I left to go to Canada, I didn't think I could cope with not being near her.'

'You think you can really love someone at that age?'

'Yes,' he said, convinced. 'I do. That was the first time I had this feeling I get when I know I'm in love. The others were called – um, let me think – Tara, Angela, Stephanie and you.' He paused. 'Yes. Helena, Tara, Angela, Stephanie and you, in that order.'

'Did you go out with any of them?'

'Just Angela.'

'And she was the one you told you loved?'

'That's right.'

'How old were you?'

He looked sheepish. 'Twelve.'

'What happened?'

'I think I scared her off. It's not like we had anything serious. Not at that age. We only went out once, to the cinema to see *Batman*.'

'You even remember the film?'

'Eritrea, you could ask me about any detail connected to any girl that I've ever loved and I'd be able to tell you.'

'Okay, what were you doing when you met Stephanie?'

'I was fourteen and I'd just had my hair cut too short and I was feeling self-conscious about it and she came along to this church youth group event we planned. We were going to see a fireworks display in Montreal city centre and she sat next to me in the bus.' Håkan sat back against the door. 'Impressed?'

'All right. Tara. What was the precise moment you fell for her?'

'The teacher moved me to sit next to her at school because he said I didn't concentrate on my work when I was sitting next to this kid called Sammy Horton. One morning she came into school when it had been raining. She had wet hair and drew a picture of Snoopy lying on his kennel and her hair touched the paper and smudged the ink and she leaned over to me and sang *All That She Wants*.'

'What about me?' She had not intended to ask that. It just slipped out, in spite of herself.

'We went up to the hill behind the base on the first day, just after everyone had arrived. Remember?'

'I remember.'

'And when we were sitting up there looking down at the vines I watched you and I thought, how can it be so warm in October? I had all the wrong clothes with me. And you were wearing this long-sleeved T-shirt. You haven't brought it with you. You must have left it in Lyon.'

'In England. I meant to pack it but it was still in the wash. I only remembered it after I'd left.'

'You hardly spoke to anyone. It was before you started spending time with Patrique.'

Neither said anything for a while. Then, Eritrea spoke. 'Do you think there's a difference between being in love with someone and simply loving them?'

'What do you mean?'

'Well, being "in love" is mostly a feeling with all these romantic connotations, isn't it?'

'I don't know if I'd put it quite that way, I suppose in some ways...'

'But if you say you just "love" someone, pure and simple, then it's something more – far more powerful – than saying you're "in love" because it transcends pure feeling. What you're saying is that whatever happens, you will care for this person. Whatever they do, regardless of circumstances. Regardless of how your feelings change.'

Håkan lifted his hands. 'I know that I love you. But I am also in love with you. The two things co-exist.'

'I know,' she said quickly. 'But I've been praying about my feelings.' She looked up at him, gently. 'I've been praying a lot about my feelings. And I know... I know that we're not allowed to make romantic attachments during the school and stuff. But it's not that. It's like, in a way, I feel as though God has given me a gift to sort of skip the "in love" stage with you. I can honestly say that I just love you. And that I truly love you. Without any misunderstandings or anything like that.'

There was something in her words that he could not – or would not – quantify. Perhaps what she wanted to say did not seem to equate with, or fit into the words that she spoke. All he thought in that moment was, does she not love me in the same way I love her? The thought went through him like cold steel.

Eritrea saw the effect of her words and was afraid, deep down. She wanted so much to back pedal, but she stood her ground. She took his hand. 'People fall in and out of love all the time. It's quite *fickle*, almost.' She thought, good grief, what am I saying. 'I don't mean it like that. I really don't. What I mean is that I can look you in the eye and tell you that I love you, with all my heart, with no confusion, no misunderstanding, and that I'll always love you, whatever happens.

'When you're in love, it's an emotional feeling – something that doesn't necessarily last. You could even say that it's a bit, kind of *self-centred*, in that you and the person you're in love with exclude other people so that you can live in the moment. But it's a moment that passes. You know, when couples have been together for so many years they may not be in love with each other in the way they were when they first met. The emotional, self-centred side of it has been burned away but what they have underneath is pure love – not anything that depends on feeling, you know? And that's the gift I think that God has given me. To love you with that kind of pure love that has no misunderstanding and that doesn't come and go. It's something solid. Something that lasts.'

A question came from Håkan's lips. 'Is it like the difference between *je t'aime* and *je t'aime bien*?' It was not something he wanted to ask, but he had to know.

'No.' Eritrea shook her head. 'It isn't. All I can say is that the feelings I have for you are stronger than anything I've felt for anyone before. But what's inside me is more than feelings. I'm attracted to you strongly, so strongly. But I don't trust my emotions or my feelings because the love I have for you goes beyond all that.'

'It does?' Håkan said.

'I love you so much.'

For a while the two sat there, each thinking their own thoughts.

Eventually, Eritrea broke the silence. 'You know,' she said, 'the leaders pretty much ordered me to stop spending any more time alone with Patrique.'

'Oh?'

'They thought I was developing some kind of exclusive relationship with him.'

Håkan understood the implications in the fact that Eritrea's train of thought had led her to think of Patrique, and he was troubled. He was tempted to ask, well weren't you? Instead, he said, 'What happened?'

'Nothing dramatic. They just spouted this stuff about appearances and the good of the group and told me that we couldn't be alone together any more. I tried to explain to them that they didn't understand. I mean, for goodness' sake, Arran and Brigitte were working together then as well and they spent more or less every waking moment together. They didn't say anything about *that*. I just felt so hurt. And... misunderstood. And that's what I wanted to say. I feel like people misunderstand me. I mean, Patrique has been really good about things. He knows the leaders are being stupid about this and he's gone along with it without complaining or anything. But it's hurtful to think that our friendship has been totally undermined because some leader gets hold of the wrong end of the stick and starts giving out orders about who I can and can't talk to, just because they doubt my intentions. I mean, they can't see inside my head.'

'No.'

'Not like you can.'

He turned to look at her, into her eyes.

'That's why I told you about Jo. I think there's something special between us. It's almost as if we've always known each other. I love it.' She leaned closer to him and rested her head on his shoulder. 'I love it so much.' She reached up and put her arms around him and held him tight, burying her head into the fabric of his sweater. 'That's why I wanted it to be clear where we stand with each other. We have such a great friendship that I wouldn't want it to be ruined by anything.'

Håkan heard her words and, on one level, understood them. But with the feel of her touch their meaning seemed to evaporate away into nothingness. All he wanted to do was to sit there and hold her and unravel in the intimacy of the moment.

Eventually, they rose to go to bed. Håkan opened the wooden door as quietly as possible, to keep the hinges from squeaking. Eritrea stepped through first, and he followed, pulling the door to, but not shutting it. The French window leading into Arran and Håkan's room was slightly ajar; Eritrea gently slid it open enough for them to slip inside, side on. She stepped through the opening into the darkness and Håkan followed. As he turned to pull it to behind him, his elbow caught the edge of a metal vacuum flask that was perched on top of Arran's rucksack. It fell to the floor, landing with a crash that sounded like a gunshot, and then rolled almost the entire length of the tiled floor, over the sand and grit, crackling like a seventy-eight rpm record. Arran leapt up in bed and shouted, '*Shit!*'

Håkan stood, frozen in the position he had been in when he had sent the flask spinning to the floor. Every muscle in his body was taut. His mind was utterly blank.

Arran said, 'What's going on? What's happening?' Over on the other side of the room Eritrea was doubled up in silent paroxysms of laughter.

Chapter 15

'Of course,' Arran said loudly to Håkan, in English, 'what he's failing to mention is that the vast majority of slaves who went through that door were betrayed, kidnapped and sold as prisoners to the traders by members of *other* local African tribes. Not members of their own tribes I admit, but their own people nevertheless. Somehow, that's a minor detail everyone seems to forget.'

The PCOM team were standing, with a number of other tourists, in the courtyard of the Slave House on Gorée Island, listening to an unofficial tour guide, who stood on one of the two stone staircases that flanked the Door of No Return. The guide was a Rastafarian with admirable dreadlocks and a multicoloured ankle-length caftan. His demeanour astride the stairs was that of Moses just returned from the peak of Mount Sinai to discover the Israelites worshiping a golden calf. 'Thousands of men, women and children,' he said, throwing his arms out in a great sweeping gesture over the heads of the tourists, 'passed through this door to the slave boats that would set off on the voyage across the Atlantic. For many of them it was the last journey they would ever make. Children were separated from their mothers, who were kept chained up in the darkness under these very stairs, unable to hear their children's cries. They sat wretched and dehydrated in the cold sea water while a few metres above them the white slave masters feasted and partied like kings. Those men were your ancestors. Wealthy men from Europe to whom the lives of the slaves meant nothing. All they cared about was money.' He spat out the word. 'Money. And nothing else.'

Håkan, like many of the rest of the gathered crowd, was looking at the ground and blushing furiously. He cast a sidelong glance at Arran, who was lounging against the wall and looking mightily unimpressed. 'This is what they do every day,' Arran said again in an undiplomatically loud voice. 'Drag another bunch of witless tourists down here, charge them five dollars apiece and blame them for engineering the slave trade. Next they'll be telling us we started the crusades, too.'

From across the courtyard, Eritrea shot him a venomous look. It was a tired-of-hearing-this-kind-of-crap look; not a look she would have given Håkan.

They had arrived on Gorée Island a couple of hours earlier and, as soon as they stepped off the boat, had been immediately mobbed by a group of trinket sellers who stuck to them with breathtaking tenacity, like limpets that suck themselves in against the rock when one has tried tentatively to prise them off. 'Don't buy anything,' Natalie said to everyone and no-one in particular. 'It's a complete waste of money.'

'So you keep telling us,' Arran said. But the sellers' tactic was to wear the group down. They followed them up and down the winding streets, when they sat down on a wall in the square to eat their sandwiches, when they made their way to the slave museum. And they drove a hard bargain, too. They pushed their trinkets at the group vindictively, as if the PCOMers had sold the bracelets to them in the first place and they were simply trying to get their money back for being conned. If they were ignored they pushed at arms and shoulders. 'Hey, I said three hundred. It's a good price. I'm robbing myself it's such a good price.'

Durant found them a guide to take them around the museum and the Slave House, perhaps in the hope that he would send them on their way, but the guide made no attempt to do so. Instead, as he took the PCOMers around the island saying, '…And this is where they filmed *The Guns of Navarone*,' or, 'This street was, during the slave trade, the busiest street on the island,' he looked right through the bracelet sellers, ignoring them as one ignores a light breeze. Only when the group finally entered the museum did they disappear to look for other prey.

Inside the museum, when their eyes had adjusted to the darkness, the group saw the rusty balls and chains used to keep the slaves on the island from escaping before making the trip to the Americas. They saw layout diagrams of the bottoms of ships, showing how the maximum number of African slaves could be squeezed together for a journey. They saw perished wooden fixtures from galleons; depictions of slave owners with feathers in their caps, striking aristocratic poses and looking lordly. And there were horrific accounts on every wall. They were written neutrally, as if the slaves had been merely units, or animals: *Deprived of food and water and kept on the brink of starvation*. Natalie read one and left the museum. Lauren waited in the doorway.

Immediately afterwards, the guide led them to the Slave House and the Door of No Return. Eritrea stood in the shadow of the wall listening. Various negative emotions pricked at the top layer of her awareness. There was a feeling of sickness towards Arran for being so desperately insensitive. There were feelings of self-loathing for being white – for being somehow linked to the people who had perpetrated the slave trade – and feelings of self-righteousness of one unjustly accused, for it felt very much as though within the guide was a bottomless well of vituperation that poured out on them. She imagined him waking every day and putting on the mantle of that hatred, nurturing it. She could not wait to get away, out of the courtyard.

When the guide had finished his spiel, Fleur told them they had an hour to look around before the boat left. Eritrea knew exactly where she wanted to go. She walked alone, with purpose, to the highest point on the island, where a sandy cliff looked westward over the ocean. Arriving at the cliff, she saw a familiar figure already sitting close to the edge, looking out over the red rock at the breakers below. She sat slightly away from him, to his left. He did not notice her.

After a few minutes, he turned and saw her sitting about five metres away from him, hugging her knees and watching. She did not turn her gaze away from him as one would when caught staring. She simply watched him, and he watched back. Her expressionless expression burned a passage through his outer senses and deep into his heart. He would have torn it out and given it to her if, by doing so, he could have had some guarantee from her that she would continue looking at him like that for a minute more. It was a wordless bond, a confirmation that put the whole world on hold.

When it was time to go, they stood up together and made their way back to the boat separately. No words were exchanged, no agreement made that they should not walk together. There was no need for spoken words. As he walked downhill towards the tiny crescent-shaped bay, Håkan heard again the sound of the flask spinning over the floor of the bedroom. But he felt no concern. It had merely been a physical occurrence; something that had happened the night before the day when she, with a look, had confirmed the soul tie between them.

On the boat she continued to watch him. There was a rush of tourists to catch that particular boat, to get off the island, perhaps driven by the overwhelming desire to escape the guilt and humiliation. The noise and the urgent seething of the crowds trying single-mindedly to force their way on to the boat provided her with a cover behind which she could hide and observe him, unnoticed. He stood next to Arran on the starboard side, holding on to the rail near the prow with one hand. The wind was blowing his hair around so much that he had to hold the other hand to his forehead to keep it out of his eyes. The wind and the guttural choke of the motor drenched all other sound. He had put on his jumper, the one that he had been wearing the previous evening. Eritrea knew how it smelled around the collar, at the base of the neck where it touched his hair. He was looking back towards the island and moving his head the way people do when they are describing something without using their hands to gesture.

The majority of the boat was filled with a group of Italians – mostly teenage girls. Eritrea watched Håkan and the girls, as a third party watches the actors and the audience from the wings of the stage, and she was jealous. From the moment the girls set foot on the boat they had been nudging one another and pointing to Håkan. Some surreptitiously took photos. He did not notice them, or at least nothing about the way he carried himself showed that he had. Eritrea thought, leave him alone. Stop looking at him. Take your eyes off him. He belongs to me. She was slightly taken aback by the intensity of her thoughts.

At Croix Blanche, Håkan was involved in making the supper. He peeled potatoes at the kitchen sink next to Didier, who was cutting carrots. He was surprised to notice that he had bitten the sides of both thumbs down to the place where the skin creased at the joint. The starchy water from the raw potatoes ran into the exposed lines of bitten flesh painfully.

He adjusted his grasp of the peeler to try to keep the skin dry, but then peeled a chunk of thumbnail by mistake.

As he climbed the stairs he sucked the injured thumb, trying not to think about the sensation of torn nail on his tongue. The bedroom was empty, but there was another note on his bed. He looked at it from the other side of the room for a second. He did not have to read it: as soon as he entered the door, he knew what it said. Instead, he hunted around in the cupboard until he found the nail clippers. He had to cut right down to the quick to round off the nail so that it would not snag. Only when he had done this did he sit down and pick up the note. It was folded in two, with the side facing up bearing nothing more than his name. Inside it said:

Håkan,

I have been ordered not to spend time alone with you any more. I can't believe it, but it looks like there's nothing I can do about it. The leaders have the last say, I guess.

I'm sorry. This is not how I wanted it to end.

Eritrea

Håkan looked at the paper. The writing seemed not to be able fully to contain Eritrea's frustration, which burst out through the angular curves of her beautiful handwritten y's. *This is not how I wanted it to end.* End? he thought. Hadn't she said that what she felt for him was something that would never end? It was hard to reconcile the previous night's conversation with the bitter disappointment in this note. He continued to stare at it for a while, then folded it up, placed it under his pillow and went back down the stairs.

In the kitchen, he felt somewhat betrayed by Didier, who stood innocently shaking salad dressing in a jam jar. He was surely in the know about the split – perhaps he had even engineered it – but he neither said nor did anything to suggest it. 'That looks painful,' he ventured shortly, about the thumb. 'You should put a plaster on it.'

And you should keep out of things that are none of your business, Håkan wanted to retort. Instead, he finished the potatoes, washed them under the tap, put them in a saucepan and lit the gas ring underneath it.

At dinnertime he and Eritrea sat at different tables. He was so careful to avoid looking at her that, for all he knew, she might not actually have been there at all. Of course, it was too late now to be concerned about what other people might think. But he was subject to feelings of such raging paranoia that he wanted to avoid the appearance of anything for which he knew he might be reprimanded. He knew that some kind of talking-to was probably waiting just around the corner and he struggled to get a handle on the mixture of bitter disappointment and anger that surfaced every time he tried to swallow a forkful of floury boiled potato.

Sure enough, Didier plucked him by the elbow as he was leaving the worship room.

'Where do you want to do this?' Håkan asked, resignedly.

'We could go to my room if you want,' Didier suggested, but the improvised effect of the comment was undone when Håkan found Fleur already waiting for them inside. 'You know why we want to talk to you,' she said.

'I think I do,' he answered levelly.

'Even so,' she said, and then lectured him at length about how Practical Christian Overseas Mission was not a dating agency. Håkan wanted to ask her, did the flask wake you up yesterday? Is that what did it? He thought about that while

Fleur talked on about previous schools and how, when people were open to God and spiritual things, they became much more sensitive to new emotions and therefore much less capable of handling the romantic feelings that inevitably sprang up for other students. She neatly pigeonholed his relationship with Eritrea as "typical of what happens during any practical outreach". She'd seen it many times before. 'And besides,' she added. 'You probably know that we had to intervene with her and Patrique. Someone like you should have known better than to get mixed up with her.'

Fleur had a very unfortunate way of giving advice, as if she were addressing some unruly spiritual force in a person, not the person themselves. It was the way she leaned forward and pointed and then leaned back and lifted her head sagely as if reflecting on the wisdom of her own advice. Mortified as Håkan felt for having, in some way, been a source of consternation to the leaders, this last comment was too much for him. 'We're only friends. We've never been anything other than friends. And I think it's going too far to say we're "mixed up" with each other.'

'She has major personal issues,' Fleur said.

'I know that.'

Fleur raised her eyebrows and retracted her chin into her neck like a chicken, in an expression that said, I'm sure you don't. The atmosphere in the room was becoming tense.

Didier intervened. 'I think we've made the situation clear,' he said. 'If it's okay with you, Håkan and I will talk alone a minute.'

When Fleur had left the room he said, 'After the school you can do what you want. We're only asking that you tone things down until the end of next week, that's all.'

'Tone things down. What things?'

'I understand that it's difficult for you.' Håkan expected him to go on and say something about how easy it was for third parties to misconstrue the nature of a friendship, especially when a group of relative strangers were living in one another's pockets, but he did not. 'Our job,' he said, 'is to look after you and provide whatever help and guidance we can during your school. We have to set limits sometimes –' his mouth shut as his train of thought moved on to things that he was obviously unwilling to share – 'and keep to them. Even if people aren't actually overstepping any mark. It's true, we're not always right, and you might not like what we decide. But whatever we do, we want it to be in everyone's best interests.'

He exhaled sharply through his nose. 'What I'm really trying to say is that whatever we decide, we don't want to drive such a wedge between you and us that you feel you can't come to us and share things that are on your heart. I hope we somehow manage to strike a balance between seeming patronizing and interfering on the one hand and genuinely expressing a concern for your feelings and... and needs on the other. If, at the end of the school, you feel that we've potentially been there for you – whether you *actually* shared things with us or not – then we can consider that we've done our job as leaders.'

'I know. It's just not that easy to swallow.'

'Understandably.' Didier seemed to have something else to say again, but he kept it back.

Now that Fleur was gone, Håkan's conciliatory side got the better of him. 'I'm sorry. Of course you've got to set limits. I'm not stupid. I just get tired of people I don't know that well telling me how I should live my life, how I should think and feel and stuff. I always seem to get people like that giving me advice. And I just get tired of it sometimes. That's all.'

'I did this school, too,' Didier said. 'And not that long ago either. Every PCOM leader has. So I know what you mean.'

'Right.'

'So if you still feel you need to talk to someone about this or anything else…'

'Yes. Don't worry.'

After leaving the room he crossed the hallway to his own bedroom. He shut the door behind him and sat down on the bed. Next to him, Arran pulled his headphones out of his ears. 'How did it go?'

'How did what go?'

Arran tried to repress a smirk, but failed. 'You must think we're pretty stupid.'

'Who? I never said that.'

'Remember when you got so annoyed with me at the Lac Rose the other week?'

'Not really.' He remembered perfectly well.

'Why do you think I gate-crashed your little twosome around the lake?'

'I don't know.'

'You didn't think it could've had something to do with how Patrique might've felt to see you two go waltzing off together?'

'No. Not when you put it like that.'

'Well, it did.'

'Okay. Thanks for telling me.'

'Don't mention it.'

'I won't.'

'Fine.' He put the headphones back on and cranked up the volume. Håkan sat with his back against the wall for a while. Eventually he signalled to his roommate to stop the CD. Arran wound up the headphones as if he didn't expect to be putting them on again in the immediate future. 'I'm just not in a particularly good mood at the moment,' Håkan said.

'What I did, I did for you, too,' Arran said. 'For both of you.'

'Perhaps I wasn't sensitive enough to see it, that's all.'

'Patrique and Eritrea were like this in Lyon —' Arran showed Håkan a pair of crossed fingers — 'and pretty much the same for the first few weeks here. You know that.'

Håkan inclined his head in a shrug. 'So?'

'So when they get broken up and she turns her attentions to you, someone's bound to get hurt, aren't they? You might not have noticed it, but I've done my level best to steer you away from situations where you blatantly go off alone with her in full view of everyone — partly to protect you two and make things easier on Patrique, and partly because every time the leaders see you alone together they come one step closer to doing what they decided to do today. The trouble is, as soon as you two fall for each other you just stop thinking, so in your mind everybody else does too. I mean sitting out on the balcony all hours of the day and night, and then coming back and shouting and slamming doors and kicking things over and stuff. You'd have been less likely to wake people if you'd gone around the house blowing a trumpet.'

'Look, last night we blew it — figuratively, I mean. But apart from that one situation I didn't think we were *that* obvious.' He thought for a moment. 'You read the note she left on the bed, didn't you?'

'And,' Arran continued, ignoring Håkan's question, 'how would you feel if, having been banned from talking to you, Eritrea moved on and spent the last week going for secret evening talks with Marcello.'

Håkan snorted. 'That's ridiculous.'

'But think about it. That's exactly what she did to Patrique. Why not do the same to you?'

'She wouldn't. And in any case, I have to say I don't feel particularly sorry for him. He's given me the cold shoulder ever since the beginning of the school.'

'I wonder why.'

'So do I. It's not as if I ever spoke to Eritrea before we came out here.'

'But I bet he knew you liked her. Or –' he wagged his finger knowingly – 'that there was potential for you two to get together, or whatever.'

'She's free to spend her time with whoever she wants. And anyway, if you think Patrique was so jealous that she might like me, how can you possibly suggest that she might go off and do the same thing with Marcello?'

'Just trying to make a point, that's all.'

'Which is?'

'What goes on in her head. See, if her desire not to hurt Patrique was directly proportional to the time they spent together before they got split up, she'd have been a lot more careful about how much time she spent alone with you.'

'I don't see what you're getting at.'

'That she is remarkably naïve. How do you think Patrique felt when he got back from Dauphin? She just doesn't think about the consequences of what she does.'

'She does. You have no idea how upset she was about the way the leaders interfered with her and him.'

'Even Lauren and Natalie say that the way she acts towards guys is not normal.'

'And the way they do is?'

'You know what I mean.'

'They're American. She's English. They're bound to relate to people differently.'

Arran lay back carefully on his sleeping bag. 'I'm not going to argue with you about this. You're right. I don't know how she feels about Patrique, and I don't know what goes on in her head. All I know is what I see and hear. Anything that I say to you is to help you.'

'Thanks.'

Tuesday and Wednesday were undoubtedly the worst days of Håkan's time in Senegal. The agony that he had touched the previous week, when Eritrea had failed to give him the confirming signs he needed, returned with a vengeance. Most of the time he experienced a gnawing sense of rejection that ate away at him, until he felt that there was really nothing left in him but pain and emptiness. Every time he and Eritrea occupied the same physical space, her failure to give him some kind of sign that she empathized or was feeling frustrated in the same way as he about their enforced separation pushed him further towards a state of total wretchedness.

He continued going about his daily routines on autopilot, as people do. In worship on Tuesday morning, he played guitar next to Fleur but was filled with such rancour towards her that he was surprised he managed to keep from breaking it over her head – especially when she belted out the high notes. She displayed no remorse for having stepped between him and Eritrea. Her body language was belligerent, openly challenging even. Opposite the guitarists, Eritrea worshiped with an expression of rapturous joy on her face, lifting her arms and praising in a way that did not befit someone who had just been told she was no longer to spend any more time alone with the one she loved. At lunchtime, she sat at a different table.

In the afternoon, when Håkan arrived back at the villa with Céline after evangelism, he could not remember who they had spoken to, or where they had been. His mind was entirely consumed with the sickness of rejection. She no longer cares about me, he thought. This break has not affected her in the slightest.

He wallowed in the feelings, feeding them with his own self-pity and allowing them to swell and expand until they blotted out every other rational thought in his head. Not for one second did he think that Eritrea might have been trying to obey the leaders or keeping a low profile in order to toe the line. In his mind, she was simply rejecting him.

These periods of utter dejection were interspersed with rare moments of delirious elation when she happened to give him the briefest of signs that confirmed her own frustration with the situation. But these moments were over all too quickly.

On Tuesday evening, quite by accident they came face to face with each other in the kitchen doorway when he was carrying out his plate after dinner. His eyes were on the floor, but he raised them just in time to catch her gently pleading, thwarted look. Then she disappeared up the stairs. She has told me that she cares, he thought. Her look said, I understand and I hate this as much as you do, but I don't know what to do about it either. For a few minutes he was sent spinning into the stratosphere. She really does love me. This is not the end after all.

But then he had to go out into the yard and pump water for breakfast the following morning. And, to make matters worse, he had to do it with Patrique, who worked opposite him in the kind of involved, diligent silence that said, now you know what it feels like. He did not talk to Håkan except to issue terse, reprimanding instructions like, '*T'aurais dû nettoyer le filtre*,' *You should've cleaned the filter*. Håkan was tempted to tell him he had been doing the job for three weeks now and was quite aware of how to go about it, but by that time the bubble of ecstatic confirmation had burst, leaving him feeling more empty and depressed than ever.

Eritrea managed, callously, to avoid eye contact for the whole of Wednesday morning. By dinner time Håkan was shocked to notice that his feelings towards her had begun to include a shade of what he could only describe as resentment. It had crept up on him unawares but revealed itself when, for the second or third time that day, she left the room talking cheerfully – this time to Natalie. He hated himself for it. He knew it was ridiculous to harbour resentment, but he could not help it. He sat in the worship room playing the guitar while it sloshed around inside him, mixing with the rejection. When he went to bed, he lay looking up at the ceiling and felt that something within him was coming undone.

This unravelling feeling was waiting for him next morning when he awoke. It tormented him throughout breakfast and kept him from being able to pray properly. His prayer times had been somewhat disjointed since Monday – partly because he had spent most of the time glancing up at the roof to see if Eritrea might be looking down – but this morning he could not even concentrate enough to formulate a sentence in his head. The day's prayers ultimately seemed meaningless as he sat on the balcony step. The painful emotions had knotted themselves into a ball that had been content, the previous night, to reside in the pit of his stomach, but now tried to fight its way up into his throat. And accompanying everything was an urgent whispering. Time is running out, it said. Things really are drawing to an end and there's nothing you can do about it. Soon it really will be over with her, just like she said.

As he struggled his way through worship he knew he could not last out, and that whatever it was that was gathering momentum within him would break over him like a tidal wave and swamp him completely. Afterwards, he went straight to Durant and asked if he could be excused from going out on evangelism in the afternoon. 'I've got some issues I need to think and pray about,' he said. It had not occurred to him that if he stayed at the villa, Céline, too, would effectively be stopped from going out. When Durant pointed this out, Håkan stood silent not knowing what to say.

'Look,' Durant said eventually. 'I'll tell you what. Youssou isn't coming until later this afternoon so I'll go with Céline for an hour or so.'

'Thanks. Really. I just wouldn't be any good to anyone today.' He turned to go but Durant called him back.

'Håkan, it's good for you to pray things through,' he said. 'There's no point going out if you've got other things weighing you down.'

He could not face lunch, but he did not want to draw attention to himself by being absent. In any case, he could not truly be alone until the teams left. If he sat up in the bedroom, he risked being disturbed by Arran. If he went to the roof, he would have to leave when the sunbathers came up.

But, for him, time was running out. Digging at the rice on his side of the bowl in a feeble attempt to look like he was eating, he knew that he was beginning to lose it and he just thought, oh God, please don't let anyone be around when this thing that is in me breaks. He swept the worship room, pumped the water. He saw Arran leave the villa. Then he went up into the bedroom and shut the door.

Lying on the bed, he saw himself standing on the edge of a high cliff, his ankle manacled to a heavy ball like those at the slave museum on Gorée Island. The ball itself was not made of metal, but was a compound of all the desperate emotions he had felt since Eritrea had stopped paying attention to him, and it was heavier than lead. At first it was still by his feet, but then it started to roll towards the edge of the precipice and tipped itself off, as it must. He watched the chain unravelling as the ball fell, gathering pace. So this is what I have been feeling, he thought. When the chain runs out I'll be pulled off the cliff, too. This must be what they mean when they talk about broken heartedness. I have committed myself to her and given my heart into her hands, but she does not return the love I feel for her. So my heart will break. He saw a flash in his mind's eye of himself years down the line, trying to develop coping tactics to paper over the cracks in the heart that was breaking right now, and there was nothing he could do about it.

Then he was plummeting down the precipice, dragged by the weight of his emotions. This is it, then, he thought, and waited for the ground to come to meet him and crush him.

But that did not happen.

Instead, he was caught in a pair of outstretched arms that absorbed his fall by giving slightly before firming up. It reminded him of the way his father had used to throw him into the air as a child and then catch him, almost without him being aware that he had been caught.

The voice that belonged to those arms that caught him now said, 'Do you really think I would let you break your heart?' Håkan's eyes snapped open because the voice was like Durant's, but Durant was not in the room.

'Your heart has been with me all the time,' the voice continued. Håkan closed his eyes again and sat still for a long time. He seemed to be suspended in mid-air now, not falling. It was as though the hands that had caught him had cut the weight that had been pulling him down. It was gone so completely that he wondered if it had ever existed, except in his own mind.

Then the physical silence around him was punctuated by another kind of silence: the silence of a voice inside his own spirit. This time, however, the voice did not speak in words, but communicated Spirit to spirit – in the way that speaks to a person's heart, mind and emotions at the same time in the language that, once heard, makes all human speech seem like one hissing mono frequency.

First came the confirmation that he, Håkan, was, and always would be, loved; the touch of love he felt on his heart as the understanding registered within him was like the cool water of peace and clarity and utter contentment. But then, alongside the heart knowledge of love, and with the assurance of love flowing all the while underneath like water, came a warning. It was the merest of suggestions, the tiniest hint of a reprimand, not unlike the glance that a parent gives a child who is on the verge of doing something forbidden. But in the ultimate gentleness of the reproach Håkan knew instantly that he had created the pain for himself, that he had nurtured it and fostered it. *That was the first time I had this feeling I get when I know I'm in love.* He remembered his own voice speaking to Eritrea from their last conversation. I idolize people, he thought. And I have made her the biggest idol in my life.

Think, then, the voiceless voice said, how your priorities have changed over the last few weeks.

And in the way that the sunlight poured into the streets and alleyways on the other side of the balcony in the morning, Håkan saw the streets and alleyways of his own motivation gradually being soaked in the blazing light of conviction. It was an ugly sight. He saw that the school, the mission, the other people around him – everything, in fact, except Eritrea – had come to mean nothing whatsoever to him. He saw how he had effectively cleared every single thing out of his path so that he could seek after her. He saw, for a second, the totally self-absorbed nature of his feelings and the vain pride that was feeding them. The sudden realization of how complete his selfishness had been made him catch his breath. But it did not end there. The light, by its nature, had to illuminate everything, the whole maze of his motivation. He saw that the noble romantic thoughts that he perpetuated – thoughts he considered of the very highest order – were not noble but hollow, for when they met with no confirming response they were ready to turn, at the drop of a hat, into thoughts of resentment and self-pity.

When his heart recognized this, he finally admitted to himself the truth of the last conversation he had had with Eritrea. *I can honestly say that I just love you. And that I truly love you. Without any misunderstandings or anything like that.* Whatever she feels, he thought, she is not in love with me in the way that I want her to be. I must remember what she has told me. I must remember that I have been fooling myself. Forgive me, Lord, for being so selfish.

When Håkan knocked on Didier's door later and said, 'I think I'd like to have that talk now,' Didier waved him in without a word.

'I could've taken her with me to Dauphin,' Didier said. 'We had to make a last-minute decision about whether to take her or Patrique, and seeing as I was in charge of the team it was ultimately up to me.'

'You're saying that if you had, we wouldn't have spent time together and caused you all this trouble.'

'You haven't caused *us* trouble. If anything you've only caused *yourself* trouble.' He considered. 'But no. That's not what I'm saying really.' He was silent again. 'Let me put it this way: I was tempted to take her because I knew it was in my power to do so, but I knew that my reasons for picking her would be wrong. Do you see?'

Håkan wondered if he was hearing right.

'In other words, take advantage of my position as a leader to have her in the team so that I could try to make her like me.'

'Surely not?'

'Oh yes.' He nodded. 'Is it really so hard to believe?'

Håkan thought about it. 'No,' he admitted eventually. 'Not really.'

'You know how people say, "There's just something about so-and-so?" Well, there just *is* something about Eritrea. Something in her that draws certain men to her. We watched Patrique succumb to it and now we've seen the same thing happen to you. If I'm being entirely honest, I have to say that I wanted to be involved with her, too. I mean, I *want* to be involved with her, even now.'

'You should've told me this on Monday.'

'No. Oh no. Fleur gave you enough of a lecture. I don't think you were in the mood to hear what I had to add.'

'Does she know how you feel about Eritrea?'

'Leaders don't know everything about each other, Håkan.'

'But you don't miss a trick when it comes to the students, do you?'

'We've done a lot of these evangelism schools. You'd be surprised how the same things come up, time and again. Different people, different schools, same issues.'

'There's an Eritrea in every school?'

'Ah now, I wouldn't put it that way. This kind of situation arises from time to time, yes, but I don't think I've ever met a girl who was so compelling. The moment I saw her, I thought, Didier you're going to have to watch out for her. But then, four months later, I find myself trying to justify having her on my team – to keep her away from someone who's mixed up with her – so I can hit on her myself. That's how strong it is. Much stronger than my own ability to reason.'

Håkan wanted to ask about the tragedy in Eritrea's life and whether Didier thought that it had somehow caused her to act the way she did. He remembered what she had said: *I think I held on to Jo's death as an excuse for going on doing what I was doing*. But he thought, that would be overstepping the mark. Even if Didier knows. Just the thought of it made him feel like a conspirator. Instead, he asked, 'So what stopped you from taking her to Dauphin?'

'I don't know. Somehow I made the right decision. Goodness knows how. But listen. I know that you feel things are clear in your mind and you know that God isn't hauling you over the coals for the way you've been acting. It could happen to any of us. Me included. I just think it would be good to give expression to the way you feel and to pray that any –' he paused – '*bad* ties between the two of you would be cut. The other day I said to you that the school would be over soon and that you could do what you liked afterwards, and that it's none of our business and so on, but I advise you as a friend – not a leader, but a friend – that you should be careful with her. You've narrowly avoided being hurt by her. You'd be silly to let it happen again.'

'She'd never hurt anyone on purpose,' Håkan said. He lowered his eyes in embarrassment. 'In fact, I think she tried to make it clear to me that she didn't want anything more than friendship.'

'What people say and the impression they give are often two different things,' Didier said. 'So in a sense it doesn't matter what she's said. It's in here that the ties are made.' He pointed to his chest. The important thing is, are you ready to give it to God and surrender it up?'

There was no evangelism on Friday, the day after Håkan and Didier had talked. As a surprise for the students, the leaders decided to pool what was left of the money and organize a ram roast. The group ate lunch as normal and cheered Fatou when she made an appearance at the back door to say goodbye.

Later in the afternoon, a man arrived at the front door of the villa holding a leash roped around the necks of two skinny goats. Durant led him through the worship room and out to the back of the house with the goats trotting docilely behind, their feet clicking on the tiles. In the back yard, the man herded them against the wall, undid the rope from around their necks and used it to loop their feet together. Then he slit their throats as calmly as if he were snipping the label from an article of clothing. The blood poured out on to the dry soil with a curious rushing sound. The PCOMers looked on with morbid, disgusted fascination and the goats stared back with wide, calm eyes as the life drained out of them. When their taut legs had stopped flicking, the man strung them up upside down against the wall, further spattering it with gore. Anne said to Durant, 'I thought you said he'd do all this before coming.'

'He was unspecific,' he coughed.

Didier stared at the carcasses and said, 'Looks like we're going to have to do some painting before we leave.'

Eritrea looked on silently while the goats, now sufficiently blood free, were taken down from the wall, further rendered and skewered on portable spits. The man had brought wood for the fire but had left it around the front of the house. When Damien and Patrique began to carry it through and arrange it under the spits, she turned to leave. There was talk of a trip to the market to look at materials for clothes. Anne, Fleur, Céline and Natalie were going. Normally, Eritrea, too, would have jumped at the chance to get out of the villa, but in this case it was a Catch 22 situation: stay back and struggle with all the impossible feelings that being there entailed or get out and suffer being near Fleur.

The news on Monday that she was now not allowed to spend time alone with Håkan either instantly sent her reeling into a state of shock, as though she had been physically punched. The humiliating repeat of the dressing down she had been given several weeks previously was too much for her. She crawled out of the leaders' room to the toilet and shed a few tears of pure rage: the kind that seep out painfully like blood from a cut. She tried not to think about annihilating Fleur.

But the initial incredulity soon gave way to a kind of gaping loathing that lodged itself like a thorn in her heart. And as the flower of her despair blossomed, the thoughts of general loathing began to turn in on herself. She felt desperately and horribly embarrassed. She thought, what is it in me that makes them punish me again and again? I must be bad. How can they be so cruel? Lying in bed that night she thought about how each of the special times with Håkan had been intentionally taken and smashed. She saw the conversations as precious things that Fleur had kicked to pieces, like some insanely jealous child. But in her heart of hearts, she was terribly afraid of her.

So afraid was she, in fact, that she kept the lowest profile possible on Tuesday. At first she longed to be able to give Håkan a sign. Even if she did not look directly at him, she saw, through the corners of her eyes, the miasma of pure distress that surrounded him during breakfast, worship, lunch, chores. But then, in the afternoon, she sat in an anonymous student bedroom and Arran's French, with its outlandish Californian drawl, became a noise in the background as she thought, can he really feel this strongly for me? Part of her knew it already, but the confirmation, the tangible outworking of Håkan's misery, still surprised her by its very intensity.

Much as she hated everything about the situation; the interference, the anger, the humiliation, there was still a tiny part of her that examined his wretchedness and related to it with a certain sense of calm. Had she been capable of pinpointing the feeling within herself she would have realized that she felt flattered – deeply flattered in fact – but that underneath this feeling was the tiniest hint of satisfaction.

After dinner, and without consciously thinking, I will put this to the test, she was presented with a brief opportunity and gave him an understanding look. The force of the relief and yearning that flooded out from him to her when she did so almost knocked her back through the kitchen door; she was enormously gratified and touched: his response was like the tearing cry of an abandoned child longing to be picked up.

By Thursday, there was uneasy cohabitation between the frustration and disappointment on the one hand, and the satisfaction on the other. It was not that she derived pleasure from Håkan's pain, but there was nevertheless something that gave her an inner sense of comfort when she observed him, his head bowed as he struggled to contain his feelings while sweeping the worship room or pumping water. She watched him from a distance, when he was not looking, and was content. Just the squeak of the pump was enough to rekindle the feeling inside her.

Part of her longed to give him the confirmation he craved, every time they were in the same room. But she had been told that she mustn't talk to him, had she not? So she doled out tiny measures of consolation, at her own discretion, the way an older sister with a bar of chocolate might taunt a younger brother, giving him little specks when he has long since devoured his own. And it was strangely satisfying to see him gobble them up hungrily and then wait impatiently, desperately, for more.

When she had sat in Fleur's room on Monday, dying another death, it had never entered her mind that the ban on talking to Håkan might have its benefits. None of these feelings were within the grasp of her conscious mind, which is why what happened on Friday completely threw her.

They had seen each other briefly at dinner in the worship room on Thursday evening and she had deliberately kept him at arm's length, starting a game of cards with the American girls, fully aware that he would not join in, as Anne was in the room. He had hung around for a few minutes unsubtly, and then left.

Then, when she saw him on Friday morning, he was different.

She could not tell exactly what it was, but as the day went on it dawned on her that he was no longer first and foremost concerned about seeking after her. He sat between Marcello and Richard at breakfast, and ignored her completely. By mid-morning she was piqued; by lunchtime, she was almost furious. After the meal, he even laughed and joked with the others and she hated him for it. Like a fisherman who plays with his catch only to reel it in and lose it at the last moment, Eritrea realized, with an awareness akin to horror, that she was staring at the end of an empty line. Suddenly and unaccountably she had no power over him whatsoever.

She was so unprepared for the sudden, inexplicable anger that rose within her that she wanted to escape from the villa, if only to get a bit of breathing space and analyse her feelings. But the only possible way to do that was to go with Fleur and the other girls to the market, and she could not pluck up the courage to be that close to Fleur. She could have wept out of sheer frustration, but one way or the other she was trapped. This free day that she had even been looking forward to in a small way was fast becoming a nightmare. Nor was it made any easier when Arran and Håkan announced that they were going for a walk. In yesterday's world order he would at least have stayed within the compound if he knew that she was there too.

When they walked out together she was left alone, completely bewildered by the strength of her anger.

In the evening, the spitted goats were placed lengthways on one of the worship room tables, which had been brought out into the yard. The man stripped meat from the carcasses as though they were giant kebabs and the team queued tightly around the table for a portion of the meat, as people do when they are just a little concerned that there might not be enough for everyone.

Eritrea scrutinized Håkan now, too. At one point during the meal, he happened to catch her looking in his direction and he smiled at her. It was the kind of smile that said, we have been a bit stupid about things, haven't we? Then he turned back to his food and his conversation.

When Fleur brought out her guitar, Eritrea excused herself quietly and went up to the roof. The sound of singing, punctuated occasionally by bantering and laughter, floated up to where she stood, mingling with the tinny sound of a radio from the house over the road.

The smile he gave her had been from a friend to friend – not a lover to a friend. She had told him, as clearly as she could, in their last conversation that she was not in love with him and that the love she offered was the love of a friend. Now he had taken her words at face value, processed them and somehow got over his feelings. It was not at all what she had expected, and now, standing on the roof, she wondered why she felt so frustrated. In effect, Håkan had done exactly what she had been hoping he would, but she nevertheless felt like someone whose bluff has been called.

Tonight, he looked very handsome to her. More so now, perhaps, than ever before. She peeped over the crenellations at the yard below and saw the top of his head, the ragged,

251

uncombed line of his centre parting. She thought of how the ends of his hair dried in freak blond curls that he dragged out of his eyes and tucked behind his ears. His hair had grown a lot since they had arrived, she noticed. He was wearing his dark blue long-sleeved T-shirt tonight, the one that he only got out on special occasions. He had rolled up his sleeves and the transparent face of his wristwatch glinted white for a second when it caught the light from the electric lamp mounted on the villa wall. The watchstrap was one that could be stretched over the hand – sometimes he played with it, pulling it open and letting the links flick back together – and it was imbued with the smell of Egoïste and his wrist, a smell which was completely Håkan. He was talking now to Lauren, and she strained to hear what he was saying, but all she caught were the low, soft rounded r's of his Canadian intonation. He was saying something about a road, but he pronounced it "r-eau-d".

Something about his being suddenly unavailable to her, out of her reach, made him seem incredibly attractive. If he had been up on the roof with her, she would have grabbed him and kissed him as hard as she could.

She heard voices echoing hollowly from the stairwell and she drew back from the wall. Marcello and Richard appeared at the doorway, laughing with the kind of secretive laugh that people share when they are doing something they know they shouldn't. They did not see her immediately: she heard the scratch of a match and for a second Marcello's face was lit up by the faint yellow glow of a flame. Then he saw her. '*On fait le scallywag*,' he commented, with a naughty giggle. The end of his cigarette hissed softly and glowed orange as he took a drag. '*Ça va, toi?*'

'*Ben, tu sais...*' She approached carefully. She had not smoked since her second year of university, but there was something appealing, comforting even, about the tiny wreaths of smoke that drifted towards her. Perhaps Marcello saw something in her eyes, for he proffered the box. It was a soft packet – he would have bought it here in Dakar. She was sorely tempted, but then thought, no, it would be crass. Really, she thought of what Håkan's reaction might be if he chanced upon her with a cigarette in her hand, or happened to smell the smoke on her breath. She raised a hand, in the negative, and Marcello concealed the packet again in the pocket of his trousers. 'It's not a good habit, it'll kill you,' he laughed, while Richard kicked, somewhat guiltily, at the base of the wall with the toe of his trainer and flicked his ash too often, the way a non-smoker does.

'Quite,' she said, contenting herself with the scent of tobacco smoke that tantalized her sense of smell at intervals, on the breeze.

The next day, Saturday, was the last official day of evangelism. It was also the day that Håkan did a very bad thing.

After praying with Didier that the soul tie between him and Eritrea would be broken, he opened his eyes a different person. On Thursday morning he had felt as though his heart would break. Now he felt clothed in a strange kind of peace; a peace he had not really felt for many weeks. Seeing Eritrea on Friday morning brought none of the gut-wrenching weight of grasping hope that he usually felt when he was in the same room as her. His soul could look her full on and say, although I will never have you in the way I have wanted you, it does not matter. He felt as though his heart were full of love for her, but of caring love, not selfish love that simply calls out for fulfilment.

The lifting of the burden from his shoulders made him feel as light as air. The Lord has been so good to me, he thought after breakfast. After the way I have behaved I did not deserve for Him to help me, but He has nevertheless been merciful.

For twenty-four hours, Håkan actually walked in the freedom that he had been given through the prayer.

But then he threw it away.

His decision was not so abrupt or deliberate; he did not say to himself, now I will discard the peace that Jesus has given me. He simply became aware of an alternative to the peace. It crept up on him stealthily and accompanied him until it was fully fledged in his mind. Then when he had entertained it for a time and it was ripe enough to drop into his hand, he acted on it.

This is how it happened: on Friday night, when he caught Eritrea's eye and smiled at her during the ram roast, he saw that his state of spiritual freedom had somehow unexpectedly turned the tables in their relationship, or reversed the pecking order. In the split second of registering the look she gave him, the awareness was born within him. You could turn this to your advantage, it whispered to him. Then he had a moment of clarity where he saw that it would be disobedient to do so. His spirit said very clearly to him, you must take this thought, pray about it and discard it now, right now.

But instead, he pretended to himself that the thoughts that had just occurred in his head had not, in fact, occurred at all. And, in so doing, he made the decision there and then to act on the awareness.

When Eritrea left the company to go to the roof, the awareness made its presence known to Håkan again, saying to him, you see her leave? She's going because she can't take the fact that she has no power over you any more. Now you can call the shots if you want to. All you have to do is re-establish the link, but on your terms. Håkan continued to pretend to himself that he was not hearing the suggestions, but they were beginning to sway him.

On the Saturday there was an open invitation to Youssou's house. His sister had laid on snacks for the PCOMers, and twelve decided to go – Eritrea and Håkan among them. It was quite a squeeze but somehow they all managed to find a place to sit within the space of the living room. Eritrea was one of the lucky ones to have a chair of her own; Håkan sat cross-legged on the floor almost opposite her, by the side of the settee. Natalie was perched on the flat settee arm next to him. Her waist was almost on a level with his head, so he was virtually hidden from view. As chance would have it, the only person he could see directly was Eritrea.

Youssou's sister brought glasses of a thick, sweet peanut drink, which were distributed around the room. Håkan sipped his and put it under the sofa so that Natalie would not kick it over.

'…So, friends,' Youssou was saying from where he stood in the corner of the room, 'if I had known but a month ago how my life would change this year, I would not have believed it.' He smiled at the gathered group. 'For years I had been living the life of a devout Muslim with the intention of one day following in the footsteps of my own teacher and becoming an esteemed leader in the Islamic faith myself. This way would have brought great honour to my family and would have sealed our social status. But, even before I knew it myself, the Lord Jesus Christ had his hand on my life and was guiding my ways. My mentor, who would have been horrified – *bouleversé* – had he known the consequences of his words, gave me a prophecy that had been supplied by none other than Christ Himself, that I would be visited by white foreigners –' here he signalled to Durant – 'and that they would tell me the words of truth and life.'

Håkan had not expected Youssou to make a speech, but from the lengthy introduction it seemed that he was gearing up to speak for some time.

Sitting on the linoleum, he was beginning to lose the feeling in his backside. He watched Eritrea from behind one of Natalie's legs. She sat slightly forward in her chair, to indicate that she was listening. The bridge of her nose was slightly shiny from the shower she had taken that morning. When she took her eyes off Youssou, they drifted across the room and rested momentarily on other group members sitting on the settee. Then she saw Håkan. For a while she almost looked through him, as if distractedly looking at an object in the room. They exchanged a gaze of pure neutrality. Then the awareness inside him reached into his mind and said, now is your opportunity.

He knew that to act on it was effectively to cast aside the peace. But how could he not? He had already made the decision. So he winked at her: a long, wicked wink. She opened her eyes slightly and looked away. When she looked back, she shot him one of her teacher-looking-disapprovingly-over-spectacles glances and the link was re-established.

Youssou talked for thirty-five minutes. In that time, Eritrea and Håkan played a silent staring game. Through each one of her looks, Eritrea deliberately let him glimpse the hunger that she had felt for him on the roof the previous night. It was as though she was opening a little gap in the curtain of her soul and letting him glimpse in at the real her, further than she had let him see before. This made the blood rush to his temples and sent his heartbeat into an absolute frenzy. He felt as though she were consciously standing opposite him and removing her clothes. In reality, she could not have affected him more if she actually *had* stood naked before him.

In all the time they had spent together there had always been a platonic edge to the physical contact they had shared. Now, paradoxically, a mere look from her was more sensual, more physical, than any of the times their physical bodies had actually touched. He felt a wild hope rising in him, a hope against hope. She had never before communicated the full force of her desire to him – neither directly nor subconsciously. In fact, she had gone to pains to conceal it. Maybe his distance from her had somehow ignited it. Men can play hard to get, too, he thought to himself. Or maybe it was the awareness still whispering to him.

Walking back to the villa, he felt almost dizzy with passion and guilt. But what have I done that was actually wrong? he challenged himself. I am just walking along the road. I haven't spoken to her. No words have passed between us. Thus he excused himself for what he had done, all the while burning up with desire for her.

What he did not realize, however, was that rejecting the peace that God had given him was a trade off. He had got back the drug-like yearning that he loved so much – it had exploded joyfully, like a fire, back into his body – but he would also get all the other, less pleasant, feelings, the side effects; the fallout, the pain. The Spirit had offered him what the Spirit had to give and he had rejected it. He could only have one or the other: the Spirit's peace, or the good and the bad of his own human desires.

So the other, less pleasant, feelings began to creep back into his heart after lunch. Well, you did invite us, they seemed to say. Don't you know how it works in the spiritual realm?

Didier and Durant had ordered a major cleanout of the villa, as the owner would be coming on Sunday to give the place a final check over.

'Why can't we just scrub it off?' Arran grumbled to Håkan as they whitewashed over the dried blood on the outside wall. 'As soon as it rains the paint'll get washed off and whoever lives here then will think we buried bodies under the garage or something.'

'The Silence of the Goats,' Håkan commented dryly, dipping his brush. But he was already trying to fend off the pain that had begun, again, to pick away at him. Eritrea was up on their balcony, of all places, painting the walls with Richard. He could hear them talking together. Somehow their English accents sounding together from behind the wall suggested a cultural understanding or complicity between them that was slightly beyond Håkan's ability to comprehend. He felt terribly excluded.

'You know Durant isn't coming back to Lyon?' Arran said.

'I had no idea.'

'He's staying here with the Tufala church to disciple Youssou.'

At once, Håkan felt a stab of conviction, as he usually did when he thought of Durant. He knew that it was not the kind of thing that he could ever do, stay behind when everyone else was leaving.

'How long for? When did he make the decision?'

'A few months, and I don't know.'

Håkan wanted to strengthen his connection with Arran, if only to keep from thinking about Eritrea talking to someone else on the balcony. He and Arran had not talked properly since their conversation on Wednesday. He wanted to say, listen, you're a good friend. I appreciate your honesty. But Arran knew that Håkan did not necessarily appreciate his honesty. It would sound insincere.

At dinner, Eritrea shot him the same smouldering look she had given him earlier. He thought he would melt down into a puddle at the table.

While he was packing that evening, the feeling that time was running out overwhelmed him. As he pushed a pile of T-shirts into his rucksack, he felt as if his longing to hold the hours that were left was like trying to hold a handful of dry Senegal sand. The sand there had been blown about by the African winds until the grains had worn themselves down to dust. It was not like the coarser, heavier sand he knew from the beaches he had been to when he was younger. It was so fine, so insubstantial, that it got into everything, lining the cracks in his penknife, choking the Toyota engine, burying itself deep into the seams of his clothes. But it was too fine to hold on to, and it was leaking out from between his fingers and flowing away. Its residue would be on him and his belongings for much time to come, but it could not be held.

The next morning he reluctantly hauled his rucksack down to the front yard, where Eritrea and Lauren had sometimes secretly eaten *baignets*. There were other suitcases and bags piled there outside the door and Marcello sat alone on the step, wearing the pitch-black Ray-Bans he had refused to take off on the first day of evangelism. Inside the villa there was a good deal of commotion and inefficient activity. In the worship room, the tables had been folded away and the room echoed as if it were a different room altogether, not the place they had sat and eaten breakfast and dinner for two months. Seeing it transformed like this, Håkan had a sudden futile desire that the PCOM team should not leave. In an hour we shall be gone and we shall never return here, he thought. He squeezed past Céline and Anne, then walked out of the door and into the back yard, which was steeped in a strange, poised silence. He had to get a look at the physical things that had been the props in his life over the last two months. He went to the passageway where he and Eritrea had sat and talked about the genie protectors. On the step was a cardboard box, containing the dismantled water pumps.

He walked to the other side of the yard; Lauren had forgotten her towel on the clothes line. He would have to remind her to get it. The goat blood was already showing faintly pink under the paint. Oh well, he thought. The sink under the balcony was bone dry. It looked as though it had never been used.

The balcony.

Håkan made his way back inside. Céline and Anne were drinking up the last of the *Schitrus* left over from the ram roast, and Fleur was calling to them from the worship room to wash and dry the cups. 'Howken,' she said as he went past. 'You packed everything? Put your bag outside, your guitar?'

'Yes, of course,' he said hopping up the stairs. On the landing was an uneven pile of sponge mattresses, mostly from the girls' room. Natalie was trying to squeeze the last of the seven-week-old air from her mammoth Li-lo. She had rolled up about half of it and there was a tight bag of trapped air near the valve. 'Please,' she was saying to Arran, who was standing over her critically. 'It doesn't weigh that much. Only five kilos.'

'You had space for it on the way over,' he mused. 'I'm sure you can find space for it now.'

'Come on. Don't be so mean. You've hardly got anything yourself.'

'Put it in with the general stuff. That way it'll just go through. Or, you *could* leave it here.'

Håkan slipped past them into the corridor that led to the girls' bedroom. Brigitte was alone in the large upstairs room, sweeping industriously. She gave him a curt nod. He looked at the space where he knew Eritrea had lain, remembering how, when his outreach group had had their planning meetings there, he had sat on her bed. Then he went back into the corridor, past the toilet where she wrote her letters, past the bickering Arran and Natalie, and into his own room. The movement of the door stirred up the dust bunnies on the floor where his rucksack had been. Now the room seemed huge and bleak. He scraped open the French window and walked purposefully to the balcony. When he tried the door he hoped, for a second, that Eritrea would be on the other side of it, but she was not. The balcony smelt of whitewash. It was not a smell he associated with it, and it somehow made it difficult for him to evoke the memories that he wanted to touch one last time before leaving.

'Hey,' a voice called from above.

He glanced up and saw her looking down from the roof. 'Something about this situation seems strangely familiar,' she laughed.

'Wait there,' he called.

When he came out of the stairwell doorway, she was still looking over the edge of wall.

'I'll have good memories about that balcony,' she said, without turning to look at him.

'I know.'

'These last few days have been strange.'

'Yes.'

He wasn't entirely sure where he stood with her. She was wearing jeans that he hadn't seen since Lyon. They widened out around the ankle and were slightly frayed at the edges where her heels had rubbed and trodden them on the ground. They made him think of her as she had seemed to him at the beginning of the school, unknown and mysteriously compelling. He wanted, above all, to say, those looks you've been giving me. Tell me they mean that you are attracted to me. Tell me they mean you want me. But he could not: he was still committed to using the small remaining measure of aloofness he had secured a few days earlier, as a lure. He felt now as though, with every confirming look he gave her, he was spending credits — eating into the aura of superior distance he had obtained dishonestly — and that soon he would have no credits left and would be penniless, without the disguise of remoteness; the same old desperate Håkan, subject to her as he had been before. He knew as he looked at her exquisitely tanned forearms, the aesthetically perfect length of her fingers, that that time was not far away. In some ways, he wanted to throw off all pretence now and reveal himself to her as he really was, fully in love, totally committed to her. Now she turned to look at him, her pupils intense and framed in the green of her eyes, and the desire to do so came upon him like a rush. But he could not. The fear of being rejected was too great.

'We're disobeying the leaders by talking up here alone,' she said. But it seemed more like a question or a request for confirmation.

'I suppose we are, aren't we? But I don't think it matters now.'

'I wonder if we'll ever come back here and see this place again.'

He did not know whether she meant just him and her, or the whole group. It was so exactly the kind of thing she would have said.

'I was thinking the same thing.'

'It's strange how attached you get to a place,' she said. 'Two months ago I didn't even know it existed. Now, for the rest of my life, I'll remember this house. One house on the west coast of Africa. Isn't that strange?'

'Not at all.'

But then Fleur was calling his name from the front courtyard. 'They're on to us,' he said edging back, reluctantly, towards the door.

'Håkan,' she said as he was turning to go.

'Yes?'

'I love talking to you. I've always loved talking to you, you know.'

He bowed his head in recognition. 'Me too.' Then he was gone, down the stairwell.

They were waiting by their bags for Didier to come back with a taxi bus when the house owner arrived. He drew up outside the compound on what sounded like a large motorbike. He entered the gate sporting a chunky leather jacket, despite the heat. Durant walked him through the house to inspect the rooms.

'Let's hope he doesn't see the blood,' Håken said, when they had gone through the worship room and out into the yard.

But the owner, obviously sufficiently satisfied with the condition of the place, was soon back in the worship room, exchanging words with Durant. He picked his way over the group sitting in the sea of luggage, lifting his head neutrally at them before revving up his bike outside the gate the way someone does when they want to advertise that they have a big and expensive piece of machinery.

Anne carried the last of the rubbish bags through the front door and deposited it on the pavement outside the compound, where five or so were already waiting in a pile.

'What are you going to do when you get back home?' Lauren asked Håkan.

'I don't want to think about it, really,' he said. Natalie and Lauren exchanged an unsubtle, knowing look of amusement.

'I'm going to have a mammoth beer,' Arran said. 'I can see it now: crisp, golden with about a centimetre of head.

263

Almost freezing cold and in one of those hourglass glasses, with condensation running down it.'

'Don't know how you can miss beer,' Lauren commented. 'You seem to drink more than enough of it on the beach.'

'What about you?' Natalie asked Eritrea.

'A hot bath. I'm going to turn on the hot tap in the bathroom and let it fill up to the brim and then just lie in it for hours until my skin goes pruney.'

'Let the bathroom fill up to the brim?' Arran said, genuinely interested.

'Oh man, hot water,' Natalie said. 'A hot shower.'

'A hot water bottle,' Håkan added sarcastically.

'A lovely hot radiator,' Arran continued. 'Wonderfully hot to the touch.'

'Idiot,' Natalie said.

'On a day like today it's quite hard to imagine anyone craving a hot shower, that's all.'

'A proper mattress,' Lauren said. 'Wouldn't you just kill to sleep in a proper bed?'

'How many people would I have to kill?' Arran said.

'The street kids are going through our rubbish,' Patrique said in French, looking through the crack between the gate and the wall. 'We should do something.'

'Let them be,' Fleur said. 'We can't leave it in the compound. If we pick it up now they'll only open the bags again when we've gone.'

Soon, Didier drew up in the taxi bus. He climbed out and opened the gate. 'Have you seen what those kids have done?' he said, rolling up his sleeves. 'Whose silly idea was it to leave the rubbish outside?'

'Shouldn't we, like, step on it?' Anne said. 'The plane leaves in three hours.'

'Not any more,' Didier said.

'Oh?'

'There's been a mix-up.'

'And?' Anne was frustrated.

'So we're not leaving in three hours.' Didier was in his element; he was not about to divulge the whole story while he was the focus of everyone's undivided attention.

'I might as well ask the driver,' she said. 'I'll probably get more out of him.'

'You probably will,' Didier said cheerfully. 'I'm sure he knows more about this than I do.'

'Get to the point,' Fleur said.

'The plane's overbooked and a full quota of people have already checked in, so there's nothing we can do except go on the next one, which leaves late tonight. In the meantime we get chauffer-driven to a luxury hotel for the afternoon, courtesy of Dakar airport.'

There were mixed reactions, mostly delight.

'What time does the plane leave?' Fleur said.

'One in the morning.'

'We won't all fit in that taxi,' she continued.

'That's quite true, which is why it will be making two trips.' He held up his forefinger and middle finger to Fleur.

Håkan was in the second group; Eritrea had gone on in the first. Before the taxi returned, he stood outside the gate with his rucksack and guitar case watching the urchins combing through the PCOM group's waste. The colourful empty shampoo and conditioner bottles, the moisturizer packaging, the empty tubes of hot oil treatment were like an indictment on Western wealth, and seeing them strewn about the pavement made Håkan feel oddly guilty. It seemed the street children had deliberately emptied the bags in front of them as if to say, and this is what you throw away? When we have nothing? But there was something desperately personal, too, about the waste; the most intimate secrets of the villa – including Marcello's empty bottle of scotch whisky – were rudely exposed for all to see.

The hotel was a collection of luxury, stand-alone cabins with a safari feel, randomly dotted around a field site by the ocean. Håkan and Richard were given a two-man cabin, which had hot and cold running water, a corner bath, a television and a mini bar. They dropped their luggage by the beds and looked at each other, suspiciously astounded.

They sat next to each other at lunch, too, which was an intricate three-course affair, with multiple layers of cutlery and a choice of red or white wine. The sheer opulence of the place was almost blinding, like a painfully bright white light. As Håkan was being waited on, he thought of the rubbish that had made him feel so guilty, and found his mental priorities reorganizing themselves. Richard said, 'Insidious.'

'Why do you say that?'

'It's funny how you get so used to simple, basic things that when you get given something luxurious, you almost can't take it. It's like Crocodile Dundee sleeping on the floor instead of the bed.'

'Yeah.'

Richard was staring at the carefully assembled dish of lamb fillet with a fan-shaped arrangement of herb-fried potatoes, that had just been placed in front of him. 'There's a prophecy about this generation of Christians that says that one day they'll be eating baked beans on toast and the next, caviar in palaces with kings.'

'But when you think about it,' Håkan said, 'even what we had at the villa was luxury. Pure luxury. You know, with our CDs and expensive clothes and stuff. All right, we had to pump the tap water, but at least we *had* tap water.'

As they were walking back to the cabin, Richard said, 'I'm not saying this isn't an incredible blessing and all, but I think I'd ultimately choose Fatou's cooking over that, any day.'

'Me too, I think.'

On arriving back, they both collapsed on their beds and fell into a deep sleep. Håkan had wanted to seek out Eritrea, but the morning's events, the culture shock and the weight of the food on his stomach were too much for him.

When he woke up, it was late afternoon. He levered himself up on his elbows feeling as if he were swimming up from the depths of a bottomless pool, or waking from a long hibernation. He had a moment of blank stupidity before he realized where he was. The throw on Richard's bed was ruffled but Richard himself was missing.

Håkan carefully swung his feet to the floor and sat for a while trying to get his bearings. Then Eritrea's form came into his mind, a single point of reference in a sea of confusion. He freshened up, left the cabin and walked purposefully to the shore. He did not know how he knew that she would be there; he just knew that she would. And sure enough, there she was, standing on the beach next to Richard and looking out to the ocean. He approached them and stood with them, without a word of greeting, and listened to their conversation.

'He has no attachments,' she was saying. 'It'd probably be harder if he did.'

'Has he done it before?'

'I don't know. He's been involved in miraculous things of one sort or another. I can say that much. Miracles seem to follow him around. He was happy to stay.'

'It's not something I could do,' Richard said, 'just like that.'

Håkan thought, you can say that again. 'You got to have your bath,' he remarked to Eritrea.

'Yes.' You'd think God was listening to us back at the villa. 'I want a bath, Lauren wants a bed, Natalie wants a hot shower. Then we get it all. And more.' She turned and looked out to sea. 'Isn't it incredible?'

'Do you think we'll make our plane?' Richard said. Håkan thought he meant the plane from Dakar, but Eritrea's answer sent a chill through his body.

'We'll be cutting it a bit fine, but if we get the earliest possible train to Paris, we should make it.'

It had not occurred to him that some of the group might have booked fixed return tickets to their own countries. The idea of Richard and Eritrea travelling away together seemed fundamentally wrong; something that belonged to the past, not the present.

'When is it?' he asked, distantly.

'Tomorrow evening, about eight or nine, isn't it?'

'Something like that,' Richard said.

'It'll be a pity not to see the guys back at Lyon,' Eritrea said. 'When are you leaving for Sweden?' she asked Håkan.

'The day after tomorrow.'

'I envy you so much. I really wish we could spend time back in Lyon together.'

Then cancel your flight, he wanted to say. Better still, don't go back to England at all. Stay in France with me. Then he thought immediately, I am beginning to lose it.

Durant was waiting for them at the airport when they arrived for check-in. He stood with his hands in his pockets, smiling cheerfully and conspicuously dressed in non-travelling clothes, in contrast to the rest of the group. He looked like a rock in the midst of the airport chaos. When he hugged Eritrea goodbye, he said, 'It was great working with you.'

Between check-in and boarding, Håkan sat in the dingy departure lounge surrounded by the backlit advertisements for duty free cognac and designer perfumes. The perfume models stared disdainfully with vain, mysterious eyes that said, we are party to great, intriguing secrets. To Håkan they looked ridiculous. He thought, you know nothing about anything. He sat with Natalie and Lauren, joking with an almost hysterical urgency. The final grains of sand were flowing through his fingers on to the tattered airport carpet with its cigarette burns and smooth black spots of ancient chewing gum.

He entered the plane and sat down in his seat, desolate. A moment later Eritrea came and sat down next to him.

'What about Marcello?' he said.

'We swapped tickets. He's sitting where I'm supposed to be.'

She reached over and took his hand.

The sunrise seeped in through the square hatches like liquid, throwing sleeping profiles into relief with its golden light. It bled through the plane, touching the fabric of the seats and the metal fixtures, infusing them arbitrarily with brilliant colour. The plane rocked gently, every now and then, and the seats made their muted squeaking complaints under the steady throbbing mantra of the engines. The cabin was filled with a kind of submissive silence. Håkan and Eritrea sat, wide awake, still holding hands. They had talked a little, but mostly sat quietly. The skin-on-skin contact he had with her, the interlocking of their fingers, seemed to him the most complete and most perfect connection conceivable between two people. The nerves in his left hand seemed to burn with a fire of completeness.

As the plane was preparing to land, she turned to him and said, 'Yesterday morning before you came up on to the roof, I knew what you were doing.'

'Oh, what's that then?'

'You were going from room to room saying goodbye to the house, weren't you?'

'Yes. How did you know?'

'It's just so you, Håkan. It's just so the kind of thing you would do.'

Lyon airport seemed desperately colourless and monochrome, all shadowy greys and blacks. When Håkan had collected his guitar and his rucksack, he walked over to where the group were gathered, waiting to scatter to the four winds. Only nine of them, including Didier and Anne, were going back to the Lyon base. The rest would soon be going their separate ways on trains or buses. In a few minutes they would all be gone from the airport and the space where they now stood would be empty. But I will say goodbye quickly, he told himself. I will not make a thing of it.

In turn he hugged each of the people he would not see again. Then, finally, he was facing Eritrea. Time had run out and he was there, the old Håkan, standing before her without any mystique left, fully exposed and with nothing to hide. They held each other tight for a moment. Then, she pulled slightly away from him, wrapped her arms around his neck and kissed him deeply, a lover's kiss. All he could think in that moment of stunned disbelief was, the leaders are watching us. Then, before he had time to respond to the kiss she broke off. She stood opposite him and studied him for a moment. Then she was gone.

Håkan walked out to the minibus. The air was cold with the chilly tail end of winter and made the warm African air seem like nothing but part of a dream. As he breathed it in, it burned a frosty trail to his sinuses – and to his heart.

Chapter 16

The day after Håkan got back to Stockholm a letter arrived for him. The post came early, at seven in the morning, but the rustling sound it made falling through the letterbox woke him instantly. When he saw the handwriting on the envelope, his heart turned over. He showered, dressed up against the cold and left his parents' apartment with the letter in his pocket.

What was left of the slushy snow on the roads had turned the colour of the tarmac, giving the illusion that the roads themselves were deeply rutted, like mud tracks. The grey dawn was filled with the dank humidity of early commuting activity, which hung in the air like an oily sheen. He walked purposefully to the metro, hopping to avoid the deeper puddles and shivering. On the train, he permitted himself the luxury of looking over the letter. He ran his finger over the biro-line scores on the envelope paper and smelt it. He studied the Marlborough address on the reverse side. It read like some brief, eloquent English poem – no prosaic numbers or letters like with Swedish addresses. Not even a postcode. Somehow it made him think of her standing holding the curtain at an upstairs window of a manor house in a period drama.

He took the letter to a particular café in Gamla Stan, the old town located on the island in the middle of the city. It drew tourists and visitors to Stockholm like a magnet; they got their free map of the city, saw "Old Town" and made a beeline for it. Håkan liked to sit quietly in a coffee shop which had an ornate silver-plated coffee maker in the window, and simply be in close proximity to the residue of travel and purposeful movement that clung to those passing through. It was the way they stood up, finished their coffee, brushed their coats down and glanced around, as people do when they know they will never return. Sometimes he almost felt that he, too, would be rising to go to the airport or the harbour.

He ordered a coffee, sat down and carefully slit open the letter with the teaspoon so as not to tear the return address.

When he had finished reading it for the third time, he put it down and looked up, reluctantly allowing his surroundings to draw him back from the sharp taste of the yellow fever tablets, the squeak of the compound gate and the floury feel of worn playing cards.

Today, there was a group of English tourists sitting near the window and talking together in lowered, self-conscious voices. He rose, paid and left. Outside, the winter darkness was grudgingly giving up the struggle against the spring. The threat of a cruel wind, far harsher even than the February Mediterranean chill of Lyon, crept around the cobblestones and the high, dark walls. Håkan could almost taste it.

She had written some of the letter in Africa. *I will kiss you when we say goodbye*, she said to him from the worship room table, or from the upstairs bathroom. *Not those dry French pecks on the cheek, but a proper kiss. I hate the formality of the way the French kiss their greetings. It precludes the possibility of expressing any genuine emotion.*

He clicked the door of the apartment shut and stood in the entrance hall listening to the tedious, everyday sounds of his family moving about in the morning: the spring in the toaster, the muffled sound of cutlery being moved in a washing-up bowl full of last night's tepid water. Eritrea was still speaking to him. *I prayed that we would be able to sit together, but I decided to leave it up to God and not to do anything to try and force it. When we went to get on the plane, I thought it wasn't going to happen, but when Marcello came up to me at the last minute and asked if I wanted to change tickets, I just thought, thank you God, thank you so much.*

He wrote back: *I think of all those empty corners in the house at Croix Blanche and it makes me sad. I feel like I'm standing in the worship room alone a day or so after we've all left and everything is empty and silent, but of course that's stupid because there's bound to be somebody there now.* At the end of the letter he asked, *Could I come and visit you some time in early summer?*

The kiss at the airport had provided him with sufficient stamina to last through the painful first months of their separation and to continue loyally trusting that their coming together was a foregone conclusion, an event waiting to happen. But the letters, too, as tangible proof of her commitment, helped to keep him going. They exchanged one or two a week, writing with such frequency that they usually crossed in the post. He cherished the letters she sent as if they were little bits of her soul or miniature representations of herself in paper and ink.

At first, she wrote about her feelings for him towards the end of the mission; how she boasted of him to Lucy. But there was a gradual, almost imperceptible, shift in the tone of the letters over the spring. *It would be great to see you,* she wrote in May. *We could organize a PCOM reunion and invite Richard and spend a weekend in London.* Håkan puzzled over this when he first read it. Then, as he reread it he began to fret about it. But I do not want to share you with Richard, he replied to the words on the paper. I want you for myself. How can we be lovers with Richard there? How could you ever stand, let alone desire, the intrusive presence of a third party?

273

Another time she said, *I'm so pleased that we were able to sort things out in the last talk we had on the balcony, before the leaders split us up. It was so important for me, coming back to England, to know that there was no confusion between us about our relationship. I don't think I have ever had a friend like you.*

Håkan felt a sort of curling horror, like the curling of a page constricting as it burns up in fire, when he read those words. At that moment, his implicit trust in the significance of the kiss began to dissolve. He fought to keep hold of it, to assert his interpretation of it. But it was no good.

Eventually, later that week, he resignedly put pen to paper and wrote, *Can I come to visit you in Marlborough in the first two weeks of July?* He read through the letter when he had finished it and saw with dismay that it looked exactly like what it was: a grasping, almost pitiful, plea. So I am completely subject to her again, he thought as he mailed it.

In England, when Eritrea read it, it sent a pang of fear through her. In her desire to communicate the intense empathy she felt for him, she wrote back a regular newsy letter saying, at the end, *Yes, come by all means,* all the while thinking, it cannot happen.

The next day, however, she took a postcard from her bureau draw. She wrote:

Dear Håkan,

I know I wrote yesterday that you could come. But it looks like it's not going to be possible. I'm sorry to take back what I said yesterday, I really am. I do hope you understand.

Love,

Eritrea

It was a horrendously clumsy and destructive message. She sat in front of it, agonizing over how else to word it. *I do hope you understand*, she had written. It defied understanding. She was tempted to add some kind of softening stabilizer, to say, *...not going to be possible this summer because things are so hectic*, or something similar, but she knew that that left some window of opportunity. She truly wanted to give him some kind of confirmation. But she could not.

She put it in an envelope. It did not fit properly; when she folded down the adhesive lip of the envelope, she had to make a new crease in the paper along the top edge of the postcard.

She sent it after lunch, to catch the afternoon post.

After that, she did not hear back from him for a long time.

★

About eight months later, almost to the day, he replied. By then, Eritrea no longer lived in Marlborough and only visited periodically, so the letter was left lying on her bureau in amidst a pile of junk university correspondence for a number of days. When it was eventually passed on to her, it caught her completely off guard. She held the unopened envelope in her hand and had a premonition of its contents. Something inside her told her not to open it but just to throw it away or to get one of her parents to write, *No longer at this address* on it and send it back. As if anticipating this eventuality, Håkan had not provided a return address on the envelope.

But then, another part of her badly wanted to know how he was, where he was. Curiosity eventually overcame her sense of foreboding and she opened it.

The letter said:

Dear Eritrea,

I know it is going to be very strange for you to hear from me out of the blue after all this time. I wanted to write to you before, I really did. I even started a few letters and gave them up or just never sent them. What I have to say probably won't be easy for you to hear, but I feel I must tell you.

Here, Eritrea began to feel as though her chest were slowly imploding. But she read on:

In Africa I fell in love with you. You know that I was drawn to you right from the beginning of the school, from the first moment I laid eyes on you. I told you I was. But I want you to be clear about this, just in case you somehow missed the signals I was giving off. I know that you tried to explain honestly to me how you felt, the time when we discussed the difference between "in love" and just "love" but I admit that, at the time, I wasn't really willing to take on board the possibility that you might not love me in the same way I loved you. I guess it was partly because I couldn't reconcile what you said and the way that we were with each other, like the things that we shared together and the bond that we had.

That's partly why, when I got your letter last year, I felt like I'd been torn up. If I'm being honest with myself, I knew that it was possible that our relationship wouldn't work out the way I wanted it to. I think God even wanted to prepare me to be ready for it. But I was living in denial, in a way, and using the guarantees you'd given me as proof that you loved me like I loved you.

Anyway, I eventually started seeing other girls, but I couldn't seem to make things work. Whenever things looked like they were progressing and that the relationship might turn into something, I realized that there was something in me that was holding me back and stopping me from committing. When I prayed about it, I felt God showed me that you "owned" a part of me, and that some deep part of me was holding out against, even opposing, any other relationship in the hope that you and I might still be able to get together.

I mentioned guarantees that you gave me when we were together. You said all along that you were not in love with me, but you gave me mixed messages by saying one thing and doing another. The kiss you gave me at the airport was not the kiss of a friend, but the kiss of a girlfriend. The looks you gave me towards the end of the outreach, the way you originally talked in your letters – all those things communicated to me that you were in love. I think Didier even warned me that what people say and what they communicate through what they do are two different things.

It was only when I started dating that I realized a part of me "belonged" to you and that the link between us was not really good. When I fantasized about you, it was in a way that I would be completely under your control. I recognize that now, and I see that it was not healthy.

I think that you wanted me to be subject to you and that – consciously or subconsciously – you made sure that I'd be in a position where you had the upper hand. What I am saying, I suppose, is that I think you seduce men in order to make them subject to you. Looking back, I think that I was very foolish about the reality of the potential we had to hurt each other. One of the things that made me realize this was the time when we were split up from each other; I felt so bad that I prayed with Didier for any unhealthy tie between us to be broken. Immediately afterwards, I realized you were aware that something was different and that you couldn't control the relationship and that you were even annoyed about it... I remember the evening of the ram roast in particular when you left and went up to the roof. I've wondered a lot why it was that you seemed so annoyed, but now I see that it was most likely because you knew you no longer had the same power over me.

When these things became clear to me, I sat down and prayed about them. I gave our relationship to God and asked him to remove anything bad, and when I did, he just transformed the way I felt. Now I feel that I can meet the right person in the knowledge that there will be nothing hanging over me or holding me back.

Really, I'm writing to you because I'm concerned about you and what you can do to people. I think that you have a great potential to hurt guys. There is something about you that draws men to you and that could end up causing them a great deal of pain if you're not careful. I see now that Patrique must have been terribly hurt when he saw us spending time together, after you and he had been so close for the first two months in Lyon. Arran told me as much, but because I was so wrapped up with how I felt, and because I didn't really like Patrique anyway, I hardly gave it any thought at the time. If you do seduce and then reject men, I don't know why you do it. I thought that it might, in some way, be connected to the death of your brother Jo.

Reading this might make you angry but I have to run that risk, because I care for you very much as a friend. Now that I've been released from this bond, I feel for the first time since we talked that I can treat you as a friend, just the way you wanted our relationship to be, without any complications. And friends are, at least, honest with each other. So, if this is goodbye, then it is goodbye.

Håkan

When Eritrea finished the letter, she was livid with him. But underneath the angry thoughts were feelings of hurt, and underneath those, fear. She folded the letter back up, and put it in a keepsake box. Then she locked the box and put it at the back of her bottom drawer.

Part III

Chapter 17

It was lunchtime on a wet, muggy Saturday in early August. There was something utterly deflating in the atmosphere; the shadows were tinged with sepia. Eritrea stood behind the bar counter of the *Dame de Coeur* in her black-and-white waitress outfit watching the sticky rivulets of rain twist their way down the front window of the restaurant like convulsing watery snakes.

It was a very fine restaurant – perhaps the finest in Swindon, the proprietor and chef Antoine had told Eritrea at the interview. He was an obsessive and fastidious man, the kind of man who bent over backwards in his efforts to be obsequiously courteous to the customers but then heartlessly cut the waitresses to pieces on the kitchen side of the swing doors. To him, reputation was the be-all and end-all, the absolute meaning of life. 'If the clientele find a reason, any reason to fault this place, then that is it. They will not return. And you –' he said, pointing to Eritrea – 'are responsible for ensuring that they never have reason to complain.' He said it as if the fate of all humankind rested in her hands. 'Do you think you can handle that kind of responsibility?'

She had almost laughed at him. Originally, Lucy had only brought the advert home from work for its novelty value. Lucy worked at the local job centre as a client advisor and often showed Eritrea some of the more ridiculous advertisements. This particular one she had picked up in January. It read:

Wanted:

Bilingual French/English waitress for cosmopolitan, high-class restaurant

Applicants must:
- have worked with silver service for several years
- have extensive experience in the catering industry
- have superb interpersonal skills
- be team players, adaptable and ready to work long and changeable shifts.

Salary: £4.50 – £5.00/hour

'So you get £5.00 if you were head waiter at the Ritz for twenty years,' Eritrea laughed, when Lucy read the advert aloud.

'Wanted,' Lucy said, 'kitchen porter for slummy downtown pub. In addition to speaking twenty languages fluently, applicants must also have a PhD in applied biochemistry and at least ten years' experience working as UN peacekeepers in Bosnia.'

'No, I've got one,' Eritrea said. 'You –' here she made a grand flourishing gesture with her hand to indicate the heading of a large newspaper advertisement – 'you have grown bored with your job as an accomplished paediatric neurosurgeon saving lives in a top Chicago hospital. Now you're looking for the kind of challenge that can only be found in mopping out the public loos in Swindon.'

Antoine interviewed Eritrea in French. She answered his ludicrous questions civilly. The irony of it all was that if applicants were truly bilingual they would be doing something considerably more significant than waiting tables, surely? Eritrea pointed this out unashamedly.

'Well, what about this, then?' he replied, lifting a thick wad of letters and CVs and waving it in her face. 'Over a hundred applications.'

People must be pretty desperate, she thought. *I* must be pretty desperate, she corrected herself. 'Would there be any chance of getting a raise after a few months?' she asked. 'After all, the pay isn't much of an incentive, is it?'

'A raise?' He looked at her aghast, as if she had casually asked to set fire to the premises.

She left thinking she had blown it for being so forthright, so was quite surprised when, a week later, Antoine called her to tell her that she had the job. Apart from the language and the interpersonal skills, she had none of the other prerequisites for the work. She was tempted, on her first day, to ask him about the hundred other applicants. But the job was sufficiently important to her to keep her from making sarcastic comments. The only real reason she had gone for it in the first place was because the restaurant was, it transpired, surprisingly near to the flat that she and Lucy rented – a five-minute hurried walk or a ten-minute dawdle.

'Until I saw the ad I didn't even know there *was* an upmarket restaurant around here,' Lucy said suspiciously after Eritrea's interview. 'What's it called?'

'The *Dame de Coeur*.'

'The Damned Cur? That's an unfortunate kind of name for a restaurant, isn't it? What do they serve there? Dog?'

'It's entirely possible.'

Eritrea was fed up, too, of the underlying feeling of guilt from living on benefit. Though Lucy never made sarcastic comments when she came home at five-thirty to find her loafing around on the settee, Eritrea still felt like she was a parasite on the state. Her father said, 'Don't think anything of it. You're just considering your options. And, in any case, it's good for us to get back some of the tax I pay every year.'

Eritrea did not see the logic of this, especially as she had, at the time, been considering her options for the six months since she had moved to Swindon. She thought, I feel bad about sponging off the state because you brought me up to see it as bad. How can you then go and condone it?

Ultimately, however, it was the bone-tired, desensitized feeling she got from still being sat in front of inane daytime chat shows at two in the afternoon that finally motivated her to apply. The restaurant was a sufficient source of minor dramas and woes to provide her with a framework for her life. If nothing else, by showing her what she did *not* want to do, it gave her the desire to start thinking seriously about what she *did* want out of her life. 'Isn't it crazy,' she said to Lucy, 'how you only seem to find the motivation to do the things you want to do when you're kept from doing them by something that you not only dislike but also consider a waste of time.'

'And,' Lucy added, 'that you only started doing in the first place because you felt you weren't doing anything significant.'

'What a deceitful paradox.'

But there was plenty to keep her occupied at the restaurant in the form of both work and petty intrigue. Learning to provide silver service was a complicated and fiddly task that Eritrea would have mastered far more quickly had she not considered it fundamentally excessive. To make matters worse, she was forced to be the apprentice of Fougère, Antoine's nineteen-year-old daughter, who, in addition to being the unofficial head waitress, was awfully spoilt. She insisted on speaking English to Eritrea when lecturing her on how to hold the serving spoons or how to stand. 'I'd speak to you in French if you understood what I was saying, but until you can speak it properly it's best that we address each other in English, to avoid any misunderstanding.'

Eritrea quickly noticed that such comments were intended to provoke, so as to provide Fougère with a reason to go tittle-tattling to her father. She also realized that it was far more of a provocation to Fougère to be humble and agree with her. 'To be honest with you,' she added once, in a moment of inspiration, 'it's a real pleasure for me to be able to help you improve your English.' Fougère, who, despite having lived in England for several years, still had somewhat of a French accent, withdrew into a world of silent inner fury at this apparently innocuous comment.

There were two other waitresses besides Eritrea and Fougère. One of them, Blouenne, was an old school friend of Fougère's from France and was in England on a gap year, supposedly to learn English, which she never actually spoke. Fougère had evidently been the master, and Blouenne the servant, in the relationship even back when they were ten-year-olds in France. When the two laughed together, it was always on Fougère's terms, and Fougère was often publicly cruel and disparaging to Blouenne. Nevertheless, Blouenne acted as her familiar, always following her lead as a sign of subservience. This involved treating Eritrea with complete disdain when Fougère was there, but being at an awkwardly conciliatory and silent loss when Eritrea and Blouenne happened to be waiting alone together.

The fourth waitress, Serena, was more or less Eritrea's age and had lived on Réunion Island for a number of years. She had been recruited at the same time as Eritrea and, like Eritrea, had none of the qualifications except the language. The common experience of being outsiders at the restaurant and bearing the brunt of Antoine's angry outbursts meant that their comradeship was a *fait accompli*, though Eritrea did not relish their role of the unjustly victimized nearly as much as Serena, who conjectured for hours about the fate of the previous waitresses. After thinking, for the first week at the *Dame de Coeur*, that they had been fired she settled on the assumption that they had probably walked out. She was fond of conspiracy theories. 'Blouenne's obviously a family friend so Antoine feels he can't shout at her, even though she's so clumsy. Don't you get the impression when he's yelling at you that the comments are really directed at her? I mean, can you imagine having to suffer for other people's mistakes for months just because the boss didn't feel he could blame the real perpetrator? I can't. I'd just leave.'

It was true. Antoine was visibly uncomfortable with the prospect of criticizing Blouenne and often tore into Eritrea for mistakes that clearly were not hers. But she did not mind. Blouenne, it seemed, understood the psychology of the situation well enough and showed it in her self-conscious movements around the bar counter when Eritrea had been subject to a vocal browbeating for something she had not done. There must be some family politics in this situation, she thought. Perhaps Antoine considered Blouenne's parents above him.

Fougère naturally exploited her favoured position to ensure that she and Blouenne were given the vast majority of the lunchtime shifts, which, despite the reduced tips, were far quieter and easier than the evenings. If one of the two French girls did work an evening shift, it was almost invariably a Monday or Tuesday. This was Serena's biggest bone of contention, even though Antoine saw to it that she and Eritrea had at least one Saturday evening off a month. This small gesture of his was the closest he ever came to saying, I am disappointed with the way my daughter acts. I wish she would find her own way in life. Eritrea knew that he sometimes thought it.

The clientele of the *Dame de Coeur* were the kind of pompous, pretentious folk that went to an extortionately priced restaurant with the sole aim of speaking another language in public. The menu was entirely in French, without an English translation, and customers looked at it down their nose, over-pronouncing the guttural 'r' in *fruits de mer*, so as to ensure their neighbours – who were doing exactly the same kind of thing – would hear. The wine list contained a number of popular quality wines alongside lesser-known and similarly priced but much poorer examples. Antoine was no fool. He had shrewdly assessed the class of the average punter and taken the gamble that they would be unable to tell the difference. When a French person actually came to the restaurant and asked for an explanation as to the exorbitant mark-up on a bottle of Costières de Nîmes, Antoine refused to come out of the kitchen.

On this particular Saturday in August, Eritrea had the luxury of working the lunchtime shift, with the added bonus of the rain, which guaranteed a quiet afternoon. Even so, she was feeling dejected, almost to the point of nausea. The soundtrack to her melancholy was the appallingly inevitable strains of an Edith Piaf record that leached from a speaker above her head like the sound of somebody being sick in a neighbouring toilet stall. There were only two CDs in the restaurant: a preposterous spoof of twirly-moustached onion-seller accordion music and the Edith Piaf. Antoine put one or the other on repeat play at the beginning of a shift, even before the doors were open to the customers, and, after a month of hearing them, Eritrea thought that she was going to go insane. It was aggressive noise pollution of the very worst kind – so bad, in fact, that Eritrea generously offered to furnish the restaurant with more music, out of her own pocket. Antoine interpreted this as some kind of veiled criticism and refused the offer.

Her shift finished at four-thirty. She walked home in the rain, unable to shake Edith Piaf from her head. She heard it as she dragged her feet up the stairs to the first-floor flat, as she kicked off her shoes, as she stood in the shower. It clashed with the theme of a glitzy early-evening game show that Lucy was half-watching from the kitchenette as she peeled an onion.

'It's a subtle form of mind control, I think,' Eritrea said, pouring herself an apple juice.

'Like that muzak in shopping malls that has subliminal messages telling you not to steal.'

'Yeah, except that this is like an insidious form of lobotomy that gradually wears you down to the point where you just do whatever Antoine wants, like a zombie.' Eritrea sat down in the living room. 'I hope that if I ever start coming home staring straight ahead and not answering questions, you'll tell me it's time I left.'

Lucy scraped the onion peel off the breadboard and into the bin under the kitchen sink. 'It's definitely time you left.'

They had lived in Swindon for a little over a year now, in the first-floor flat of a converted town house located near to the Magic Roundabout.

The Magic Roundabout was a confusing maze of several interconnected roundabouts that could only be described as a scandalous waste of public money. Not even long-term residents were a hundred per cent sure about the finer details of who had ultimate priority. As for tourists and foreigners, they were just plain stumped. There was a local joke that the cost of insurance claims from accidents caused by the roundabouts far exceeded the cost of designing and building the thing to start with. And the Magic Roundabout had to be a joke; but no, there was the road sign in green and white plainly indicating that it was coming up ahead. Drivers gripped their steering wheels in fearful anticipation as they drew near, steeling themselves to run the gauntlet.

The main entrance to the house led into a dark corridor ending in a staircase that served as a thoroughfare for all the residents. The front door of the flat occupied by Lucy and Eritrea opened into a windowless reception area with two doors off to the left, one directly ahead and one to the right. The two doors to the left led to two bedrooms that looked over the little square of garden owned by the couple downstairs. 'Think how guilty they must feel,' Lucy said, when they moved in. 'Whenever they have a barbecue they know that the other three sets of residents above can see them and smell the food and know they haven't been invited.'

The door opposite opened into a bathroom that was just a little too small, and the door to the right into a longish living room-cum-dining room looking over the main road, with a kitchenette squashed awkwardly in one corner. The pavement down below, outside the front of the house, was so narrow that when double-decker buses happened to get caught in queues and pull up opposite the window, the passengers on the top level would almost have been able to reach right into the girls' living room, were it not for the layers of glass separating them. Once, Lucy had been caught sitting topless on the sofa opposite the window when a bus drew up. It was not a mistake she had repeated. They put up a pair of muslin curtains that gave them a modest amount of privacy, while still letting in the light.

This was their second summer in the flat. Lucy had suggested that they move in together in June of the previous year, as soon as she got confirmation of her job. She had mentioned it half-jokingly, off the cuff, hardly expecting Eritrea to take her up on the offer, so had been somewhat taken aback when she had immediately started asking about the practicalities.

'But why would you want to leave home? They don't even ask you for board.'

'No, but if I don't get out now I never will. Anyway, I can get housing benefit, can't I?'

So, to Lucy's surprise, within a month of her first airing the idea they had moved. She started at the job centre in July, while Eritrea filled in forms for housing benefit and half-heartedly looked for part-time work.

Lucy worked weekdays nine to five as a client advisor helping people to find employment. The job fitted her character and temperament so well that after two weeks she wondered if she would ever have been able to do anything else. She sympathized profoundly with the vague, unmotivated twenty-somethings like Eritrea, who sat opposite her and shook their heads slowly as if in a stupor when she suggested what kind of work they could realistically expect to get with a degree in classics from Bath.

There were others, too: disillusioned but well-spoken executives who had been the victims of unexpected curtail-ment measures and were at pains to express the import of their many years of experience. It was almost touching how they continued doggedly to dress in their designer spun-wool suits, as if by doing so they could somehow claw back a shred of the dignity of their former occupation or cling on to the illusion of affluence. They addressed Lucy slowly, with slight chopping motions of the hand. They had had to talk to many unsympathetic whippersnappers who knew nothing of the reality of the mortgage payments they were facing.

Then there were hard-bitten, bearded travellers with worn standard-issue green army jackets, grey hooded tracksuit tops and faded jeans, who stared at Lucy with expressionless eyes and sighed through their nose at her, but usually said nothing at all.

When Eritrea got the job at the *Dame de Coeur* in January, she started seeing less of Lucy in the evenings. Previously, Eritrea had done the lion's share of the cooking. Now, if she had an evening shift she was usually out of the flat by five, before Lucy even arrived home.

Chapter 18

After the service proper had finished, Lucy sat alone in her chair and watched Eritrea cry while being prayed for. She could not hear what the counsellors were praying – their voices were masked by the general post-service chitchat and the sensitive choruses being played by the music group – but their eyes were screwed shut as they held their hands over Eritrea's shoulders and they nodded as they asserted the words of their prayers. The church was filled with the usual hubbub: parents exchanged weekly burdens energetically, somehow managing to ignore the children who tugged in vain at their sleeves, nearly falling over with the effort of pulling. Groups of teenagers stood together finalizing the evening's social agenda, interjecting periodically with comments like, 'I most certainly *did not*,' and making exaggerated expressions of incredulity as they stirred their tea. But through the pockets of social activity and the people sitting with their elbows on the backs of chairs, Lucy watched Eritrea. It was heart-rending for her to see her best friend crying again.

Recently, Eritrea had been going forward for prayer fairly frequently and almost invariably ended up in tears. And they were not tears of joy. One time, Lucy herself had been involved, against her better judgement, in the praying, and had stood next to Eritrea as she cried the kind of fraught, painful tears that make the head throb after only a moment of crying – the kind of tears Lucy understood well. Now, Lucy observed the way Eritrea's body hunched in anguish and she could barely keep from crying herself.

As they left the church building, Eritrea wiped her eyes on her sleeve. The brilliant midday sun had dried out the previous day's rain except around the cracks and joins in the paving stones, where the concrete was still dark. In the glaring light Eritrea's face looked blotched, and her eyes were bloodshot and swollen.

'Eritrea –' Lucy said, gently.

'I'm fine,' she replied, swallowing. 'People must think I'm quite pathetic though.'

'They don't think anything of the sort.' She wanted to add, I'm worried for you, but she said nothing. Something told her that Eritrea did not want to be burdened with the pressure of having to reassure her friend that she was all right.

As they walked slowly back to the flat, the few people they passed, instantly noticing the telltale signs of Eritrea's tears, seemed to shrink into the pavement in their efforts to communicate self-effacing unawareness. Eritrea appeared not to mind that she could be seen like this. Lucy thought, if only we could be at Glenfield now.

When they had moved, she had suggested making the journey back to Glenfield. 'It's not far,' she had said to Eritrea. 'Only twenty minutes by car. And the traffic's not bad on a Sunday morning, either.'

But, oddly, Eritrea had not been keen. 'I'd like to try one of the churches here,' she had said. 'I honestly don't want to stop you from going if you want to, but I just think it's time for me to move on.'

It seemed strange that Eritrea should want to leave behind what they had at Glenfield. But, when she thought about it, Lucy realized that it must be even harder for Eritrea than it was for her to go there and remember Jonah, to see him in everything and everyone; reflected in the faces of the people there. There had been, and still was, so much love and kindness at Glenfield towards the Trent family following the tragedy. As she thought about it, it occurred to Lucy that perhaps even the best-intentioned sympathy was wearing for Eritrea. Perhaps she wants to be in a place where she has no history, she thought. Really, I have no idea of what it must be like for her.

Lucy did make the trip back to Glenfield every now and then; she missed the ease of being around Joanne and the other people with whom she had grown up. Most of the time, though, she accompanied Eritrea to the local church she had settled on in Swindon – not the church Paul and Rowena had attended, to their obvious disappointment. But it was not a bad solution, and Lucy being Lucy had quickly ensured that they established a niche there. However, at times like this when Eritrea was sad, Lucy wished she would agree to go back to Glenfield and just let herself receive the love and care only available from those who had some idea of what she had suffered.

They ate lunch together, as Eritrea was doing the evening shift at the restaurant.

Sometimes, when they sat in silence like this, Lucy longed for them to be able to talk about Jonah again, as they had done at the beginning when Eritrea had come back to faith. But it had been a long time now since Eritrea had broached the subject and Lucy simply did not feel that she had the right to do so, even though she was sure it was the cause of Eritrea's sadness.

After the meal, she stood washing the dishes and felt completely helpless. More than anything she wanted to help Eritrea, but as familiarity with another person gradually demarcates the boundaries that you may not cross in your interrelation with them, so the time they had spent together prevented her now from being able to do anything more than say, I am here for you.

When Eritrea had left for the restaurant, Lucy prayed for her. She knelt by her bed with her face in her hands. 'What can I do for her?' she supplicated. 'How can I help her?' But she had been thinking about the situation so much that afternoon that her thoughts were all jumbled and confused. A solitary car drove down the path beyond the back garden and turned off on to the main road. She buried her head in the duvet cover. It smelled musty; too much like skin and too little like detergent. When did I last wash it? Her thoughts wandered until she came to thinking about whether she could fit the whole duvet into the drum of the washing machine. 'I'm sorry, Lord. I just can't concentrate. Please help me to keep my mind focused on you.'

She got up and sat on the bed, and half-prayed, half-thought, about Eritrea. The thought that kept playing over and over at the back of her mind was: What can I do for her, Father? After a while, she opened her eyes and slipped off the bed. She walked to the window and looked out at the empty garden below. In her head there was an answer of sorts, but it was not the kind of answer for which she was looking.

When Lucy had originally made the decision to start walking in the Spirit, she had found it hard to discern between the intuitive voice of the Holy Spirit and the other voices that crowded her mind and suggested any number of things: she had sometimes gone up to complete strangers in fear and trembling and asked them if their name was such-and-such, out of a desire to do what she thought the Spirit might be telling her to do. Eventually, she had received teaching from wiser people on how such leadings were often from the soul, or elsewhere. 'In some cases,' Judith had said, 'people who open themselves up to the leading of the Spirit allow themselves instead to be led by lying spirits who set themselves up as the Holy Spirit and who start telling them to do all kinds of ridiculous things.'

'But how could God let anyone who truly desires to live by the Spirit be led astray?' Lucy asked.

'You know the passage, "the sheep follow him, for they know his voice",' Judith said. 'And why would Jesus have told his disciples not to be deceived if there was no chance that they could be? People have done some very foolish and destructive things, sincerely believing that the Lord Himself had asked them to do them.' Lucy remembered the way Judith raised her eyebrows and turned up her palms in the semblance of a sardonic shrug. 'You know that. I've heard of Christians going up to people and telling them things about so-called secrets in their lives that were blatantly wrong "in the name of the Lord". It's even happened to me before.'

'What did you do? I mean, what do you do when that happens?'

'People these days seem to get so little good teaching on prophecy and words of knowledge and stuff like that. A lot of false words come about because people who've been convicted by God about a particular thing in their own lives can't handle it, so they go and project it on to other people instead of taking it on board themselves. They go around like a bull in a china shop ordering people to do or change things that actually *they* should be dealing with. Even if there's a hint of truth in what they say, they often don't realize that God doesn't usually give people words that will ultimately be anything other than a confirmation to those they're intended for. When people come up to me and tell me about problems or issues I'm supposed to be struggling with, I pray about them and if, in all sincerity before the Lord, they don't seem right – or even have the tiniest potential to be right – I just discard them. And if I'm wrong and I should've listened and the Lord wants me to take what I was told on board, or whatever, he'll tell me again clearly enough.' She laughed. 'Life's too short to fret over some of the nonsense that people put forward as prophetic knowledge. There are some "words" that you can ignore outright. The classic one is when a man tells a woman that the Lord's ordering her to marry him.'

'But what about really borderline things that might be right, but you just don't know? You know, when it seems so right but you're not a hundred per cent sure and you wind up agonizing over it?'

'It's all about peace. If you're living in the peace that the Spirit gives, you learn to see when a thing that a person brings to you is not of the same Spirit. It just takes away your peace. So, if someone comes to you with a word or something, and you're not right with the Lord or with another person, the first thing you have to do is to pray and ask forgiveness for whatever it is that's not right, or go up to the person you've argued with or whatever, and sort things out with them, to get back the peace. Then, when you have the peace again you can concentrate on praying for discernment about the word you've been given. I mean, how can someone seriously expect the Lord to give them discernment in one thing if they're holding out against Him in another, much more serious area? And this is my point. I believe Jesus lets us hear ridiculous words. He wants us to get better at hearing him and knowing the difference between His voice and other voices, so that we can be more discerning. Never underestimate how He uses anything and everything for our own good, to help us mature in the faith.' She considered. 'Take the example I just gave you. God might allow someone to hear a false word simply because He knew that they'd go and sort out something far more serious in order to get back the peace to discern the truth about the word – which might be something completely inconsequential, by the way.'

'But what about giving words to other people? Sometimes I just don't know if I'm hearing from God, or whether it's just coming from me. I hate the thought that I might go around doing and saying things that hurt and confuse people.' She thought. 'Or being Satan's agent.'

Judith laughed. 'Well. That's the thing, isn't it? But first and foremost, you shouldn't worry about it. You shouldn't worry about anything, actually. That's Biblical too, you know. Just keep praying for discernment. With time, you get to know the difference between what the Lord tells you in your spirit and the sudden, insistent must-do-it-now-or-else *commands* –' she stressed the word carefully – 'that come from other... sources. Often a sign that it's not from the Lord is that there's some kind of do it "or else" feeling attached. Good grief, the devil just *longs* to set himself up as a counterfeit Holy Spirit in our lives, telling us to do all kinds of things – not just giving words to other people – and hauling us over the coals if we don't. It's a sure-fire way to know what the source of a word is: God uses conviction, but the devil uses condemnation. If there's this feeling that you should feel guilty for not doing something or telling a person a thing then I think you can safely say that it's not of God.'

'So how do I know when it *is* God?'

'The peace. Always the peace that passes all understanding. I've made stacks of mistakes, I admit. There've been times when God clearly asked me to do something that I didn't do, and then the opportunity just passed me by. Afterwards, I just had in me a certainty that I'd missed an opportunity – but no guilt. And knowing that made me all the more dedicated to making sure I obeyed the next time. You see the difference?

Firm conviction and a clear direction – you know, to obey the next time – rather than a sense of raging guilt and a voice telling you that you failed God and let him down.'

'The accuser,' Lucy thought out loud.

'Exactly,' Judith answered. 'So many people don't know that very basic truth and crawl around for years under the weight of burdens that they should have done a million and one things that God never asked them to do. The devil is such an opportunist and if we let ourselves get taken in he'll just load up that yoke with guilt and more guilt. Do you see?'

'I think so.'

She thought she saw now; she had been leaning with her face pressed up against the window. Now when she pulled back she saw that her nose had left a greasy mark on the glass. She didn't feel any guilt about possibly not doing the thing she thought the Lord was asking her to do. It was just a rather strange thing – the kind of thing that seemed to be in the same league as going up to someone in the street and trying to discern their name. But this thing would not hurt Eritrea. How could it? There were no other ramifications for anybody else. And it wasn't even a word. It was just strange. Well, she thought. I'll wait until tomorrow and if I have the same peace, I'll do it.

On Monday afternoon, Lucy returned from work later than normal. She found Eritrea in the bathroom in her waitress gear, hurriedly putting on makeup in front of the mirror and clattering the makeup bottles against the sink in her rush. The door to the bathroom was wide open and the air was thick with shower and conditioner.

'Where've you been?' Eritrea said, not looking round. The voice sounded like a ventriloquist's: her lips were stretched slightly over her upper teeth as she painted a dark line around them. 'Careful,' she said, motioning briefly with the lip-liner pencil when Lucy made as if to step into the bathroom. 'Floor's soaking wet.'

'I brought you something,' Lucy said cautiously, standing conscientiously on the hall side of the threshold and showing Eritrea a straggly little posy.

'That's nice,' she said, barely looking round. 'What is it?'

'Jasmine,' Lucy said.

'Oh. Thanks. I've got to rush. My shift started, like, five minutes ago. Could you put it in some water?'

'Okay.'

Eritrea stepped back to examine herself. She seemed almost satisfied, but then noticed a spot on her shirt. 'How could there be food on it?' she groaned. 'I just put it on and it's already stained. This is so typical.' She whirled around and yanked the toilet roll, which spun round unravelling accordion layers of tissue on to the floor. She blew out of her mouth angrily as she wet a wad under the hot tap. 'So typical. Sooo typical.'

Lucy retreated into the kitchen with the flowers. She placed them on the sideboard by the sink and ran the water. She opened cupboards looking for a vase, but there did not seem to be anything small enough to house them comfortably. Eventually, she decided to put them in a glass. Eritrea could still be heard muttering under her breath, rushing from the bathroom to her bedroom, zipping her bag closed, swiping at her keys. 'My black shoes!' The voice was frantic. 'Where are my black court shoes?'

Evidently they were quickly found, as, a moment later, she was pulling the apartment door closed with her foot. It slammed loudly. The stressed-out din around her followed her like a cloud as she ran down the stairs two at a time, out of the front door of the house – another loud slam – and down the street, her heels clicking loudly with the stressful rhythm of late-for-work-again.

The commotion followed her around the corner of the street, and an almost surreal silence enveloped Lucy, who stood stock still in front of the sink, the cold tap still running. She turned it off distractedly and put the glass of flowers on the dining table. The tendrils looked sinewy and ugly in an untidy sort of way; not the kind of flowers one would give to another person as a gift. She stood and looked at them for a while, her head full of conflicting thoughts. Eventually, she left the room, leaving the door ajar behind her.

Eritrea came back after midnight, legs aching dully and feet burning with the kind of heat that can only be generated by an evening of striding back and forth from kitchen to table, wearing tights and shoes, in a restaurant with inadequate air conditioning on a summer evening. She let her bag slip from her shoulder on to the hallway floor and kicked off her shoes as she walked into the living room to wind down for a few minutes before going to bed. The air was close – Lucy had forgotten to open the window again – but it was permeated with a faint, heady aroma that grew stronger in the living room. Eritrea had intended to fling herself down on to the sofa, in a manner befitting the end of a desperately tedious evening of work, but instead she sat down slowly, somewhat warily. The muslin curtains of the window looking out over the road were open and the street lamps glowed a dull yellow. She sat back on the sofa and watched the dining room table for a while. Then she stood up purposefully, strode over to the table and breathed in the fragrance of the jasmine. It was sweet, almost nauseatingly so.

In the early hours of the morning Lucy woke up and reached over to her bedside table to pick up a cup that wasn't there. You only ever want a drink of water in the night when you've forgotten to take any to bed with you, she thought hazily, padding to the living room. Most days your bedside is cluttered up with day-old water, but when you actually want some... She stood over the sink, running litres of lukewarm summer water over her hand and down the drain before it cooled sufficiently to satisfy her. She had run herself a glass, downed it and was already making her way back to bed before she noticed Eritrea sitting, silent as stone, on the settee, shrouded in shadow and still in her waitress outfit. It was the way her eyes shone like black glass in the reflection from the window that made Lucy stop in her tracks, the fog of sleep instantly evaporating from her brain. 'Are you okay?'

'Yes.'

'It must be two o'clock.' Lucy looked up at the clock, but in the darkness it was hard to see the hands. 'How long have you been sitting here?'

No answer.

'What is it?' Lucy pulled her nightshirt around her legs and sat down next to Eritrea.

'I don't know.'

'Something happened at work?'

'No.'

'You're worrying me. Please tell me what's wrong.' She sat exaggeratedly attentive, the way people do when waiting for a response. None was forthcoming. Eventually, Lucy's body folded back into the settee and her muscles relaxed.

After an eternity, Eritrea said, 'Will you take the flowers away?' She breathed it in a whisper, so faint that Lucy barely heard the words.

'You don't like them? I mean, they're nothing to look at, but they smell okay, don't they?'

'It's not that. They're beautiful.'

Lucy waited.

'Will you take them away for me?'

'Of course.' She touched Eritrea's knee. 'Have I hurt you?' She was deeply troubled. 'I would never have wanted to upset you. Not in a million years.'

Eritrea shook her head.

Lucy stood up, her heart twisting with worry, went back into her room and pulled on a pair of jeans. She took the glass with the jasmine in it and emptied the water down the sink. Then she took the flowers, opened the apartment door and went down the stairs. Outside the front door, she opened the lid of the bin and laid the jasmine gently on top of a black rubbish sack. Back inside the flat, she looked round the living room door. 'They're gone,' she said to Eritrea, feeling confused and guilty. Eritrea still sat in the same position she had been in when Lucy had first entered. The smell of the jasmine still lingered in the air and Lucy was at a loss as to what to do. She stood for a while in the doorway. Eritrea neither moved, nor offered any explanation. Lucy sensed that she should leave her alone. She retreated silently, pulling her bedroom door to behind her.

Chapter 19

On Tuesday afternoon Lucy arrived home weary, with a head full of forms and brown postage-paid envelopes. Inside her was the semi-hopeless feeling of knowing there are still three long days to surmount before the weekend.

Her routine was first to wash the invisible residue of the second-hand human contact of the office, its plastic drawer and door handles, from her hands. This done, she shed her work clothes. The white shirt had a faint cream line, like a tiny screen-printed border, around the inside of the collar, where the sweat from her neck had soaked into the creased fabric. In the winter, a work shirt might last three days. This one she folded up and put by her door to take to the laundry basket in the bathroom.

She slipped on her most comfortable cotton tracksuit bottoms and a baggy T-shirt. As she trailed towards the kitchen to get a glass of something cold, she was almost beginning to feel human again.

Opening the door of the fridge, she took out a carton of juice. It only had half a glass's worth left in it, so she drank the dregs straight from the carton before flattening it and slotting it into a space down the side of the packed bin. The flat was quiet, but not, she sensed, in the way it would be if it were empty. 'Eri?' she called, tentatively.

Glancing into the hallway, she saw that the door of her flatmate's bedroom was closed. 'Eritrea?'

She went to the door and stood outside it with her hand raised, considering whether to knock. 'Are you in there?'

She waited a moment before turning the handle.

Eritrea lay, curled up in bed, her knees hunched up under the duvet, looking at the door.

Lucy stood opposite her. 'I didn't mean to come in without knocking...' It was a question really, but it was left unanswered. She formulated it better: 'Have you been in bed all day?'

'Yes.'

'Didn't you have a lunchtime shift today?'

'Yes.'

'But you didn't go.'

'No.'

Lucy perched cautiously on the edge of the bed. Eritrea shifted her legs slightly – with effort – to accommodate her. 'Can you call Antoine and tell him I'm sorry I couldn't make it?'

'You couldn't call him yourself?' She meant earlier in the day, before the missed shift.

Eritrea shook her head.

'What do I tell him? He'll want an explanation.'

'I don't know.'

'Are you ill? Have you got 'flu?'

'Yes,' Eritrea said, after a time. 'Tell him that, will you?'

She lay still, as though cast in a mould, and listened to the telephone conversation from the hall.

'No, she's been in bed all day,' Lucy said. 'She's not herself at all.'

After this came a period of quiet where Antoine would be venting his wrath. Somehow, the silence of Lucy's listening ear sounded worse than the angry words themselves might have done. It seemed an age before Lucy answered, 'No, she won't be able to make it in tomorrow either.'

There followed another pause. Eritrea thought vaguely about the pedantic workings of Antoine's mind, how any kind of disruption to his carefully planned routines was anathema to him. Lucy said, 'She hasn't missed a shift before, as far as I know.'

It touched Eritrea to hear Lucy defend her. He might well fire me, she thought. But she didn't care.

After putting the phone back on the hook, Lucy went into Eritrea's room. She did not mention the conversation. She did not even bring any of the displaced traces of Antoine's stress into the room: Eritrea loved this about her.

'Can I get you anything?'

'Honestly, I'm all right.'

As Lucy left the room her own words came to accuse her from the past. Satan's agent, they sounded hollowly in her head. You are Satan's agent.

★

There is something in the wretchedness of lying in bed alone on a hot summer's day that suffocates the heart, especially the morning after a sleepless night. At seven o'clock come the first, disjointed sounds of human activity: the rumble and grind of a rubbish lorry and the scrape of plastic bins, pierced at intervals by the curious, impenetrable calls in the workers' dialect. This is followed by the swelling crescendo of commuter traffic and pairs of feet on the pavement. Then there is a period of relative calm, disrupted periodically by the irregular scuffle and tap of someone half-walking, half-running in high heels. By now, the closed curtains can hardly withstand the blazing inevitability of the day outside.

At ten or eleven, Eritrea lay in bed and looked at the bubbles against the side of the glass of water that Lucy had placed on the bedside table the previous evening. The sheets were damp and creased as they can only be when they have been occupied for two solid days. Despite the growing heat outside, her feet were cold and the spaces between her toes wet with old perspiration. Other people were going about their important business: showered and dressed, with their hair done and makeup on, and engaged in the day's activities with the natural purpose born out of daily routine. Soon they would be having lunch with their friends and discussing the trip to the coast for a long weekend of sand and suntan lotion and salty evenings walking along the promenade. And here am I, thought Eritrea. I shall never get out of bed. I shall stay here forever. She had thought briefly about rising, but the spirit within her died at the thought: all physical energy drained out of her. It required a gargantuan effort of will to summon the strength into her legs even to go into the bathroom. She caught a glimpse of herself in the mirror during one such visit, even though she tried to keep her eyes to the floor. It can't be me, she thought. The hair was limp and dead, the face drawn and tired.

When Lucy came back to find Eritrea still in bed, she was afraid. 'You must eat something.'

'No. Please.'

'I'll tell you what,' Lucy said. 'I'll make you up a tray, then you see what you think. Okay?'

The tray, when it came, had the trademarks of concern written all over it: lightly buttered toast and a carefully boiled egg, apple juice and tea. 'Oh Lucy,' Eritrea said, 'you shouldn't have.' But she made no effort to sit up in bed, as Lucy tried to fit the tray on the bedside table, next to the water.

'Try and eat something. For me.'

'I'll try.'

When Lucy came back in, the tray was untouched except for the tea. She didn't pick it up at first, but looked at it as she sat down on the bed. 'Eritrea.'

'Hmm?'

Lucy smoothed out a crease in the duvet. 'I've been thinking and I was... I just thought that you might be able to go and see Judith. That she might be able to help you.'

Eritrea looked at Lucy dismayed, her face pale as a candle. 'Oh I couldn't do that.'

'She's a good person.'

'I couldn't. I just couldn't.'

'Listen. I've got most of tomorrow afternoon off. I could drive you over to Marlborough at two-ish. I don't want to pressure you. I don't even have to tell you that.'

'I know.'

On Thursday, when Eritrea showered, she felt as though her pelvic bones were sticking out like sharp edges, trying to pierce her skin. She crawled down the stairs behind Lucy, clutching the banister like an invalid.

When they sat in the car outside Judith's house, Eritrea said quietly, 'I don't know if I can go through with this.'

'I'm eating with my parents this evening.' Lucy tried to keep the anxiety out of her voice. 'Call me there whenever and I'll come and pick you up.'

'They don't know I'm coming here, do they?'

'I haven't told anyone, you know that.'

Eritrea got out of the car, pushing the door to. It clicked but did not shut properly. She had asked Lucy the previous evening not to call Judith to say that she would be coming. She had prayed a prayer: Lord if it is not right for me to see her, then don't let her be in. It was a feeble, pathetic prayer, but it was all she could manage. She walked down the path towards the front door, more afraid perhaps than she had ever been. Lucy would still be waiting in the car. She could still turn back. She reached up cautiously and rang the bell. Then something truly terrible dawned on her and she froze. But it was too late.

Judith came to the door, wiping her hands on a tea towel. Her demeanour was one of a person wrapped up in humdrum daily activity. 'Hello Eritrea.' She said it almost as though she was expected.

'Is my mother here?' Eritrea whispered.

'No. Should she be?'

Eritrea shook her head. 'No.'

Judith did not say, were you looking for her? or some other similar thing. Instead, she put the towel over her shoulder. 'Come on in.'

Eritrea followed her down the corridor. 'I've been baking, amazingly enough,' Judith said easily over her shoulder. 'Phillip always goes on about how much money we waste on bread. So I said, "If you're so concerned about it make some yourself." So he did.' She placed the towel on the sideboard. 'And it was a complete disaster. Tea?'

Eritrea fought back the fear that clawed around her tonsils as the water boiled. Judith swilled out the pot with water from the kettle and put three teabags into it. She put the kettle back on to boil and filled the pot when it clicked off again. Her movements were instinctive, unthinking; rounded and smooth like a pebble from a beach. 'Sugar?'

'No. Thank you.'

Only when they were sitting in the lounge did Judith say, 'Well, what can I do for you?'

There was no way for Eritrea to build up to it slowly. I have come this far, she thought. Surely I can go a little further. 'Judith,' she said. 'You must think it's odd of me to come here out of the blue, without calling you or anything. Actually –' she stared at the film of tea at the bottom of the cup – 'it was Lucy who put me up to it. But I knew anyway that you might be the only person who could help me. You knew him so well, you know, and I thought you'd probably understand better than... I mean I couldn't tell mum or dad...' She cut herself off: she was paddling round in a circle with one oar.

Judith sat patiently, not interrupting.

Eritrea had been cradling the warm teacup in her hands. Now she put it on the floor and breathed in. 'When I first heard that Jo died, I thought it was suicide.' She stared at the cup on the floor for a long while.

'But you knew it wasn't,' Judith said eventually.

'Later, yes. But not at first. Not right at the beginning. I... dropped the phone and it broke. I only heard that he was dead.'

Judith waited.

'There used to be a tree at the bottom of our garden, that we played in when we were young. But it got waterlogged in the storms one year and couldn't hold its own weight and it fell down. We were about thirteen, I think.'

'What made you think about it?' Judith asked.

'Jasmine,' Eritrea answered. The corners of her mouth turned down, against her will. 'Jasmine.'

Chapter 20

When the Trents first met Nigel Stephens, he was already spinning out of control. Though he still inhabited his physical body, his mind and soul were almost fully immersed in the absolute misery of personal hell, although he was too blind to see it that way.

When an inexperienced skier stands at the top of a ski lift and consciously decides to go down the black run, he is fully aware of what he is letting himself in for. He knows how steep and dangerous it will be because he has been warned by the sign. As he skis down the slope, each turn he commits to increases his speed, until he is literally flying down so fast that it is no longer possible for him to stop.

This is how it was with Nigel.

In his mid-twenties he had made a Christian commitment and walked in it for a while. As with all Christians, the devil was waiting and biding his time to find and take advantage of a weakness in Nigel and draw him away from the faith. He did not attack right away, while Nigel was still in the honeymoon period of his faith; rather, he was patient and hovered in the fringes until the right set of circumstances came together and Nigel was at his weakest and most likely to succumb to temptation.

About five years after coming to faith, Nigel was living alone in Marlborough. He had originally been going to St Peter's for pretty much the same reasons that had motivated Paul Trent, but unlike Paul, he was a bachelor. Though he desired with all his heart to be the catalyst that brought about lasting spiritual change in the church, he was working and praying for it alone, without support – prayer or otherwise – from anyone. Over time he became very lonely.

In the days he worked as a caretaker and odd-job man in an office building, but it was hardly the kind of work that enabled him to meet many people, let alone develop friendships. Although there was another caretaker, as well as an electrician and a plumber, in the service of the firm, Nigel had gone too far too soon in sharing his Christianity with them, so they treated him with open disdain and gradually closed him out of the circle of their social interaction. The enormous amount of free time that he had outside working hours was the plain physical proof of his loneliness. It depressed him to the point that he decided to throw himself into all kinds of activity. At St Peter's he was already doing the Sunday school and sat on the Parochial Church Council but he decided additionally to involve himself, two nights a week, in voluntary work at the local private hospital, visiting people – some perhaps lonelier than himself – who were ill or dying. Though his original motive for doing this had been quite honourable, it was ironically through Nigel's friendship with a contact at the hospital that the devil saw his opportunity and seized it.

Roger was ninety-seven years old when he died. Like a number of the people receiving treatment, he was very wealthy and subject to various parasitical relatives who were becoming impatient with the consequences of his longevity, especially those of his medical bills. Sometimes Nigel would arrive when an elderly cousin or middle-aged niece was in the room with him, clasping his hand and giving him insincere advice about keeping warm, or suchlike. They looked at Nigel through narrowed eyes, trying to assess how far his intentions in this friendship were purely financial. 'I hate talking to them,' Roger coughed when they had gone. 'They should issue a restraining order on anyone who's looking purely to diddle me out of my possessions. Just because I'm a relic doesn't mean that I'm stupid.' More than anything else, he wanted to go home. 'Ah, at home I had satellite television in my room and I could watch the football, and I'd told the nurse not to open the door to scrounging family members...'

'I love football,' Nigel said.

It was a throwaway comment – the kind of meaningless remark a person makes when they want simply to acquiesce with someone, to indicate that they're listening. He said similar things to other patients all the time, and he was no great fan of football either.

When Roger passed away and his hospital room was cleaned and tidied with the practised, almost callous, efficiency that removes all trace of the deceased as though they had never existed, Nigel received a phone call from one of the relatives. It shocked him out of his skin to hear the telephone ring and he had no idea who it could be. 'He left you the satellite dish and the receiver, so you'd better come and pick them up if you want them.' She said this in a condescending, supercilious way, as if saying, ha, if you thought you were going to get cash, you're quite mistaken.

After he had put down the phone, the Holy Spirit said to him, call this woman back and tell her that you don't want it. The advice was so clear that Nigel even picked up the receiver, to dial the call-back number, but after holding it in his hand for a while he put it down. And made his decision.

'He had some kind of annual subscription,' the relative said when Nigel dropped by at Roger's house. 'Complete waste of money of course. Never even watched the thing.'

'It's very kind of him,' Nigel replied courteously.

'Well I'm just pleased we can get rid of it,' she said in a tone that sounded anything but. 'I hate all this new technology. I can't even work the video on my own, so if you hadn't wanted this we'd have had to throw it away, or something.'

Or sell it, Nigel thought.

The satellite system came with a card for decoding the scrambled football broadcasts. There were no instructions, so Nigel had to set up a system of mirrors around the house that reflected the television screen from where he stood on his roof waving the dish around to try to find the signal. Satellite television was still relatively state of the art, so there was only one other household on the street with a dish to give Nigel some idea of what direction to point it in. When he finally managed to get it working one weekday night he found that only five or so channels were tuned in, although the receiver had a memory function to store one hundred and fifty. He had no idea how to operate the remote control so he cut his losses, left it and went to bed.

For a while Nigel contented himself with watching the few non sport channels already tuned in, when he came in from work. But then, late one evening as he was flicking through the other channels, he saw through the snowy interference that there were potentially many more not properly tuned in. He set about trying to fathom the remote control and after a few minutes managed to work out how to get it to tune the channels.

He had tuned about ten – mostly foreign news and the like – before he came up against one that had a scrambled screen and a white on black message instructing him to insert a card. Again, in his heart he heard a clear, almost audible, warning from the Holy Spirit, but he rose from his chair and picked up the card that had come with the equipment from where it was lying on top of the tuner. When he inserted it, the picture unscrambled and something like a shot of energy passed through him. He sat down and watched for a moment while his pulse quickened and his hands began to quiver. Then he thought, oh my goodness what am I doing, and switched it off altogether. He got out of his chair to make a drink and vaguely self-righteous thoughts like, of course I'll have to make sure I don't watch any more of *that*, ran through his head.

He drank his tea watching the blank grey screen and not really thinking anything any more. And in his state of not-thinking, he picked up the remote control and switched it back on to that same channel. He watched for ten minutes or so. Then, another thought dawned on him. What if there were other similar channels that could be accessed with this card? The same shot of energy passed through him with the thought. Soon, he had found and reorganized four such channels so that they were next to each other and he could flick between them.

When he finally rose, he was surprised to notice that it was past two in the morning; he could not remember the last time he had turned in so late. He went to the bathroom.

Afterwards in bed, he thought, gosh I never go to bed this late, but underneath was a kind of constricting revulsion. He fought it down.

The next day, after work, he was on hospital duty and did not arrive home until ten-thirty. He made his supper slowly and deliberately, spreading the butter evenly on the toast, stirring the soup with a flat spatula to keep it from burning on the bottom of the pan. But his hands were trembling with an unfamiliar, though not altogether unpleasant, excitement, and only one thought was in his head.

The following evening was free and he was prepared. On arriving home, he removed the card from its slot in the tuner and put it in the kitchen dustbin. He went upstairs to his bedroom, sat on the bed and prayed. 'Father,' he said, 'forgive me for what I have done. I'm so ashamed of myself. I hate myself for giving in to these feelings. I feel so weak for giving in to them. Please help me to stand firm and not let myself give in any more.' He prayed earnestly for almost an hour and then stayed on the bed thinking things through. In his post-prayer state of near clarity, the Spirit spoke to him again, saying, it is still not too late. Go up to the roof now, take down the dish and destroy it. The alternative is far worse.

But Nigel thought, destroy the dish? How could I do that? It's an expensive piece of equipment. It would be wrong to smash it up. It would be... it would be bad stewardship. It would be ungrateful to the memory of Roger's kindness. Yes, that's what it would be.

Then, shortly afterwards, he went back downstairs and fished the card out of the bin. It had some banana slime on the magnetic strip, which he rubbed down carefully with a damp cloth before putting it back into its slot.

The Holy Spirit did not give up on Nigel despite his disobedience. When the Trents arrived at St Peter's a year later, Nigel knew, after his first conversation with Paul, that here was a person, if there was anyone, with whom he could share his problem. By this time, he was like the skier careering out of control, hardly able to turn from his downhill course.

He had renewed the subscription for the card a few months previously, and had taken the opportunity to subscribe to other channels, too – the kind that were generally advertised by word of mouth because no satellite magazine would willingly house written advertisements for them.

He lived, almost literally, in hell. He existed through the day with a gradual escalating anticipation of the moment in the evening when broadcasting began. He sat up until three or four in the morning glued to the screen and then rose, the sweat cold on his body and his head spinning with fatigue, and dragged himself to bed. When he fell asleep, he saw nothing but degrading picture after degrading picture of human bodies. But worst of all was the feeling of utter desolation that greeted him when he awoke in the morning. In all of his life he had never, ever, felt so bad. The feeling was like a physical wound that festered on him and crippled him; like a poisonous compound of the worst guilt, self-loathing, uselessness and emptiness that he thought it was possible for a human to be subject to.

Nigel's life became one of complete contrasts. When, in the evenings, he was drawn to start watching, the desire in him was by then so urgent and so overwhelming that it blotted out everything else, especially rational thoughts about how he would feel the following morning. In the morning, without fail, he was subject to exactly the same heartache and pain. Every single day. He felt as if his body was inhabited by two different people: a morning person who stood on and watched broken-hearted and dismayed, and a night person who wanted pleasure and fulfilment whatever the cost. This night person drank and drank from the cup of lust but, over time, and like an alcoholic, was unable to feel assuaged and had to move on to something stronger. He was not even overly surprised to notice that he had begun to feel attraction to men. And why not? By dint of the sheer volume of debasing material he had viewed, it now seemed quite normal.

He was like a zombie at work, going through the motions as the morning guilt and turmoil started to give way, at lunchtime, to the nagging desire for more. At the weekends he slept all day Saturday, which he was thankful for because it enabled him to recover just enough composure to get through the Sunday morning act.

One night, he had a dream of hell. Not the hell he lived in on earth, but the real eternal hell with all its horrifying dead-end finality. In the dream, he was in a kind of subterranean cavern with many chambers and walls that glowed blood-red. The chambers were filled with naked humans who went from one room to the other satisfying themselves with anyone they chose. There were also grossly distorted forms with additional bodily organs where naturally there should be none, involved in the sexual acts. But there was a horrible, fearful urgency in the humans, born out of the eternal knowledge that they had this, but nothing else. In every cavern room the people knew that they could only fundamentally receive the fulfilment they needed through Jesus, but that it was truly too late to do anything about it.

When Nigel woke up, he was physically sick.

He stepped up his efforts to extricate himself from the self-perpetuating lifestyle. He even managed, in his own strength, to go a few nights without watching, but the desire for satisfaction grew and grew until it raged like a fire within him. He became hypersensitive to the tiniest of stimuli. When he saw so much as a woman in a bikini in a breakfast cereal advert, it sent his heart rate into overdrive. In shops he was painfully aware of the top-shelf magazines. He could not even look at a woman – any woman – without undressing her and fantasizing. Defeated and compromised, he went back to the pornography.

It was at this point that he considered telling Paul about his addiction. The Holy Spirit used what little was left in him that could listen to truth to urge him to do so, saying, look, your accountability to them could be a wonderfully precious thing, like a diamond. He had a vague understanding that fellowship with the Trents was something that God was offering him as a lifeline, which he could grab on to and receive the help he needed to get out of the hole he was in. He knew that his old excuse of being lonely as a reason for indulging in the habit was, through the prayer meetings, nullified now that the Trents were reaching out a hand of friendship. But alongside that knowledge was the soul-deep embarrassment of having to come clean about the reality of his life, the horrible lurid details. Would Paul consent to have him as a friend, knowing the truth? He thought, it doesn't matter. I can take that. The embarrassment is better than the pain. But then a voice said to him, ah but can you take living without the pleasure?

He considered it. The reality of having to live a life without the pornography was so fearful to him, it almost prevented him from being able to think straight. He decided not to speak to Paul just yet, and shortly afterwards decided to leave the Parochial Church Council too. At this point, the night person began to win out, as it must with so many conscious decisions to satisfy it.

Jonah and Eritrea had been going to Sunday school for quite some time when Nigel made this final decision, and, in so doing, took the hot iron to his own conscience and seared it. But it was a few months before the thing he had nurtured within himself started to demand more.

He was very friendly to the twins always – as he was to everybody – but underneath the outer crust of friendliness a part of him was scheming. He tried with all his strength to shut the thoughts out of his head, but they ran over and over like a running river, a constant stream of suggestions at the back of his mind.

As a friend of the family, he had been fairly tactile with them from the beginning, putting his hand on their shoulders or ruffling their hair, but after a month or two of teaching them at Sunday school he decided to nudge things on a stage.

One Sunday, when they were the only two there, Eritrea noticed that he had another bag by the table. Normally he had only one bag with him – the shoulder bag that he used for carrying the papers and pens for the morning's activities. She was naturally curious and asked him, 'Nigel, what's in that bag?'

'Ah, now that's a surprise,' he answered mysteriously.

'Show us,' Jonah said. 'Go on.'

Nigel put his head on one side and smiled. 'If I were to show you now, then it wouldn't be a surprise, would it?'

He taught them the morning's lesson, knowing all the while that they were burning up with curiosity. Abel Thacker's sermon lasted twenty-five minutes almost to the second, so with five minutes to spare he wound up – they weren't listening anyway – and said, 'Let's have a look at what's in the bag, shall we?'

He unclipped it slowly and with great ceremony and the twins gasped with surprise. It was absolutely full to the brim with chocolate bars and sweets – more than they had ever seen outside a newsagents. There were bars of milk, plain and white chocolate, toffees, fudge, mints; every sweet they could possibly have imagined. Nigel said, 'You can pick a bar each, if you want. But –' and here he raised a warning finger – 'you *must* eat it here before you leave and you mustn't tell anyone else about this. Firstly, because it wouldn't be fair on Tom to know that I gave you chocolate, and secondly, because you know what parents are like about eating sweets before lunch.'

The twins nodded. Oh, they certainly knew.

As they chose a chocolate bar each, Nigel said, 'This is really a little reward for you for being so good here in Sunday school. I'm not going to give one to Tom because he hasn't been as good as you. That's why I waited until he wasn't here to reward you, so he wouldn't get jealous.'

322

When the children had finished eating, he collected the empty wrappers from them and put them in his pocket, 'so that nobody will know'. To the twins' dismay, he closed the bulging bag and put it over his shoulder.

'But you've got so many sweets left,' Eritrea moaned. 'You're not going to eat them all are you?'

'Oh, I don't really eat sweets,' he said. 'But don't worry. They're not going to go anywhere. I'll bring them back when it's just the two of you and you can have some more then. All I ask for in return is a little kiss from each of you as a thank you to me.'

Eritrea leaned up and guilelessly kissed him on the cheek. Jonah, though slightly embarrassed, eventually did too.

The following week they were alone again with him. Sure enough, towards the end of the session he opened the bag and let them have their pick. This time he demanded a kiss and a hug.

The week after that, he repeated the routine.

On the fourth week, Tom, the only other member of the Sunday school, turned up. The sweet bag was conspicuously absent and Nigel neither said nor did anything to indicate that he had ever given the children chocolate. Eritrea, who had a very sweet tooth indeed, was almost bursting with frustration and shot pleading looks in Nigel's direction whenever Tom was not looking, but Nigel bowed his head slightly and put his finger to his lips. When Sunday school finished, Tom and Jonah left the church hall, but Eritrea stayed behind. 'Please,' she begged him. '*Please*. I know you're hiding them somewhere. Just one chocolate.'

He shook his head slowly. 'I told you that if Tom comes I can't give you any. It would only make him jealous.'

Eritrea sulked.

'But,' he continued, 'I've decided that next time Tom's away we'll have a feast. A secret feast.'

'What do you mean?'

'Well, there'll be almost all the chocolate you can eat and I'll get you whatever you want to drink, too. Won't that be nice?'

Eritrea was inconsolable. 'I suppose.'

Nigel put his arm around her shoulder and touched her ribcage with his other hand. She thought this was a little odd. 'What would you like to drink?' he asked comfortingly.

'Orangeade.'

He moved extremely slowly, with the kind of utmost caution that parents exercise when approaching a sleeping child to put the blanket back over it. And like the parents who know that if they approach silently and stealthily enough the child will not be woken when they reach its bedside, so too Nigel knew that if he took things slowly enough, he would be able to reach them without them really guessing what he intended to do. He took tiny, painstaking steps forward; sometimes he did not move at all. Inside him, a voice said, you have time. Don't worry about that. And he covered his tracks. Oh, he covered them so well.

The sweet-giving stage lasted for a number of months. At first he distributed sweets to both of them together in the upstairs part of the hall. Then he devised a system of rewarding them separately down in the vault underneath the hall. He would praise them personally for their conduct, sometimes giving one twin more sweets than the other with a warning not to say anything about it to the other, to prevent any jealous squabbling. At the same time he was tactile with them – but never more than he thought he could get away with.

Apart from losing their appetite for Sunday lunch, the twins' behaviour gave no other indication whatsoever that

Nigel might be up to something. Paul and Rowena had a strict policy on sweets, which Nigel had heard about quite by accident and had then been able to turn, propitiously, to his advantage. He also had an inkling that Tom's parents were planning, at some stage, to leave the church. By the time they actually did he had primed the twins to the point that they were absolutely desperate – as it were – to be alone with him.

Now he was sure that, most of the time, they would be alone with him for Sunday school, he began to lock the church hall door from the inside. He had a system: during the first hymn he would look around the congregation to check whether there were any other children of an age to go out to Sunday school. If there were, he neither locked himself and the children in the church hall, nor gave any sweets. If it was just him and the twins, as was usually the case, he turned the key in the lock and left it in the door.

The second or third time, Jonah asked, 'Why did you do that?'

'Just to be on the safe side,' Nigel replied. 'If your parents saw me doling out sweets they probably wouldn't even let you come to Sunday school any more.'

In his head he had another explanation ready for Paul and Rowena if, for any reason, they should happen to go out of the church, cross the courtyard and try the door during the service. You know the trouble there's been with tramps on the church premises, he would tell them. More than once they've been sniffing around the door of the hall during Sunday school, so it's better to lock it.

He had explanations and justifications for everything; he even used the manufactured lie about the tramps to convince himself that he was actually acting in the children's best interests.

Then, when the twins were used to the door locking, Nigel started teaching his version of the Creation, all the while sugaring the pill he had for them with gifts of sweets and orangeade. He taught them how, when Adam and Eve ate the fruit from the tree of life, it was very wrong and in their wickedness they covered themselves up. It was a great sin for them to do that because God never intended for people to wear clothes.

After one such session when he was downstairs alone with Jonah, Nigel took a magazine out of his bag. 'Look,' he said to Jonah, showing him the glossy pictures. 'This is how God intended us to be.'

Jonah knew that something about this was fundamentally wrong. The women were only wearing high heels and the men were wearing nothing at all. The pictures were rude. His conscience told him so instantly, like a ripping through his mind. But they were also somehow interesting, and here was Nigel with his soothing siren song telling him that it was all right. He was still just a little too young to equate the conflicting feelings within him. He looked at them and felt a strange feeling in his belly, unlike anything he had felt before.

Nigel said, 'Do you like them? Do you think they're pretty?'

Jonah did not say anything. He was innocent, but he was no fool.

'If you want to, you can touch yourself.'

Jonah squirmed and shrugged his shoulders, embarrassed. 'I don't think so. Not now.'

'Well, Nigel said gently, 'what we can do is this: I'll cut some of these pictures out for you, and fold them up nice and small so that they'll fit in your pocket. That way, you can look at them when you like and nobody has to know about it. Not even your sister. It can be our little secret. Would you like that?'

Jonah was silent for a while. Nigel closed the magazine and went to put it back in his bag, but then Jonah said in a small voice, 'Okay then.'

Soon afterwards, Nigel began to talk about giving them a proper appraisal with feedback and better rewards for their work over the spring. He built up to it slowly, promising that they wouldn't be disappointed because he was really pleased with their good behaviour.

Because Nigel's going to different shops to buy small quantities of chocolate so as not to arouse any suspicion, and his locking the church hall door on the inside, were motivated physical acts, they required him to blank out the section of his mind that tried to tell him what it was he was ultimately building towards. It was rather like the way a person breathes through their mouth when they are eating something unpleasant, so as to avoid having to taste it: if they manage to convince themselves strongly enough, they may even think they are not eating the very thing that is in their mouth, such is the power of the mind's persuasive abilities. Nigel became very good, adept even, at forcing himself not to think of anything at all when he was out on his little shopping trips. He refused to give reason a look-in, because his subconscious soul knew that were he to do so, he might stop moving towards the goal. He never looked directly at this goal, but ran towards it with his eyes to the ground, or looking off to the side. Every week he was closer to it, but his soul said to him, you don't really know what you are aiming to do, so it's quite all right.

In fact, he became so good at deceitfully fooling himself that he was actually able, the week before the promised appraisal, to buy condoms and odourless baby oil without knowing why he bought them. Then, afterwards, when he selected and paid for the personal stereo that Eritrea had said

327

she wanted during a previous appraisal down in the vault, he saw himself as doing nothing more than performing a noble and generous deed.

On the appraisal day itself, part of him was terrified that Paul or Rowena might actually come over to the church hall, but the compulsion within him was an insatiable force that overrode everything else – even the fear of being caught. It controlled him so completely that he could no longer make any decisions, except about how to satisfy it. It had been a long time since he had thought of consequences.

He knew that he had exactly twenty-five minutes from the moment he started walking across the car park with the twins, the muffled sound of the pre-sermon hymn in the background. He locked the church hall door as usual. Today, the children were so excited that they didn't even notice him take the key out of the door this time. He sat Eritrea down at the table upstairs and took Jonah's hand. 'We'll be about ten minutes,' he said to her. From the look in her eyes, he knew she thought this was too long. 'But you mustn't come down and disturb us under any circumstances, because if you do, you won't get any reward at all. Do you understand?'

She sat alone up in the church hall for what seemed like an eternity. It was one of those hot summer days where time seems to stand still. The air in the hall was warm and permeated with the smell of old wood and the dry stale odour of the heavy brown curtains. The only sound was that of a bluebottle buzzing and thumping frantically against the glass of one of the windows.

Eritrea wanted so badly to get up and creep down the stairs to the vault. It had been a fair time since she had actually seen the rewards that Nigel gave her brother and she naturally thought, the way a sibling does, he is bound to be getting something better than I am. But she was afraid, too, that Nigel would be true to his word. On more than one occasion he had refused to give her sweets, simply because he had come back up with Jonah to find her waiting on the top step of the vault stairwell, trying to eavesdrop.

When Nigel eventually brought Jonah back up into the church hall, she saw him pocket an electronic game, one that he had wanted for quite some time. She thought, I'm going to get the personal stereo. The thought excited her so much that she hardly noticed how pale her brother looked, or that he wasn't smiling.

Afterwards, Nigel instructed the twins on pain of death to hide their gifts away. Then he sent them out to play on the grass on the other side of the hall – not the space between the hall and the church. They did not protest. He himself walked from the church hall towards the main nave door, but then changed his mind and instead slipped around the side of the nave, intending to enter unobtrusively through the door to the vestry. The trembling exhilaration within him was still so great that he did not see Rowena Trent until it was too late. She was kneeling on the ground near the steps leading down to the vestry, almost completely concealed by the tall summer grass. In the split second after noticing her, as he was thinking, I've got to make sure she doesn't see me, she looked up. When their eyes met his heart almost stopped beating.

Her face was worn with the effort of crying.

The terror of comprehension was like a slap in the face; he felt his inner self melt like wax and he thought, this is where it all ends. She knows something. Somehow she has seen or discovered something. He asked her blankly if she was all right, all the while his mind backtracking frantically to try to discover where he had slipped up and given himself away.

But I have been so careful, so very careful, he lamented inwardly.

His fear of being faced with the truth of what he had just done – for the sake of his own twisted conscience as much as anything else – was so intense that it took a moment for the realization to dawn on him that Rowena actually knew nothing about him and was upset about something quite different. When the penny dropped he felt a rush of relief that nearly knocked him off his feet. She was saying something about next week, the children; could he walk them back home after church? She was angry with her husband. The understanding washed over him. He agreed.

Then he asked, 'How long will you be gone?'

The following Sunday, he said to the twins, 'Because you have been so incredibly good, there will be another appraisal, but this time at home after church.'

The memory of the first rape both existed and did not exist as an event in Eritrea's mind. Objectively, she knew that it had happened, but the memory, in its state of virtual non-existence, became like the constructed memory of a thing that has taken place in someone else's life, and that she had been told about. Her mind refused to compartmentalize it, so it hung there outside the chronological continuum of things that had happened to her, like a file that will never be found because it is in the wrong folder.

What she did remember of that first Sunday was the musty smell of the vault, with its empty white spaces and the metal-framed chairs with their green canvas backs all stacked up against the walls – nothing more.

That first time, before he presented her with the personal stereo, he had said to her, in an absolutely straight voice, 'Now, if you ever tell anyone about this you will burn in hell. Your parents will send you to a home for disturbed children and everyone will know that you are dirty.'

Originally, she had no memory of these words, just as she had no memory of what happened in her own bedroom the following Sunday after Nigel walked them home, or the Sunday after that, or the remaining two Sundays before Paul Trent finally plucked up the courage to speak to Abel Thacker and take the family out of the church.

Nigel, however, remembered his words. They were always with him. When he had originally uttered them, another Nigel, not the one speaking, was shocked to hear them coming out of his mouth. If he had been told as a child, this is what you will one day do, he would not have been able to believe it.

He tried mentally to block out the constant crushing accusation of these words of his, but they were always there just audible in the background. He could never escape from them.

*

'I was more scared of coming to see you,' Eritrea said, through the tears, 'than I was even when I knew that he was going to hurt me again. Can you believe it?'

'I can.'

'It was the jasmine that made me remember. When Lucy brought it into the flat I hated the smell of it. I didn't even know why. Something inside me just said that it had to be got rid of. And I lay in bed wondering why I hated it so much. I didn't want to think about it, but I couldn't stop myself from remembering that it was the smell of our tree house. So I thought, why do I hate thinking about the tree house? And then I remembered how I used to feel when I sat up there.' Her eyes filled up again with tears. 'I thought it was the only place where I could be safe.'

'Let me get you a tissue,' Judith said, rising and touching Eritrea on the arm. She left the room and Eritrea sat alone, feeling as though her life were dribbling away. Chunks of afternoon sunlight hung suspended in the air. There was no sound other than the measured tick of a clock.

When Judith returned, Eritrea said, 'Phillip will be home soon, won't he?'

'No, he's not coming back until later tonight. He's in London.'

'I'm sorry. Taking up all your time like this. I should go soon.'

Judith ignored the comment. 'That's why you thought that he committed suicide? Because of what happened?'

'I didn't think about it clearly like that, but underneath, yes.' She blew her nose and drew a ragged breath. 'I'm sorry to descend on you uninvited and burden you with all this stuff.'

Judith looked at Eritrea with eyes full of compassion. 'Eritrea. When people have experienced similar things to what you have gone through, it sometimes takes many, many months before they have the strength to even speak about what you were ready to tell me when you came.'

Eritrea gave her a look, desperate for further confirmation.

'Most of the time people who have been sexually abused –' despite what she had shared, the comprehension of the stark reality of these words, spoken out by Judith, cut through Eritrea – 'come to me to talk about something completely different. They're struggling with feelings of depression or inadequacy, or things aren't going well in their marriage, or whatever. Only after talking for a long time do the real root causes of the hurt come to the surface. I've got no doubt whatsoever that Jesus has been strengthening you and building you up to be able to recognize what happened and talk about

332

it right now. He doesn't do things at the wrong time. So you're not taking up my time and you're not burdening me.'

They both sat silently for a minute. 'Eritrea,' Judith ventured, 'what you've told me is very serious, and I really think we should meet up and talk again, as soon as you can. You have my word that I won't tell anyone else about what you've said. Not Phillip. Not your parents. Not anyone.' She let this sink in. 'But before we go any further, or do anything else, I think we should pray about the things you've shared, just to give the whole situation to the Lord so that he'll guide us and show us what to do.'

'Oh, I don't know about that.'

It nearly broke Judith's heart to see the terror in Eritrea's eyes. For a moment, she was looking at Eritrea the eleven-year-old again. She reached forward and took her hands. They were shaking. 'I have no way of knowing how hard this has been for you. I can only guess. For you to have the courage to come and tell me was a great thing in itself. Really, more than some people ever manage in their lives. But I know in my heart that Jesus has been waiting until the right moment to help you with this. He loves you so much and he hates to see you suffering, but he will never, ever force you to do anything against your will. And he can only help you if you agree to let him.' Judith spoke these words and thought of Nigel – some role model – telling the twins, after he had manipulated them and forced himself on them, that they would burn in hell. She squeezed Eritrea's hands. 'Will you let him?'

Judith watched her battle with the fear; fear of the unknown.

After a long time, she said, 'All right.'

'Jesus,' Judith began. 'You loved us so much that you died for us, even when you had no guarantee from us that we would turn to you. We praise you for doing that, Lord. For loving us so much. And we praise you too that you have a time for everything and that you don't show us things until you know we're ready to see them.' She paused and thought. 'Thank you Father for giving Eritrea the courage to come and share these things with me. We just want to come before you and pray that you will guide us as we talk together and that you will heal these hurts in Eritrea, Lord, one by one, as we know you will.' Here, she stopped praying and said to Eritrea, 'Will you let him – just agree to let him – come in and heal those hurts?'

Eritrea said nothing for a long time. Judith waited. In her mind, she was preparing the words she would say if Eritrea remained silent. Don't worry. It's okay. We can take this slowly.

Then Eritrea said, 'Yes.'

'Father, Eritrea has asked you to come in and to heal her, so we just invite you, Lord, by your Holy Spirit to enter those areas of her life that have been under lock and key for so many years. Please come and shine your light into those areas now Lord –'

'Judith,' Eritrea said. 'I think I need a bowl.'

Quick as lightning, Judith was out of the room and back with a bucket. She sat next to Eritrea with her hand on her shoulder.

In all her life, Eritrea had never brought up so much. She retched until she thought her stomach would tear itself apart, litres and litres, it felt like. And it was as black as coal. Just as she thought she could take it no more it stopped. Judith stroked her hair comfortingly.

Eritrea sat up slowly, painfully, the cold wet of tears in her eyes. She looked dizzily at the bucket for a moment before starting to cry. 'I'm scared,' she sobbed. 'I haven't eaten for three days.'

'Don't be,' Judith said. 'Don't be afraid. Come on and I'll get you a glass of water.' She helped her to her feet and accompanied her to the kitchen. While Eritrea rinsed out her mouth, Judith supported her shoulders.

Later, when they were sitting back in the living room, Judith said, 'Would you like to stay the night?'

'You'd have space?'

'There's always a room made up downstairs.'

Eritrea thought, yes, I suppose there would be. It dawned on her that, previously, she had not given much thought to what it was that Judith actually did. 'Lucy's still here in Marlborough. She said she'd pick me up when I called her.'

'If you feel up to it.'

'I think I'll go back with her. I'm grateful for the offer. I really am. It's just that she's been worried about me.' She smiled, weakly. 'She's very good at looking after me.'

'She is. But Eritrea, I want you to come and see me again as soon as possible. Can you make it tomorrow?'

'Yes. But... don't you have other people to see?'

'I see a lot of people about a lot of different things. But there's nothing going on tomorrow that can't wait.'

When Eritrea was leaving the house, Judith said, 'What happened earlier – don't be afraid about it. The spiritual and the natural, you know, they overlap. Sometimes, when God is working, things happen that you can't explain humanly. But don't let it worry you. It might seem like things are out of control. But they aren't.'

'It's hard not to be scared.' Eritrea turned at the gate and looked back at Judith, standing on the doorstep.

'I know. But He has you in His hand. Like this –' she cupped her hands together.

Eritrea nodded. 'See you tomorrow.'

'And,' Judith called, when Eritrea was outside the gate. 'Have something to eat.'

When she had gone, Judith stood still in the doorway for a while and listened to the sound of the car fading into the distance. Her heart ached for Eritrea with a kind of drawing pain. She was afraid for her, for she could see what Eritrea, in the immediacy of her suffering, could not see: the reality of the journey she had before her.

In her mind, the memories she had of the twins were reorganizing themselves independently of her will. Each image that materialized in her head – Jonah looking out of the window of the minibus, or the twins pointedly ignoring each other at church – was being tainted by the reality of Eritrea's revelation, as a jar of clear water is tainted when the dirty paintbrush is dipped in. She stood there, touching the doorframe, and all the formless doubts that she had ever entertained regarding them fell into place with diabolical precision and made a complete picture, but it was a horrific picture. She felt as a person does when they watch a tragic film for the second time – there is always a vague, impossible hope that the characters will not be drawn into the tragedy. And as the fluid of her scattered memories of the twins congealed and clotted into a lump of incontrovertible truth, there was a kind of laughter accompanying it. See my handiwork, it said. See my handiwork.

Yet, despite the horror that wrung her with the registering of the truth behind each memory, her spirit looked on with a far greater calm, like the calm of the sea, and said, you shall not have the last word in this.

The sun had begun to sink down behind the house and half the lawn was engulfed in shadow, but the afternoon was warm; almost affectionately so. Judith stepped back into the

336

porch and clicked the front door shut with the utmost care, deep in thought.

Driving home, Lucy wanted so badly to ask Eritrea what had happened. But out of love, she did not. Eritrea sat in the passenger seat, folded in on herself, looking more vulnerable than she had ever seemed to her.

When they got back to the flat, Lucy made Eritrea a sandwich, without asking. Eritrea ate it slowly and in silence. 'Thank you,' she said, when she had finished.

Chapter 21

To Eritrea's surprise, Judith did not suggest that they pray on Friday when Eritrea arrived in the morning. Instead, she asked Eritrea to talk, nothing more. 'Why don't you want to pray for me?' she asked, confused. 'You wanted to yesterday.'

'Yes. And I think it was right to give our times of sharing to the Lord. But now that we've done that, I feel it would be good to hear more from you about what you remember. Whatever you have the strength to tell me.'

So Eritrea talked. From time to time, Judith asked short questions, always gently probing, urging her to say more if she could. Every now and then, she said, 'Any time this is too much, or you feel you're going too far, we'll just stop. All right?'

Eritrea replied always, 'I'm okay, really I am.'

After a couple of hours, though, she was so drained that she felt she might faint from the effort of speaking out the things that came from within. She was surprised at how completely it sapped her energy; each word that she spoke about the memory of the abuse seemed to tear itself from the physical fabric of her body, like the tearing of a scab that has not yet developed enough to heal properly. Eventually, she felt as though she were speaking from within a glass box. Although she could have reached forward and touched Judith with an outstretched hand, she seemed to be miles and miles away from her, as if there were an inseparable gulf between them. Yes, she thought. Around me there is a vacuum. A void that cannot be crossed.

She did not realize just how far out of herself she had drifted until Judith touched her on the shoulder and handed her a cup of coffee with the sugar already stirred in. 'Drink it,' she said. 'It'll do you good.' Eritrea had not even noticed that Judith had been out of the room.

Somehow, receiving the cup and feeling its heat triggered a fit of shivering in her. Her teeth chattered as she held it in both hands and felt its warmth seep through the china and into her skin. When she yawned, it made her shoulders quiver convulsively. 'It isn't cold in here,' she said, through the shaking. 'It isn't that.'

'I know,' Judith replied. 'Relax for now. *I* think it's time we took a break.'

They ate lunch together, in almost complete silence. Afterwards, Eritrea said, 'I want to talk some more.'

Judith looked doubtful. 'Are you sure you're up to it?'

'You said it was good for me to get it out of my system.'

'I did. And it is good. But only what you can manage.'

'Am I doing this wrong? Is this not how it should be?'

'Eritrea, there is no wrong or right way in this. What you are comfortable with – that's the right way. Nothing else.'

She let Eritrea speak until she sensed that she was beginning to flag. They had a break and more coffee. Only then did Judith consent to speak herself.

'A person's body is like a house with many rooms,' she said. She was sitting on the floor of the living room, leaning on one hand and holding her shin with the other. It was about three in the afternoon. 'The body belongs to Jesus Christ because He has redeemed it. But we're all works in progress. Like Paul says, He wants to do with us more than we can possibly imagine, and He works in us at His own pace, as we give Him permission to come further in. But, like I've said to you, He doesn't do things in us against our will. There are

339

some rooms in our house that are open and are illuminated immediately with the light of Christ, as soon as He enters our lives. But as we go on in our walk with him, He starts to knock on those doors that are shut or locked. He doesn't ever barge His way in. And the saddest thing is that, if we choose not to let Him into those places, though we're redeemed and saved, we can go through our whole lives hurting or spiritually crippled in some areas because those places are untouched by His light.' She looked out of the window, and Eritrea was surprised to see tears in her eyes. 'And yes, I've seen people go through their lives and die with great hurts, even though Jesus repeatedly gave them the opportunity to be healed.'

'Why?'

'Fear, mostly. Fear of the unknown.'

Eritrea gave Judith a look of slight incomprehension.

'I'm getting away from the point,' Judith said. 'Let's say that in your body there are a number of rooms that have been open to Jesus from the moment that you gave your life to Him, but that under the stairs there is a space that has been under lock and key for years. Maybe it was locked long before you became a Christian.

'You are the master of the house and always have been, but say, for argument's sake, that this space under the stairs has been locked for so long that you've forgotten it even exists. When you invite Jesus into your house, He knows it inside out already. He knows all about that locked door, even though you don't remember it. Eventually, when the time is right, He reminds you that it's there and offers to open it for you. If you agree to let Him, He does. What happened the other day was just that. The trouble is that these dark spaces in our lives have been under the control of other things, not the Lord Jesus. It's like they've been occupied by −' she paused for a second − 'a squatter. Someone who has no right to be there but has settled in without your really knowing it and made a little... nest, if you like. But as soon as Jesus opens the door, the things inside are exposed to His holiness and light and they just have to leave immediately. They just can't tolerate it and they can't stay. What made you sick was like the eviction of the squatter, the beginning of the healing process. And Jesus could only do it because you gave Him permission.'

'The beginning? When will it be dealt with properly?'

'Eritrea, I have to be honest and say that I don't like the term "dealt with". It sounds so draconian, you know. The Lord Jesus loves us and looks after us because we're His children. When He's healing us, the devil likes to make a noise or give us a scare – like trying to go out with a bang – when his influence in us is being cut off, so that we make a connection between the scary supernatural things that sometimes happen and God. It's a ploy to frighten us – nothing else.' Here, she lapsed into silence. She shifted her weight on the floor and looked past Eritrea into the distance as though she were watching memories of past episodes playing like video films before her eyes.

'I don't know if what happened yesterday was unprecedented. Certainly only a very few people that I have ever counselled have been able to share so much, so quickly. But that does not mean that the process of healing will take less time. Up until yesterday you were living in the abuse. It was over you. It kind of covered you.' She searched for a way to express herself. 'The things that happened to you twelve years ago formed – to a greater or lesser extent – the framework within which you lived your life. The series of events that Jesus set in motion and that led up to what Lucy did for you to help you remember have enabled you to start the move from that chapter of living *in* the abuse to a new chapter of living *with* the abuse. But this new chapter of living with it won't be something that you can work through more quickly... just because you want it to be behind you. The work of the Holy Spirit in you – there are no short cuts to it.'

Eritrea bit her bottom lip hard. 'It's hard to hear you say that.'

'I know. But there's no point in trying to speed things up. It's no good.' She seemed to want to go further. 'Eritrea,' she said in a voice full of tenderness, 'you were always so single-minded and determined. I remember that about you. When you knew what you wanted, nobody could stop you. There was this dynamism in you, even back then, so soon after it happened. You and Jo were so different in that respect. He was never like you. But the time has come to let go of that. You can if you want to. You don't have to run any more. Not here. Not with me. The Lord is inviting you to stop running and to rest. Just to rest now.'

This caused the emotion to break the eggshell of Eritrea's inhibition again. She cried for a while. When she had finished, she said, 'I studied a year of English literature at university. Did you know?'

'No. I didn't.'

'One of our professors gave an interpretation of a poem by Yeats. It was called *Leda and the Swan*, or something. His interpretation was that the swan was like the virgin Mary, and that God forced Himself on her and raped her. That she had no choice in the matter. It was a horrible thought, but as much as I hated it, something in me said, what if it really was like that? It's like a part of me has always been afraid that God would hurt me, too. So it's kind of hard to see Him as inviting me to rest. You know?'

'I do, Eritrea. I really do. But people like the English professor love to pin evil attributes on God because it gives them an excuse not to be accountable to him. If you say, and

342

let yourself believe, that God is a manipulator, then you can justify in your own mind not having to feel bad about rejecting Him. But God is not a manipulator. It is the devil who is the manipulator. We who are born of the Spirit know that it is Satan's kingdom that is based on control, not God's. It's just that the devil does everything in his power to ensure people see it the other way around. The reason something within you was afraid that the professor might be right was because your own life was manipulated in the cruellest way by a person who was supposedly God's representative to you and who, after gaining your trust, violated it and hurt you. It's only natural that deep down inside you'll feel that way. But you know that yesterday you could've walked out of here, pushed the hurt back down and eventually continued living your life as you did before.'

'Yes.'

'And a part of you must have been telling you yesterday just to walk away.'

Eritrea nodded.

'But you didn't. And it was God who gave you the strength to be able to stay, because He loves you so much.'

When Eritrea arrived back at the flat that evening, Lucy was sitting in front of the TV in her after-work clothes. Without saying so much as hello, Eritrea went into her bedroom, shut the door, delved in the chest of drawers opposite her bed and fished out the box containing the letter from Håkan. She had not touched the box since putting the letter in it, months before.

Later, when she went into the living room, the first thing she noticed was that the volume was muted. Seeing Eritrea, Lucy switched the television off altogether. 'How did it go?' she asked, failing to keep the concern out of her voice.

'Well… Very well,' Eritrea replied.

'Can I get you something to drink?'

'Not unless you're having something.'

Lucy stood up and stretched. 'I think I will, actually.' She went to the kitchen and ran some water into the kettle.

Eritrea sat on the sofa arm and watched Lucy rinsing out a mug. 'Be patient with me.'

'Don't worry.'

'I want to tell you about what's happening, I do. I just can't talk about it yet.'

'You don't have to say anything.' Lucy dried the mug and put a teabag in it. 'You don't have to give any kind of explanation.

'You've been so understanding.'

'I don't know. I don't think I'm a particularly patient person.'

'If it wasn't for you, I'd never have gone to see Judith. You must know that.'

'Well.' She went to the fridge, opened the door and stood looking into the depths. Then she turned around. 'I'd never want to pressure you to tell me if you didn't want to but… I'm just so scared that I hurt you by getting you those flowers. I can't help it. I don't understand. I didn't think getting them could possibly have hurt you. I wouldn't have done it if I'd known.'

Eritrea's eyes softened. 'More than anything I want to tell you what's happening. I'm just not ready.' The thought of invoking again the same terrible fatigue she had felt with Judith, by talking about some of the same things to Lucy, was too much for her to bear. It was not even that she did not want to share with her. The effort would simply have been too much. 'I can't even get my own thoughts together in my head. But trust me when I tell you that God used what you did to speak to me the other day.' It was the most she could say. 'What you did was absolutely necessary and I'm very grateful.'

'You are?'

'Very.'

Lucy shut the fridge door. 'Changing the subject, Antoine called. He wants to know if you're going to be well enough to work tomorrow night.'

'I thought he'd have called to fire me. No such luck, obviously.'

'No. He says they miss you there.'

'Ha. I don't believe it.'

'He wanted you to call back before eleven if you were going.'

'I'll be going back over to see Judith tomorrow morning. Can I borrow your car again?'

'You know you don't even have to ask.'

'I should be back before five though.' She stood up and went into the hall.

Lucy called after her, 'I told him you probably wouldn't be going and not to wait for your call.'

'I think I'll be all right.'

'You don't have to. I told him you were still feeling bad.'

As she dialled the *Dame de Coeur* she thought, Lucy, what would I do without you?

On Saturday, Judith once again encouraged Eritrea to talk. 'When you speak about things to me,' she said, 'the burden that you've been carrying alone is immediately shared between the two of us. You could see it as me standing outside the cupboard under the stairs while you go through it with a torch, passing me the things that are in there. Some of the things that you pass me will be very heavy – too heavy perhaps for you to lift them out alone, which is why I'm here to help you.'

'Judith... You say that. I want to do it so badly. And it's so tiring for me.'

'It is. This fighting spirit in you. It makes you... push yourself. We can stop whenever you want. You can take it slower. Really you can. Remember that Jesus is in there with you all the time. Don't forget that.'

'No.'

'And there's another reason for doing it this way. When you speak about something that has previously only been a feeling or a fear, it crystallizes and becomes something tangible that you can hold and that you and I can both see. It was no less real when it was only a feeling buried inside you, but by putting words to it, you clothe it in reality, so that I can see it too. That is the action of passing out to me the things that are in that space. I couldn't go in there for you and take things out, because I couldn't necessarily see them, and even if I could guess at what was in there, I would have no right to do that. All I can do is stand in the doorway and encourage you in whatever way I can to pass out to me the things that you find in your hands.'

'Somehow I was expecting... I thought...'

'That I could pray for you? That you wouldn't need to talk about it?'

'I suppose so. I don't know. I *did* think that we'd pray more. People have been praying with me a lot recently at church.'

'Yes —' Judith said this in a somewhat guarded way — 'not that they were to know, of course, but even that can be unhelpful sometimes.'

'How so?'

'This time, when the pain is so near to you, is a time for you to get in touch with your feelings. We can take things at your pace. But it's good that we've known each other for so many years, and that we've shared some — some — of the same pains and hurts. I know that you've been pushing yourself to talk to me over these last couple of days. There's nothing wrong with that. But there's a danger with praying too much at the start.'

'Danger?'

'Mm–hmm. In the past I've known situations where victims of abuse, who received a lot of prayer in the beginning, sort of "hid behind" the spiritual words in the prayers, before they ever really let themselves get in touch with the reality of what they had gone through. You can't get ahead of yourself in this process.'

So again, Eritrea talked. By the afternoon she was not overly surprised to hear herself telling Judith about PCOM. She talked about Lyon and Africa, building up slowly towards Håkan's final letter.

Judith listened without interrupting once. When Eritrea had finished, Judith digested the information and then raised her eyebrows in slight disapproval. 'Unhealthy ties, eh?'

Eritrea did not know how to respond to this.

'It sounds like jargon to me.'

'Jargon?'

Judith thought, yes, jargon. People love to stick these labels on things they know nothing about and then sit back and feel good about themselves. But she did not say any of this aloud. 'You say Håkan knew about Jo?'

'Yes. About his death, at least.'

'That letter must have been deeply hurtful.'

Eritrea did not reply.

'A lot of people that I counsel aren't even Christians so they don't know anything about the way the Holy Spirit works. But with you it's not the same. It's a wonderful thing that God made it possible for us to meet up and share, because of the things that we have both seen, my friendship with your

347

mother, Jo… everything. For many people who go to seek help it's not like that.' Eritrea could see that she was thinking of other events, other victims. 'You know, I never intended to be in on Thursday afternoon. I only happened to be home because I felt God was "telling" me that it would be obedient to Him for me to stay home and bake. I was like, baking? Why would He want me to bake?'

'Really?'

'Really. But you see that He ordained for us to speak. And that's a good starting point. Anyway, what I'm trying to say is, you've been to PCOM and done a school. God's let you see and hear a lot, so I feel I can tell you things I wouldn't necessarily tell other people. Well –' she considered – 'not immediately, anyway.'

'Don't say that, as if I was spiritually mature or something. Looking back at the things that have happened over the last few years is so embarrassing. Like, because I'm a Christian I should've known all this stuff before. I mean, the conversations I've had with people about spiritual things… Just thinking about it is almost too much.'

Judith shook her head. 'Locking the door to the room that contained the memories of what Nigel did to you was a coping tactic. Some things that happen to us are so painful that our mind wills to forget them. Psychologists call it suppressed memory.'

'I know. I've seen TV programmes about it.'

'Yes. But, in a way, why should a TV programme about suppressed memory make you remember something, if your mind has chosen to forget that the thing ever happened in the first place? You can have conversations about spiritual or Christian things with other people, without ever thinking about the things in your life that have been hidden away. The human soul is incredibly good at suppressing feelings or emotions or memories – or even creating them. It's like your English tutor, totally convinced in his own mind, no doubt, about what God is like. But with you, this closing and locking of the door enabled the bad that got a foothold through what Nigel did to fester and, with time, to thrive. And though you shouldn't feel guilty about it, these things *have* had an effect on you over the years. Despite what you've seen and done as a Christian.'

Eritrea looked at the floor.

'Knock-on effects from things like that filter down into our characters. They work themselves into the fabric of who we are and they start affecting the way we relate to the world – and to other people. They can start developing very soon after the bad things have happened to us, but however quickly or slowly they develop, there comes a time when we start to feel that we can't live without them, or that we were always like that. Even if we know that we were once different, we sometimes like to hold on to the things anyway. Evil as the catalyst was that created them, the knock-on effects can sometimes be turned to our advantage. Quite beneficial, even. You know what I mean, Eritrea?'

'In a way, I think.'

Judith looked at Eritrea long and hard, but her eyes were filled with compassion. 'The door of the room with the bad memories has been opened and the cleaning begun, as it were, but there are still the consequences of what happened, the knock-on effects, the habits and the lifestyle that will need to change. Do you see?'

'That letter Håkan sent… It terrified me,' Eritrea said.

'I'm not surprised.' Judith sighed. 'People get a little knowledge about someone so they think that they have the God-given right to start telling them to sort themselves out. It must've been very hurtful.'

'He thought I did what I did because of Jo. Because he died.'

'There you go. He had no idea what you'd really gone through. But... maybe God used the letter after all. Perhaps it was a link in the chain of events that's been leading you back to see the past.

'The funny thing is,' Eritrea said in a small voice, 'reading it reminded me of how I felt when you and I used to be in the same room together. If I'm being honest, I've always been scared of you, in a way. Ever since we met.'

'Why do you think?' Judith said in a voice that suggested she already knew.

'I always felt that you were disapproving of me, or *judging* me. I can't explain it. I felt the same way about Fleur. It seems so irrational.'

'Not at all. When you and Jo first came to Glenfield there was something in the way you were, your mannerisms, that kind of concerned me. I was this close to mentioning it to your mother. But I didn't. Obviously, for whatever reason it just wasn't the right time. You could say that this has been a serious lesson for me, too. I suppose, at the time, I thought, humanly – stupidly – that it couldn't be possible. That nothing like that could've happened to you.'

'You *knew* something?'

'No. It's not as clear cut as that. I just felt –' she searched for a way to put it – 'well, there were sort of... signs. But what I meant to say was that perhaps you recognized this part of you had no control over me. Just as it had no control over Fleur, or Håkan – ultimately.' She leaned forward and picked at something on the carpet. 'Let me put it plainly. I'm in no way condoning the way he went about things, but I think that he was possibly right, in a manner of speaking. One of the knock-on effects of what Nigel did to you was, indirectly, to create in you the ability to seduce people. I'm sorry if I sound harsh, but there's no point in beating about the bush any more. I've always recognized in you this immense capacity to draw others to yourself. From what you've said to me about Africa, I think you do, too. Now that I know what happened at St Peter's it makes perfect sense. But, really, I'm not telling you anything you don't know already, am I?'

Eritrea did not answer.

'This power that you had was both a weapon and a shield. A weapon that you used – first and foremost – to bring men under your control, so that you could later reject them to punish them for what Nigel did to you all those years ago. And a shield because if men were subject to you and you had ultimate control over them, you could always reject them before they had a chance to hurt or reject you, and in so doing, protect yourself.

'I said that we sometimes turn the effects of the bad things that happen to us to our advantage. What I mean is that when you realized you had this power over people and especially over men, you probably subconsciously saw it as something that was quite an asset, quite a useful personality trait, not as something that was bad or the result of the abuse. When Håkan put to you the truth of what you did, even though he didn't know *why* you did it, it was a threat to you. But you were still suppressing the memory that caused you to be that way in the first place, so you simply had to shelve it. He probably sat back and felt great about the fact that he'd sorted things out in his own mind, leaving you with the pain. It must've been a shock to the system, how much it hurt when you got that letter, right?'

'You keep saying that. And it was. It was terrible. But how can you know?'

'It's quite ironic, really. You told Håkan not to come here – which he took as a rejection. But later he used what little he knew about you to reject *you*. I'm sure he didn't see it that way, but there must have been a small part of him that actually wanted you to feel bad. Maybe to give you a taste of your own medicine. In a sense that letter – or what it represented – was the one thing you've spent your adult life trying to avoid.'

'A rejection.'

'Exactly.'

'You make it sound like I went out of my way to hurt people.'

'But didn't you?' Judith sat up slightly. 'There's a very simple but deep truth here. It's this: if people were truly aware of what they did that hurt other people around them, in most cases they'd try to avoid doing it. Often, the reason they do those hurtful things is because they quite honestly do not know what they are really doing.'

Eritrea blushed to the roots of her hair. 'I *did* tell Håkan that I didn't feel for him the same way he felt for me. I suppose I even knew how I could hurt him. That's why I wanted him to be clear about where we stood.'

'Definitely. And he should have known better, let's be clear on that. But that doesn't change the fact that you were not entirely in the right either. What was in you was stronger than your ability to do the right thing, so whatever you said, you couldn't help giving him these mixed messages.

'Everybody does these kinds of things, Eritrea. In different ways. It's part of the human condition. I sometimes counsel people who have manipulated others – their families, their friends – for years. To those outside the situation it's plain what's going on but, nine times out of ten, the person doing the manipulating is completely unaware of it. However, that doesn't change the fact that it needs to stop.'

'Yes.'

'In the same way, you have become the way you are because of the hurt. So it's understandable that you hurt men in the way you do. But the fact that it's understandable doesn't mean that it's justified, or that it should continue.'

Eritrea nodded her head.

'The idea of letting go of it scares you, I'm sure.'

'It petrifies me.'

'Do you know why?'

'Not really, no.'

'Do you remember me saying that one reason some people go their whole lives without letting Jesus heal the hurt is due to a fear of the unknown? Literally, they've lived with the hurt and the consequences of it for so long, that they're afraid of what life might be without it. God doesn't patch us up and leave the job half finished. He wants to go back and heal everything – not just the root cause but the consequences, too. And that means that the power you got over men as a result of what Nigel did has to go too. In your mind, you probably think, but if those things that define who I am are taken away from me, what will I be left with?'

'I suppose.'

'Let me reassure you Eritrea. Jesus knows exactly what you are going through because He went through it, too. In fact, anyone who truly lives out their faith in Christ has done what I'm suggesting and let go of things – not necessarily the same things, or the same pain, but they've gone through the same process, nevertheless. I've gone through it –' she laughed – 'I *go* through it. Daily.

'The cross has become such a trite subject in Christian circles. It's been talked about so much and people have heard so much teaching on it that they think there's nothing more they need to know about it. But they're *so* wrong. Jesus said, "For whoever would save his life will lose it, but whoever loses his life for my sake will save it." People – and I'm talking about everyone, not just non-Christians – who live simply to satisfy themselves don't comprehend that they'll never truly find themselves if their motives are selfish.' She shook her head in disgust. 'Living for yourself is a religion these days. It's pathetic. It's become some kind of noble and respectable quest in life. But when people go on a quest to find themselves by doing whatever *they* want to do, they don't realize that the sin of their selfishness will eventually overtake them and destroy them from the inside out. But if you take the road of the cross and die to yourself, you *will* find yourself in Jesus. It's the madness of the cross, the stumbling stone, like Jesus said. Just before He went to die, He said, "Father if you are willing, remove this cup from me. Nevertheless, not my will, but yours, be done." He was terribly afraid. Just like you are now. And why would He have been afraid if it was not fear of the unknown? Even on the cross He called out, "My God, my God, why have you forsaken me?" Being forsaken by God was a new thing to Christ. For all eternity, He and the Father and the Spirit had been together, but then suddenly He was thrown into a situation where He was subjected to the very thing He had feared – the thing He had never known or experienced. Do you see?'

'I think so.'

'When people become Christians they make a fundamental decision to live by the cross – by the principle of the cross – but so many either immediately renege on their decision or fall into a way of being that denies its reality. The process of dying to yourself is a daily one. There are big one-off things that God reveals to you and asks you to die to and then there are smaller things, the potential to fall into habitual sin, and so on, that you need to die to every day. I mean crucify them with Christ. I don't think you become accountable for some things until you understand them, and you can only understand them when God reveals them to you. Some people hold on to things tightly knowing that they should have been put to death ages ago, but in your case these things – the way you relate to men and so forth – are only just becoming clear to you now.'

'But once I understand them, then I become accountable for them.'

'Yes. That's it. But this process is a perfectly normal part of Christian life. When a person becomes a Christian, what they're in effect doing by giving their life to Jesus is saying that they're willing to make the way of the cross their whole approach to life. They make one major decision at the beginning, which is also a commitment to make the many smaller decisions that they will face in their walk with the Lord.

'Becoming a Christian is the single most radical decision a person can make. When Jesus went to the cross, He – the most powerful man ever to walk the earth – threw everything away. He could've had legions of angels to help Him. He said it Himself. If the devil had known that by giving up His life Jesus would reconcile us to God, you can rest assured he'd have done everything in his power to make sure there was no crucifixion. But the devil had no idea that by giving Himself up, Christ would be resurrected and would conquer death. By dying, Jesus gave us the ideal to live by, which is that personal victory only comes through absolute self-sacrifice. Do you see?'

'I've never heard it put quite like that before.'

'So when a person makes the decision to be born again they're technically saying to Jesus, "I embrace Your example and make it my way of life, too. I will die to anything and everything that stands in the way of me and fellowship with You, because You died for me first, before I even knew You."

That's why Jesus said that we should count the cost before making a commitment. This is one of the simplest truths of the faith, but you'd be surprised how many Christians seem to have conveniently forgotten it.'

'Not that surprised, actually.' Eritrea laughed, but it was a laugh tinged with irony.

'Everybody is moving in one direction or another. Towards God or away from Him. I don't think that anyone can honestly say they are standing still. And anyone who thinks they are is probably drifting backwards.' Judith laughed. 'Every time God faces me with something He wants me to die to, I think, oh no, Lord, not that. Anything but that. But if I refuse to give it up to Him, how can I really expect to grow as a Christian in other areas? Maybe I think I can, but when I really come back before Jesus He always faces me with the very thing I refused to let go of again.'

'It's hard.'

'Eritrea. It is the hardest thing in the world. Think of it: a human being throwing away their independence. Jesus first, for us. Then us, as we follow Him. I reckon that you can only fully embrace the way of the cross when you've recognized that it is, in fact, the hardest thing in the world.'

Eritrea started to say something, but then stopped.

'I'm not softening the blow, am I? That's what you want to say, isn't it? People who think that Christianity is a crutch, it makes me laugh. It shows they have absolutely no idea. None whatsoever. It's living for yourself that's the crutch, the easy way out. It's just that when people have suffered, their priorities change and they're more ready to let go of the selfish things in their lives. Think of where you are now. I don't know why you've suffered the way you have. In all the time I've been counselling I honestly don't think I've met anyone who has suffered with the things you've had to.' She seemed somehow to come back to herself when she said this, as though the words were a reminder to her, too. 'These conversations that we have had these last three days have been incredible. But like I said when we were talking about praying, there's a danger that because things have gone so well and so fast now, we could easily fall into thinking that all will be sorted out soon. Maybe I'm guilty of not recognizing that. So little steps. Always little steps.'

'But about this giving up, of these things in me?'

'Yes… As we go through this process, there will be a time when you will need to give these things about your personality over to God and to die to them. Not just yet, maybe. But as you do, He will turn the pain and the sorrow around in the most amazing way. He is already doing it now. It's perhaps the greatest and most precious truth in the universe. If you die to things, God will bring new life. Jesus showed that first through the cross and now you, as His child, have the chance to follow the example of His death as you give up things in your own walk, as a sign of obedience to Him. Of course, you think, how can I possibly cope if I willingly give up to Christ the human ability to protect myself from rejection? But I can tell you now that in return He will give you something far greater. Imagine no longer being afraid of rejection. Imagine that. You just have to have the faith to believe that Jesus loves you so much that when you step off the precipice into the unknown He's going to catch you.'

'This love is hard.'

'Yes. But if it wasn't all that it is, how could it be the answer to everything that we as people utterly and completely long for?'

On the way to the restaurant, Eritrea fretted briefly about the explanations Antoine might demand about her absence. But she need not have worried. He was surprisingly mild towards her, giving the subject a wide berth and limiting his questions to whether or not what she had was catching and was she really up to working, after all? She was a little surprised at this uncharacteristic and almost caring attitude, until she saw herself in the mirror behind the spirit bottles.

The evening was not without its trivial dramas. Fougère made it manifestly obvious that she was angry with Eritrea by refusing to speak to her and giving her stony looks. At first Eritrea was mystified, but then she realized the looks were intended as some kind of punishment, presumably because Antoine had put his foot down and made his daughter work evening shifts, during Eritrea's absence, that she would otherwise have avoided. But Fougère's sulkiness did not touch Eritrea. It seemed utterly inconsequential. Once she had figured out why Fougère was so angry, she thought, oh that's what it is, and then forgot about it immediately.

There was the typical Saturday evening nit-picking clientele. One man, possibly on a romantic dinner date with his wife, called Eritrea over to the table to complain about gritty mussels. 'It's just not good enough,' he said, 'in an establishment of this calibre.'

Eritrea was still somewhat surprised to be at the *Dame de Coeur* at all. While the husband made his feelings about the food known, she wondered why Antoine had not fired her. Underneath, she mused, isn't it strange how life goes on. How people are like blind creatures pushing at one another while the current continues to pull them forward together. She felt as though she were being drawn, lifeless, in the current while this man struggled and pushed at her from the side. Soon, however, he would be pulled away in a different direction. Why could he not be more gentle with her now in this, the only contact that they would probably ever have?

When he had finished ranting, she said dreamily, 'Well, we do soak the mussels in fresh water while they're still alive. It's quite funny. When they go into the bucket the water's completely clear, but after a night of soaking there's a layer of sand on the bottom. We try our best to make sure there isn't any left inside them.'

The unexpectedness of this response seemed to pull the rug out from under his feet. He changed tack. 'And the Côtes du Rhone my wife ordered is corked.'

The woman opposite him kept giving him infuriated "time out" looks of embarrassment. He answered the looks with words. 'But I have to say something, honey. It's expensive wine.'

As the target of the criticism, Eritrea might normally have made a show with apologetic body language and mollifying comments for the sake of the customer, but she was so detached and unbothered tonight that she could not even go through the motions. The conversation seemed like some kind of comedy act. 'Sir, I'm sure I stayed at the table after opening it while your wife tasted it,' she thought aloud. 'I don't recall there being any complaint then.'

'Yes, well. *I* hadn't tasted it then. Now I have and I think it's corked.'

The Côtes du Rhone had an impressive aged-looking label with a fancy antiquated font and the writing all in French, but Antoine made up the cost of an entire crate on one bottle. 'I'll get you another one,' Eritrea said. 'There's not much I can do about the mussels, I'm afraid, but if you'd like something else, then I'd be happy to oblige. At no extra cost.' She remembered that Antoine had been stressing about the fact that the lobster special would not last past tonight. 'I can recommend the lobster,' she added.

'Hmm. Well,' the husband said. 'I suppose that will have to do.'

I suppose it will, she thought, as she headed back to the kitchen with the wine and the mussels. The man was saying, to his wife – to himself perhaps, '– and it's always the same. You only ever go to a nice restaurant like this on a special occasion, so you feel that you can't complain when the food's no good. It's just not on. People shouldn't take advantage of the fact that they know you won't want to ruin a special occasion by complaining…'

By the time she had sorted them out, a new customer had come in and sat down at one of the small tables along the wall, under the framed prints of Renoir's Swing and the River Seine. She recognized him as someone who had been there before. She'd seen him from behind the bar and only remembered him now because Fougère had thought he was cute. So much so, in fact, that she had ordered Eritrea and Serena to let her serve him should he return. Cue more drama, Eritrea thought, as she went to the kitchen.

'There's someone on table two that you might want to deal with,' she said to Fougère, who was crouched over her pad with her father, ticking off a list of main courses. She gave Eritrea a look of venomous fury. 'Can't you see I'm busy? I've got this family of five to deal with.'

'But you specifically asked –'

'Are you really so lazy that you can't handle it yourself?' She spoke as if her father were not present.

'I'm happy to take over from you if you like. It's just that you wanted –'

'Eritrea. I can't believe I'm hearing this. I don't care how ill you've been. It doesn't mean you can dump customers on me just because you feel like it.' Then a thought dawned on her. 'You want the tips from the family. That's what it is. Unbelievable.' Then she turned her attention back to her father. 'Two beef, one guinea fowl.'

Eritrea went back into the restaurant proper and over to the table where the man was sitting, poring over the menu. He had a goatee beard. If Eritrea had known him better she would have suggested that he shave it off. 'Are you ready to order?' she asked, envisaging Fougère's fury on exiting the kitchen.

'I um… would be, except that I can't speak French.'

'Oh. Right.'

'What would you recommend?'

'Well, what kind of food do you like?'

'I always have a steak. But that's because I can never think of what else to order.'

'Do you like fish?'

'Yes. I suppose so. But not floury, tasteless fish, you know, the frozen stuff. Even if it's been spruced up.'

Eritrea failed to stifle a laugh. 'I can assure you we don't use frozen fish.' This conversation is insane, she thought.

'Oh, in that case I'll have some fish.'

'There's salmon, perch, mussels, red mullet. Oh yes, and lobster. Which is on special.'

'What's the least bony?'

'The lobster, probably.'

'Except shellfish.'

'Then it would have to be the salmon.'

'Okay, that sounds good.'

'Would you like some wine… sir?' she said, remembering the decorum.

'Um. Yes. Do you have a house white? I mean, I'm not particularly…' he left the sentence hanging.

'Certainly,' she said. 'And a starter?'

'Might be a bit problematic,' he said, with a slight cough. 'Salmon's fine.'

As she turned to go back to the kitchen, she saw that Fougère had just come out through the swing doors and seen

361

the man at table two. As she passed Eritrea, she gave her the kind of look that suggested she would like to exterminate her.

Chapter 22

'I wish I could go back and change everything,' Eritrea said. 'I feel like I've wasted so much time.' It was Wednesday, almost two weeks since she had first gone to see Judith. She was sitting on one of the high stools in Judith's kitchen while Judith stacked the dishwasher. 'Just thinking about Africa makes me feel... I don't know. I just wish the ground would swallow me up. During the outreach they got me and Patrique doing this mime called *The Heart*, where I was this seductress who played around with his heart and broke it before he found God. Then the leaders went and broke us up because they thought I was seducing him. You'd think it was orchestrated or something.'

Judith was trying to fit the handle of a greasy saucepan in the lower rack without it impeding the sprayer nozzle. 'You shouldn't think like that,' she said.

'Goodness knows why they even let me into PCOM in the first place. Why couldn't they have been discerning enough to realize that I wasn't ready?'

'Eritrea.' She shut the dishwasher and switched it on. The kitchen was filled with the familiar and comforting sound of the cycle. 'Don't think like that. Didn't it occur to you that perhaps the PCOM leaders might have guessed that the issues surrounding Jo's death mightn't have been the only ones you had? Okay, so they didn't know any details, but still. They don't wait until people are perfect before letting them do a school. It's the same with God. He entrusts us, His imperfect

363

children, with all kinds of things. And God uses even the worst and most embarrassing things for good in those who love Him.'

'You have an answer for everything,' Eritrea said.

'Huh. It would be nice if I did. I'm only trying to say that we see things according to our own rational priorities. If God worked the way we wanted him to, we'd be instantly transformed into perfect beings without even the potential to do wrong as soon as we were born again. But what would we learn from that? I mean, how would we learn to trust God? Would a parent want their child to be able to walk and talk as soon as it was born? Of course not. Even though it looks like a mess now, there will come a time when you look back at what happened in Africa, even at what's happened over these last weeks, and see that God was always working according to His perfect plan.'

'I wish I felt like that now.'

'It's about perspective. I was driving past a field of cabbages once and thinking about exactly this thing. When I looked out of the window at the cabbages they seemed to have been planted all crooked and I remember thinking, why on earth did the farmer plant them like that, but when I turned along the other side of the field, they all miraculously lined up and I realized I'd just been looking from the wrong angle. Do you get what I mean? You're seeing things from one angle but there'll come a time when you've travelled a bit further and you'll see from quite another.'

'All the same, I wish things could be more cut and dried right now.'

'The way God works, His timing... These things overlap. You prayed for a miracle in Africa and, as a result, that Muslim leader came to know the Lord. At that time the memories of Nigel and St Peter's were still buried deep inside you. God knew about them, but He didn't say, I won't let Eritrea be involved in this miracle because she's got problems she doesn't know about. It's not the way He works.

'I don't know, maybe that was the single biggest thing that happened in your school. The one reason God wanted the school outreach to be in Senegal in the first place. And you were involved in it.'

Eritrea considered. 'I need to hear that, you know.'

'Of course you do. Because it proves that God entrusts us with things before we've become adults in the faith. It's a way of showing us that legalism means nothing to him.'

'I'm not with you.'

'It's the human legalistic attitude of our soul that tells us we ought to be totally perfect according to our own priorities before we can be used for God's purposes. But by entrusting great and honourable tasks to us in our unfinished state, God shows us that He doesn't care about that. His priorities are different. By using you to bring that Muslim to Him –'

'Youssou.'

'Yes, to bring Youssou to Him, He showed you that He trusted you even though there were unresolved things in your life that you knew nothing about. And there's another principle here, too. God wants to turn the bad around not only to heal you but to bring wonderful things out of this. I was saying the other week that when you make a conscious decision to die to things – habits, unhealthy thought patterns, revealed sin, whatever – God turns the bad around to create good things that bring glory to Him. Much more powerful than the bad.'

'I'm still finding that hard to believe.'

'Yes. You're still very close to the pain, now. I know. But imagine that when Nigel hurt you it was like him stepping into a pool of water and that the consequences of the things he did were like ripples that spread out from him, affecting you first then, through you, other people that you had contact with.'

'Patrique, Håkan –'

'Whoever. In fact –' she broke off and thought for a second – 'it's quite possible that Nigel himself was abused and that he was a ripple, too, if you like.'

'I didn't think of that.'

'That's the way the devil works, using people to create shockwaves that spread out and cause the maximum amount of damage. But what God does for all those who come to Him for healing and help is to take those bad things and transform them, so that what were weaknesses in you as a consequence of what happened, are turned into strengths. Strengths that you would never have had if the bad things hadn't happened to you in the first place. Beauty for ashes.'

'But I have to be willing to die to the things that God reveals to me. You said so yourself.'

'I did. I think maybe I was taking things too fast. That's why I haven't wanted to talk about it since then.'

Eritrea ignored this. 'To die to the things that God reveals to me,' she persisted.

Judith nodded. 'Like Jesus said, a seed can only bear fruit if it dies first. What I'm saying is that God takes the bad and makes it good, so that the good is much more good than the bad was bad. Like when you break your arm. It's not a nice thing to happen, but when it heals, the calcium around the part of the bone that broke is usually stronger than before it was broken.'

'Yes, but then you could almost say it's good for a person to be abused, because when they get healed they'll be stronger in that area, or whatever. You could even say that God let it happen because it was "part of His plan".'

Judith thought of Eritrea at university, hearing the interpretation of the poem about the swan. 'The wounds are open
at the moment and it's tough. I know… You have every right
to be hurt.'

Eritrea felt her eyes welling up. 'Good grief. All I seem to
do is cry these days.'

'I mean it. There's nothing wrong with letting the pain
come out. It's right for you to let it happen. It's the best thing
you can do. In counselling situations, the counsellor usually
needs to encourage the person, to create an environment where
they feel they can share. The funny thing is, when I talk to you,
I always feel that it's exactly the opposite. That I keep needing
to help you to relax, not to worry, so that we don't take things
too quickly.'

'Too quickly? I don't feel like I'm anywhere, really, at the
moment.'

'Eritrea, it's the hardest thing to understand why it is that
God allows these things to happen. Sometimes we suffer as
a result of other people's disobedience. But God doesn't
orchestrate for us to be hurt. Satan's main aim is to do things
that make us think that's the case, because if, in our hearts, we
see God as a manipulator then we can't ultimately trust in
anything.' She went over to Eritrea and held her.

'I'm messing up your top,' Eritrea cried.

'I don't care.'

'Deep down, I suppose I know that God didn't make Nigel
hurt me. I just hate myself for what I did to Håkan and other
people because of what Nigel did to me.'

'You mustn't carry a burden about that. All things work
together for good in those that love God. Håkan wouldn't have
been hurt unless God were doing something in him and using
you to teach him things he needed to learn about himself, and
that he couldn't otherwise have learned.'

Eritrea let go of Judith's shoulders. 'It still bothers me. I hate to think of him being hurt.'

'Let me get you some paper.' She reached over, picked up a kitchen roll and tore off a couple of sheets. 'You had an excuse for what you did.' She handed her the paper. 'For all I know, he didn't.'

'But still, I want him to know that I didn't mean to hurt him. I felt so flattered by him, I couldn't help what I did. I was in love with him, in a way. But I was too proud to admit it to myself.'

'Eritrea. Guilt should never be our motivation for doing things,' Judith said gently. 'But,' she added, 'if you really have peace in your heart about apologizing to him now – with or without explanations – then I'm sure it won't do any harm.'

Later, she said, 'Eritrea. I want us to continue meeting up on a regular basis. There's so much that we still need to talk about, especially to do with Jo. But we can't always do it secretly. I see a lot of Rowena, after all.'

'I know. I think about it every time I come here.'

'I would never force you to tell them or anyone else about what happened. I promised you that at the beginning and that promise still holds.'

'I know what you're going to say. He did it to me, so what's to say he hasn't done it to other people, too.'

'Yes,' Judith said carefully. 'I've prayed that he won't be able to do anything now, and I believe that God will honour that prayer... But something will, at some point, have to be done. I would never break your confidence without your permission, though.'

'No. I know. But you're right. I just need a little more time.'

'I understand.'

Chapter 23

The restaurant was quiet on Wednesday evening. Eritrea and
Serena were working together, and for the first hour the girls
sat on chairs outside the kitchen. They were mostly shielded
by the bar, but their heads looked over the top, like soldiers
entrenched in a dugout, waiting for an onslaught. Antoine sat
in the kitchen, so uptight about the lack of custom that the
waves of worry almost pushed the swing doors open. Edith
Piaf gargled away in the background.

'I wish I'd get sick with whatever you had,' Serena said.

The comment was so absurd it made Eritrea laugh out loud
– an incredulous, humourless laugh. 'I don't think you do.'

'You've lost so much weight. Look at this.' She untucked
her shirt and showed Eritrea her belly. 'At least if I got sick I'd
get a bit thinner.'

'You should go to Senegal and drink tap water. You'd
be surprised at how quickly you lose your appetite. And the
weight just drops off you. I mean, not that you need to, of
course.'

The restaurant door opened and a party of four came in.
'I'll deal with them,' Serena said.

'I don't mind.'

'It's okay. Take it easy.'

While Serena was taking their order, the door opened
again. It was the man with the goatee beard whom Eritrea
had served a week-and-a-half earlier. She stayed where she
was while he removed his jacket. Instead of placing it over the

chair so that the wooden frame supported the shoulders from the inside, he hung it so that the lining of the jacket was between his own back and the chair. When he pulled it in to sit down, the inside pocket, which was hanging open at an angle, spilled a wallet and other paraphernalia on to the floor. Eritrea watched from behind the protective barricade of the bar and smiled.

When he had picked up the fallen possessions, she approached the table.

'What would you like today?' There was the faintest waver of amusement in her voice.

He passed her the menu. 'I'm not sure.'

'Still can't speak any French?'

He looked at his shoes in embarrassment and she immediately knew who he was.

'I quite liked the fish, actually,' he said, looking at her but not seeing her.

Can he not know who I am? she thought, as she went into the kitchen with his order.

Later, when he was paying, he said, 'The wine was a bit fizzy. Is it supposed to be like that?'

'Yes,' she answered, studying him. It was the beard. That and the fact that his hair was so different. Yes, that was it. 'Wine made from Muscadet grapes has a tendency to go bad quickly if it's exposed to oxygen, so instead of putting it into new barrels after fermentation they leave it lying on its own sediment – the *lie* – until they bottle it. That's what gives it its slightly sparkling taste.'

'I'm impressed,' he said, signing his credit card receipt. He handed the paper to her and she scrutinized the signature suspiciously.

'Just part of the job.' A mine of useless information, she thought.

When he left, she stared at the door to the street as if expecting him to come back in and tell her, look, I'm only joking. I know who you are really. But he didn't.

She must have been standing like that for a while, because Serena came up to her and said, 'You can't have him. He belongs to Fougère.'

'You what?'

'He's taken. If she were here now she'd never have let you serve him.'

'Is that a fact?'

'Better believe it, girl.'

'He's not my type. Anyway, I hate goatee beards.'

'Oh yeah.' She gave Eritrea a reproving dig in the side.

It was not too late when she arrived home: Antoine had reluctantly let her and Serena leave five minutes before the restaurant was actually due to close.

Outside the flat, the sky was the English blue-grey of summer night, but Eritrea nevertheless distinguished the faint glow of Lucy's bedside lamp under the crack of her bedroom door. It made her feel guilty. But, I have to do this first, she thought as she pushed her own bedroom door to.

She sat at her desk and prayed in her mind, Father, help me to know what to say. She picked up a pen and started writing.

Much later, when she had finished reading through what she had written, she folded the paper and put it in an envelope. Then she put on her nightshirt, cleaned her teeth and went to bed. Sleep would not come to her immediately; she stared at the ceiling and thought about her words:

...I think you were right about the fact that I made men subject to me, it was just the reasons you were unclear about. I see now that I did it with Patrique to some extent, just like I did with you.

There's a couple of other things I have to tell you, though. In Africa I made sure I told you clearly that I didn't return the same kind of love that you had for me, but if I'm being completely honest about things, I did fall for you. I wanted so much to keep myself from falling in love with you like that, but I couldn't help my feelings. I felt so flattered by you, by the way you treated me and the attention you gave me. I didn't want to admit my feelings to myself. I want to apologize about the confusing messages I gave you. I really do.

But as I'm sure you see, there was another reason why I wrote to you and asked you not to come here. It wasn't just because I was rejecting you… A part of me just couldn't handle you actually coming to Marlborough. At the time, I didn't even know why I felt like that, but now I understand that the part of me that still remembered something of the pain just couldn't cope with you being so near to where the abuse actually took place. In my mind it was like, home is one world and Håkan is another, and the two can never meet.

I'm sorry that I hurt you. I really am. But I'm not simply writing to apologize. I also want to say that whatever we did wrong, I look back on Africa with good memories. When I thought back over what I did, bad as it was, I see that I didn't mean to do anything wrong. I had a clear conscience at the time, even before the leaders. I'm ashamed now, whereas then I was just angry and confused. I want to tell you this so that you won't judge me. I never intended to hurt you, Håkan.

You've had to wait a long time for this letter, but I hope you understand that it was as soon as I could manage.

Early on Thursday evening, Eritrea walked towards the *Dame de Coeur*. Over the past two weeks, she had become used to the ever-present fatigue that walked with her, wherever she went and whatever she did. Going to work somehow exacerbated the tiredness – not simply because, in her fragile state, the harsh oblivion of her work colleagues cut into her more deeply, but because going to work was, in itself, tantamount to suffering without ultimate reason. The conversations she had with Judith were inherently more painful, but they were, at least, like stepping stones that led – albeit slowly – upwards to the top of the mountain she was attempting to scale. The shifts at the restaurant, however, were nothing more than awkward, unavoidable sidetracks through rocky gullies; needless detours that wore her out even more and brought her no closer to where she was trying to go. For this reason, there was always an added heaviness in going there, and in her attempts to muster whatever strength she could to last through the hours of her shift.

Today, however, as she walked something was slightly, ever so slightly, different. The weariness accompanied her, as always, but it was somehow tempered with something, or the possibility of something, like the vaguest of hopes, that moved near to her. It walked softly, just beyond the reach of her consciousness, beyond her grasp, and its intermittent touch on the edges of her mind was insubstantially light, like the touch of butterfly wings. But somehow, in its very lightness, it took away just a little of the burden of pain and fatigue. Odd, she thought, as she went through the door. Serena greeted her with a dazzlingly wide smile.

'You did lunch, didn't you?' Eritrea said.

'I did indeed.'

'And you're doing tonight, too.'

'It certainly looks like it.'

'Why?'

'Swapped with Blouenne,' she said. 'I'm going away tomorrow for a long weekend.'

'I knew there had to be a reason. You couldn't possibly be this radiantly happy about doing two shifts back to back.'

'Oh, it's not that,' she gushed, taking Eritrea by the sleeve and dragging her through to the kitchen.

Antoine was fussing over the salad garnishes on plates of goose liver pâté. On the table next to him was a bunch of red roses, wrapped in cellophane. Antoine worked with exaggerated concentration, as if trying to pretend that the flowers were not there.

Eritrea turned to Serena. 'They're lovely,' she said. 'Who sent them?'

'They're for you, you idiot.'

'Oh.' She remained standing where she was.

'Aren't you going to read the card?'

'I might do.'

She walked over to where they were lying on the table. Antoine gave her a hurried nod of greeting that communicated, you can look at them, but only if you're quick about it.

Eritrea picked them up self-consciously. Where they were cut off, the stalks of the roses were encased in a kind of cellophane balloon filled with water to keep the flowers fresh. The card read: *To the waitress who knows so much about wine. For you, I'd consider learning French, and that's saying something.*

'They'll be okay like that for a few hours, won't they?' she said to Serena, as she did up her waiting apron in the bar area. But Serena was not listening.

'You should have seen her face,' she said, kissing her thumb and forefinger. It was *un moment parfait.*

'I don't know if I want to hear it.'

'Oh, but you do. You do. He came in at lunchtime and Fougère thought they were for her and he goes, "Is the waitress with the brown hair here?" and she goes, "No," so he

374

goes, "Could you give them to her from me?", and she's like, "Okay".'

Fougère is going to crush me to dust, Eritrea thought.

'You should have seen her fa-ace,' Serena sang.

When she walked home, the few Thursday evening passers-by glanced at the flowers with the mild, irrepressible curiosity of the English. The sensation she had felt walking to work was gone. In the flat, she unwrapped the cellophane and breathed their cool velvety crimsonness, the smell that is all rose. After trimming the stalks and putting the flowers in water, she knocked on Lucy's door. Lucy answered it in her pyjamas.

'It's not too late, is it?'

'No. I was reading.'

'I'm ready to talk now.'

'Only if you're sure. Not for my sake. Honestly.'

'Shall we go in the living room?' Eritrea asked.

'Goodness,' Lucy said when she saw the flowers. 'Who gave you those?'

For a moment, Eritrea toyed with the idea of asking Lucy to guess, just to see if she might eventually come up with the right name. 'Someone I met at work.'

'An admirer?'

'You could say that.'

'I should've got you a bunch of roses,' Lucy mused aloud. 'Not jasmine.'

'Sit down,' Eritrea said gently, patting the settee.

Lucy obeyed.

'Do you remember when our family came to Glenfield? When Jo and I first started coming to Sunday school, when Judith was leading it?'

'Of course.'

'Do you remember when it was that I stopped coming?'

'I'm not sure. It could have been a year or so after, I suppose. There was a time when you came on and off before you left altogether.'

'Did you have any idea why I stopped coming?'

Lucy shook her head blankly. 'I don't think I saw things the same way then. Maybe I thought that it was peer pressure at school. Going to a church not exactly being a cool thing to do and all that.'

'Mum and dad hated me not going. We had this long psychological battle before they eventually gave in and let me stop coming along. But I had to stop.'

'And James. He used to annoy you so much. Jo even said that's why you left. He used to irritate me enough, and he didn't even fancy me.'

'Oh, I'd forgotten that. But that's not the main reason.'

'It isn't?'

'No. Would you believe it if I told you that I was scared of Judith?'

'Come on.'

'It's true.'

'I would *never* have guessed.'

'Even after I came back from Africa I was still scared of her. That's part of the reason I wanted out of the church as soon as possible. I wanted to get out of Glenfield – and Marlborough.'

'I thought it was because of Jo,' Lucy said carefully. 'Because being at Glenfield reminded you of him.'

'That's why you never made anything of me wanting to move here so quickly. You were being tactful.'

'Partly. I was flattered, too. Despite what we'd been through, I still didn't think you'd want to share a flat with me. I've always been paranoid like that.' She was thinking as she spoke. 'Oh my goodness. Suggesting that you go and see Judith the other week can't have been particularly easy to swallow.'

'You can say that again.'

'But *Judith*? What did Judith ever do to make you afraid of her?'

'It seems impossible, doesn't it? One of the reasons I went to see her was to face it. To face things square on. For a long time I thought it was just irrational, but there *was* a reason. In the past I just couldn't see it, that's all.'

'Does this have anything to do with the jasmine I gave you?'

'Yes,' Eritrea said. 'Surprisingly enough it does.'

At one-twenty in the morning, Eritrea stretched and rose to get a drink. 'I'm having hot chocolate. You want one?' she asked Lucy.

'Mmm.'

She poured milk into a pan and added three heaped tablespoons of powder from a carton in the cupboard. Some of the powder fell on the sideboard and she wiped it up clumsily with a dishcloth, leaving behind a faint smear on the work surface.

'The way that God used the jasmine to speak to me, I can hardly believe it. It was the most gentle thing He could have done, when you think about it. Isn't it?'

'When I was praying for you,' Lucy said, 'I struggled so much with whether or not to go ahead and act on the word. Then, once I'd decided to do something about it I couldn't find any jasmine anywhere. None of the florists round here had any. I was pretty close to giving up.'

'So where did you get it then?'

'I drove to this garden centre and they'd sold out, but just as I was leaving one of the sales assistants who'd overheard the conversation said there was some growing up the wall in the staff car park. I didn't even have to pay for it.'

'How funny.'

'Well, it seemed fairly amusing until I saw your reaction.'

Eritrea stirred the milk and poured it into two mugs. It had burnt a brown crust on to the bottom of the pan, which she half filled with water and left in the sink. 'I was on the edge. You must've known that or you wouldn't have been praying for me in the first place. I'd been on the edge ever since Håkan sent me the letter. But I needed something to push me over it. To remind me. I can hardly express to you in words the importance of what you did.'

'That's a relief. I've spent the last two weeks going around thinking –'

'I know. I know. And I'm sorry. I wanted to tell you, but I couldn't until things were clear in my head.'

They sipped their cocoa in silence. When Lucy reached the dark grit at the bottom that hadn't dissolved properly she said, quietly, 'Jo tried to talk to me once about St Peter's.'

'He did?'

'It was in Wales, just before he died. The day before he died. The rest of the group went out mountain climbing and Judith and I stayed behind to be with him.' She broke off and sucked her teeth, the way people do when fighting back the emotion. 'That day I was more concerned about the fact that Judith might think I was trying something on with him than I was about him being ill. Isn't it strange how your priorities, in retrospect, condemn your motives?'

'Don't. Don't blame yourself. We've agreed on that before.'

'We were sitting in the field where we were camping and we got talking. He tried to tell me about a time when he had a carol service at St Peter's and he was embarrassed in front of other people, or something.'

'How so?'

'I honestly don't think I can remember all the details.'

'Try.'

Lucy had been turning her mug so that the wet cocoa silt made wavy patterns up the inside of the china. Now she put it on the floor. 'He got told off about something that wasn't his fault and one of the teachers made him stand in the aisle in front of the other boys. Something like that.'

Eritrea pictured the scenario in her mind. It did not bear thinking about. 'The thought of Håkan being in my bedroom, occupying the same space where Nigel had once been was too much for me to contemplate. Imagine how it must have been for Jo to have had not only to go back to St Peter's but then to be made to suffer like that.'

'Don't,' Lucy said, almost choking. 'I remember... He started saying something about how he felt bad because he'd heard your father saying they abandoned the church when it really needed them. How could I have known what was really the matter? I hardly gave him the chance to tell me about it. I just talked on, like an idiot.'

'Don't beat yourself up. You couldn't possibly have known. We did a pretty good job of hiding it.'

And yet, and yet, Lucy thought. Even then, all those years ago, there was something about the way he was, his stubbornness. Even the way he just put up with meningitis until it killed him, that should have warned me. People are rarely like that without a reason. She said, 'I miss him so much. Sometimes I want to talk about him but I don't because I'm afraid of upsetting you. I know you've always hated people's oversensitive sympathy.'

'Judith says she doesn't think I've grieved properly for him because of all these suppressed memories and stuff.'

'Oh?' But Lucy knew it was true.

'She says she doesn't know of anyone who has ever had to suffer the things I have.' She said it in a bluff, matter-of-fact way. 'I don't really know what it means to grieve properly. *Is* there a proper way? Sometimes I still tell myself that he's just gone away for a while and that he'll be back soon.'

'He loved you a lot. Do you mind me saying that?'

'No.'

'He said that… that you were a good person and that I shouldn't judge you. He was trying to tell me about what you'd gone through, I think.'

'Do you think he forced himself to forget, like I did?'

'Not in the same way, maybe. I don't know.'

The two sat with their own thoughts. 'Eritrea,' Lucy said after a while, 'where will things go from here? With Judith, I mean.'

'I don't know. We've been meeting for two weeks but we've hardly even prayed together about it yet. I don't even know how to relate to the things I've told her. Sometimes I feel like I'm running on ahead wanting to strip everything away, to get to the bottom of everything, as soon as possible. Other times I wake up in the morning and feel that I've gone nowhere, like I'm waking up again on the morning after the first day we talked.'

'What about your parents? Have you thought about when you might tell them?'

Hearing these words evoked in Eritrea's mind an image: that of a long, cylindrical tunnel. She was standing at one end and looking down through it. The circle of light at the other end was almost impossibly small. And the immense distance of the tunnel was like the expanse of incomprehension that separated her from her parents, who stood, like tiny blurred dots, in the light at the other end. 'Judith has asked me that, too,' she said. At this point, she knew that the ability to express her feelings in words that could be understood was beyond her. She cut her losses and said, 'It's just too early for me at the moment.'

The words were so two-dimensional. They did not say what she meant to say. But they had to do.

She did not get to bed until almost three in the morning, but when she slept, she dreamed. She walked in a field under a benevolent sun. A wind was blowing and rippling over the grass in the aimless, restless way it does on those hot days when it seems that there could never be any other season but summer. And it was a warm wind that warmed the roots of her hair. The buttercups touched her legs, leaving traces of mustard-powder pollen on her skin. And Jonah was there walking with her, twisting a blade of grass between his thumb and forefinger.

'How funny that there should be white clover here,' she was saying, looking at the ground.

'Why should that surprise you?'

'Do you remember we used to pick clumps of it at the bottom of the garden and suck the honey out of the flowers?'

'I remember.'

They walked together for a while. Presently, something occurred to Eritrea.

'Should I be grieving for you?'

'I don't know,' he said. 'It's not something I know much about any more. But you certainly shouldn't worry about me.'

'Worry?'

'You worry about what I couldn't fulfil on earth by dying. But that comes of being afraid that when someone dies with unresolved issues, they'll never be sorted out.'

'Do I worry?'

'It's the secret fear of so many Christians. The human fear that heaven is somehow not everything that earth is or that what we have on earth is somehow greater, somehow more real than what we will have here. You think that I've missed so much – the things that you've seen and done and realized since I've been gone. And that I died without coming to terms with what happened.'

'But that's true, surely?'

'No. It's not like that at all. It's hard when you're in the body not to think of all things from the point of view of the physical, and to see the bad things that happened in the physical as the final word on the matter, on my life. Back there it's terrible for someone to die young and not experience adulthood. It's even worse if they had a big unresolved hurt. That's what you worry about when you think of me, isn't it?'

'I suppose it is.'

'But you mustn't.'

'I can't help it.' She had stopped walking.

He turned to face her and put his hand on her shoulder; they had never really touched each other as teenagers, but it felt comfortingly normal to Eritrea, like arriving home. 'On earth, people want their kind of happy ending. It helps them not to have to think about the eternal.'

'But when it's all you have –'

'Back there, people feel sorry for me. But if they chose to let Him show them how it really has been for me, then the way they live their lives would change. And in their spirits they know that. It's part of what He wants them to learn – about trusting Him. He always whispers to us on earth and tells us not to concentrate on the things down there. Do you see? Even *you* think that I suffered much more than you, but it's not like that. The truth is that you've suffered far more than I ever did. If you knew how it was for me you would only want to be here. You'd hardly be able to bear living out your life on earth.'

Eritrea looked at him in confusion.

'As humans, we're afraid of the unknown. We want to be with Him, but our physical body is afraid of not being corporeal anymore. Even some of the greatest children of God, in moments of weakness, fear heaven.'

'You want me to admit that I'm afraid?'

'Eritrea, if anyone ever had a reason to be afraid it's us. You and I. But other people do, too. It's normal. Our humanness says to us that we can never do without the body, without the physical ability to choose to do the things that will sort us out and bring us closer to that arbitrary place of perfection. On earth, we fear losing the body before we've had the chance to reach that place in our own strength.'

'Or the physical ability to protect ourselves.'

'Yes.' Then he laughed as though the memory of what she meant had just returned to him. 'That too.'

'I miss you, you know. There's so much I want to talk to you about.' She looked down at the ground.

'I know. And you will, soon. But in the meantime, don't worry about me. Grieve, if you need to, but don't worry.'

'I'll try not to.'

'And Eritrea –'

'Yes?'

'You are different.'

It was hard for her to comprehend what he meant.

'You wanted to know if you were.'

'I did?'

'Yes, you did.'

Chapter 24

Håkan's reply came soon, as Eritrea had known it would.

You said you sent the letter as soon as you could manage, and you were worried it was probably not soon enough for me. But I'm glad that you didn't write back for so long, because I think God wanted to show me some things about my motivation that I wouldn't have understood or been able to tell you about if you'd written earlier. I needed the time to learn and to know those things to tell you, because the way I relate to what we had and what we were in Africa has completely changed. If you'd written to me immediately after I sent you my frustrated letter all those months ago, I would have expected and wanted an apology. Now that you've sent one, I have to tell you that it's not you who should be apologizing to me but me to you.

Knowing the truth about what happened to you has convicted me – again – about the way I behaved, not just in Africa, but afterwards. My last letter was full of anger. I felt that you'd played with my emotions and then let me go. I was hurt and disappointed, and though I genuinely wanted to help you deal with whatever issues made you treat me that way, I also wanted to get one up on you and make you feel the way you'd made me feel. It was hypocritical of me to say that I cared for you as a friend but still to write that letter to you. Part of me wishes I had never written it. Thank God that He uses all things for His glory in those that love Him. It's hard for me to believe that such a hurtful letter could have been a link in the chain that led you to rediscover your past. I'm pleased if that's the case, but I also can't help but feel guilty about it anyway. I was so ignorant about the things that happened to you and I was wrong to use what you shared with me against you.

But there are other things I feel I should tell you: I said I needed this time of silence between us to come to terms with things I'd never seen in myself regarding the way I behaved in Africa. In the last letter, I criticized your reaction – at the ram roast – to the broken bond between us. What I failed to mention is that I went on and used the power I gained over you to manipulate you. I honestly had no idea that I'd done it until I thought and prayed about things recently. Praying with Didier did give me some kind of freedom from you, but the freedom also gave me power over you, which I used as leverage to get guarantees from you. The ironic thing is, the more I tried to flaunt the fact that I was no longer subject to you, the more I actually became subject to you, until I was right back in the emotional turmoil I'd been in before Didier and I prayed.

It doesn't matter what you did or didn't do that was wrong. The fact of the matter is that I took the freedom and the peace that God gave me and exploited them to achieve my own selfish goals. I wanted you so badly, and I needed to hear you say, and see you show, that you loved me. I was desperate, but that doesn't mean I was right. After the ram roast, I had the chance to make our relationship good. Instead, I deliberately re-established the soul tie between us and put us back into a position where we could hurt each other.

As for the reasons why you asked me not to come to Marlborough, I just feel terrible. I had no idea that my being there would be hard for you because of what happened there in the past. I just went and wrote you a letter that made you feel worse.

So, for all these reasons, you see that actually I am the one who should be apologizing to you. Not you to me, but me to you. Even if you didn't know what was motivating you, you still tried to avoid hurting me, but I did pretty much everything in my power to lead you on, making it almost impossible for you not to hurt me. Then afterwards, I blamed you, even though I've never had to live through anything like the kind of pain you've experienced.

You could sum up everything I've said in two words: Forgive me. I behaved badly and that's that. But I also wanted to tell you that now I feel the same way you do about Africa. Like you, I look back on our time there with good memories. I wish I could also say, like you, that I had a clear conscience back then, but I didn't really. Looking back over my diary I see that I didn't fully understand my motivation, even though the Holy Spirit tried to warn me not to do certain things. If I had been faced with, and understood, what I was doing, I'd like to believe that I wouldn't have done it. I was childish towards you, but I think that I've learned a lot through it and I can look back on the whole experience as what it was: a gift.

How extraordinary, Eritrea thought when she finished reading, that Håkan should say the same thing as Judith: that if we were really aware of the things we did that hurt other people, we would try not to do them.

She folded up the letter and put it back in its envelope. This time, though, she put the envelope in the drawer of her bedside table.

★

There was an evening function at the *Dame de Coeur* on the last Saturday of August. It was one of those stifling evenings where the heat is claustrophobic: impossible to escape it wherever you go. Half of the restaurant had been cordoned off for the function. The eyes of the other patrons sometimes drifted uninterestedly over the fixtures on the VIP side of the restaurant, but they were really checking to see that the party was not getting better service or food than them. Blouenne and Fougère were seeing to the needs of the big group and Eritrea was looking after the other few non-function people. There was a distinct air of paranoia among Eritrea's customers: the party was made up of French people, who spoke real French and who could fling their hands around or lean back in their chair and guffaw without looking pretentious.

As the evening was beginning to boil dry, he walked in. In keeping with the ultimate denouement that the meeting was destined to be, he entered at a moment when Blouenne, Fougère and Antoine were all out of the kitchen and the room was as crowded as it could be. Eritrea was carrying an armful of empty plates. He gave her a hopeful look, communicating a desire to speak, but she had to go out to the kitchen and could not signal with a shrug or other appropriate body language that she would shortly be back. She did not look at Fougère as she shouldered her way through the swing door. When she came back out, Fougère had immersed herself in courteous waitress–customer conversation with one of the VIPs. But somehow, in her polite requests about whether the crème brûlée met with expectations, there was a burning anger – an intense awareness of Eritrea approaching the man she had stolen from her. Eritrea thought, Lord, I did not ask for this situation. I did nothing to lead him on. As my conscience is my witness, I did not lead him on.

'Did you come in to eat?' she said more curtly than she intended. 'If so, we're closing in a minute.'

'No,' he said, self-consciously. 'I… Actually, I came to see you.'

'This really isn't the time or place.'

'Oh. Well. Okay.' But he just stood there.

The function started to break up. Some of the members of the party got to their feet. The minor flurry of activity afforded Eritrea a little cover. She looked him square in the eyes. 'Why are you playing this game with me?'

She saw the self-incriminating words "What game?" in his eyes and on his lips, but he did not utter them. 'I don't understand what you mean. I'm not playing a game.'

'What is it then?'

'It's… I don't know. Aren't I allowed to buy you flowers?'

Eritrea saw, in his answer, that her tone had been overly aggressive. 'It was sweet of you. But there are all kinds of reasons why…' she let the sentence drop away, wanting to add words like, "worst possible timing" or "truly not interested". How can I make him go away? she thought. She was not angry with him – she was more fearful than anything else. These people that knocked against her in this caustic reality that was her work life were like jagged rocks on the paths of these needless detours.

'We could go somewhere quiet to talk when you finish,' he said. 'I could wait for you outside, or something.'

'No, that's no good,' she answered instinctively, almost incredulously.

'There's a quiet pub near here,' he said desperately. 'It's open until twelve.'

'I don't think so.' But an idea of how to rid herself definitively of him, without hurting him, was beginning to form in her mind. 'I don't know.'

'I understand if you don't want to. I mean, for all you know I could be a killer or something.'

I find that hard to believe, she thought. 'You're trying to persuade me to talk to you – knowing that I don't want to,' she said, 'and you suggest that you might be a killer. It's not the best way of going about things, is it?'

'No.' He was at a complete loss, now. They stood opposite each other for a while. Eventually Eritrea felt she had to acquiesce, if only to break the impasse and bring the situation to a swift end. 'Okay. Wait on the corner. I'll be out in about ten minutes.'

He turned to go. She wanted to call after him, please don't expect anything, though. I'm just not in that place. But he was gone, out of the door.

While the party dispersed, Eritrea formulated in her mind the words that she would say to him, to ensure that the message would be well and truly driven home. She wondered, when the closed sign had been put up, if she should say something to try to appease Fougère, but she knew that this would only be interpreted as deprecation. Why do these unfortunate things have to happen to me now? she half-thought, half-prayed. Why are you letting this happen, Lord?

Outside, she saw him waiting expectantly under a lamp-post. He went to say something, but before he could, she asked, 'Which way are we going?' and continued walking. It was rude, she knew, but there was no point in explaining that Fougère was still inside and would burst a blood vessel if she happened to come out and see the two of them loitering together. Damage limitation, damage limitation, she told herself as they walked.

When they arrived at the pub he offered to buy her a drink. She scanned the tables for a place they could sit undisturbed but not unseen. She picked a corner table and plonked herself down, dumping her bag by the chair. The air was full of the summer pub smell of sticky, yeasty beer and smoke. The other patrons might be looking at her in her waitress outfit, but she didn't care.

He came back presently with a pint of something coppery and a glass of bar soda for her. 'I always like to try the local brew,' he began. 'It's not usually that good, but sometimes –'

'Please let me get to the point,' Eritrea said. 'I don't want to seem rude or ungrateful. The flowers were beautiful and unexpected and all that, but you wouldn't be interested in me. I'm a Christian. But not just a Christian. I'm sold out to Jesus Christ. I'm the kind of religious nutcase who would embarrass you in public by talking openly about how life means nothing whatsoever without the saving power of the cross.' The rehearsed words came out quite fluently.

He was taking a draught of his beer when she began and she saw his eyes widen over the rim of the glass. When he put it down he was silent. She thought, there. That's closed the door.

He put his hand, palm open, on the table, like a question. 'You're born again?'

'Yes.'

'And you're not involved in some kind of weird cult or sect, are you?'

'No.'

'You believe in the baptism of the Holy Spirit?'

She looked at him askance, now. 'Yes.'

'Have *you* been baptized in the Holy Spirit?'

'Yes.' The conversation was not going as she had expected it might.

'That's good.'

'You... I mean you must be –'

'I am. I have been, yes.'

This dialogue was quite bizarre to her. But she had to continue, to explain. 'When you came into the restaurant, I didn't do anything to lead you on did I? It wasn't as if I –'

'No.'

'I didn't intend to. If I gave you the wrong message, I'm very sorry. I never intended to lead you on.'

'You didn't give me any message whatsoever.'

'So what attracted you to me? I mean, I don't want to sound big-headed or anything, but you did give me those flowers. Is it because of… before? Is that what it is?' Other words she had in her head were left unsaid.

Before? he thought. 'You seemed so… fragile. How can I put it? When I saw you, it was as though you needed protecting.'

She felt a strange rush, not unpleasant, on hearing these words. But she fought it away. She said, 'The other girl at the restaurant. The one with the straight black hair. She thought you were interested in her. When you brought the flowers it put me in a real situation. I always seem to hurt people. Especially when I don't want to.'

'Before?' he said now, aloud.

'Listen. It's all very well us pretending and so on, but let's at least be honest with each other.'

'I wasn't out looking for anything. At first, I only came into the restaurant to get something to eat. To try something different.'

'Not that. I mean me. Do you really not know who I am?'

He shook his head. 'Should I?'

'We were in the same class at school. And Bebidas club. Well, it used to be called that anyway. Does that ring any bells?'

He sat back in his chair stunned. It took him a while to say the word: 'Eritrea.'

'How can you possibly not have known?'

'You look different. I saw what I wanted to see – not who you are.'

'You really didn't have the faintest idea?'

'You look… different.' He was somewhat shocked.

'You're not the first person to tell me that recently.'

'I'm not surprised. The funny thing is, it's not that you *look* different. You just *are* different.'

'You're a Christian,' she said, pointedly.

'Yes.' He had made a number of fundamental re-evaluations in his head and now looked at her slightly differently, with the weight of the shared history in his eyes. 'We all have our stories.'

'This isn't some kind of stunt is it?'

He went to deny it, but then realized something and laughed. 'Actually, I suppose it is. But not one that I engineered.'

She didn't know what to say to this. Then the bartender rang for last orders.

'You were saved by the bell,' he remarked, as he walked her home.

She noticed that he kept at a respectful distance from her as he walked, and that they were walking much more slowly than they had been on the way to the pub. And that she was setting the pace.

Outside the main door of her house he said, 'Well. It's been good to see you again. Strange, but good.'

'Yes. Strange, but good,' she echoed.

'So.' He rocked up and down on his heels and toes. 'I'd better be going. I'm going away tomorrow, so I've got to be up fairly early.'

'You're not going to ask if we can see each other again?'

'I wouldn't want to push my luck just now after starting World War Three between you and the other waitresses. But… I'm not worried about it.'

'Oh.'

'Okay,' he said, seeing the surprise in her face, 'can I see you again?'

'Perhaps.' There was just the tiniest hint of humour in her voice. 'But you were right. I am… kind of fragile at the moment. The last thing I'm looking for right now is a relationship.'

'That's okay. If nothing happens, I'll understand.'

'You might have to wait a long time.'

'I can wait,' he laughed. 'I'm used to that. But,' he said pointing a finger, 'I do know where you live now.'

'Well. Better that you contact me here than at the restaurant.'

'I realize that now. But. But, but.' He was thinking aloud. 'You're right. I'd rather you made the next move. And if you don't, that's okay.' He said it a little reluctantly, despite himself.

'But I've got no way of getting in touch with you.'

'Of course.' He gave her a card. It made her think of his accoutrements falling out of his jacket pocket at the restaurant.

'What if I don't call?'

'I'll just have to live with that possibility.'

She put the card in her bag.

He said, 'Well, I'd best get going then.'

She opened the door. Standing in the open doorway she turned and said, 'Goodbye then.'

'Goodbye, Eritrea Trent.'

She went to close the door, but he quickly leaned up and stole a kiss on the cheek. She felt it in her toes and coccyx. 'I mean the next move after that,' he said, embarrassed. He turned to go and she smiled to the inside of the door so that he wouldn't see it.

As she climbed the stairs, she felt again the feeling she had had walking to work a few days previously. It came without warning, silently, in a rush, and brushed her spirit as it moved past her. She stopped in her tracks and waited, holding her breath. As she lingered there, it seemed to come back to her – almost timidly – and alight on her head, in the fleeting way that a butterfly might land on a flower. She did not want to move, for fear that she would disturb it and make it go away. She did not want it to leave her again. Very cautiously, she began to climb the stairs. Despite the tiredness, she felt light.

'Are you too tired for a chat?' she asked Lucy, on entering the living room.

'I'm never too tired to talk. You know that. I need a drink though.'

While Lucy hunted for clean cups, Eritrea said, 'Lucy.'

'Yes.'

'I'm ready to go back to Glenfield now.'

Lucy stopped what she was doing and looked up. 'Are you sure?'

'I'm sure.'

'How soon?'

'How about tomorrow? We could drive over if you want.'

'Is it what you want to do?'

Eritrea nodded. 'At the moment. It is.'

When they were sitting down, Lucy said, 'That person you were talking to just now.'

'How did you know I was talking to someone?'

'I heard you, down there on the pavement. Was it the same one who gave you the flowers?'

'Yes.'

'Well, who was it?'

'It was Neil Baker.'

'What, from school?'

'The very same.'

Later, Eritrea brushed her teeth, put on her nightdress and got into bed, all the while accompanied by the thing that had settled on her when she was walking up the stairs. Still, she did not want to make sudden movements in case it took flight and left her. She settled slowly into bed and lay there for a while with her eyes closed. The part of her mind not seeking sleep tried to analyse the feeling. But it seemed to elude her somehow. Eventually, her conscious desire to understand overcame her physical tiredness and she sat up in bed.

This something, she told herself, is not simply a feeling. It is more of a knowing or an assurance. It is a thing that has touched me, yet I am lighter for its touch. How can that be? It has come to be with me, and while it is here with me, it has also taken something away from me. But if it has taken something away that has always been in me, but is now not there, how can it feel so good, so right? She sat silently in the deadlock of confusion, struggling with her thoughts for a moment. And then it dawned on her. She gasped. A rushing, like a tingling of joy or great anticipation, touched the sides of her head behind her ears and flowed through her. So this is what it feels like. She opened her mouth and, in the semi-darkness, whispered to the walls of her room, 'For the first time, I am not afraid.'

Acknowledgments

First and foremost my thanks go out to Jacques More for his help, advice and guidance. Thanks are also due, in no small measure, to those others who helped make this book a practical reality: Dan O'Brien, Aleks Kääriäinen, Sarah Widdicombe and Samantha Barden.

I am very grateful to the following people for their encouragement and feedback: Bruce and Serendipity Garner, Mum and Dad, Pat and Martti Kääriäinen, Phil Cowell, Robin Hart, Chris Huff, Peter Williams, Dan Weeks (whose creative energy has always been a massive source of motivation to me), Hanna Ranssi-Matikainen and Ari Puonti (whose sermons inspired many of Judith's words), and everyone else from Helsinki Vineyard.

Last, but by no means least, I want to thank my wife Sue for her moral support and unshakeable belief in this project over the years and through the various drafts. Without her, this book would have remained just another file on my computer.